ARIZONA JUSTICE AND THE LONELY GUN

ARIZONA JUSTICE

CHAPTER ONE

Rowan Locke drew rein as he topped the low ridge which bordered the sluggish Rio Mescalero. He shoved back his battered campaign hat and slowly rolled a smoke. The rolling country to the east was colorful and quiet under the afternoon sun of New Mexico. Smoke drifted up from a ranch on the southern bank of the river. In the distance the sun baked the sprawling town of Llano on the north bank of the river, which wound its way down to the distant Pecos.

Rowan would be spotted as an ex-cavalryman even without the faded gray shirt he was wearing, with the darker patches between the elbow and shoulder where chevrons had been cut off. His cavalry breeches, still with their yellow stripes, were neatly tucked into cowman's boots. It had been less than a month since he had taken his discharge at Fort Bowie, Arizona Territory.

"This is Llano, Jim," he said to the bay. "Somewhere around here is the man that drygulched Cousin Larry." He touched Jim with his spurs.

The hoofs of the bay drummed on the plank bridge which spanned the Mescalero. There were but four dusty streets in Llano. The main street ran north and south, crossed by three east and west streets. Hipshot ponies dozed at saloon hitching racks. White-faced cattle with Box R brands milled in a peeled-pole corral near the river. A ranch wagon rattled by, raising a plume of dust. A poke-bonneted woman drove a blue-painted buckboard past Rowan, turning a little to eye him as she touched up the mules with her whip.

Rowan swung down from Jim in front of the livery stable. He eased his crotch. It had been a long trip from Fort Bowie, through Lordsburg to Socorro, where he had stopped to see Judge Heard sworn in as a Deputy U.S. Marshal for southern New Mexico Territory; then across the northern end of the dread Jornado del Muerto, through the Capitans, toward the Rio Mescalero. Rowan was unknown in Llano, although he had been there five years before when Larry Forbes and he had bought the spread they had named the Lazy LF. Rowan had stayed in the service while Larry had run the spread. The news of Larry's death had come to him a month before he had completed twelve years' service. He had taken his discharge, asked for and received a recommendation for a U.S. Marshal's job, and had left the service forever.

A man broke through the batwings of the Union Saloon across Front Street, and hurried into Sim Short's General Store. A moment later he was back out in the harsh sunlight again, accompanied by a tall, gangling man who wore a white apron. "Mayor," the first man said, "the Black Donigans are in the Union talking war again."

The name struck home like an Apache lance to Rowan. Larry had been found near the Donigan place with his back full of shotgun pellets.

Sim Short spat. "Get Marshal Hayden," he said. "Better tell him to take two special police with him. Tell him to round up the members of the Vigilante Committee, too. He'll need 'em!"

The man hurried down the street. Men began to gather in the shade of wooden awnings, watching the

Union with sober eyes. Loud voices broke the afternoon quiet. A man yelled in the saloon. A broad-shouldered man paced deliberately up the street, the sun glinting on his marshal's badge.

Marshal Hayden pushed through the batwings, followed by two other badged men. There was a moment's quiet. Then a bottle came through a front window of the saloon. Glass tinkled to the boardwalk. The batwings crashed open and the marshal lit on his rump on the walk. Blood flowed from his mashed nose. He got to his feet in time to meet the tigerlike rush of a tall, dark-haired man. Fists bounced off the marshal's jaw and he went down hard, rolling over to avoid the feet which lashed out at him.

The marshal got to his feet and raised his fists, but three smashing blows drove him down again and he lay still. The batwings swung open again and four tall men came out onto the boardwalk, laughing as they looked back over their shoulders. They were all of the same breed. Tall and wide of shoulder, with dark curly hair showing beneath battered straw hats. Huck shirts were thrust into faded denim pants and they wore heavy work shoes instead of boots. Hard blue eyes looked from one onlooker to another.

The first man dusted his knuckles. He rolled the unconscious marshal over and ripped his badge from his vest. He rolled him back and pinned the badge to the seat of his pants, then he lifted him easily and carried him to the horse trough in front of Rowan. He dumped the marshal into the green-scummed water and laughed harshly. Rowan jumped back as the marshal's body overflowed the water onto the walk.

The storekeeper gripped a man by the arm. "Go get Deputy Busch," he said. "I've had a bellyful of these damned Black Donigans!" The man ran up the street.

Rowan eyed the five tall men. They were brothers without doubt. Ranging in age from about eighteen to thirty, the oldest being the hellion who had felled the marshal. Their features were finely chiseled, and their eyes gave them a rakehell air. Something was wrong about them and Rowan suddenly realized that none of them carried guns in a land where a man would as soon go without his trousers as his six-shooter. Three of the brothers held chair legs in their big fists. One of the others, obviously the youngest, had picked up a rock.

The men who had followed the marshal crowded in closer and suddenly all hell broke loose. The Donigans charged into them with waving clubs and lashing fists. The townsmen broke and fell back, sullenly watching the five laughing men who stood out in the hot sunlight, defying the whole town.

A shotgun bellowed in the street, and a short, stocky man carrying a smoking double-gun pushed his way through the crowd. He stopped in front of the first Donigan.

"Wash Donigan," he said, "I'm arresting you for breaking the peace, assault and battery, and resisting arrest!"

Wash Donigan spat at the deputy's feet. "Busch," he said thinly, "if you don't get outa my way, I'll take that scattergun away from you and bend it over your head."

Busch looked behind him. He was all alone facing the five. He stepped back. Wash grinned.

"Let's go, boys," he said. "Pa will be worried about us." He turned his back deliberately on the crowd and walked to his horse. The Donigans mounted, leaving Busch standing white-faced in the center of the street gripping his scattergun. The brothers thundered over the bridge, raising spurts of dust from between the rattling planks.

"You, Busch!" the storekeeper yelled. "You ain't worth a damn! Badge and all! You had him cold-decked!"

Busch turned slowly. "I didn't see *you* out here facing them!"

The storekeeper raised his hands in disgust. Rowan pulled the marshal from the water trough. The store-keeper ripped the marshal's badge from the seat of the soaking pants and threw it in the street with a look of disgust. Rowan couldn't help but grin. Short cursed. "What's so damned funny?" he demanded.

Rowan rolled a smoke. "Seems funny to me," he said easily, "five unarmed men treeing a whole town."

"Maybe you think *you* could have arrested Wash Donigan?"

Rowan nodded and bent his head to light his cigarette. "Yes," he said matter-of-factly, "I think I could have."

The storekeeper picked up the badge and held it out toward Rowan. "Take it then. Go get him!"

"I'm just passing through."

"You oughta keep your big mouth shut then!" roared Deputy Busch.

Rowan eyed the red-faced deputy. "Be careful how you run off at the mouth," he said quietly.

Busch glanced down at the plain-handled Colt and then into the cold gray eyes. He flushed and turned on a heel, walking rapidly up the street.

Rowan led the bay into the livery stable and then crossed the street to the saloon. Two broken chairs lay on the floor, broken glass littered the bar. One of the men who had entered the saloon with Marshal Hayden was moaning softly as he dabbled at his smashed nose with a bandanna. The other man lay unconscious over a table. The bartender was wiping blood from the corner of his mouth. He glanced angrily at Rowan.

"Well?" he asked.

"Rye."

The bartender slid a bottle and a glass down the bar. "Damned dirt farmers," he growled. "Come in here at least once a week to raise hell. Break chairs, bottles and jaws, and then defy the whole damned town to stop them. Makes a man sick to his gut!"

"Who are they?"

"The Donigan brothers! The Black Donigans. The oldest one is Wash Donigan. That's the one who threw Marshal Lem Hayden outa here and told Busch to go to hell. The others are Adams, Jeff, Mad and Monroe."

"Queer names."

"Yeh. Old Mike Donigan named them after the first five presidents. Washington, Adams, Jefferson, Madison and Monroe. He shoulda named them after Apache chiefs!"

"They sure have hurrahed Llano."

Sim Short came into the saloon and thrust out a hand. "I'm Simeon Short," he said. "Mayor and run the general store. I'm sorry about the way I talked to you awhile back."

Rowan smiled. "I guess you were riled up a bit. The name is Rowan Locke." He gripped Short's hand.

Short looked at the issue shirt and trousers. "Ex-soldier?"

"Yes. I was top kick of A Troop, Sixth Cavalry."

"Looking for a job?"

"Not particularly."

Short got a glass from the bartender and filled it with rye. "Those damned Donigans have made fools out of every marshal we've ever had. I hired Hayden three days ago after the Donigans choused the last marshal clean out of the county. Hayden is tough. At least we *thought* he was. You saw what Wash Donigan did to him."

Rowan downed his drink and Short refilled his glass. "I noticed they don't carry guns," he said.

Short looked up at the ceiling and raised his eyebrows. "Yeh. Old Mike Donigan don't believe in hand guns. Says they're only used for killing men. Won't allow the boys to carry six-guns. Those boys ain't afraid of guns, either. Matter of fact, they ain't afraid of anything that walks, crawls, flies, or swims. Last week I rounded up a Vigilante Committee of ten men when the Donigans was breaking up the Union here. We were between marshals, so to speak. When the dust cleared around here, five of the vigilantes was on the ground and the rest were running for the hills. Locke, I've seen hard cases in my day, but them nesters are rough as a cob. The sheriff went out there one day to pick up Wash Donigan for rustling. He had four men with him. The Donigans forted up and opened fire with scatterguns. The posse raised dust, I'll tell you, getting off Donigan land. Sheriff Claypool sent Busch, his deputy, to Llano to handle the Donigans. You saw what happened to him."

The bartender shook his head. "There ain't a man in this area that can handle 'em. And the old man is the worst of the lot."

Sim nodded. "To top it off, they're sitting on John Ripsey's land. Squatters they are. John has missed fifty head in the last three months. Them Donigans are always selling fresh beef to the butcher, the restaurant and the hotel, and no one has seen more than a dozen or so cows on their land! Locke, will you take on the marshal's job?"

Rowan shook his head. "I'm sorry. I'll only be around here a short time."

A man pushed through the batwings and swayed a little as he came toward the bar. His face was swollen and one eye was shut completely. "Rye," he mumbled.

"What happened to you, Loco?" asked Sim Short.

The man wiped a trickle of blood from the corner of his mouth. "I was at the Donigan place trying to get Nelly back. My mule strayed yesterday and I trailed her out there. I figured as long as the Donigan Boys were in town I could get her offa their land. The old man caught up with me from behind with a pick handle. Liked to beat me to death. And he's still got Nelly."

Rowan looked closely at the swollen face. "By God,"

he said. "Cass Dawson! You were in A Troop of the Sixth at Fort Grant three years ago."

Dawson peered at Rowan with his one good eye. "Sergeant Locke. Well I'll be double-damned!" He gripped Rowan's hand and looked at the other men. "Best damned yellowleg that ever forked a McClellan!"

"I'm out of the service now, Cass."

"What are you doing here?"

"Passing through. Figured on buying a small spread. I like this country."

Dawson downed his drink and refilled his glass. "Well, get on your cayuse and head outa here. Any man buys a spread around here won't have his cows long. Rustling going on all the time."

Rowan shrugged. "I'm in no hurry. You know, Cass, I never forgot you. Remember that time up at Cibecue when you saved my life?" Rowan looked at the others. "A big Tonto buck got at me when my horse was killed. Pinned my left arm to the ground. Cass grappled with him until I caved the Tonto's head in with a rock."

Dawson spat. "Wasn't nothing, Sarge."

Rowan rubbed his jaw. "You've had trouble with the Donigans before?"

"Hell! Who hasn't?"

"Your mule still there, Cass?"

"Call me Loco—everybody else around here does. Yeh. The old man has it in his corral. I'll never get it back. Anything strays on Donigan land it stays there."

"I'll get Nelly for you."

"They oughta call *you* Loco, instead of me. Leave her be, Rowan. It ain't worth the trouble you'll get into."

"I'll get you deputized," said Short.

Rowan shook his head. "No. I'll do this on my own."

Loco traced a map, using his finger which he wet in his rye. "Look. You ride south from the bridge a piece. You'll see a road cutting off to the west. You follow that two miles. You'll see the Donigan place right where the road cuts south again."

"Take my advice," said the bartender, shaking his bald head. "Fork your cayuse and get outa town. You don't want anything to do with them."

Rowan walked to the door. "I'll go," he said.

A tall man came into the saloon and eyed Rowan. His dark hair was shot with gray. His clothing was of fine material, from his white hat down to his finely tooled Mexican boots. The eyes were flat and cold. Gambler, thought Rowan.

The man sat down at a table and waited for his liquor. Loco Dawson came up beside Rowan. "Dane Grenville," he said softly. " 'Bout the only man around here ain't afraid of them Donigans."

The cold eyes held Rowan's for a second and then lowered. Rowan had a feeling similar to that experienced in looking at a rattler at close range. He walked out into the hot sun and across to the livery stable. He unsaddled Jim and shifted the saddle to a sorrel the liveryman said he could use. As he swung up on the sorrel, he saw that Sim Short and Loco Dawson were watching him over the batwings of the Union.

The Donigan place was set on high ground not far from the Mescalero. Smoke drifted up from the low, rambling house. There was a neat, tight look about the place. A barbed-wire fence encircled the ranch buildings and a large pool of clear water. A sign hung from the cross pole of the gate. "Keep out! The Donigans," read Rowan as he dismounted to open the gate. He led the sorrel up toward the house. There were flowerboxes at each window of the house; neat curtains showed through the clean glass.

A mule bawled from the peeled-pole corral as Rowan dropped the sorrel's reins. The kitchen door opened and a young woman came out, drying her hands on a gingham apron. She was tall and slender, with blue eyes and dark, lustrous hair. There was no doubt in Rowan's mind that she was a Donigan.

"Can I help you?" she asked.

"I'm Rowan Locke," he said, taking off his hat. "Seems as though Loco Dawson, a friend of mine, had a mule stray onto your land. Loco asked me to get it for him."

Her eyes were troubled. She glanced at the barn. "There is a stray mule here," she said quietly.

"May I take it?"

She hesitated and placed her hand at her throat. "Yes. It does belong to Loco Dawson. It's in the corral. Take it. But please get it out of here in a hurry. I don't want my father or brothers to see you with it."

Rowan tilted his head to one side. "Why? It isn't your mule."

She flushed. "My father had words with Loco about it."

The mule bawled plaintively. "Is that Nelly?" asked Rowan.

"Nelly?"

"Yes. The mule."

She laughed. The sound of it sent a strange feeling through Rowan. "Yes, that must be Nelly," she said. "Do you work for the Box R?"

"The Box R?"

"You must be a stranger. Everybody around here knows the Box R. John Ripsey's ranch. Just about the biggest in this part of New Mexico, with the exception of John Chisholm's Long I spread."

"I was just passing through Llano. Loco asked me to get Nelly."

Her eyes held his and something unsaid passed between them. Rowan didn't want to leave.

"I thought you must be a stranger, to come on Donigan land without permission," she said quietly.

"You must be one of the Donigans."

She glanced at the barn again. "I'm Joan Donigan."

Rowan felt vastly relieved that she hadn't changed her name. It was a puzzle, because in this country a single woman could pick and choose her man. "Do I have your permission to be on Donigan land?" he asked.

"Of course! But hurry! I'd rather not have you here when they come back."

Rowan smiled. "I'm only picking a stray, Miss Donigan. Nothing wrong in that, is there?"

She tucked back a wisp of dark hair. "No. But please go now."

Rowan hesitated. "I'd like to call on you," he said.

"No."

"Are you spoken for, Miss Donigan?"

She reddened. "No." She turned and hurried back into the house. As Rowan went to the corral to get Nelly, he knew Joan was watching him from the window. With five hell-raising brothers and an old hellion for a father, he knew why she hadn't been spoken for. He got the mule and led it to the sorrel.

"Where the hell you think you're going with that mule?" an angry voice shouted.

Rowan turned. A tall, gangling man was walking swiftly toward him, carrying a manure fork. "Loco Dawson asked me to get it," said Rowan.

Mike Donigan had the flashing blue eyes of the tribe. He was easily sixty years old, but his back was straight and he carried himself with the easy grace of a much younger man. "I run that snooping little fool outa here awhile back. Now, mister, you just take that mule back into that corral!" Donigan raised the manure fork.

Rowan took out the makings and began to roll a smoke. "I'm taking the mule," he said quietly. "Stop waving that manure fork."

Thin lines etched themselves at the corners of the old man's mouth. "Maybe you don't know where you are?"

Rowan lit his smoke. "You're Mike Donigan, aren't you?"

"Yes."

"Then this is the right place and the right mule."

Joan was watching them through the half-opened kitchen door. Donigan looked past Rowan and smiled thinly. "I'm sorry for you, stranger," he said. "Here come my boys. You still got time to ride through the pasture and get across the river."

Rowan turned. Five men rode swiftly up from the gate and drew rein twenty feet from him. The man in front was big Wash Donigan. His eyes were as cold as ice. "Who's this jasper, Pa?" he asked. The four behind him slid from their saddles and eyed Rowan.

"A friend of Loco Dawson's. Come to get Loco's mule."

Wash rubbed his jaw. "That damned mule been on our land again?"

"Yeh. This *hombre* says he's taking it back to Loco."

One of the Donigans laughed. They looked at each other as though sharing some great, secret joke. The youngest one picked up a rock and threw it up and down, eyeing Rowan. Wash opened and closed his big hands. "Mister, you're green around here. You just get on that sorrel and ride outa here."

Rowan flipped away his cigarette. "The mule goes with me."

Wash smiled. "Guess I'll have to beat some sense into your thick head."

Rowan looked Wash in the eye. "The mule goes with me," he said quietly. "You tell your little brother to stop playing with that rock."

The kid telegraphed his movement. Rowan dropped his right hand, cleared leather with his six-gun and fired a shot inches above the kid's head. The noise of the shot echoed softly from the hills behind the ranch. The kid dropped the rock. His face was white and set.

Mike Donigan spat. "You're a fast man with a cutter," he said sarcastically. "A coward's weapon! Take off that gun and put up your fists! Let's see how good you are with *them.*"

"Yeh," said Wash. "Take any of us, from the old man down to Monroe there."

Rowan walked to his sorrel and mounted, holding the mule's halter in his left hand. He rested his arms on his saddle horn and looked down at the six angry faces. "I'm taking the mule," he said. "Now get out of my way. The next time I shoot will be for record. Savvy?"

Rowan spurred the sorrel. The Donigans broke to get out of the way. Old Mike Donigan raised his manure fork. Wash looked at his father. "Let him go," he said. "We'll get him soon enough."

Rowan looked back as he reached the gate. The young woman was standing on the front porch watching him.

He rode along the fence line, wondering where Larry had been shot down. He half expected a pursuit, but the six men stood watching him. Sim Short had called them "nesters," but it looked as though they had been there a long time. Neatly kept fields attested to their skill as farmers. It was the girl who stayed in his mind as he rode toward Llano. She looked lonely. Try as he would, he could not get her out of his mind.

CHAPTER TWO

The sun had died, tinting the sky rose and gold, when Rowan led the mule into Llano. Loco Dawson came out of the Union and stared at him. He shouted over the batwings:

"He got Nelly, like I said he would! You owe me a bottle, Dandy!"

Sim Short crossed the street from his store. "How did you make out, Locke?" he asked.

"I got the mule."

"The marshal's job is still open."

"No, thanks."

"I'm buying," said Loco. He put his arm around the mule's neck. "Maybe I ought to buy one for you too, Nelly."

As Rowan walked into the Union, Grenville left, eyeing him sharply as he walked past him.

Dandy put a bottle and glasses on the bar. "Maybe there wasn't anybody there?"

"They were all there," said Rowan.

Loco slapped Rowan's back. "I told you he'd do it!"

Dandy shook his head. "If I was you, I'd pull outa Llano. And keep going. No one around here ever bucked up against them Donigans and got away with it."

"Them nesters," said Sim Short. He spat. "Old Man Ripsey has been trying to chouse them off his land for a year now. Can't get nowhere. He's got thirty hell-raising cowpokes and even *they* can't pry them Donigans off Box R land."

"Actually they got a right to stay," said Dandy.

"How so?" asked Rowan.

"Well, Ripsey got a surveyor to run lines. Got a slick lawyer to make out the papers. Ripsey homesteaded by proxy all along the Rio Mescalero. Every *vaquero* who worked for Ripsey got a quarter section of that land. Built a claim shack on it and did a few improvements. After three years, when the claim had been proved, John Ripsey would buy the land for a hundred dollars or so, and then file the deed. Old John even got some Mexicans to file. He claims *all* the land, clear back to the hills, on both sides of the Mescalero. Then he bought up Government paper, and scripped thousands of key acres to shut out the nesters. Any of them who got a foothold he bought off with five hundred dollars or so. Those that wouldn't, he had his boys pester until they were choused. The Donigans refused to go. They fought fire with fire. Donigan's barn went up in smoke. The next night one of Ripsey's barns went the same way. Ripsey's boys cut Donigan fences. Donigan's boys cut Ripsey's fences. They been hanging on for two years now, and Old John has been sweating over a year trying to boot them off what he thinks is *his* land."

"You'd think Ripsey would have enough land by now," said Rowan.

Dandy snorted. "Not King Ripsey! Besides, when the Rio Mescalero dries up in season, there's a top spring on the Donigan land that ain't never run dry in the history of this country. Ripsey wants it."

Sim nodded. "And that ain't all them Ripseys want. Pres Ripsey—the old man's only son—has had his eye on Joan Donigan ever since them Donigans showed up from

Kansas. Jeff Donigan— he's the third Donigan boy— caught Pres sparking around Joan when she came into town to do some buying. Jeff worked over Pres and then flattened a Box R waddie who horned in. Pres ain't never forgot it."

Rowan shoved back his glass. "I'll have to get a room," he said.

"The Plains House is your best bet," said Dandy.

"The job is still open," said Short.

"I'm heading up north toward the Canadian River." Rowan left the saloon. Loco followed him and they stopped on the walk. Loco came close.

"Listen, Rowan," he said softly, "seems to me you had a cousin around here. Owned the Lazy LF."

"So?"

Loco looked up and down the street. "Seems funny to me, you dropping in here, out of the service. You always was army."

"Keep talking."

"That cousin was Larry Forbes. Over a month ago he came down this way from the Lazy LF spread looking for rustled cows. He found some hides with Lazy LF brands in a shed behind Schwab's Butcher Shop. The butcher claimed he bought them from the Donigans. The brands had been blotted, a sloppy job, but they were Lazy LF all right. The Donigans called Schwab a double-barreled liar. Forbes got a warrant for the arrest of Wash Donigan. It was never served. Larry Forbes was found out near the Donigan place, his back full of shotgun pellets. Murder by a person or persons unknown was the coroner's verdict."

Rowan eyed the little ex-soldier. "Forbes was my cousin. I'm half owner of the Lazy LF. I came here to find the murderer. No one else around here knows Larry was my cousin, Loco."

Loco gripped Rowan's arm. "You can bet I won't open my mouth, Rowan!"

"I may need your help."

"All you need. I work around town most of the time, doing hauling for the merchants. That's why I had to have Nelly."

"Keep your ears and eyes open and your mouth shut."

"I'll freeze onto anything I hear."

"I think I can trust you, Loco."

Loco nodded. "We rode the river together, didn't we?"

Rowan took the sorrel to the livery stable and got his war bag. He registered at the Plains House and sat for a long time in a chair near a front window looking down into the lamplit streets of Llano. Then he took paper and pencil and composed a letter to Marion Forbes, Larry's widow on the Lazy LF. It was slow going. There wasn't much he could write except the fact that he was in Llano and meant to stay there until he found the man who had killed Larry. He put it in an envelope and took it to the post office to drop it in the slot. He stood for a long time in front of the building, trying to marshal his thoughts. The odor of food drifted to him from a hash-house across the street and he suddenly realized he was very hungry. He went into it and ordered a steak and trimmings, idly wondering if the meat came from a Lazy LF beef.

Rowan slept uneasily that night, thinking of Larry, but always the clear blue eyes of Joan Donigan seemed to drift into his vision.

He was eating breakfast the next morning when a stocky puncher limped in and stopped by Rowan's table.

"I'm Wasco Barnes," he said. *"Vaquero* for John Ripsey. He wants to see you, Locke."

"Where is he?"

"Out on the Box R."

"If he wants to see me, I'll be here in Llano."

Wasco scratched his bristly chin. "Damnit," he said finally, "Old John will rowel me raw if you don't come back with me."

"Why does he want to see me?"

"Damned if I know, unless it's about you bluffing them Donigans."

"How did he hear about that?"

Wasco shrugged. "Old John knows everything that goes on around here."

Rowan stood up. "I'll come," he said.

They walked down the street to the livery stable and Rowan got Jim. As he and Wasco rode south out of Llano, he saw Dane Grenville watching them from his seat in front of the Union. The man's dark, enigmatic eyes followed the two horsemen until they were out of sight.

"Do you know Dane Grenville, Wasco?" said Rowan as he offered the makings to Wasco.

"Yeh. Gambler. Cold-gutted as a shark. About the only man around here the Donigans won't hurrah."

"Why?"

Wasco shrugged. "I don't know. Grenville just don't seem to worry about anybody, even Old John."

They cut off just before the bridge and followed a good road west along the northern bank of the Rio Mescalero. About five miles from the town Wasco drew rein. "There it is—the Box R," he said, a note of pride in his voice.

A double row of giant cottonwoods stretched in front of them along a level slope. A large knoll was situated in a fine bosque of trees. A huge adobe house squatted in the bosque. There were enough outbuildings to form a small settlement. White-faced cattle dotted the slopes to the west, below the purple hills.

They rode between the cottonwoods and halted in front of the adobe. The door, thick and studded with handhewn bolts, was set deep in the thick wall. Wasco dismounted. "Go ahead," he said. "Miss Laura don't like us cowpokes in the house. We stink, I guess."

"Miss Laura?"

"Old John's daughter. Queen of the Box R." There was a note of sarcasm in Wasco's voice as he led the horses off.

Rowan rapped on the huge door and waited. In a few minutes the door opened smoothly. A Mexican woman looked at him. *"Quién es?"* she asked.

Rowan answered in cowpen Spanish. "Ripsey wants to see me. I'm Rowan Locke."

"Yes. He is expecting you. Please follow me."

The long hallway was cool, the floor waxed to a high degree. They crossed a shady patio. The woman tapped on a door and then opened it. "Please to go in," she said.

It was a big room, with carved vigas supporting the ceiling. It was delightfully cool after the harsh sunlight of the day. A beehive fireplace was filled with pieces of vertically stacked mesquite and piñon wood. The heavy furniture of the room was polished, reflecting the sunlight that crept in through the partially closed shutters. A set of long-horns was mounted over the fireplace. A man coughed and entered the room from a small doorway.

"Rowan Locke?"

"Yes."

Hard dark eyes studied Rowan as they shook hands. "Sit down," said John Ripsey. He wore a well-trimmed Vandyke and a shaggy dragoon mustache. John Ripsey sat down behind a littered desk as broad as a bunkhouse table. He shoved a box of cigars toward Rowan. "Drink?" he asked.

Rowan took a cigar. "Don't mind if I do."

Ripsey filled glasses from a silver decanter. Rowan had the distinct impression that Ripsey was probing into his brain, trying to snatch every fleeting thought.

Ripsey sipped his liquor. "Where are you from?" he asked.

"Fort Bowie, Arizona Territory."

"Just discharged?"

"Yes."

"How many years' service?"

"Twelve."

"Why did you leave?"

Rowan stood up. "I was told you wanted to see me, Ripsey. I didn't come here to be cross-examined."

Ripsey waved a strong brown hand. "Don't get riled. I like to know a little about the men I hire."

"I'm not working for you."

"You will."

Rowan couldn't help smiling. "You're damned sure of yourself."

Ripsey leaned back in his chair. "Yes. I am. I drove a trail herd here from Texas in '67. Built the Box R up from that herd of two hundred head. Today I have twenty thousand cattle and a ranch about the size of Rhode Island. I was dead broke when I got here, Locke. Fought Comanches, Navajos, Jicarillas, Mescaleroes and Mimbrenos to keep my land."

Rowan inspected his cigar. "Very interesting."

"You're an independent one!"

Rowan grinned. "Just a man who likes to swing a wide loop."

"I heard that you called a Donigan bluff yesterday."

"Let's say I talked sense into them."

Ripsey nodded. "What are you doing in Llano?"

"I'm on my way to the Canadian River."

"I have a feeling you mean to stay around here."

"I may."

"The Donigans are a hard lot—from the old man down to young Monroe. They've bucked me every inch of the way."

"So?"

"They've poisoned my cattle. Burned down a barn. Cut fence. Shot up two of my line shacks. Half a dozen of my *vaqueros* beaten up. Jeff Donigan beat my boy, Pres, because he spoke to Joan Donigan in Llano. They're a thorn in the side of the whole township."

"I've heard that you've done a little chousing yourself."

"Legally I'm in the clear."

"What do you want from me?"

Ripsey refilled the glasses. He glanced down at Rowan's plain Colt. "I want them run out of here. You're the only man I know of who has managed to ride off their land with a whole skin. Now, I don't care how you do it, but I want them rooted out!"

"I'm no killer, Ripsey."

The dark eyes seemed to veil themselves. "I can get you sworn in as deputy-sheriff. Say the word and you'll start today."

"Who will I be working for? The county or John Ripsey?"

Ripsey smiled. "I like you, Locke. Tell you what I'll do. I'll pay you two hundred a month and expenses, over and above your deputy's pay, to do the job."

"No."

"You drive a hard bargain. There will be a bonus for every Donigan hide you nail on my barn' wall. Say two hundred dollars apiece."

Rowan stood up. "You'll have to hire another killer."

Ripsey chewed at his cigar. "All right! All right! You don't have to do any killing. Consider yourself a stock detective. Just scout around and watch those Donigans. If you catch them in any deviltry on Box R land, you can report it to me. I'll take care of the rest."

"I'm sorry."

"You can consider the proposition. I'll give you a few days to think it over."

"Thanks."

Ripsey stood up and thrust out a hard hand. Rowan was surprised at the strength in it. "If you change your mind, just let me know."

Rowan left the room and crossed the patio to the hallway. A young woman was standing in the hallway eyeing him. She was tall, with honey-colored hair and light eyes. The odor of heliotrope drifted faintly to him.

"I'm Laura Ripsey," she said. "Are you working for Father?"

"Rowan Locke. No, ma'am."

She raised her eyebrows. "Father *always* gets his own way, Mister Locke."

"He didn't this time."

She laughed. "That's a change! Are you staying long in Llano?"

"For a time."

"Maybe we'll see more of you."

"I'll be busy, Miss Ripsey."

"So? You're rather abrupt, Mister Locke."

He smiled. "I'm an old army man, Miss Ripsey. I'm unused to pleasantries. You must forgive me."

She glanced down at the faded patches on his sleeve. "You have better manners than most enlisted men."

"I didn't know that manners were issued only to officers."

"Touché!" She opened the front door and walked with him toward the stables. "You must forgive me. I've spent so much time with rough cowmen that I sometimes forget my own manners." She tilted her head to one side. "Why did you enlist?"

"I was restless. Wanted to see the West."

"And you've seen a lot of it."

He looked toward the salmon-colored slopes, studded with mesquite. "Yes," he said quietly. "And I have no desire to return to Missouri."

She wrinkled her pretty nose. "I hate it. I spend as much time as I can away from here. But Dad likes to have Pres and me here with him. It seems to suit Pres. He likes to play the role of a rich rancher, though Heaven knows he doesn't do much work."

"Does he have to?"

"No. Dad has more money than he knows what to do

with. I want him to go East with me this fall and visit Philadelphia, New York and Boston. Perhaps even see Europe. The Grand Tour, you know. But he can't stay away from the Box R."

"I don't blame him, Miss Ripsey."

Her face changed, flooding with pent-up emotion. "I hate it!"

Wasco led up Jim. He waited as Rowan said goodbye to Laura and watched her go back into the house. Laura had given Rowan's hand a slight pressure as she held it. Wasco scratched under his arm. "You've made a hit," he said. "You working for the Old Man?"

Rowan mounted. "No."

Wasco raised his shaggy eyebrows. "Do tell! Well, I'll stand you a drink in Llano sometime. It'll be worth it to find out what you said to Old John."

"I just told him I had other plans."

"Yeh," said Wasco, with a grin. "That's why I want to hear what he said. Watch them Donigans, Locke. They're all mean, but Wash is the worst by far. No one around here has ever beaten him in a fist fight."

"There's always a better man, Wasco."

"Yeh . . . but where is he?"

"That I don't know. *Adios,* Wasco."

The puncher shook his head as he watched Rowan ride down the cottonwood lane. He glanced at the huge house and shook his head again.

As Rowan neared the gate, he saw a tall man riding a fine black come through it. The sun glinted on silver *conchas* on the saddle. The man drew rein as he saw Rowan. He nodded. He had John Ripsey's dark eyes and features, but there was a handsomeness about him that had been denied to John Ripsey. He wore finely tailored range clothing and a *buscadero* belt with twin ivory-butted, nickel-plated Colts.

"You're Locke," he said.

"I am."

"I'm Pres Ripsey."

"Pleased to meet you."

"When do you start working for Father?"

"I don't."

Pres frowned. "Didn't he offer you enough money?"

"More than enough."

"You leaving the country?"

"Not for a time."

Pres raised his head. His dark eyes were hard. "Maybe you'd better learn right now that John Ripsey runs this country. One word from him and no one else will hire you."

"I work for myself, Ripsey."

Pres stroked his thin Mexican mustache both ways. "Independent, eh?"

"Yes."

"The Donigans will take some of that out of you if you stay around Llano."

Rowan held the younger man with cold eyes. "I understand Jeff Donigan took some starch out of you not long ago."

Pres dropped slim hands to the butts of his ornate Colts. "Watch your lip!"

Rowan grinned. He touched Jim with his spurs and rode past the young man. "Get a checkrein on that temper, Pres," he said. "It might get you into trouble." He did not look back as he rode through the gateway.

As Rowan rode slowly toward Llano he had an uneasy feeling about the Box R and the three Ripseys. They were used to having their own way, riding roughshod over those who opposed them. The Donigans were of the same ilk. Rowan rolled a smoke, watching a roadrunner scuttle awkwardly out of the mesquite and race ahead of the bay. There would be big trouble in the Rio Mescalero country. The signs were plain to see.

CHAPTER THREE

R owan went into Schwab's Butcher Shop when he returned from the Box R. Schwab was busy with a woman customer. Rowan looked about the big shop. There were at least three beeves represented in the piles of meat on the long counter. Through an open door Rowan could see a locked shed. There were several barrels of offal beside it. Rowan studied Schwab. He was a burly man, almost as broad as he was high. In a country where most men acquired a deep tan it was surprising to see the fresh, almost pink complexion of the butcher. He spoke with a slight German accent. When the woman left, he looked at Rowan with clear blue eyes.

"What can I do for you, sir?" he asked.

"I may have some beef to sell."

Schwab wiped his hands on his apron. "Where do you get it?"

"I thought I might pick up some money by buying cows from the Mex ranchers in the hills and bringing them down to your slaughterhouse."

"I don't have a slaughterhouse."

Rowan glanced at the shed. "I see offal out there."

Schwab waved a huge hand. "Only the calves I

butcher here. The rest I get from Sid Coates and Slip Wellman. They got a slaughterhouse out to Salt Creek." The blue eyes studied Rowan.

"Maybe I can make you a better deal."

Schwab shook his head. "Them Mexicans don't have good beef. I don't want my customers should think Oscar Schwab would give them poor meat."

Rowan shrugged. "I was only trying to make a little money, Schwab."

The butcher leaned across the pile of fresh meat on the counter. "Listen," he said, "I know you. You're the man who went out to the Donigan place and got Loco's mule back for him. Now I give you good advice: you forget about getting beef for me or anyone else in Llano."

Rowan rolled a smoke. "Why?"

Schwab looked out through the front window. "You're living on borrowed time around here. Bad enough you should bluff them Donigans. Worse yet you should try to sell beef here in town."

"The Donigans are farmers, aren't they?"

"Yes." Schwab hesitated. "Sometimes I buy beef from Wash Donigan. I don't want to, but I got my shop to think about."

"You're afraid of him, too?"

Schwab colored. He raised a thick arm and touched the hump of bicep. *"Him* I could break in two pieces yet. But there are six of them, counting that old devil of a father. You want I should lose my business?"

"If it's good beef, what's the difference who you buy it from?"

Schwab raised his big head. "There was a man came in my place over a month ago. Nice fellow. One night he looks in my shed out there and finds some hides. Lazy LF brand they were. He talks to me about it the next day. I tell him I don't buy rustled beef. He claims the hides are from his cows. I tell him I bought the beef from Wash Donigan. I don't want to, but like I said, I have to play along with them dirty fellows or have my place wrecked yet. This man gets a warrant for Wash Donigan. He never gets it served. You know why?"

"No."

Schwab lowered his voice. "They find the poor fellow dead near the Donigan place with holes in his back. Ach! I am sick. Not only because he was a nice fellow, but because Wash Donigan probably knew I told this man where I got them Lazy LF hides. Wash said he never sold them to me. He is a liar!"

Rowan smiled. "I'm sorry we can't do business then."

"You get some other work. Maybe better you should leave Llano. It ain't healthy you should ask questions about beef in this town."

Rowan walked out of the shop. Loco Dawson was unloading supplies from his wagon in front of Sim Short's store. Rowan walked past him. "Come down to the livery stable when you're done," he said.

Rowan waited for Loco in the coolness of the big stable.

"What's on your mind, Rowan?" the little man asked when he ambled in.

"What do you know about Sid Coates and Slip Wellman?"

"They got a slaughterhouse out on Salt Creek."

"Where do they get their beef?"

"Quién sabe?"

"They legal?"

Loco scratched under his arm. "Legal as anybody, I guess."

"You ever haul for them?"

"Once in awhile."

"Beef or hides?"

"Beef mostly. Carried some hides for them to Alamogordo once."

"What brands?"

Loco looked at the ceiling. "Bar K. Double E. Some others. They were all local brands."

"Any Lazy LF?"

"No." A light dawned in Loco's eyes. "I get it. Listen! Sid and Slip been away for a time. Why don't you go out to their place and look around?"

"I intend to."

"Take the road north about two miles. Turn off on a dirt track to the west. Follow that about a mile. The slaughterhouse is in a hollow near the crick."

"Keno."

Loco eyed Rowan. "How'd you make out with John Ripsey?"

"Turned down a job."

Loco shook his head. "Old John will be on the prod for you. Watch out."

"I'll be all right." Rowan saddled Jim. "What kind of a man is Oscar Schwab?"

"He's all right. Does a good business. You been talking with him?"

"Yes."

"He don't know who you really are, does he?"

"I didn't tell him."

"He'll keep his mouth shut."

Rowan swung up on Jim. "I'll take a pasear out to Salt Crick. See you, Loco."

Rowan rode north and followed Loco's directions. The slaughterhouse squatted in a hollow. The door was padlocked, but it didn't keep the odor from creeping out into the clear air. Rowan wrinkled his nose. He grounded his reins and walked around to the back of the building. There was an empty peeled-pole corral there. He tried the back door but it was locked. One window was partly open and he pried it up with a stob of wood and climbed into the stinking interior. At one end of the building there was a small partitioned area. He crossed to it and looked in. A box held some papers. He riffled through them. There were bills of sale from half a dozen ranches, but none from the Lazy LF.

A few dried hides were piled at the back of the building. They were branded Bar K. Rowan left the building and rolled a smoke to get the stench out of his nostrils. He looked about the corral. On a rack beyond the corral he found four green Double E hides drying in the hot sun. He went back to the front of the building and walked up the creek. On the far bank he saw a place where the earth had been disturbed. He waded the shallow water and climbed the far bank. An animal had been rooting in the soft earth. He pushed some of the earth aside with his boots. The corner of a hide appeared. He uncovered enough of it to see that it was branded Box R. He got a branch and pried at the hides below it. The third one down was Lazy LF. There were three others below it.

Rowan replaced the earth, went back to Jim and rode down the creek. Locusts whirred in the willows and cottonwoods as he rode past. Suddenly there was a sound as of a snapping stick. Smoke puffed from a clump of brush on a knoll two hundred yards to his left. The gun cracked again and a slug rapped into the cantle of his saddle. He bent low and set the steel to Jim, dusting the trail to the road. When he reached it and looked back, there was no sign of life.

Rowan rode slowly back to town.

———

THERE WAS a familiar black horse in front of the Union when he tethered Jim to the rack. Pres Ripsey's blooded mount. Rowan took out his case knife and pried the slug from his saddle cantle. He examined it. The base was not mutilated and Rowan guessed it was fifty caliber. He dropped the slug into his shirt pocket and went into the Union. Pres Ripsey was seated at a back table with Dane

Grenville. He glanced at Rowan and then went on with his conversation.

Dandy grinned as he saw Rowan. "What's your pleasure, Locke?" he asked.

"How's the beer?"

"Rotten, but it's cold."

"I'll try it."

Dandy placed the bottle in front of Rowan. "A little different from the army, hey?"

"Some."

Dandy polished a glass and placed it on the back bar. "How'd you like to work for me?"

Rowan grinned. "As swamper?"

"Hell, no. You just be on call. When them Black Donigans come in you just stand at the bar and eye them. It'll be worth it to me."

"I may not always be lucky with them, Dandy."

"Sho! Lucky? Hell, you just didn't pull freight for the tules when they stood up to you. Ain't everybody can do *that!*"

Rowan emptied his beer and waited for another. The batwings pushed open and two of the Donigans stood there, straw hats pushed back from their curly black hair, hard blue eyes taking in every man in the room. The tallest one was Jeff Donigan, the third son, while the other was young Monroe, the kid who had picked up the rock the day Rowan had been at the Donigan place. For a moment Jeff's eyes clashed with Rowan's and then he looked past him, saw Pres Ripsey, and spat.

Dandy lowered his hands beneath the bar. "I don't want no trouble from you men," he said quietly. "I've had just about enough outa you after that last fracas."

"Hell!" said Monroe with an easy grin. "We just want a beer to cut the throat dust, Dandy."

Dandy glanced at Rowan and then back at the Donigans. "I got a sawed-off scattergun under here," he warned.

Jeff shrugged. "Just keep it there," he said.

"Belly up to the bar then," said Dandy.

"I'm buying," said Rowan.

Monroe laughed. "For a Donigan?"

"No hard feelings," said Rowan.

Jeff leaned on the bar. "Wash ain't forgot you, Locke," he said.

Monroe drank his beer. "Wash ain't never been licked yet," he declared.

Rowan downed his beer. "There'll come a time," he said. "See you, men." He walked from the bar. A buckboard with two horses tethered behind it was in front of Sim Short's place. Rowan walked into the general store. Joan Donigan was at the counter.

"Good afternoon, Miss Donigan."

She turned quickly. "Hello," she said.

Sim looked nervously from one to the other of them and then through the front window at the Union.

Joan Donigan handed her list to Sim. "I'll be back in a few minutes for this," she said.

Sim flushed. "Well," he said, "there's a little matter of an unpaid bill."

She raised her head. "We always pay, don't we, Sim?"

Sim rubbed his jaw. "Yes, but your father raised the devil in here some time ago about what you bought."

"For instance?"

"Some of them canned vittles. He said sow bosom and Mex strawberries were good enough for his family."

"I'll pay you the next time I'm in town."

Rowan was embarrassed. He watched the girl walk to the door. "Couple of boxes of .44/40 shells, Sim," he said. "No, not those dusty ones. The fresh boxes in the back of the case."

"They're all good shells," grumbled Sim.

"Then it doesn't make any difference which boxes I take, does it?"

Sim grinned. "Fussy, ain't you?"

Rowan took the boxes and slid them into his pocket. Sim looked out of the window. Joan was standing by the buckboard. "Nice girl." Sim scratched his lean jaw. "Damned if I can figure her out. She's a lady. As fine as they come. Make a nice wife for some man."

Rowan grinned. "Providing he can lick Old Mike and the five little boys."

"Yeh. Yet she ain't afraid of any of them. I look for her to run off some day. Beats me how she's stayed there as long as she has."

"No accounting for tastes, Sim."

Sim nodded. "You still want that job?"

"No."

"I'll keep asking."

"I'll keep saying no."

Sim waved his hands in disgust as Rowan walked out of the store. Joan was still standing by the buckboard. Rowan stopped. "I'm sorry I was in the way in there," he said.

Her clear eyes studied him. "Don't apologize. I'm used to it, Mister Locke."

"My name is Rowan."

"Rowan, then." She glanced across the street. "You'd better not be seen speaking with me, Rowan."

"Why?"

"People will talk. It seems that I'm tarred with the same brush as the rest of my family."

He smiled. "I'm worried."

The batwings of the Union swung open and the two Donigans stepped out. Jeff wiped his mouth, stared at Rowan and then crossed the sunny street with short, plunging steps. He stopped ten feet from Rowan. "Get moving," he said.

"Why?"

"My sister don't talk to men like you."

Monroe leaned against the wagon and watched his

brother and Rowan. Rowan looked at Joan. "What do *you* say?"

"Jeff, Rowan has been very nice," she said quietly.

"Rowan?" said Jeff sharply. "What's been going on here?"

Joan raised her head. "Did you miss something, Jeff?"

Jeff's face was set and white. He looked at Rowan. "You got the guts to take off that gun?"

People had stopped to watch the little scene. The only one who was unperturbed was young Monroe. There was an expectant grin on his face as he watched his brother and Rowan.

"Jeff," said Joan quietly, "I don't want a scene."

Jeff ignored her. "You hear what I said, Locke? You got the guts to face a Donigan without a gun?"

Rowan looked at the girl. "Go ahead," she said quietly. "I won't stay to see it." She got into the buckboard and unwound the reins. She spoke to the mules and turned the buckboard.

Rowan looked at the set face of the third Donigan. Jeff was about his build but taller. His muscles were the muscles of a man used to hard manual labor in contrast to the long flat muscles that corded Rowan. Rowan slowly unbuckled his gunbelt and hung it over a hitching rack. His eyes never left Jeff's as he took off his hat and jacket and placed them on the walk. Jeff moved his head from side to side, pleased and expectant.

A man looked over the batwings of the Union.

"It's one of them Donigans again! Jeff, this time! He's going after Locke!"

Pres Ripsey and Dane Grenville were among those who came out of the Union to watch the two men in the street. Suddenly Rowan stepped off the boardwalk and raised his fists. Jeff spat back over his left shoulder and thrust out a long left arm, shuffling his feet in the thick dust. Rowan grinned. He moved in. The long left shot out, and Rowan blocked it easily with his right forearm, testing his man, waiting for the real attack. Jeff bobbed awkwardly and drove in. Rowan measured him with a left and clipped him neatly with a right hook. Jeff came in fast. There was a rapid interchange of blows, leaving Rowan with a puffed lip while Jeff's left eye was a little red.

The dust rose as they circled. Jeff landed a smashing left to the gut and drove up hard with a big right fist for the jaw, but Rowan sidestepped, caught Jeff under the right ribs with a punishing right and hit him behind the ear with a left. Jeff grunted with the pain and backed off. Monroe spat. "Go get him, Jeffie."

Jeff came in, bobbing and weaving like a belt winner. Rowan blocked three blows with elbows and caught Jeff in the lean gut with a short left, then pulled the snapper on his cocked right. Jeff went down in the dust. He leaned back on his hands and stared at Rowan. A trickle of blood crept down his jaw. Rowan stepped back and drew in a deep breath. He was caught flatfooted. Jeff came up off the ground like a raging fury, disregarding all science. He threw punches so fast that Rowan was flat on his back on the boardwalk with blood leaking from his nose and a loose tooth flooding his mouth with blood. Jeff's face was a mask of white rage, streaked with blood.

Rowan shook his head. The street lifted a little and then seemed to settle. For a moment he was sure that he saw two shuffling Jeff Donigans moving about in the harsh sunlight.

"Get up, man," said Sim Short behind him.

Rowan got up in time to meet another rush. His shirt was ripped from a slashing hook. His ribs, ached from a devil's tattoo. He covered up and hung onto his man, trying to draw the hot air into his lungs. Jeff threw him back and drove in a punch. Rowan saw it coming but couldn't avoid it. He turned his head and caught it on the neck. He staggered back. There was a low, triumphant growling in Donigan's throat as he charged in.

Rowan shot out a left, which Jeff brushed aside. He clipped the taller man on the jaw and staggered him. Jeff whirled like a lassoed maverick in time to meet a piston left to the jaw and a jarring right which sent him backwards with arms outspread for balance. Rowan drew on his reserve strength and followed. He threw a wild right which shut the blinds on Jeff Donigan. The man went down flat, seeming to bounce as he hit the boardwalk. Blood flooded from his slack mouth and onto the dry wood of the walk. Monroe Donigan ran to his brother.

"Jeff, you're fooling! Get up!" he yelled.

"He ain't fooling," said Sim Short dryly.

Monroe snatched a piece of board from the ground and rushed at Rowan. Rowan slid behind a post. The board slashed splinters from the post.

"Donigan!" a man called.

Monroe tried to circle behind Rowan. Rowan glanced at his gun. He'd never make it. The kid would cave in his skull like a melon.

"Donigan!" the man called from the center of the street. It was Dane Grenville.

Monroe spat and hunched his shoulders, eyeing Rowan warily. Suddenly he raised the board. There was a sharp crack. Monroe grunted, dropped the board and gripped his right bicep, staring foolishly at the blood between his fingers. Grenville pocketed the tiny pistol which had seemed to leap into his hand from nowhere.

Monroe reached down for the board with his left hand. Grenville smiled. "I have another bullet in the other barrel," he said softly. "I *aimed* for your right arm, Monroe. It could have been between the eyes. *Let that board alone.*"

Rowan wiped the blood from his face, watching the cool gambler and the tense kid. "Thanks, Grenville," he said.

"My pleasure. Killing a man with a board is a messy business."

Rowan picked up his hat and jacket and put them on. He looped the heavy gunbelt over his left arm and walked toward the general store. A woman was watching him from across the street. Laura Ripsey. Rowan turned away and walked into the store. Sim Short came in behind him.

"Doc Beardsley will take care of the kid," he said. "My God, Rowan! That last punch was a heller!"

Rowan drew in a deep breath and looked at his shredded knuckles. He ached all over. "A man is a fool to fight," he said quietly.

Sim pulled a bottle from beneath the counter and handed it to him. Rowan drank deeply and wiped his mouth with the back of a shaky hand. Sim looked admiringly at him.

"I damned near got beat, Sim."

"Hell! Jeff can't hold a candle to Wash."

Rowan drank again. "That's what I was afraid of," he said.

Sim tugged at Rowan's sleeve. "Look," he said, "I knew she'd be across the street before long."

Rowan turned. Laura Ripsey was in front of the store looking down at the bloody face of Jeff Donigan.

"Why?" he asked.

Sim spat. "Likes blood, is all."

"What do you mean?"

Sim lowered his voice. "For all her airs, and schoolin', and her talk about hating the West, she fits in all right. Somethin' mighty peculiar about that young woman. Fact is, there's something peculiar about the whole damned family."

Suddenly Laura looked through the window at Rowan, and then, as though he were a total stranger, she turned and walked swiftly out of sight. There was a cold feeling in Rowan. Once in the Chiricahuas he had turned a shoulder of rock, walking silently in Apache moccasins, to see a mountain lion crouched on the bloody carcass of a deer. He remembered the blood-smeared muzzle, and the cold, baleful eyes. He gripped the bottle and drank deeply. A sudden revulsion for Llano came over him. Yet he had set his feet on the trail. *"Dih asd-za hig-e balgon ya-hi dont-e shilg-nli dah,"* he said in Apache.

"What the hell is that mush?" asked Sim.

Rowan looked at the storekeeper. "This I have done and what has resulted therefrom is all the same to me," he translated. He buckled on his gunbelt and walked to the door.

Sim Short scratched his chin. "Well, I'll be damned," he said softly. "The whole damned town has been eating jimson weed, it appears like. Shoulda listened to my mother and become a man of the cloth!" He picked up the bottle and drank deeply.

CHAPTER FOUR

Rowan was in his room, lying on the brass bed, watching the wreathing tobacco smoke waver and then drift swiftly out through the partly open window. Spurs jingled in the hall and Rowan rolled over and cleared his Colt from the holster hanging from a bedpost.

Knuckles tapped on the door. "It's Loco, Rowan! You asleep?"

"Come in, Loco." Rowan sheathed the six-gun.

Loco came in and closed the door. His sagging jacket pockets held two bottles. He whistled as he saw Rowan's face. "Who won?"

"I wonder," said Rowan drily.

Loco placed the two bottles on the table. He grinned, wrinkling up his seamed, homely face. "I got Volcanic Oil for the outside and Bacanora mescal for the inside."

"Forget the liniment."

Loco shook his head. "Shuck outa that undershirt. Your ribs will feel like a busted barrel tomorrow."

Rowan watched the little man as he applied the oil, whistling "Cotton-eyed Joe" in time to his deft rubbing of Rowan's battered rib cage. Loco stepped back and tilted his head to one side. "That'll do. Put on your shirt."

"What's the talk about town, Loco?"

"The odds are even on you and Wash Donigan now."

Rowan shook his head and accepted a bent cigar from Loco. He lit while Loco filled two glasses from the squat mescal bottle. "I've been wild as a Nueces steer in this mess, Loco," he said.

"How so? You can name your price around here now. Sim Short will hire you for twice what he paid Lem Hayden, and *that's* something. Sim is stingy enough to kill a flea for his hide and taller. Old John Ripsey will hire you at a better price. You planning to stay around here, you'd better take one job or another."

Rowan walked to the door and listened. He opened it softly and looked up and down the dusty hall. It was empty. He closed the door and turned to Loco. Rowan needed help. He had made a public figure out of himself by facing down the Donigans and whipping Jeff. Loco was a good man, eccentric as a hill-nutty prospector, but he was the only one Rowan could rely on. They had ridden the river together in times past. Loco handed Rowan a glass and raised his in salute.

They drank and Loco sighed. "Mother's milk," he said.

Rowan sat down on the bed. Loco dropped into the creaking platform rocker near the window. Rowan took out his marshal's badge and tossed it to Loco. "Look," he said quietly. "Now you know why I don't want the marshal's job here."

Loco whistled softly. "I had an idea you wasn't just pirootin' in Llano."

"My orders are to get the man that killed Larry and also to round up some of the big loopers around here."

Loco shook his head. "You bit off a chunk, *amigo*. Whoever killed Forbes vanished like a damned *chisos*. As for rustlers, they're thick as fiddlers in hell in the Pecos country. In the last year they've had all kinds of lawmen drifting around here. Stock detectives, U.S. Marshals, sheriffs and deputy-sheriffs, Pinkerton men and Association men. Some of them give up. Some of them get scared off." Loco drained his glass and looked at Rowan with half-closed eyes. "Some of them are Pecos-ed. Shot, gutted, and dropped into the Pecos, so they don't float up again."

"I was out at Coates' and Wellman's slaughterhouse this afternoon. Found some green hides buried across the crick. Box R *and Lazy LF.*"

"It figures, Rowan."

Rowan puffed at his cigar. "You think they do the rustling themselves?"

Loco shook his head. "They don't have to. They peddle meat all over the Rio Mescalero country."

"Who's supplying them?"

Loco picked at a tooth with a match. "It ain't the Donigans."

"You sure?"

"Positive. The Donigans get their beef from cows that stray on Donigan land. Or so they say."

"They have to have a bill of sale."

Loco shook his head. "You don't have to have a bill of sale for a fallen hide. They bring in Box R, Bar K, Double E, or any other brand, claim it's a fallen hide and get away with it."

"And they make them fallen hides, is that it?"

"Keno!"

"The beef delivered to Schwab could come from any brand. If they pick up a cow without a bill of sale, they bury the green hide. Any beef they buy legitimately they have a bill of sale for and can sell the hide."

Loco refilled the glasses. "Your job is to get the coward that drygulched Forbes."

Rowan reached in his pocket and took out the mutilated slug which had struck the cantle of his saddle. He handed it to Loco. "Take a look at this. You were an armorer once. What do you know about it?"

Loco eyed the slug. "About .50/95, I'd say. Probably from a Winchester."

"Common caliber in the Pecos River country?"

Loco scratched his jaw. "No . . . mostly .44/40 around here. Quite a few .38/40. Some .32/20, but they ain't too common. Most of the vaqueros carry Winchester Model 1873 rifles. Some old Spencers and Henry rifles kicking around. Damned if I can recall any of them being .50/95, though."

"Think, Loco!"

Loco looked at the ceiling. "I worked for Old Honus Kiser in El Paso about a year ago. Best damned gunsmith west of San Antonio. Saw rifles in his shop I never knew was made."

Loco got up and paced back and forth. "Wait a minute!" he said. "The Winchester Model 1876, that's the Centennial Model! Old Honus had a couple in the shop, including a 'One in a Thousand Model.' The '76 came in the special .45/75, .45/60, .40/60, and later in .50/95. The .50/95 was called an Express. Came out in '79."

"Anything else?"

"Yeh. The .50/95 Express had a shorter barrel than the other calibers. Twenty-six inches, as compared to twenty-eight in the other calibers."

Rowan nodded. "Some drygulcher fired twice at me along the Salt Crick trail. That slug hit the cantle of my saddle."

"Well I'll be dipped. You see him?"

"Nothing. I jumped up a lot of dust skiting out of there."

Loco lit a cigar. "Coates and Wellman ain't been around for awhile. Been up around Fort Sumner, I think." Loco worked his cigar to the other side of his mouth. "Couldn't be one of the Donigans. They're dirty but I never seen them with a saddle gun. 'Bout the only thing they ever use is a shotgun."

They looked at each other. "Yeh," said Rowan. "That's what got Larry—a shotgun."

"I'll keep my eyes open for anyone that carries a '76 Winchester, although it might not mean much, 'lessn it's Coates or Wellman. Might be they just wanted to scare you off, providing it *was* them."

Rowan stood up and swung his gunbelt about his waist. He picked up his hat. "Come on," he said. "I'll stake you to a meal."

Loco was out of his chair like a shot. "Well, I ain't hungry but you talked me into it." He handed Rowan the mutilated slug and the badge.

They left the hotel and walked down the dimly lit street. "I can't figure out why Grenville stepped in today," said Rowan.

Loco shrugged. "Damned if I know. Grenville was a gentleman somewheres. He's like a lot of card sharks, polished on the outside, but shaggy inside."

They ate quickly and Loco invited Rowan to the Union for a drink. A lean-looking man stood at the end of the bar wearing a Mex hat, ornamented with coin silver filigree. His shirt and trousers were black, his boots of the same color. His slender hands were cased in tight black gloves. Loco whistled softly as he saw the man. "Chisos Ahrens," he said.

"Who is *he?*"

"Works for John Ripsey. Graduate of Hays, Ellsworth, Dodge City and Tascosa. Wrathy to kill, that *hombre.*"

The saloon was well filled but Chisos stood alone, staring moodily at his whiskey glass. Rowan threw a silver dollar on the bar. At the ring of the coin, Chisos looked up slowly, directly at Rowan. The eyes were a startling light gray in the lean tanned face. The thin mustache accentuated the thin line of the bloodless lips. A cold finger seemed to trace the line of Rowan's spine. He had seen the notorious Doc Holliday in Tombstone many times, as well as John Ringo, and the similarity between them and this cold-eyed man at the bar was marked.

Dandy served Rowan and Loco. He eyed Rowan's bruised face. "Good fight, Rowan," he said.

"Thanks."

Dandy glanced down at Rowan's big-knuckled hands. "That last punch was a ring-tailed roarer. By God, I thought you broke his jaw and your hand."

Chisos shifted a little and then walked toward Rowan, his big Mex spurs jingling musically. "You're Locke, aren't you?" he asked in a voice that was flat and quiet.

"Yes."

"Bueno! John Ripsey is in town. He wants to see you."

"Now?"

"Now!"

For a moment Rowan was tempted to tell the gunman to go to hell. Then reason applied the checkrein. He downed his drink. "I'll come. Where is he?"

"At the Stockman's Bar."

Loco wet his lips and looked back and forth between the two lean men. Rowan threw another dollar on the bar. "Drink up on me, Loco," he said. "I won't be long."

They walked down the street. Men stopped to watch them pass, like two great cats. Chisos did not speak until they reached the saloon. "Mister Ripsey is in Dan Tolliver's office at the back of the saloon," he said. He looked Rowan full in the eye. "Ripsey is a good boss. I like him."

"Why?"

Chisos smiled thinly. "He always pays off what he owes."

"Wages?"

"Yes . . . and everything else."

Rowan shrugged and walked into the saloon, past the long bar, garishly decorated by a long oil painting of a fleshy nude, tastefully draped in transparent painted gauze. Rowan grinned as he saw a neat bullet hole through the buxom damsel's navel. Rowan tapped on the office door. "Come in!" called Ripsey.

Rowan went in. John Ripsey was seated in a leather chair studying a large ledger. He looked up from the pool of light on the desk. "Set," he said.

Rowan dropped into a chair, crossed a leg, and rolled a smoke. Ripsey closed the book and shoved it to one side. He filled two glasses from a bottle and shoved one toward Rowan. "Sure make yourself at home here, Ripsey," said Rowan.

"I ought to be able to, seeing as how I own it. Dan Tolliver went broke a couple of years ago and I bought the place, leaving Dan as the figurehead."

"Nice arrangement."

Ripsey nodded. "Laura doesn't like the idea of her old man being a saloon owner."

"An ancient and honorable profession."

Ripsey grunted. "I hear you locked horns with Jeff Donigan today."

"I did."

"You beat him."

"That's a fine point. Look at my face."

"The point is—*you did beat him.*"

"I wouldn't bet on the next fight."

Ripsey lit a cigar. "Jeff Donigan beat my son badly. Then to pile it on thicker, he whips Ranse Norton, one of my best boys. You've got the Donigans treed, Locke."

"I have my doubts about that. I wasn't trying to, anyway."

"You have. Now, when do you start work for me? I can have you sworn in tomorrow."

Rowan shook his head. "I'm on my own, Ripsey." He ground out his smoke and eyed the cold-faced man across from him. "Besides, if you're so damned afraid of the Donigans, why don't you sick Chisos on them, like you did me."

"I only asked him to tell you to come here."

"Supposing I had refused?"

"Hell's fire, man! Don't be so damned ornery!"

"You didn't answer me, Ripsey!"

John Ripsey spat. "Nothing would have happened."

"You're a liar!"

Ripsey's face went white. A nerve twitched at his jaw. "One of these days," he said softly, "they'll put a bandanna over your face to keep the clods from dirtying it."

Rowan stood up and placed his hands flat on the desk. "I'm no yahoo from up the crick," he said. "You sent that cold-gutted killer to put the fear of God and soft-nosed slugs into me. For a 'dobe dollar, I'd whip you, Ripsey, if you were big enough and young enough."

Ripsey wasn't afraid. He took the long cigar from his mouth. "I've tangled with your type before," he said. "You go on your you-be-damned way like a skunk in the middle of the road until you're cut down like any other man with a chip on his shoulder. Now you listen to me!"

"I'm listening."

"One word from me and Chisos will corner you into a gun fight, and *he won't lose!*"

Rowan laughed thinly. "Six gunless men have John Ripsey, King of the Rio Mescalero, crying for help. They whipped that gutless son of yours and Ripsey blood can't stand it. Isn't that the truth?"

Ripsey went fish-belly white. "Get out of here," he muttered.

Rowan turned and walked out. The bartender and the men at the bar eyed him curiously, and he realized the door had been partly open and their voices must have carried out into the bar. He pushed through the ornate batwings. Chisos was leaning against a post, a cigarillo pasted in the corner of his mouth. "When do you start work?" he asked.

"I don't."

"Ripsey won't like that."

Rowan sucked in a deep breath. He had been choused enough that day. "Let his kid fight his own battles," he said.

Chisos straightened up. "I could have killed Jeff Donigan for what he did to Prescott," he said coldly. "I don't fight a man who ain't got the guts to wear a gun. *You got a gun, Locke.*"

The saloon light cast a sickly glow over the lean face of the gunman, giving him the look of a death's-head. A man stepped out of the shadows on the far side of the street, saw the two figures in the light of the saloon and stepped quickly back.

"You got a gun," repeated Chisos. He slowly raised his right hand and took the cigarillo from his mouth. "Draw," he said softly.

Rowan dropped his right hand. Chisos moved like an uncoiling spring. He dropped the cigarillo and his hand flashed down. Rowan forgot about his Colt. He blocked the right arm of Chisos, which had come up with frightening speed, cocking the long-barreled six-gun. Rowan swung the whole strength of his muscular body into a chopping blow at the corded throat. Chisos gasped in pain even as the Colt roared, awakening the echoes in the dark street. It roared again, whipping a slug through Rowan's hatbrim, half-blinding him with smoke and flame. He gripped the gunman's right wrist and drove it upward, snaking his free right arm under Chisos' upper arm and locking his right hand on his left wrist. The Colt cracked, sending a slug through the wooden awning over them. Rowan bent the arm back. There was a sickening snap as the gunman's wrist broke under the terrible pressure. The Colt bounced from Rowan's left instep, making him wince with pain.

Chisos cursed. Rowan freed him and measured him with a left. Chisos staggered back, flapping his useless right hand. Rowan followed him, smashing at the pain-filled face. Chisos turned to run and hit the adobe wall of the livery stable. Rowan gripped him by the right shoulder and whirled him about. His right came in like a maul, smashing Chisos' head back against the wall so hard that dried flakes of adobe hit Rowan in the face. Chisos slid down silently and fell sideways. Rowan stepped back, dragging in lungfuls of the thin hot air.

Boots pounded on the boardwalks and thudded in the thick dust of the street. A door banged open across the street. Men ringed Rowan, looking down at Chisos in awe.

Deputy-Sheriff Busch pushed through the crowd. He knelt beside the battered gunman and examined the blood-streaked face. He ripped back the fine black shirt and placed his ear against the naked chest. He looked up at Rowan. "He's dead," he said quietly.

Rowan felt the white worms moil in his gut. The white-hot fury which had sparked his attack drained from him, making him feel weak. Busch stepped close to Rowan and slipped his Colt out. "I'm arresting you for the murder of Chisos Ahrens," he said. "I warn you that anything you may say will be used against you."

CHAPTER FIVE

Rowan watched the sun ease itself up across the plains to the east, flooding the gray sky with light, and tinting the puffs of clouds which hung over the valley of the Pecos. There had been no sleep for him; the pale face of Chisos Ahrens had seemed to float before him when he had closed his eyes. He had killed before. He didn't know how many men. In his twelve years in the cavalry he had seen only two men who kept a blood tally. A white civilian scout who was nothing more than a killing machine; a man who killed with a cold desire because of some twisted trail in his brain pattern. The other had been a naturalized German, a veteran of Berdan's Sharpshooters, a man skilled in the use of the long gun, who placidly filed a nick on the butt plate of his issue carbine every time he accounted for an Apache. Yet there had been no malice in him. To him, it had been just a job; a job he had done with the thoroughness of the Teuton.

Rowan rolled a smoke and lit it, watching the blue wreath drift between the bars. He had killed perhaps a dozen men in his life. Apaches, a crazed trooper who had tried to knife a quartermaster sergeant, several Mexican raiders. He could hardly remember them. But Chisos

Ahrens had been different. Ahrens was a professional gun-slinger, hired to draw blood, doing his job with coldness and skill. His Colt could probably have been notched to look like a bear-cub's teething ring. But the killing of Chisos Ahrens had been so unexpected, a sort of extra handicap thrown into the bloody, secret game Rowan was playing. He cursed and sat down, grinding the cigarette butt beneath his boot heel and looking down at his raw-knuckled hands. There was almost something obscene in killing a man with bare hands, a reversion to the primitive.

The sun was well up when Coon Ellis, the turnkey, brought Rowan his breakfast, unlocking the door to place the tray on the rickety table in the cell. "How you feel, Locke?" he asked curiously.

"Lousy!"

"Yeh. I know. Busts a man all up inside."

Rowan nodded.

Coon filled his pipe and watched Rowan eat. "Figger it this way, Locke. Chisos woulda shot you down and drawn his bonus from John Ripsey without turning a hair. You was the better man, is all."

"You think Ripsey wanted him to kill me?"

Coon shrugged. "It's been done before. Killing a man, any man who crosses him, ain't nothin' to slow Old John down."

"Ripsey didn't mean to have Chisos kill me."

"Mebbe . . . but Chisos tried. Yuh gotta figger this angle: Chisos was a mad dog. A first-rate killer. Probably treated like a dog when he was a kid, and aimed to take it out on the world. He wasn't the kind of *hombre* you could bunk with, split a bottle or a smoke with. A lone wolf. But Old John treated him like he wanted to be treated. Like a *man,* paying his wages, and acceptin' him like an equal. You crossed Old John. That was enough for Chisos. A one-man dog don't have no rules to follow except to stick by his master."

Rowan looked up at the old man. "Coon, I think you've been reading books."

"Me? Hell, no! But I been working around jails since I was a young man. I've seen killers cry for their mothers when the time came to dance at the end of a rope. Onct, in the Indian Nations, I seen one worry about who was gonna take care of his pet mouse when he left this vale of tears by way of a rope necktie. I had to take care of the squeaking little bastard, too, like I said I would."

Rowan smiled. "Takes all kinds, Coon."

"You finish that food! You'll be gaunt as a gutted snowbird if you just drink coffee."

"What happens next?"

Coon lit his pipe. "Coroner's jury. This morning about eleven."

"Fast work."

"Old John made a few calls early this morning. He gets things done around Llano."

"Why don't they call it Ripsey instead of Llano?"

Coon grinned. "He's too modest."

———

JOHN RIPSEY WASN'T in the little courtroom when the jury convened. Rowan sat in a chair with Deputy Busch behind him. The coroner was Addison Pritchard, a massive man, gone to loose flesh, with a pale face and pale green eyes. Partway through the testimony of the bartender of the Stockman's Bar, John Ripsey came in, followed by Pres. They sat at the back of the room. Sim Short, Loco Dawson and others of the townspeople were there. The testimony droned on. When the bartender finished, his testimony was substantiated by the men who had been in the bar. Now and then Ripsey's hard eyes steadied on Rowan. There was no mercy in them. The gist of the testimony was that Rowan had argued with Ripsey and had left the saloon in a rage, meeting Chisos on the way out. None of the witnesses had seen the altercation which had led to the killing. Busch testified, stating that Chisos had been beaten to death.

It was after twelve when a tall man entered the courtroom and leaned against the back wall. It was Jeff Donigan. His face was still battered and swollen from his battle with Rowan. He did not look at Rowan, and also ignored the hard-faced Ripseys.

Addison Pritchard raised his head as the last witness finished his dull statement. The clerk waited expectantly, shuffling his papers. "If there are no more witnesses," said Pritchard in a dull voice, "we will hear the statement I prepared on the cause of death of Leonard Ahrens, known to us as Chisos Ahrens."

The cause-of-death statement was read slowly by the clerk. Rowan shifted in his chair. Joan Donigan was standing beside her brother. She spoke quietly with him, squeezed his arm and left the room, glancing back at Rowan.

Pritchard raised his massive head again. "As there are no more witnesses, we will proceed with the instruction of the jury."

Rowan raised his head. "No statement was taken from me," he said quietly.

Pritchard's eyes swiveled and settled on Rowan. "You will be quiet," he said.

Rowan tried to stand up, but Busch shoved him down in the chair. Jeff Donigan walked quickly to the front of the courtroom. "I have a statement to make," he said.

"In reference to this case?" "Yes."

"You are not a witness, Mister Donigan." Donigan glanced at Rowan. "Yes," he said quietly, "I am."

Pritchard turned quickly. "Swear him in." Donigan was sworn in. "I was in town last night, looking for Rowan Locke, the man accused of the murder of Chisos Ahrens. I had been in town for an hour waiting for a chance to meet Locke. It was after dark when I saw him leave his hotel, with Loco Dawson. They ate in the restaurant. Then they crossed the street to the Union and I waited outside to catch Locke alone. They was only in the saloon a short while when Locke came out with Chisos and walked down to the Stockman's Bar. Chisos stayed outside. Locke went inside and was gone about fifteen minutes. Chisos Ahrens was still outside. I was in the shadows across the street. I figgered Locke would leave Chisos there but they started to talk so I waited. Then Chisos drew on Locke. Locke didn't try to draw. He blocked Chisos' draw. Chisos' six-gun went off. Locke gripped Chisos' gun arm and I guess he broke it. The gun went off a few times. I don't remember how many. Locke left his gun in its sheath and fought Chisos with his bare hands. Chisos got killed when he hit the wall. Locke never drew on Chisos."

In the silence that followed, Rowan looked at the battered face of the man he had fought. Pritchard coughed and looked at the clerk. "You get all that?"

"Yes."

Ripsey's face was a set mask. His son bit his lip and dropped his hand to the butt of his Colt.

Pritchard looked at Busch. "How many shots were fired from Leonard Ahren's pistol?"

"Three," said Busch.

"How many from Rowan Locke's pistol?"

Busch hesitated. He glanced at the Ripseys and then down at the floor. "There was five cartridges in his Colt."

"Then one was fired?"

Busch shook his head. "The hammer was resting on an empty cylinder hole. The gun hadn't been fired at all."

Sim Short grinned. Loco waved at Rowan. Pritchard turned to the jury. He instructed them in the difference between premeditated murder and killing in self-defense, and they left the courtroom. Jeff Donigan sat down on a window ledge and rolled a smoke.

The jury was back in twenty minutes. Andrew Home,

the foreman, stood up and looked at a slip of paper in his hand. "We, the jury, impaneled and sworn in this case, do, upon our oaths, find the Defendant not guilty."

Rowan felt the cold sweat work down his sides. Busch nodded to him. Rowan stood up. The Ripseys had left the room upon hearing the verdict. Jeff Donigan followed them. Addison Prit-chard waited until the clerk had written out the verdict and until it was signed by the jury and then he read it in his flat voice:

"Verdict. Territory of New Mexico, County of Lincoln. An inquisition holden in the county of Lincoln, territory of New Mexico, on the 16th day of September, 1883, before me, Addison Pritchard, Coroner of Lincoln County, New Mexico Territory, upon the body of Leonard Ahrens, there lying dead, by the persons whose names are hereto subscribed. The said jurors upon their oaths, from the evidence do say that the said Leonard Ahrens came to his death by fist blows administered by Rowan Locke, causing his decease by the impact of his skull against a wall, thus fracturing it and causing instant death, on the 15th day of September, 1883, in the county of Lincoln, territory of New Mexico."

Pritchard read the names of the jurors and turned the verdict over to his clerk. He nodded at Rowan. "You are free to go now," he said in his dull voice.

Busch coughed. "Your Colt is in the rack at the *calabozo,*" he said. "Coon will give it to you. You're a lucky man, Locke."

Rowan spoke, his eyes never leaving Busch. "Yes," he said. "Damned lucky that Jeff Donigan was a big enough man to save me from a hanging when he could have kept his mouth shut."

Busch picked at his lower lip. "You ain't out in the clear yet," he said.

"What do you mean?"

"Old John will get at you some way. He's got ideas of his own when it comes to justice."

Rowan walked out of the courtroom, pausing to accept the proffered hands of Loco and Sim. He stepped out into the harsh sunlight. Joan Donigan was seated in her buckboard across the street. Rowan doffed his hat and stopped by the wagon.

"I want to thank your brother," he said.

She smiled. "He told me of it late last night."

"It was a fine thing for him to do, after the fight we had."

She tilted her head to one side. "Perhaps you misunderstand Jeff, *all* of us Donigans, in fact. We're all fighters, but *clean* fighters. My brothers like a fight as well as any man, but they like justice too."

Boots grated on the hard *caliche* and Rowan turned to see the scowling face of Jeff Donigan. He looked past Rowan. "Well," he said to his sister, "we've wasted the morning coming in here. We got work to do. Let's go."

Rowan held out his hand. "Thanks, Donigan," he said.

Jeff ignored the hand. "I ain't forgot what you did to me," he said. "Someday we'll see who is the better man."

Joan smiled. "The rest of the boys have ridden Jeff pretty hard about losing that fight," she said.

Jeff spat. "Be quiet," he said. He got into the buckboard and took the ribbons. He looked at Rowan. "You might as well know she talked me into coming here."

Joan adjusted her bonnet. "I told Pa what you had said about seeing the killing, Jeff. You know very well he ordered you to come in and testify for an innocent man."

Jeff slapped the reins. The buckboard pulled away. She looked back as it reached the plank bridge and waved, and Rowan forgot all about Chisos Ahrens, the Black Donigan brothers, and Old John Ripsey in that brief moment.

Rowan turned and walked slowly toward the *calabozo*. Pres Ripsey was on the porch in front of the Union, a cigarette pasted in the corner of his thin mouth. Rowan drew level with him. Pres slowly took the cigarette from his mouth.

"You got off easy, Locke," he said.

Rowan looked up. "Maybe you got fooled, Ripsey."

Pres stepped off the porch. "You've set yourself in with the right crowd," he said. "Now I know how we stand."

Rowan looked the angry young man in the eye. "I don't think you and I would ever stand together on anything, Ripsey."

Pres looked down at Rowan's empty gun sheath, then he smiled thinly. "You've roped out a nice filly there," he said. "Slender in the pasterns, smooth of flank."

Rowan went cold. "What do you mean?"

Pres laughed. "That Donigan bitch."

Rowan moved like a cat. Pres dropped his hands to his twin Colts. Rowan flipped his hat from his head, throwing it at Pres's face. Pres cursed, trying to draw up his cutters, but Rowan drove in a left to the gut, a right to the jaw, kicked a dropped Colt under the porch, slapped the other from the nerveless hands and clipped Pres behind his left ear, driving him back against a post.

Pres cursed and ran at Rowan, thrashing out with both arms. Rowan threw a right jab which pasted lips and teeth together in a bloody hash. Pres hit the boards of the Union and slid down, falling sideways, his slim hands scrabbling at the dusty wood beneath him.

Rowan looked up into the agate eyes of John Ripsey. Ripsey walked slowly forward, his right hand clawed over his Colt. "Draw, you hellion," he said quietly. "See if you can whip the old man!"

Rowan looked down at his empty sheath. "I'm unarmed, Ripsey," he said quietly. "Your boy tried to draw on me."

"So?"

"He called a fine young woman a bitch."

"Who?"

"Joan Donigan."

Ripsey faltered. He dropped his hands. "Get out of my sight," he said.

Rowan stepped back. Pres Ripsey staggered to his feet, spitting blood and teeth. "Get him, Dad," he mouthed.

Ripsey stepped back up on the porch. His right hand lashed out. "You fool!" he said. The hand caught Pres across his damaged mouth, splattering blood. "You can't fight! You won't work! You insult a lady! God alone knows why Locke stopped when he did. I would have killed you. *Get home!*"

A small crowd watched Pres Ripsey pick up his nickel-plated Colts and drive them hard into their sheaths. He walked to his horse and mounted, setting steel hard into the smooth flanks of the black. It reared and then settled, racing for the plank bridge. John Ripsey turned to Rowan and looked at him through a veil of bitter dust. "We've got a score to settle, Locke," he said softly.

For a moment Rowan saw John Ripsey as the man he had been. The cattle king. There was no fear in the hard eyes. Rowan realized that if he had had a gun, Ripsey would have shot it out with him then and there. Ripsey turned, raised his right hand helplessly and dropped it to slap his holster. His shoulders were bowed as he walked to his horse, mounted it, and rode slowly out of Llano.

CHAPTER SIX

For two days after Rowan's acquittal, there was an uneasy quiet in Llano. Rowan decided to ride to the Lazy LF and see his cousin's wife and the baby. He had a packet of food prepared and got Jim. As he rode past Schwab's Butcher Shop the big German came to the door and beckoned to him. Rowan swung down and followed Schwab into his shop.

"You are leaving Llano for good?"

"Just a little trip, Schwab."

"So? You are all man, Locke. Yet there is some things about you that don't fit together in my mind."

"Such as?"

"You were a soldier. I know. I was a soldier myself in the old country many years. I leave only because I hear of this fine country where a man is his own boss if he work hard. So I come. I am soldier again in war, fighting for my new country with Franz Sigel. You know of him?"

"A good soldier."

"Ja. For a time I think maybe I should stay in army, but there is a wound in mine leg what hurts in damp weather. So I come here where it is dry and become butcher. But you—you are still soldier at heart. Yes?"

"In a way. I like ranching, too. The army's all right as long as there's action. The rest is dross."

"Ja. I see." Schwab rubbed his round face. "Yet, as I say, things about you don't fit exactly. I am a thinking man. Many books I read. About people. People I like to study, such as the great Bismarck, Frederick the Great, George Washington, Abraham Lincoln—and Franz Sigel yet."

"You have me in good company, Schwab."

The butcher waved a big hand. "You are no drifter, no saddle tramp, as they say in this country. With the hands you fight well, and the gun is not worn for show. It is the eyes that tell. You are always looking for something."

Rowan rolled a smoke. "So?"

"So I show you something yet." Schwab led the way to his shed behind the shop and unlocked the big padlock. He went in and turned. "Shut the door. I light the lantern."

Rowan shut the door and yellow light flooded the shed. Schwab pulled a hide from behind some barrels. "See? Here is a brand. Look. What do you see?"

Rowan eyed it. "Looks like a Lazy 4B brand."

Schwab spat. "There is no such brand in this country. Look again."

Rowan studied the green hide. Schwab moved the lamp about. Rowan touched the brand. "This wasn't done with a stamp iron, Schwab. See? The edges are rough. This brand has been blotted with a running iron."

The butcher traced the letters with a thick finger. "See here. This first letter was an L, the second letter maybe an I."

Rowan shook his head. "No, it was an F. Lazy LF."

They looked at each other in the flickering light. "It is the brand that young man looked for just before he was killed by them dirty Donigans."

"Where did you get it?"

"Sid Coates came in this morning with it. I need fresh

meat. I am in a hurry. I cut the meat and sell it. Then I check this brand. I think maybe this is what that young man wanted to learn."

Rowan puffed at his cigarette and handled the green hide. "Yet you said the Donigans sold those other Lazy LF beeves to you."

Schwab wiped the sweat from his face with a thick arm. "Yes, they did. But it is said they take any cows they find on their place, kill them, sell the carcasses and say they are fallen hides."

"It's being done all over the West."

"A dirty business, but it is hard for a lawman to prove anything."

"How many hides do you have like this?"

"I had three beeves this morning. This was the only one."

"You have the bills of sale?"

"Yes . . . but the Lazy 4B don't look right."

"Let me see it."

They left the shed and Schwab got the bill of sale. Rowan studied it. "Looks all right."

Schwab shook his head. "See. Here where the brand is marked. It has been erased and written over. Very well done." Rowan nodded. "You take it with you."

Rowan eyed the big man. "Why?"

Schwab smiled. "Look! I do not say you are a lawman. None of my business it is. But I am good citizen. I like United States, my adopted country. I like New Mexico, for here my wound does not bother me. I like Llano because here are my friends. I am taken into lodge. I run with the fire engine when there is a fire and go to beer parties with the boys when there are no fires. They like Oscar Schwab. Big Oscar they call me, sometimes Dutchy, although I am good German, not Dutch. I do not like this dirty business. Do you understand?"

Rowan nodded. He took out his marshal's badge. "You're a damned good citizen, Oscar. Better than many who have been born here. Save that hide. Buy any others they bring. Save the hides. Another thing . . . keep your mouth shut."

Schwab waved a meaty hand. "I listen, see, but I do not talk, like the three monkeys."

Rowan grinned. "You were close," he said.

"Sid Coates is at the slaughterhouse, but he says Slip Wellman is visiting friends in Santa Rosa. Maybe he is visiting ranches at night to get cows."

"Maybe." Rowan shook the big man's hand. "I'll take a pasear out to see Sid. Thanks again, Oscar."

"It iss nothing."

Rowan left the shop and mounted Jim. He rode north out of town. It was the first real lead he had. Rowan picketed Jim in a hollow a mile from the slaughterhouse and took his field glasses from a saddlebag. He took his Winchester with him and worked his way along the south bank of the creek into a motte of cottonwoods. There were half a dozen steers in the corral but he couldn't make out the brands. A tall man walked between two of the buildings, too fast for Rowan to focus his glasses. A thread of dust rose behind the slaughterhouse and Rowan caught a glimpse of the tall man riding a gray, west toward the hills.

A thin man came out of the slaughterhouse and went into a shed, only to reappear carrying a shovel. Rowan shaded his glasses with his hat and studied the man. His face was thin and gaunt. A ragged dragoon mustache drooped over his upper lip. He walked into the slaughterhouse and came out carrying a green hide. He splashed across the shallow creek and into the willows. Rowan cased his glasses and cut down to the creek bank and through the thick brush until he could hear the grating of the shovel on hard earth. He looked through a natural lane between the tall trees. The man was uncovering loose dirt. He threw it aside until he was down two feet and then laid the hide flat, weighting it down with flat rocks from the creek bed. He was whistling "Sally Gooden."

Rowan waited until the man went back across the creek and then he uncovered the hide. It was branded with a sloppy-looking Lazy 4B, but it was easy to see where the running iron had changed the original brand, a poorly branded Lazy LF.

Rowan covered the hide, wiped the sweat from his face and went back to Jim. He squatted in the shade of the bay and rolled a smoke. He could arrest the man at the slaughterhouse, but it wasn't time for closing in. He finally mounted Jim and rode out, turning north on the main road.

Rowan camped that night in an eroded adobe beside the road, riding on the next morning just before dawn. By late afternoon of the second day out he drew rein on a ridge which overlooked the Lazy LF. It had been a long time since he had been there. He studied the well-built ranch buildings through his glasses. Smoke drifted up from the cookhouse. Rowan lowered his glasses. The place was just as Larry had said it would be, well-built, with plenty of water and shelter. Rowan had financed the original outlay with money won over the green-covered tables of Tucson, Benson, and Globe. Once Larry had started the first work on the spread, Rowan had stopped his gambling. Larry, for all his youth, knew ranching. It would have been a place for Rowan to end his days after leaving the service.

Rowan led Jim down the slope and watered him at a rock pan sheltered by trees. He thrust a foot into the stirrup and then suddenly raised his head. An odor had come to him on the fresh wind, tainting it. The odor of burning hair. He grounded his reins and jerked his Winchester from its scabbard. He padded through the trees, up a rocky slope and halted among some scrub oaks. Below him, in a natural cup of rock, were a dozen cattle. A huge man squatted over a fire, eyeing a running iron. He threw a loop over a steer and dogged it down, with a strength that seemed incredible to Rowan. Big enough to hunt bears with a switch, thought Rowan.

The big man turned for the running iron. His face was almost childlike in contrast to the huge body which must have tipped the scales at close to three hundred pounds. The broad face was caked with dust through which the sweat had cut runnels, giving the big man a curious striped look. He took the iron from the fire. Rowan could see the stamp-ironed brand on the steer's flank. Lazy LF. The man began to work, slowly and clumsily, his pink tongue hanging out of his mouth in his intense concentration. The stench of burning hair came to Rowan. The steer thrashed a little and the big man cursed, smashed a huge fist down on the steer's head.

Rowan eased down the lever of his Winchester and loaded it. He slipped down the ridge to stop twenty feet from the concentrating giant. The rustler was trying to transform the original brand into a Lazy 4B. Rowan raised the rifle.

"Calf rope!" he said loudly. "Grab your ears!"

The rustler stopped short. The running iron raised a thread of acrid smoke from where it rested against the hide. Then the man turned to eye Rowan. There was a look of childish fear on the great face, and then Rowan knew he was dealing with a natural. The man got up slowly, dropping the running iron. His Adam's apple bobbed spasmodically. "Who're you?" he said hoarsely.

"United States Marshal."

The man wet his thick lips. "These is my cows," he said with a sickly grin.

"So? Keep those paws up! Who are you?"

"Slip Wellman."

"Sid Coates' partner?"

"How'd you know?"

Rowan shoved back his hat. "Sid confessed to rustling

up this way," he lied. "Said you'd be doing some brand-blotting around here."

"Sid wouldn't do that to Slip Wellman!"

Rowan spat. "Old Sid is in a bad way in the *calabozo* at Llano. We found half a dozen brand-blotted green hides buried across the crick from your slaughterhouse. Sid resisted arrest. We had to beat him around a bit with a gun butt before he agreed to come along."

The big face hardened. "Ain't no one gonna hurt Sid," he said. "I take care of Sid in fights. Who did it?"

"Some posse-men. They've been combing the country for you."

The eyes went sly. "You talk a big wind, stranger. Ain't no one gonna bother me and Sid."

"So? Sid is being bothered and you're going to be bothered a lot, too, Wellman."

The giant laughed. "Look!" he said. He bent down to get the running iron. Rowan raised the rifle. "Don't shoot. I wanna show you how tough Slip Wellman is." The iron came up in the huge hands. The big man strained. Slowly the bar of metal began to bend. He threw it down with a loud laugh. "See? Who's gonna bother me now?"

Rowan smiled. "You got strength enough to pull yourself up a rope?"

"Pretty hard for a big man like me," the giant admitted.

Rowan shook his head. "When that old noose tightens and you dance on air, you'll want to climb that hemp necktie."

Wellman paled. "I ain't gonna hang."

"Sid said you were the brains behind this rustling deal."

"Sid wouldn't say that!"

Rowan shrugged. "I'll show you his confession."

"I can't read."

Rowan took out an old letter and held it up. "This is it, Wellman."

Slip shuffled his huge feet. "Sid did all the planning," he said. "We was up here a while back and Sid tole me to brand-blot these critters and drive 'em south."

"Lazy LF, aren't they?"

"Yes."

"What other brands have you altered?"

"A dozen different ones maybe."

"How about Box R?"

The broad face went sly. "We ain't *that* stupid! We run *them* off over the Capitans and Jicarillas, through a pass in the Sierra Oscura and then across the Jornado to the Rio Grande. We got some *amigos* that pick 'em up there. Sometimes they drive 'em clear into the San Simon in Arizona. Them Box R's we don't run off we kill, skin, and then sell the beef to Oscar Schwab and other butchers around the Rio Mescalero. We bury the green hides like you said."

"Lower your hands slowly. Draw out that cutter and toss it over here. Careful now! I've got an itchy trigger finger!"

Wellman did as he was bid. Rowan jerked his head toward a rock. "Sit there." Wellman sat down.

Rowan leaned against a rock, covering the big man with his rifle. "Sid says you killed Larry Forbes of the Lazy LF."

"That's a lie!"

"I thought so. He did it, didn't he?"

"I should say he did, to get even, but I won't. I ain't like him, telling lies about my *amigo.*"

"Who did then?"

"Them Donigans."

"Which one?"

"How the hell should I know?"

"Who works with you?"

Wellman scratched himself. "Some of the Seven

Rivers boys. Some of the boys from up around Santa Rosa."

"Anyone else from around Llano?"

Wellman rubbed his bristly jaw.

"Well?"

"No one."

"You don't run those cattle west without a lot of help."

"I said we had *amigos.*"

"You must have, to take Box R steers."

Wellman laughed. "We ain't afraid of Old John and his *vaqueros.*"

"Why?"

"We just ain't."

"Ripsey runs the Rio Mescalero country."

Wellman spat. "He ain't so much. Useta be, but times is changed. That old mossy-horn ain't the king no more. Sid says all a man needs to make money around here is to have a rope, nerve, and a running iron."

Rowan shrugged. "Cut that cow loose!"

Wellman plodded to the steer and cut it loose. "Get your cayuse," said Rowan.

He followed the big man into another hollow where the rustler pulled up the picket pin of a huge *trigueno.* He led the horse back to the rock hollow. Rowan motioned him away from the *trigueno* and jerked a rifle from the scabbard. It was a battered Spencer. "What caliber is this?" asked Rowan.

".36/36. Why?"

"No reason. What caliber rifle does Sid carry?"

"Winchester .44/40."

Rowan jerked his head. "Lead your horse up that slope and down the other side. One careless move and I'll drill you, so help me God!"

They went up the slope and down to Jim. Rowan mounted. "Head for the ranch, Wellman. I'll be right behind you." Rowan slid Wellman's Spencer into his own

sheath and carried his Winchester across his thighs,
following the big man down a long slope toward the
ranch buildings.

"What are you going to do with me?" asked Slip.

"Throw you into the juzgado. You'll sing like a little
bird, Slip."

"Can't I see Sid?"

"Some day. Providing you don't hang in separate
towns. I can arrange it so you can hang together."

A shudder went through the big frame. Slip eased his
dirty bandanna. "We was only making a few pesos," he
said.

"Free roping, she's an easy life, is that it?"

"Yeh. But I ain't so sure now. I tole Old Sid to stick
with me, but Sid got a message to come back in a hurry.
He tells me to get them cows and bring them down
when I get done with 'em. Tole me to bring them in at
night."

A woman came out of the ranch house and shaded
her eyes, watching the two dusty horsemen. A man
limped out of the bunkhouse and stood beside her.
Rowan reached the gate and the woman began to run
toward him. It was Marion Forbes. Rowan waved to her.
"Wait there, honey!" he called. The man limped toward
them. "You're Rowan Locke," he said.

Rowan jerked his head at Slip. "Get down," he said.
"Up with those hands."

Marion waited for Rowan. "This is Hash Bryce," she
said. "Foreman here, Rowan."

Rowan handed the rifle to the grizzled ramrod. "Keep
it on that big moose," he said. "If he breaks for it, plug
him through the legs. Had a dozen Lazy LF steers up
over the ridge blotting the brands."

"I hope he *does* make a break for it," said Hash.

"I won't," promised Slip.

Rowan kissed his cousin's wife. Marion Forbes was a
pretty blonde, a city girl from Denver who had followed

her husband to the Lazy LF. She held Rowan close. "Oh, Rowan," she said, "we've missed you."

"I came as quickly as I could."

They walked to the house. Rowan turned to Hash. "Lock him up and set a man to guard him. He's likely to break through a wall if you don't."

"Keno," said Hash. "Move along, you maverick!"

"I'm goin'," growled Slip.

Rowan followed Marion into the kitchen of the house. "Where's the baby?" he asked.

"Asleep."

"Can I see him?"

"If you're very quiet."

Rowan followed her into the bedroom. Little Larry was fast asleep, his tiny hands gripping the edge of the coverlet. Rowan touched one of the hands. "Looks like Larry," he said.

"He has my eyes," she said.

He put his arm around her. "I'm glad."

They went into the kitchen. She sat down. "Tell me about your trip. You were awfully slow, Rowan."

Rowan took out his badge and showed it to her. "I stopped at Soccoro to get sworn in."

She touched her throat with a slim hand. "You're not going to get mixed up in this thing?"

Rowan rolled a smoke and lit it. "Larry's killer is still loose," he said. "Tell me everything you know about why Larry went down to Llano."

"We had lost quite a few steers. There was a gunfight over near the waterhole and one of our men was wounded. That night the rustlers got away with thirty prime steers. Larry notified the sheriff, and a posse went out but lost the trail the next day. One afternoon a man came by the ranch and said he had information that might be of interest to Larry. He told him of Lazy LF steer hides being seen in the Llano area."

"Who was the man?"

"I didn't see him. Hash did, though."

Rowan stood up. "I'll talk to Hash."

"I'll get dinner ready. You must be starved."

"I could eat," admitted Rowan.

He left the house and walked toward the bunk-house. Hash limped toward him. "Yuh see the baby?" he asked. "Ain't he something, though?"

Rowan offered Hash the makings and they squatted beside the bunkhouse. "How's it going, Hash?" he asked.

"Not too bad. Lost quite a few cows, but no more than other spreads around here. I had Missus Forbes hire a few more *vaqueros* and it slowed the stealin' down a bit. But the boys have had a lot of work to do here lately."

"That big oaf wasn't more than a mile from the house doing his blotting."

"He ain't too bright from the looks of him."

"That's why he did it. Up until this time he's been working with someone a lot smarter than he is."

Hash lit up. "That wouldn't be hard."

"He had a dozen cows up there, a fire and a running iron."

"Guess he figgered he'd blot them and run them outa there tonight. There's been some cows loose up there the last few weeks and we didn't get up there to round them up. Damned careless of me, Rowan."

"Forget it."

"You're staying here now?"

"I'm after the snake that killed Larry."

Hash nodded. "Figgered you was. The little lady's pining for the city life. Her mother wants her to come back home. I think she'd go if she had a chance."

Rowan rubbed his jaw. "I'll buy her out if she wants to sell, or let her stay in, whichever she likes."

"It's a fine spread, the Lazy LF. You'll make money here, Rowan."

Rowan watched a hawk circle high overhead. "Marion

said something about a man coming through here tipping Larry off about some Lazy LF hides being seen in Llano."

"Yeh."

"What was his name?"

"I disremember."

"Describe him."

"Tall *hombre*. Nice clothes. Dark hair. Little gray in it. Wore a white hat. Mex boots. Cold eyes. Gambler, I'd say."

"Dane Grenville!" said Rowan.

Hash spat. "How did you know? That's his handle all right. I remember now!"

Rowan had been looking for pieces in a puzzle, trying one here and one there, without much result, and now he had a big piece which seemed to throw the whole puzzle out of kilter. Why would a man like Grenville bother to tell a rancher about illegal hides?

Hash inspected his smoke. "Anyways, Larry was hot to go down to Llano and poke around. I argued with him, but you know how ornery he was when he got an idea someone was taking him. Waal, Larry takes off. Next thing we know he's dead. Broke the missus up considerable, but she's made of whang leather and steel under that pretty little figger. I tells her Old Hash will run the place 'til you get here if she wants to take a pasear up to Denver for a spell, but she says no, she's waitin' for you."

A horse whinnied sharply from the corral. A cowpoke paced in front of the shed where Slip Wellman was confined. "Damn you!" he yelled in a window. "You'll eat. You act like a summer boarder waiting for his hash! Now shut up, or I'll pump some hot lead into that big belly to fill it!"

Rowan eyed the shed. "That big *ladino* knows more than he'll admit," he said quietly. "He's got a mortal fear of hanging, Hash."

Hash raised his eyebrows. "He has? My! My!"

"You've got rope, of course?"

Hash waved a hand. "A few yards here and there."

"Enough to make a hemp necktie?"

"How you talk! Why, certainly! One thing, though, I don't know of a tree around here would hold the weight of that bait of meat."

Rowan stood up. "There's a big beam in the barn. I'd admire to have you and a few of the boys join me in a bluff hanging this evening."

Hash stood up and bowed. "You'll want us to dress formal, of course?"

"Oh, just come as you are! Find some sacking and make some hoods with eyeholes cut in 'em. I aim to put the fear of God into that hunk of dumb meat. He'll sing tonight!"

They looked at each other and grinned. Hash punched Rowan on the arm. "All we got to do is keep a straight face."

"That's why I want the hoods. Get a few of the boys who can put this thing across."

"Don't worry. We got the biggest bunch of pranksters on this spread you ever saw. I'll tell them what we want."

"Get them together about midnight. I'll have a bottle for the boys after we're through."

"You know, Rowan, we're going to like having you around."

Rowan started toward the house. Slip Wellman would talk. He knew enough to give Rowan the information he wanted. But Dane Grenville was the puzzler. He shook his head as he walked into the house.

CHAPTER SEVEN

Rowan left the ranch house just before midnight. Marion was fast asleep. Rowan walked over to the bunkhouse. Hash handed him a hood made from sacking. Two grinning punchers were with Hash. "This skinny galoot is Slim Orris, the ugly one is Joe Ruffin. Dort Perkins is with the big fellow."

Rowan nodded. "Slim, you go in and hang a noose from one of the beams. Joe, you leave off the hood and go tell Perkins to take Wellman into the barn. Blindfold him."

Rowan had a cup of coffee with Hash and then they walked to the back door of the barn. Slip Wellman was standing in the middle of the barn with his hands lashed behind him. The noose hung just in front of his face. Dort Perkins was standing behind him with a six-gun against the rustler's broad back. Rowan, Slim, Joe and Hash put on their hoods. A shaded lantern cast a dim pool of light in the barn. The conspirators walked in and seated themselves on boxes arranged by Hash. Rowan nodded at Dort. He removed the blindfold. Slip looked at the four grim figures seated in front of him. Dort put on a hood and stood behind a post watching the big man. The noose swayed a little in the draft. Slip swallowed.

"What the hell is this?" he asked in a hoarse voice.

There was no answer.

Slip looked behind him and saw the figure of Dort Perkins. He looked back at the four men. "Can't nobody talk?"

Nothing but silence, broken by the creak of the barn door as it moved a little in the wind.

Slip shuffled his huge feet and tested the bonds about his wrists. "This ain't no legal court," he said.

"There is no legal court for such as you," said Rowan in a muffled voice.

"No legal court," repeated Hash.

Slip eyed the four grim figures. "Who are you?"

Rowan shifted. "Vigilantes of Death," he said.

"I want a lawyer," said Slip. "Old Sid said you should always ask for a lawyer."

"No lawyer," said Slim Orris.

Slip spat. "What's the rope for?"

Hash laughed. "He wants to know what the rope is for."

"Your neck," said Joe.

Slip jerked as a coyote gave tongue in the hills behind the ranch.

"The coyotes are hungry," said Dort Perkins.

"They're always hungry," said Hash.

"They'll eat tonight," said Slim.

Minutes ticked past. "What you want to know?" asked Slip. Sweat beaded his broad simple face.

"Who is your leader?" asked Rowan.

"We ain't got none."

Rowan raised a hand. "Place the noose about the defendant's neck."

Dort walked forward and placed the noose over the big head. Slip looked down at the loop. "This ain't right."

"It works," said Slim.

"It still ain't right, I tell yuh!"

Slim raised both hands and then pointed at Slip. "Who killed Larry Forbes?"

"Them Donigan Boys."

"A lie," said Rowan.

Slip wet his lips. "Wash Donigan did it."

"How do you know?"

"He alius was the leader of them Donigans."

"Did you see him do it?"

"No."

"Then how do you know he did it?"

"I was guessing."

"Why aren't you afraid of the Box R *corrida?*" asked Rowan.

"We just ain't."

"Why?"

"I *told* you why!"

"Why?"

"Let me alone!"

"Why aren't you afraid of Old John Ripsey? Everyone else is."

Slip shifted a little. "We got protection."

"What kind of protection?"

"I don't know. Sid never told me."

Rowan stood up. "Get a horse."

Slim got a horse from its stall and fastened the end of the rope to the saddle horn. "Old Pecos here can haul up any weight," he said. "Pulled up four sticky loopers in the last two years. Easy as sin."

Slip swallowed hard.

Rowan pointed a menacing finger. "Your time has come, Slip Wellman. You may pray."

Slip swayed a little. His face went fish-belly white.

Rowan nodded to Slim. Slim led Old Pecos forward, drawing the noose up tight about the big man's neck. Slip gasped.

"Talk," said Hash.

Slip shook his head. Slim slapped Old Pecos on the rump. The rope drew taut and began to raise Slip's head. "I'll talk!" he gasped hoarsely.

Rowan raised his head. "Who is the brains behind the rustling?"

"I'll get killed if I tell."

"The Vigilantes of Death will protect you."

Slip breathed deeply as Slim eased the line. "Pres Ripsey works with us. He and Sid cooked up the deal. Before God, that's all I know."

"Pres Ripsey hasn't the brains to run a slick deal like that," said Rowan.

"All right! All right! He ain't got the brains then, but he works it so we get Box R cows easy. We usually run them over the mountains, like I said."

"Then there is another man?" asked Rowan.

"Yes. But I swear I don't know who he is!"

"Any of the Donigans?"

"No!"

"Deputy Busch?"

"He's John Ripsey's man."

"Oscar Schwab?"

"That dumb Dutchman? Hell, no!"

"What's Pres Ripsey's angle?" asked Rowan.

Slip wet his dry lips. "His old man won't give him enough money."

"So he steals his own cows, is that it?"

"He *has* to!" blurted Slip.

"Why?"

"He owes a lot of money."

"To who?"

Slip waggled his big head. "I don't know! I just don't know! Lemme go, willya?"

Rowan leaned forward. "Does Pres Ripsey owe money to Dane Grenville?"

"How should *I* know?"

The barn was silent, broken only by the occasional

stamping of Old Pecos. Hash looked at Rowan. "All right," said Rowan.

"Suits me," said Slim. He slapped the horse on the rump before Rowan could stop him. The line drew taut and lifted Slip a few inches from the floor. Rowan leaped to his feet and whipped out his clasp knife. He slashed the line and Slip slumped to the floor.

"By God," said Joe Ruffin. "He's out cold!"

Rowan pulled off the hood. "Hash, I'll be leaving for Llano in the morning. Send two of the boys into Santa Rosa with him. Have him locked up. I'll write a note to the sheriff there. I want him held there incommunicado."

"What the hell is that?" asked Slim.

"You ignorant *hombre,*" said Joe with scorn.

"Well," asked Slim, "what is it?"

"Damned if I know," said Joe.

Rowan walked out into the coolness of the night and rolled a smoke. Hash limped after him. "You learn enough? We can work him over again."

Rowan lit his cigarette. "No. He doesn't know anything else. Poor Slip."

"Yeh. He's like a kid, ain't he?"

"He'll get off with a light sentence."

Hash laughed as he accepted the makings from Rowan. "I'll bet he follows the straight and narrow after this."

They walked to the ranch house and Rowan got a bottle from his war bag and they took it to the bunkhouse. Hash filled tin cups. Rowan rubbed his lean jaw. "Try to keep the cows together. Set double guards at night. If there's any more rustling, send me a message. Leave it at Schwab's Butcher Shop."

"Keno!"

Rowan drank his liquor and went in to bed. He had more leads now. Pres Ripsey was in on the deal. But Rowan still didn't know who had dry-gulched Larry Forbes. Dane Grenville was mixed up in the deal, and he

was the one who worried Rowan. It was one thing dealing
with men like the Donigans, Sid Coates, Slip Wellman
and Pres Ripsey. But Dane Grenville had brains with his
deadliness. There was more to the thing than Rowan had
anticipated.

CHAPTER EIGHT

Rowan reached the Llano area after dark. There was a faint new moon as he rode toward the slaughterhouse on the creek. The place was deserted. On an impulse, he headed west along the fence line of the sprawling Box R, but the place was as quiet as a cemetery. He skirted the fence line for a mile and then turned south to follow a jog in the line. He drew rein on a rise where he could overlook the ranch buildings, dimly seen through the great trees. There were a few lights in the massive pile of buildings. Rowan shoved back his hat and studied the spread. John Ripsey had planned well. The ranch extended for miles south, past the back of the Donigan place, beyond the Rio Mescalero. Then the Box R extended down to the road beyond the Donigan place, hemming it in. Ripsey's cattle empire went west, including the dim line of hills.

Rowan touched Jim with his spurs and then drew rein again. A faint flicker of light showed at the back of the big barn which squatted darkly at the edge of the river. Rowan leaned forward and watched it. The light was brighter. A tongue of flame lapped at the dry wood. Rowan cursed. He set the steel to Jim, cleared the low fence in front of him and set off at a hell-for-leather pace down the long rock-studded slope. The flames were higher now, lapping beneath the broad eaves, lighting the side of the barn. Rowan cleared a sagging fence and hammered for the ranch buildings. The flames were licking hungrily beneath the eaves. A runnel of fire traced its course toward the front of the big barn.

Rowan saw a man dart from behind a shed and sprint for a ground-reined horse in the brush. He stared at Rowan for a moment and then swung up on his horse. He set steel to the horse and plunged through the brush even as Rowan jumped down to open a gate. When Rowan urged Jim through the gateway the man was gone but Rowan had caught a clear glimpse of Madison Donigan.

Rowan circled the bay just short of the bunk-house. "Fire! Fire! Fire!" he yelled. He circled the bay again and headed for the barn, but the bay balked. Rowan slid from the saddle and ran toward the barn. Smoke billowed toward him as he jerked the door open. A horse screamed like a frightened woman. Rowan ripped off his jacket and darted into a stall, narrowly avoiding the lashing hoofs of a panicky gray. He threw the jacket over the gray's head and led him through the wreathing smoke. He slapped it on the rump as he reached the water trough and turned to run in after another horse. Men were yelling hoarsely above the steady crackle of the burning wood.

Rowan got a bayo coyote from a rear stall and cursed as a fat spark seared his neck. Two *vaqueros* darted in and threw shirts over the faces of two other horses. A plank snapped high overhead, sending down a shower of sparks which set fire to the straw-strewn floor of the barn. Rowan got the bayo coyote out and saw Old John Ripsey running toward the barn. A dozen men were filling buckets at the trough and throwing them on the roaring flames. Rowan whirled and went into the smoke-filled interior for the third time, fighting savagely with a sorrel mare which lashed out with flying hoofs in her panic. Rowan was blinded with the smoke. He coughed and his eyes filled with tears. The mare fought all the way but Rowan got her into the open and turned to go back.

"Don't go in there again!" a man yelled. It was Wasco Barnes.

Rowan saw Laura Ripsey watching the battle. John Ripsey was shouting orders like a madman. The fire was out of control. Dimly Rowan heard the flat crack of a gun out in the brush along the river bank. He ran down the side of the barn to see if there was another entry, but the wall had only windows. Smoke lay low on the ground. Rowan turned back, half-blinded. He ran to the front of the barn and recoiled as a tongue of flame licked hungrily toward him. He ran in as it receded; he could hear a horse screaming in panic. A board dropped on Rowan's right arm, burning through his shirt. He slapped at the flames and dropped to his knees to look for the horse. A spark seared his face. A wall of flame extended across the barn, sealing the horse to a terrible death. Rowan coughed harshly and weaved toward the door. His burned arm stung like fury. He reached the open and wiped the watery sweat from his scorched face. The flames had full control now, dancing and snapping across the wide roof.

The horse was still screaming when the sealed loft, filled with hot air, suddenly exploded, scattering flaming splinters and sparks far and wide across other buildings. "Forget the barn!" roared Rowan to the firefighters. "Douse the other buildings!"

Thick ropes of smoke drifted about between the buildings. A grass fire started behind the barn and ran swiftly into the dry brush, sending it up in roaring joy. The whole area was lit with a devilish light. Fire licked eagerly across the roof of a shed. Fine wood ash began to settle on the ground, coating everything. The tart smell of burning pinewood shingles filled the nostrils. Oily soot swirled upward, intermingled with soaring sparks.

"Get back!" yelled John Ripsey. "Get blankets! Wet

them and cover the roof of the house. By God, we'll save that, anyway!"

The cursing, panting men scattered like smoky goblins to do as they were told. Rowan touched his blistered face. Laura Ripsey came toward him. "Let me look at those burns."

"It's nothing," Rowan said.

"Come," she said.

Rowan walked beside her toward the great house. Cowpokes were dousing blankets in the water trough and passing them to others who spread them on the flat roof. The brush fire was raging westward, driven by the wind. A wall of the barn collapsed outward, carrying the roof with it. Sparks shot outward like a Brock's Benefit. The noise of the fire was a steady roaring. But the great house was safe now as the increasing wind drove the flames and sparks away from it.

John Ripsey was cursing at his men like a first sergeant. He glared at Rowan with red-rimmed eyes and crossed the gap between them with short, plunging steps, tugging at his Colt. Rowan dropped his hand to rest on the butt of his six-shooter. Ripsey thrust out his left arm. "You—" he said thickly.

Laura Ripsey stepped in front of Rowan. "He saved some of the horses, Dad!"

"Damned funny! Sets fire to the barn and then saves the horses!"

Laura thrust a hand behind her and gripped Rowan's right wrist. "I saw him ride across the field *after* the fire had started."

"What was he doing here in the first place?"

Laura squeezed Rowan's wrist tightly. "There was someone else at the barn," she said. "He ran off just after the fire started."

John Ripsey spat. "Seems to me you saw a helluva lot tonight, Laura."

She raised her head. "You can take my word for it," she said. "Rowan Locke did *not* start that fire!"

For a moment the agate eyes stared at Rowan and then John Ripsey whirled and stalked back to bellow orders at his sooty firefighters. The brush fire had died away three hundred yards down the river bank, leaving a black area dotted by smoldering brush stumps.

Laura still held to Rowan's wrist. She drew him toward the house. Rowan let her lead him into the big house through a deep doorway and into a dark hallway. There was an uneasy feeling in him; a feeling that Laura Ripsey had found a new plaything.

Laura opened the door of a room and turned to Rowan. "My room," she said. "Wait here while I get something for those burns."

Rowan took off his sooty hat as he walked into the big, low-ceilinged room, gingerly avoiding the thick throw rugs with his filthy boots. Everything about the room was indicative of the young woman who lived there. The bed was a refined four-poster, the furniture too spindly for a ranch in the heart of the Southwest. Magazines were piled on a small table near the bed. A low fire flickered in the beehive fireplace in one corner of the room. A polished wardrobe was partly open, revealing a neat row of frocks and gowns with a row of dainty little shoes beneath them. The faint odor of heliotrope hung in the room intermingled with that of the burning piñon wood. There was something missing and it took Rowan a moment or two before he realized what it was. For a rancher's daughter, there wasn't one thing in the room that indicated New Mexico or the West, beyond the room itself.

Footsteps sounded in the hall and Laura hurried in carrying bandages and a small medical kit. She led Rowan to a chair near the fire and deftly cut back his right sleeve. She bathed the arm, salved it and bandaged it neatly. Then she washed his face, treated the burns, and smoothed his hair back. She smiled. "Is that better now?"

Rowan shifted uneasily. Her body had brushed hard against him as she worked. She hovered over him like a mother hen. He smiled. "Yes, thank you. Now I had better leave. I'm not too popular on the Box R."

She tilted her head back. "As long as I am with you, you'll be all right, Rowan."

"You've been more than kind."

"I like to help people."

"Then help me to get out of here."

She walked to the door and shut it, turning the key. She placed her back against the polished wood and pressed her slim hands flat against the door. "You're safe with me," she said. She came slowly to him. "I expected to have you call on me."

"I might have, Laura," he said quietly, "but you know what your father and brother think of me."

She shrugged. "Dad still admires you. You are a great deal alike, you two. You know what you want and go after it. Pres is nothing. My mother spoiled him. He was always protected and catered to. Secretly Dad is ashamed of him." She raised her head and smiled. "I'm more like Dad."

You know what you want and go after it, thought Rowan, *a new plaything, clothes, luxuries . . . men.*

She touched his face with a cool hand. "You will come and see me?"

"Please, Laura. Let me get out of here before hell breaks loose. We can see each other again."

"I said you were safe."

"Look, I'm a mess. Perhaps some other time— soon?"

Her eyes held the conspirator's look. "Yes. Very soon. I'll look about outside and see what is happening." She unlocked the door and hurried away. Rowan put on his hat and padded to the door. The hallway was dark. The front door creaked a little. Rowan crossed the hallway and stepped into a deep doorway, pressing his back flat against the door. Spurs jingled softly in the hall. Rowan drew in his breath and eased his hand down to his Colt. A man passed between Rowan and the shaft of light from Laura's room. Pres Ripsey, trailing a rifle. He peered into Laura's room. "Laura!" he called. He pushed the door open and looked in, then turned and walked down the hall toward the patio door. It closed behind him.

Laura's quick steps sounded on the hard floor. Rowan crossed to her room and stood where he had been. She came in and closed the door, locking it behind her as before. "Something has happened up the river," she said. "All the men are up there. You'll be all right."

Rowan turned toward the door. "This is my chance to get out," he said.

"No!" she said fiercely. She put her arms about his neck and drew his face down towards hers, seeking his lips. Suddenly she stepped back, walked to the harp lamp and turned it down to a small flame. She was back in an instant, holding tightly to him. Rowan pushed her back. "Wait," he said.

"Laura! Laura!" It was the voice of Pres Ripsey in the hall.

"For God's sake, woman!" Rowan said. "Answer him!"

"Laura! Are you in there?" called Pres.

She smoothed her gown over her body and walked to the door. "What is it, Pres?"

"Where's Locke?"

"Outside somewhere. Why?"

"I just wanted to know."

Rowan walked to the window. It was up. He pulled the dainty curtains aside and shoved the shutters out. He thrust a leg through and stepped outside. The area about the house was deserted. Jim was near the burning pile of the barn. Rowan looked back at the dark house which held so many secrets. He wiped the sweat from his face. John Ripsey had spawned two children who would make his late days a hell on earth. He went to Jim and mounted. "The sins of the fathers shall be visited on the sons, Jim," said Rowan.

A waddie came toward Rowan. Rowan turned Jim and gripped his Colt. It was Wasco Barnes, smoke-stained and sweaty. "You leavin', Locke?" he asked.

"While I can."

"Yeh. Pull leather. There's hell to pay."

"What's up?"

"Found a dead man down in the brush. Charred all to hell."

"Fire got him, eh?"

Wasco looked up. "Got the *dead* body all right."

"What do you mean?"

"Corpse has a bullet hole in the back of the head." Wasco shoved back his hat. "Like I said, there'll be hell to pay. *It's Madison Donigan.*"

"Who did it?"

"Damned if we know. I picked up a hull at the edge of the burned area." Wasco opened his hand to show Rowan the brass case.

"Let me have it, Wasco."

"Why?"

Rowan drew his Colt. "Give it to me!"

Wasco's mouth sagged open. "Sure! Sure! No need to get riled!"

The cowpoke handed the case to Rowan. Rowan fished a ten out of his wallet. "Here. Keep your mouth shut."

"That case ain't from your saddle gun?"

"No."

Wasco shrugged. He eyed the bandaged arm. "Miss Laura patch you up?"

"Yes."

Wasco rubbed his bristly jaw. "She's good at that." He grinned.

Rowan touched Jim with his spurs and rode swiftly

toward the gate between the cottonwoods. The case was a .50/95. Suddenly he remembered hearing the shot that had cracked out during the fire. Then he remembered Pres Ripsey walking down the dark hallway trailing a rifle. It had been too dark to see what type of rifle it was, other than a lever-action repeater. Rowan urged Jim out onto the river road, looking back at the smoke which still lifted over the buildings of the Box R. As Wasco had said, *there would be hell to pay.*

CHAPTER NINE

Rowan was in his room at the hotel the morning after the fire when knuckles hammered on the thin door. "Who is it?" he called.

"Wasco Barnes!"

"Come in then."

Barnes opened the door and came in. He closed the door behind him. "You got time for a little palaver?"

"*Sí.*"

Barnes dropped into a chair and scaled his hat onto the bed. He eyed the bottle on the marble-topped table. Rowan filled two glasses. Barnes downed his drink and waited while Rowan refilled his glass. "What's on your mind, Wasco?"

Barnes dipped stubby fingers into the pocket of his cowhide vest and took out something. He tossed it to Rowan. It was a mutilated slug. Rowan looked curiously at Barnes. "So?" he asked.

Barnes wiped the sweat from his broad face. "John Ripsey asked me to bring Mad Donigan's body into town in the buckboard this morning. On the way I got to thinking about you. Now why would Locke want that brass hull, I asks myself? He ain't a collector of relics like Levi Acton, the druggist. So I think with my thick head.

This Locke comes into town, trees a few Donigans, gives Old John a lot of lip, kills Chisos Ahrens with his bare hands, shows up mysteriously at the Box R and then helps save Old John's pet horses. A curious duck, I says. Then he throws down on Wasco Barnes with his cutter and takes a cartridge case away from him. Why?"

Rowan glanced at his holstered Colt hanging from the brass bedpost. "Why?" he echoed.

Wasco downed his drink. "Because he's a lawman, I thinks."

Rowan stood up and refilled Wasco's glass. Swiftly he gripped his holster and ripped the six-gun from it, cocking it in a fluid motion, and turning toward the puncher.

Wasco did not move. "Put it up," he said. "I ain't opening my big mouth. I work for Ripsey because he pays well, treats me like a man, and serves the best hash in the Pecos River country, but I'm an honest *hombre*, Locke, and things are going on around here that I don't cotton to."

Wasco jerked his head at the slug lying on the table. "I dug that outn' Mad's skull, figgerin' you might want to add it to your collection."

Rowan picked up the slug. The base was still intact. He took out the brass case and fitted it to the neck, working it in against the spreading caused by the explosion of the gas behind the slug. He looked at Wasco. ".50/95," he said.

Wasco rolled a smoke. "There's only one .50/95 on the Box R," he said. "Model 1876 Winchester. Centennial Model."

"Who owns it?"

"Pres Ripsey. Fancy deal. Breech chased in silver with ducks, geese and suchlike. Got some words on the barrel. 'One in a Thousand,' it says. Extra accurate barrel. Got a fine wood stock, some kinda special walnut. Pistol grip too, only one I ever seed around here."

Rowan remembered the two shots that had been fired at him the first time he had visited the slaughterhouse on Salt Crick. Yet Pres had been within his rights to kill Madison Donigan if the man had set fire to the barn. But there would be a blood trail now in the Rio Mescalero country.

Wasco lit his cigarette. "I left the body over at George Mitchell's undertaking parlor. George sent a man out to the Donigan place to notify Old Mike and the boys. I've had enough of this hassling."

"What will you do?"

"Buy me a cayuse and head north to the Canadian River country."

"You think Mad Donigan fired Ripsey's barn?"

"*Quién sabe?*"

"It looks like it."

"Mebbeso, but I don't blame them Donigans too much. One of the Donigan mules strayed onto the Box R. Pres Ripsey hit it at three hundred yards with that fancy saddle gun of his. Pres ain't much with a six-gun but he handles a long gun real fine."

Rowan tossed the cartridge that had killed Madison into the air and caught it. "Yeh," he said dryly, "he sure does."

Wasco stood up. "Well, I'm moving on."

Rowan gripped the homely *vaquero's* hand. "You know where the Lazy LF spread is?"

"Up north toward Santa Rosa."

"Keno! Go there and ask Hash Bryce to give you a job, Wasco."

"Friend of yours?"

"Yes. He'll tell you about it when you get there."

Wasco grinned. "Right nice of you, Rowan." He picked at his lower lip. "Watch your back, Rowan. There's dark things goin' on around this country. More killings. Fifty head of prime cows got driven off the Box R coupla nights ago. There was a gun hassle and a Box R man got creased. Another thing: you keep away from Laura Ripsey. She's man-hungry."

"I think I know what you mean."

Wasco hesitated. "Dane Grenville fooled about with her. Ripsey run him offa the Box R, but Grenville saw Laura a few times after that. In Santa Fe. Another time in El Paso. I know because I drove her both places. Last year that was. Grenville ain't been near her for a time. He and Pres get together over the cards quite a bit. Grenville is deep into Pres, from what I hear, and the Old Man would kill Pres if he knew."

"I can see why you're pulling out of this mess."

Wasco nodded solemnly. "Coupla nights ago I dreamed of a preacher and a gray mare on a Mississippi River steamboat."

"So?"

Wasco shook his head. "You sure don't know your dream book. Bad luck, that is, mortal bad luck. I'll see you, Rowan." The waddie left the room.

Rowan looked down into the street. The undertaker was taking a tarp-wrapped form from a buck-board. Madison Donigan. Rowan buckled on his gunbelt and shrugged into his coat. His arm bothered him quite a bit. He placed the cartridge case and slug into his coat pocket and left the hotel. Men were standing beneath the awnings eyeing the tarp-enveloped form. As Mitchell took it into his shop the men began to talk among themselves, glancing apprehensively toward the bridge that spanned the shallow Rio Mescalero. Waiting for the Donigans.

Rowan walked into the Union. The place was quiet. Dane Grenville sat at a green-covered table, riffling cards through his slim hands. He nodded when he saw Rowan. Dandy mopped his round face. "Beer," said Rowan.

"A melancholy drink," said Dandy, with a shake of his head. He placed the bottle in front of Rowan.

"See what Grenville will have." Grenville stood up

and came to the bar. "Bourbon," he said. "Thanks, Locke."

Dandy looked over the batwings. "This is a terrible thing," he said. "The killing of a Donigan on Box R land."

Grenville leaned easily on the bar. "What did you expect?" he asked. "I've been surprised that one of the Donigans hasn't been shot down by now."

"Blood on the moon," said Rowan. "True," said Grenville. "Like a Kentucky hill feud."

"Right and wrong on both sides," said Rowan. Grenville nodded. "I saw the same thing in Colorado some years ago. Two families living side by side. Three brothers and a father in one family. Two brothers and two cousins in the other. Over a period of two years, two of the brothers and the father in the first family were dead, and one of the brothers and a cousin in the other."

"You're from Colorado?" asked Rowan.

Grenville shook his head. "Not originally. But I lived there for some years. Denver. Fine city, Denver."

"I've never been there."

"You'd like it. Some fine families there."

"Plenty of gambling?" asked Dandy with a grin.

Grenville looked at the bartender. "Yes," he said coldly.

Dandy hastily mopped the bar.

Grenville sipped his bourbon. "You've been with us some time, Locke. I must say it has been exciting."

Rowan shrugged.

"A lesser man would have left here before some of the things that have happened to you would have occurred."

Dandy reached under the bar and brought up his saw-off shotgun. He broke the breech and checked the shells.

"I'll pay, Dandy!" said Rowan.

Dandy looked up quickly. "Dammit," he growled. "This is a helluva time to be cheerful."

Grenville eyed Rowan. "You seem to have been scorched a bit, Locke."

"I was. There was a helluva fire on the Box R last night."

"So we heard this morning. How did you get involved?"

"I saw the fire start. Spread the alarm. It was a mess."

Dandy snapped the shotgun together and stowed it under the bar. "Who done the job to Mad Donigan?"

Rowan shrugged. "I left about the time they found the body."

"Burned to a nubbin, we hear," said Dandy.

"I didn't see it."

Hoofs thudded on the hard street. Rowan walked to the door and looked over the batwings. John Ripsey was coming with his *corrida.* The old man rode straight-backed, looking neither to right nor left, his left hand holding the reins of his fine gray, his right hand resting lightly on the butt of his Colt. Half a dozen Box R *vaqueros* rode behind him. All were young men, wind-burned, loose and easy in their fine saddles, eyes slitted against the dust rising from the hard street. Their hands were firm on the reins. *Young, wiry and cruel,* thought Rowan as he watched them riding like nobles up the sunlit street.

"Pres is conspicuous by his absence," a dry voice said behind Rowan. It was Dane Grenville, eyeing the Box R men through half-closed eyes.

John Ripsey drew rein in front of the Union and dismounted. "There will be no drinking," he said flatly.

The Box R men dismounted and tethered their horses. They lounged on the shady porch, rolling ciga-rettes and spitting casually with a you-be-damned look on their tanned faces. Sim Short hurried across the street. "My God, John," he said. "Get those men outa town before the Donigans get here."

Ripsey drew his gloves through his left hand. "Get back in your shop," he said quietly. "We have a right to be here."

Short waved an impotent hand. "I'm mayor here in Llano. I got to think of the people here."

"I know you're the mayor. Get back and sell your beans and bacon and think about your people."

Short was not to be bluffed. "I'll have to get Deputy Busch," he said.

Ripsey spat. "Damn you," he said thinly. "Get the hell out of my sight!"

Short walked back across the street talking to himself.

A tautness settled over the sunlit street. Men eyed the lounging *vaqueros* nervously. Dandy shuffled up and down behind his long bar. "Why do they have to use this place as a battleground?" he asked plaintively.

Rowan drained his beer. "I'll be getting on," he said.

"See you," said Grenville easily. Rowan stepped out on the porch. Ripsey glanced at him, tugged impatiently at his right ear and looked away. The waddies eyed Rowan insolently. They were the Ripsey clan, loyal to their boss and to hell with everybody else. Rowan crossed the street and walked up on the porch in front of Sim's store. The planks of the bridge rattled. A buckboard was coming fast into town, followed by two horsemen. Wash Donigan drove the buckboard. Old Mike sat beside him with a shotgun across his lap. Jeff and Adams Donigan rode behind the vehicle. The sun glinted from the barrels of their scatterguns. Dust wreathed up and settled behind them as they came straight up the middle of the street. John Ripsey gripped the hitching rail and watched them. They drove right past the Union and halted in front of the undertaking parlor. They went in. The dust settled and the street was quiet again.

Sim Short spoke to Rowan through the open door of his shop. "I won't offer you the marshal's job today," he said. "I like you too much, Rowan."

"*Gracias.*"

Sim wiped his sweaty face. "This oughta be good. Skite through here if they open fire."

Five minutes drifted past and then Mike Donigan stepped out into the street and walked up to John Ripsey, followed by his three big sons.

"Who killed my son, John Ripsey?"

"I don't know, Donigan."

"You admit he was found along your side of the river with a slug in the back of his head."

"I own *both* sides of the river."

"Admit it!"

Ripsey nodded. "We had a hell of a fire. A shot was fired while we were fighting it. The body was found where the brush fire had raged. None of my men were near where Madison had been killed. That's all I know, Donigan."

Donigan thrust out a long finger. "You have smitten my son to the ground! The blood of his soul will be on your hands. Your mouth has been full of cursing, deceit and fraud. Hell will welcome such as you!"

Ripsey spat. "You sanctimonious fool! Prating holy language at *me* when you back your play with shotguns."

Wash Donigan lowered his shotgun barrel from where he had cradled it in his arms. The muzzle pointed at John Ripsey. Jeff and Adams separated a little from the eldest brother and gripped their scatterguns. The Box R men had straightened up now, and stood with strong hands hanging near gun butts.

John Ripsey raised an admonishing finger. "Now you listen to me, Mike Donigan! Your boy was killed on my land by some unknown. Not one of my men! If I find him, I'll turn him over to the law. That should satisfy anyone. I'll forget about the burning of the barn. I don't like the death of that young man any better than you do. That's what I have to say."

Mike Donigan moved swiftly, jumping forward to grip Ripsey with his left hand. Ripsey cursed. His strength was no match for Big Mike. They swayed together. The punchers started forward and then realized they couldn't shoot.

"Oh, my God," said Sim Short. "It's here!" The two old men turned, pitting their strength against each other. A Box R man jumped off the porch, but a blast over his head from Wash Donigan's shotgun stopped him where he was. Ripsey clawed down for his Colt, but Mike butted him with his head. Blood streamed from Ripsey's mouth. He was tiring fast. Mike dragged the smaller man to the center of the street. Ripsey stamped on the old man's instep and took advantage of the surprise to break free. Ripsey jerked at his Colt, cursing wildly. Adams Donigan jumped to one side and raised his shotgun. A Box R puncher dropped behind a barrel and freed his Colt. Rowan jumped back into the general store as the Colt barked. A shotgun roared, shattering one of the Union's windows. Ripsey freed his six-gun and raised it, but Adams Donigan fired his second barrel just as Mike Donigan moved into the line of fire. Mike's right arm jerked like a puppet's as the concentrated charge ripped into it, scattering blood and cloth against the startled Ripsey.

Mike Donigan swayed in the center of the street as the firing stopped. He gripped his shattered arm with his left hand and stared wide-eyed at his enemy before he pitched forward on his face, the blood soaking into the hard earth beneath his awkwardly twisted right arm.

Adams Donigan threw down his smoking shotgun and ran to his father. John Ripsey slowly wiped the blood from his white face. The Box R men started for the Donigans, but an imperious wave of Ripsey's hand halted them. "Let's go home, boys," said John Ripsey. "He got his blood."

Rowan turned to Sim. "Get the doctor." Rowan crossed to the fallen man and swiftly cut away the huck shirt, staunching the flow of blood by arterial pressure. "Get some whiskey," he said to Jeff Donigan.

"He don't drink."

"Goddamn it! Get that whiskey!"

The old man opened his eyes. "Curses are the language of fools and ungodly men," he said, and then fainted dead away.

Rowan watched the Box R men, led by set-faced John Ripsey, mount their horses and start away. Wash Donigan raised his shotgun. "Put it down, you damned idiot," said Rowan. "You want the street paved with blood?"

"Go to hell, Locke," said Wash.

The doctor came up the hot street at a run. People gathered swiftly. Rowan stepped aside as the sawbones knelt to render first aid. He wiped Donigan's blood from his hands with his bandanna and walked into the Union. "Rye," he said.

Dandy wiped his bald head. "That was sure close. The old man will lose his arm, no doubt."

"No doubt."

"I wonder why Ripsey came into town?" asked Rowan.

Dane Grenville toyed with his drink. "I think he wanted to make sure no one thought he was behind the killing of Mad Donigan," he said. "And at the same time he wanted to show Mike Donigan that he wasn't afraid to face him."

Dandy shook his head. "Two damned old mossy-horns fighting in the street. Scandalous."

Rowan rolled a smoke. He glanced over the bat-wings. Donigan's sons were carrying him away. "This isn't the end of it," he said.

Dandy rubbed his plump face. "I heard tell one time, quite a while ago, that Mad Donigan was stuck on Laura Ripsey."

Grenville gripped his glass tightly.

Dandy wiped the bar. "Waddie who useta work for

the Box R seen them talking one time over the fence at the border line of the two ranches. Very cozy like, he said. Ain't no doubt that Madison Donigan was the best looking of the boys."

A cold feeling came over Rowan as Dandy finished. He looked into the mirror behind the bar to meet the eyes of Dane Grenville, cold and enigmatical.

"I hear tell Laura Ripsey is man-hungry," said Dandy. " 'Course I ain't had no personal experience."

Grenville's hand cracked across the fat face of the bartender. "Keep your filthy thoughts to yourself," he grated. "Keep a lady's name out of this hole of a saloon." Grenville turned and walked out of the saloon, wiping his right hand on a fine handkerchief.

Dandy touched his face in wonderment. "Now why the hell did he do *that?*"

Rowan looked after the tall gambler. "I wonder," he said quietly. "I need another drink, Dandy, and you look like you ought to have one yourself."

"Yeh," said Dandy, "yeh. Broken window and slap in the phiz. Why the hell should my place always be a battlefield?"

Rowan downed his drink. The memory of Laura Ripsey came back to him, and he felt the bile rise in his gorge, as though he had overturned a rock and seen something disgusting beneath it.

CHAPTER TEN

The evening of the day Mike Donigan suffered his shattered arm, Loco Dawson came to Rowan's room. "I got something for you," he said. "I been poking around quite a bit. Coupla nights or so ago there was a hassle out at the limits of the Box R. Box R boy got skinned by a slug. Ripsey lost forty or fifty cows. Now, I was coming back from Encinosa after delivering some staple goods for Sim Short up thataway, and it was dark as the inside of a beegum hat. Damned mule got a stone in its hoof. You know how Nelly is."

"Yeh," said Rowan. "Get on with it!"

"Waal ... I was down getting the stone out when I hears cattle bawling amongst the hills to the east of the road. I figgered it was too damned dark for any *honest* man to be driving cattle, so I leads Nelly into the brush and scouts down the road. All of a sudden here comes fifty or so head of cows, making a racket like the devil beating tan-bark. Three or four waddies chousing them along. When they cross the road one of the *vaqueros* drops behind. He yells something about holding the cows near Carrizo Peak. The *hombre* he was talking to says to hold them there for further orders before driving them through to the Rio. Then the cows was gone."

"Must have been Box R beef."

"Too dark to see, but I did see one thing."

"So?"

"The *hombre* that tells them to hold the cattle was Pres Ripsey."

"It figures."

"Rustling his own cows?"

"Yes. I'll tell you about it later."

Loco nodded. "Anyways, I heads back to Llano. A little while ago I see Sid Coates in town. Sid tells Schwab he won't have any beef for him for a coupla days."

"Where is Sid now?"

"He was having a beer at the Union when I last saw him. Said something to Dandy about taking a ride west tonight."

Rowan jumped up. "Get my horse!"

"You trailing him?"

"Yes."

"Not without me, you ain't. You been playing a lone hand too long, sonny. I'm in on this."

"Fair enough. Get a cayuse."

Rowan pulled on his boots and grabbed his hat as Loco left the room. He checked his Colt and Winchester and hurried down the stairs after Loco. Loco was in the livery stable saddling Jim while the liveryman saddled a blocky grullo. Rowan looked across at the Union. Sid Coates came out, wiping his ragged dragoon mustache both ways. He swung up on his buckskin and rode quickly out of town to the north. In a few minutes Rowan and Loco were after him. The moon was lighting the sky as they saw Coates turn off on the Salt Creek road. They followed him through the trees. Coates stopped at the slaughterhouse for a few minutes and then left it, following a dim trail which paralleled the creek.

"Trail leads to the Encinosa Road," said Loco.

The moon was full up when they reached the road. Loco rubbed his belly. "We forgot to eat," he said.

"Take a Spanish supper, Loco. Tighten your belt a notch."

It was late when they caught sight of Sid again, riding steadily on the road. They let him get a lead. Loco drew rein at a dim trail which cut off to the west. "This is the quickest way to the peak," he said.

Rowan saw a pile of horse dropping in the trail. He swung down. "Dropped a short time ago," he said. "Let's take a chance and follow this trail."

They kneed their horses from the road onto the trail. It was midnight by Rowan's repeater watch, under the dim bulk of Carrizo, when they heard a steer bawl up the canyon. Rowan slid from Jim. Loco took the two horses and picketed them in among the trees. The two men took their rifles and followed the rough trail. The odor of wood-smoke came to them as they rounded a curve in the trail. Ahead of them a fire glowed through the trees, revealing the white faces of Herefords. Five men squatted about the fire. They were eating from tin plates. "I'm famished enough to ask them for some grub," said Loco.

Rowan dropped behind a rock. One of the men finished eating and poked at something in the fire. One of the other men dogged down a steer. Coates took a glowing object from the fire and applied it over the brand. Smoke rose and the stench of burning hair came to the two watchers. Loco spat. "Blotting out a brand with a flat iron," he whispered.

Sid put the iron back into the coals and took out a stamp iron. He applied it to the flank of the steer and nodded to the man beside him. The steer was released. Five more times a brand was blotted and rebranded. The steers were corralled in a rock hollow. The fire began to die out and the men rolled up in blankets, leaving one of their number on guard.

"Now what?" asked Loco.

"I have a feeling Sid will drive those six steers back to the slaughterhouse."

"So we sit it out and wait for him to do it?"

Rowan nodded.

"Chihuahua! It'll be cold tonight."

"You wanted to come along."

"Shut up!"

Rowan took his slicker from his saddle and put it on. "Take the first watch. Wake me if they move those cows." He scuffled some leaves together and dropped down on them.

During the night Loco and Rowan spelled each other. Rowan was aroused by a hand shaking his shoulder. "Dawn," said Loco. "Coates is getting ready to leave."

Rowan got up stiffly and yawned widely. The men were cooking their breakfasts. The odor of sow bosom drifted up to the two watchers. Coates ate and saddled his buckskin. He drove his six steers up the trail. Rowan and Loco faded into the thick brush. Coates passed, and they followed him.

"You ever eat *sopapillas,* Rowan?" asked Loco.

"Don't recollect."

"The greasers take squares of short biscuit dough, fry them in deep fat. They puff up like a balloon."

"You mean *bunuelos.*"

"The hell I do! I mean *sopapillas!*"

Rowan spat. "What the hell is the difference? We haven't got any."

"Useta have a Mex gal named Elena. She could surely cook enchiladas. Dripping with cheese and covered with chopped raw onions. You could taste them for a week afterwards." "Shut up!"

They reached the Encinosa road. Fresh cattle droppings littered it. They followed the trail northeast.

The sun was well up when Coates could be seen *cara-joing* his steers down a slope toward the Salt Creek trail. Rowan and Loco followed the plainly marked path of the rustled steers. Coates reached his slaughterhouse and drove the steers into his peeled-pole corral. Then he roped a big steer and led it into the slaughterhouse. "Let's go get him," said Rowan. They left their horses among the trees and padded forward on foot. Rowan darted to the side of the slaughterhouse and heard a grunt as Coates smashed a sledge down on the head of the steer. He walked quietly to the front door, motioning Loco to go to the back of the building.

Rowan drew and cocked his Colt. He raised his right foot and booted the door open, racing through into the semidarkness. There was a startled exclamation from Sid Coates, who was bent over the dead steer. Loco rattled at the back door. Coates threw a heavy sledge at Rowan. Rowan jumped behind a post, afraid to shoot for fear of hitting Loco. Sid leaped the steer and jumped behind the thin partition at the back of the building.

"Surrender!" yelled Rowan. "United States Marshal!"

There was a scuffle of feet as Loco ran alongside the building. A revolver flamed from the end of the partition. The slug slapped into the post behind which Rowan was standing. He fired into the semidarkness. Sid cursed. He fired twice. Rowan dropped to the floor and crawled behind the steer. He could see Sid peering into the shadows. Rowan's boot hit a box. Coates whirled and fired. He pulled trigger again but the hammer hit a dud cartridge. Rowan came up from behind the steer like an uncoiling spring. He fired over Sid's head. Sid turned and hurled his Colt. It hit Rowan on his bandaged right arm and the pain made him drop his gun.

Loco came through the doorway, blinking. "Where the hell are yuh, Rowan?" he yelled.

Coates sprinted for the back door, but Rowan snatched up a board and threw it between his churning legs. Coates went down hard. Rowan dived on him and met an upthrust knee which knocked the wind out of him. He gasped for breath and rolled to one side. Coates turned to meet Loco head-on. Loco took a straight smash to the jaw and up-ended over the steer. Coates snatched up Rowan's Colt and fired. The slug rapped into the hard earth inches from Rowan's head. Loco came up fighting mad. He belted Coates alongside the jaw and the two men tangled in a wild flurry of boots and fists, punctuated by pistol shots.

Pulling himself to his feet, Rowan laid a boot alongside Coates' skull, ripping through the flesh with his spur. Coates grunted in pain. He broke loose from Loco and turned to meet a blue norther which Rowan launched from mid-thigh. Knuckles merged with jawbone and Sid Coates flipped backward with the impact of the haymaker, driving Loco back over the dead steer again. The rustler lay still.

Loco passed his hands over Coates' body and pulled a double-barreled derringer from a hip pocket.

"Tie him," said Rowan.

Loco limped to a coil of rope hanging on a peg. "Where do we take him?"

"You'll take him to Santa Rosa and throw him in the juzgado with Slip Wellman. In separate cells, mind."

"You mean you got Slip, too?"

"In the cooler."

Loco scratched his head. "When the hell do we eat?"

"I'll give you money."

"Can't eat the filthy stuff."

"I want him out of the Llano area. Cut a bait of meat off of that steer, courtesy of John Ripsey. You can cook it on the way."

"Keno! But what about you?"

Rowan picked up his Colt and reloaded it, ramming it down in its sheath. "We've only picked up the penny-ante boys. I'm after the plungers."

"It'll take some doin', Rowan."

Rowan looked at Loco. "That's what I'm here for, *amigo.*"

They carried Sid outside and lashed him over his horse. They mounted and rode for the Llano road. Loco turned north after Rowan handed him some bills. Rowan touched Jim with his spurs and rode south.

CHAPTER ELEVEN

That evening Rowan dismounted from Jim at the gate of the Donigan place and led the bay up the lane to the house. There was a light in the parlor. He stepped up on the porch and tapped on the door. "Who is it?" a woman's voice called out.

"Rowan Locke," he said.

Joan Donigan opened the door and eyed him. "How can I help you?" she asked.

Rowan stepped in and removed his hat. A fire blazed in the fieldstone fireplace.

"I came to see how your father is."

Joan smiled. "Neighborly of you," she said. "Dad is resting. He's very weak. He is under drugs now and will be for some time. I'll tell him you were here."

"I haven't left yet."

She colored. "Please sit down. The boys are out somewhere."

A cold feeling came over him. He looked quickly at her. She raised a hand. "They have promised me that they will not start trouble."

He smiled. "You seem to be able to control them better than anyone."

"I've been sister, mother, nurse and cook for them.

They have their faults, as I have, but they have been good to me."

He took out his makings. "May I smoke?"

"Certainly."

Rowan rolled a smoke. She watched his big hands. "You do things so easily," she said. "Somehow I feel as though you could do almost anything you set your heart to. Soldier, ranch, build, almost anything. I believe in hands. Yours, for example, strong and capable."

He tilted his head to one side. "I'm glad I have one redeeming feature, Miss Donigan."

She flushed and looked away. "I'm sorry. I don't often get a chance to speak with men outside of my brothers and my father. Perhaps I talk too much."

"I could sit here a long time listening to you. Do you never go to dances and parties?"

She shrugged her shapely shoulders. "I used to, but young men learned to stay away from me when they knew of my brothers." She smiled. "Once I went to a dance out at the Double K. Jeff dropped me off. I had a wonderful time dancing. I especially liked the Varsoviana. It seems such an unusual dance for New Mexico."

He lit up. "I've heard that it came from Mexico, imported by the Austrians who came to Mexico with Maximilian. Like all things in America, it is of foreign birth, but has fitted into our way of life."

She continued. "There was a young man there from an outlying ranch who took me home when Jeff didn't return in time. We got along famously until he turned the buckboard up the lane. He just went pale and asked me if I was the sister of the Donigans. When I admitted it, he couldn't wait to get me out of the buckboard. The last I saw of him he was cutting the bend in the road on two wheels with his coattails straight out behind him like a board." She laughed gayly.

Rowan was fascinated as he watched her. "Your

brothers can't expect to keep you corralled here for the rest of your life, can they?"

"They won't!"

"You'll have to leave then to get your own way."

She stood up and placed a piece of wood in the fireplace. "No. I knew some day a man would come here who would stay to speak with me and face my brothers."

"Like me, perhaps?"

She turned slowly. Her lips were parted. "Yes. *Like you,* Rowan."

"You know nothing about me, Joan. My background. My past."

She came closer to him. "I know you're an honorable man, and I think my family does, too.

They admire courage and respect a man for standing up to them."

For a moment she looked as though she would come closer. There was a low moan from a bedroom opening into the living room. She placed a slim finger to her lips and hurried into the room. Rowan flipped his cigarette into the fire and walked softly to the bedroom door. She was bent over Mike Donigan, who was propped up in the big bed. A night lamp cast a soft glow of light on her. Rowan knew he had found his woman. She turned, lowered the lamp a trifle and closed the door. As she turned, she bumped into Rowan. He drew her close and her arms went around his neck, drawing his face down to hers. Rowan kissed her. She clung to him, kissing him again and again. Time seemed to drop out of existence as they stood there. Then the distant beating of hoofs came to them from the road. She drew back, deftly touching her hair. "My brothers! You must leave!" she said.

Rowan shook his head. "They'd better know right now," he said.

"We'd better meet them outside then," she said.

He grinned. "You think there will be a ruckus?"

She pressed his arm. "You know my brothers." They

went out on the moonlit porch. Four horsemen were coming up the lane. They saw Rowan. The four brothers slid from their horses.

Monroe led the mounts away. Wash Donigan leaped the low picket fence that surrounded the front yard of the house. "You! Locke! What are you doing here?"

"He came to ask about Dad," Joan said.

Wash thrust out his chin. "Well," he said, "you've asked. Vamoose!"

Rowan turned to the girl. "I'd like to talk with Wash," he said. "You go into the house."

"You telling *my* sister what to do?" barked Wash.

Joan looked her tall brother in the eye. "Yes," she said. "And I'm *listening!*"

Jeff and Adams were waiting at the fence. Rowan could hear their low voices as they talked. Wash looked over his shoulder. "You hear that?"

"Sure did," said Jeff.

Joan walked to the edge of the porch. "Rowan has my permission to be here, and also to leave. I don't want any of you to bother him. Hear?"

The girl turned to Rowan. He knew she expected him to kiss her, but he had a feeling he would be flattened under an avalanche of rocky Donigan fists if he did. "Good night," he said.

For a moment she hesitated and then she went into the house. Rowan took out the makings and rolled a smoke. He lit it and walked down the fence. Wash was right behind him. Rowan turned.

"Go ahead," said Wash. "She's covering you. You're safe. But I'll thrash hell outa you if you come back."

Rowan took his cigarette from his mouth. "I'm coming back," he said. "Whenever Joan will see me."

"You hear that, Jeff?" asked Adams.

"Yeh."

Wash Donigan's face was a set white mask in the

moonlight. "Git!" he said thinly. "Or I'll work you over right here."

Rowan dropped his smoke and ground it out deliberately. He looked Wash in the eye. "We might as well settle things right now," he said quietly. "I hear tell you're the kingpin in these parts with your fists. I aim to come back whenever she'll have me."

"Then you'll fight *me!*"

Rowan nodded. "Let's get away from the house. Your father is restless. Besides, Joan won't like it."

"The barn is fine," said Adams eagerly.

Wash looked at Rowan. "All right with you?"

"Keno."

They crossed the moonlit yard to the barn. Jeff lit two extra lanterns and hung them up. The barn was big and well kept. The Donigans cleared tools and boxes out of the way, leaving an open area lit by the lanterns.

Wash turned to Rowan. "How do you want to work this?" he asked.

Rowan shrugged. "Just keep them off of me."

"They won't bother you, even if you whip me."

"Hawwww!" brayed Monroe.

"Shut up!" snapped Jeff.

Wash rubbed his lean jaw. "How'd it be if we was to square off in here alone? The man that walks out is the rooster around here."

"Suits me."

Monroe cursed. Jeff looked at Rowan. "We'll take that gun," he said.

Rowan unbuckled his gun and handed it to Jeff. There was no fear of dirty work in him, but Wash was unarmed. Wash turned to his brothers. "You keep Joanie outa here. She comes to the barn I'll whale hell outa all three of yuh!"

The three brothers reluctantly left the barn and closed the door behind them. Wash looked at Rowan. "They won't bother yuh," he said.

"I believe you."

Wash shucked his shirt and undershirt, revealing bunched muscles. There wasn't an ounce of fat on the man. He moved easily, like a great lean cat. Rowan stripped off coat and shirt. He hung them up and pulled his undershirt over his head. He tightened his belt about his lean waist and worked his shoulder muscles a little.

Wash eyed the tight bandage about Rowan's right arm. "What's that?"

"Burns."

"Bad?"

"I'll be all right."

"I want no advantage!"

Rowan smiled. "You'll get none."

"Rough and tumble, or rounds?"

"You pick it out."

"Rounds. A man's knee touches the floor he calls time. A knockdown is a round. I can get one of the boys to referee."

"No need."

"Let's have at it then."

Rowan raised his fists. Wash came in swiftly, wasting no time. He feinted with a long left, and drove out a piston right. Rowan blocked the right high with his elbow and brought an underhand blow to the lean middle of the tall man. Wash backed off, bending his handsome head behind his fists, eyeing Rowan cautiously.

Rowan circled, letting Wash bring the fight to him. He didn't have long to wait. Wash feinted with his left, drove out the right, held it short and then swung an axe-blow left that stung Rowan's left jaw. He was down on one knee before he realized it. "Time," said Wash. He backed off, shuffling his feet, spitting over his left shoulder, his blue eyes watching Rowan.

Rowan got up and raised his hands. Wash came in fast. Rowan threw a looping left and followed with a right, but Wash had drawn back at the split-second time the right came across. He circled about, bobbing and feinting, waiting for a chance. Rowan forced the fight, getting home a left hook before he was smashed to the straw-littered floor by a right he never saw coming. "Round," said Wash. He stepped back and placed his hands on his hips, breathing lightly.

Rowan touched his jaw, feeling a cracked tooth with his tongue. He sat up and shook his head and then got to his feet. Wash came in differently this time, leaving himself wide open, throwing his head about tauntingly. Rowan threw half a dozen futile punches that seemed winners, but skinned by the lean jaw of the tall man. Wash slammed a jolting left to Rowan's jaw, dropped it, and hit hard over Rowan's heart, then followed through with a right which Rowan knew would floor him. It did. His head bounced from the hard floor. "Time," said Wash.

Rowan sat up and gingerly touched the back of his head, and he knew he was in for a hell of a shellacking. Rowan got up and sparred about, saving his strength. Twice he tied the taller man up by locking his arms under his own armpits, riding him about, leaning heavily on Wash to tire him. Rowan's sweat was greasy on his sides and Wash slipped his hands free, tapped Rowan tauntingly on the nose, and danced back.

Rowan had learned something. Wash invariably dropped his left when he threw a right. Twice Rowan tried to cross the dropped left without success. Then Wash drove in a left cross, lowered it, and fanned across a swift right. Rowan crossed the left with his right and smashed Wash from left ear to the tip of the nose. Wash staggered back, fighting for balance, caromed from a post and hit the floor. "Time," panted Rowan.

Rowan didn't know his man. Wash came up off the floor like the opening blade of a spring knife. He forgot his science and fought with rage. Punches cracked another tooth of Rowan's, started his nose bleeding and threw him back against the barn door so hard a pitchfork clattered from its peg. He slid down to the floor and dazedly wiped the blood from his aching face. Salt sweat stung the partially healed burns beneath the bandage on his right arm. "Time," said Wash easily. "Had enough?"

Rowan grinned crookedly. "I should say yes, but I think I can lick you, Wash."

"Get up then!"

Rowan got one leg under him, placed the tips of his fingers on the floor and came up fast, driving in, leaning far off balance, throwing punches from wide out. Wash retreated, but Rowan hooked his left inside Wash's right and hammered one to the kidneys. Wash whirled Rowan around but was off balance. Rowan chopped at the base of the neck and then at the kidneys again until Wash broke free.

Rowan backed off, flinging sweat from his forehead with a hand, drawing in the thin, hot air, deep, deep, and finding little relief in it. Wash came at him and Rowan saw the dropped left and once again snapped in the right that dropped Wash. Wash shook his head and spat blood. He looked up at Rowan with a partially closed eye. "You can fight, Locke," he said.

Rowan grinned, although the floor seemed to lift and fall a little beneath his feet. "So can you, but we're not done yet."

"Hell, no!"

All science was gone now. Blows battered at bellies, hearts, jaws and noses until blood streaked them from crown to waist. Their hearts seemed to slug at each other when they clinched. They threw each other back as though trying to rid each other of the other's presence and then closed again. There was no sound but their labored breathing, the shuffle of feet in the straw and the solid thud of punches landing home.

Wash threw Rowan back and lanced in a left jab which threw Rowan off to one side. As Rowan came up,

Wash uppercutted. Rowan's head snapped back. He threw a looping right which cracked solidly against the taller man's jaw. Rowan hit the floor, tried to get up, felt the barn roll

slowly over once or twice, and lay there helpless, knowing he was licked as he had never been before. He closed his puffed eyes and drew in deep breaths. There was a weight on his long legs, and for one awful moment he thought they had been injured. He raised his head and looked full into the battered face of Wash Donigan. Donigan's body was across Rowan's legs.

"Get up, Wash," said Rowan weakly. "You won!"

Wash spat out a tooth. "I can't," he said. "I feel like a damned chopping block."

They stared bloodily at each other. Suddenly Rowan laughed. Wash rolled off of Rowan and got weakly to his feet. He blew on his abraded knuckles and coughed hard, spitting out blood. He drew in a deep breath. "Well?" he said.

Rowan sat up and pressed his hands down on the floor. He tried to get up and sank down again. He cocked his head and looked up at the tough man above him. Wash reached down and gripped Rowan by an arm, pulling him to his feet. "Come on," he said. "We've both had enough—and proved nothing at all."

Rowan took his clothing from the hook and draped it over his free arm. He staggered a little as he headed for the door. Wash placed an arm about Rowan's shoulders.

"They're done!" said Monroe, outside. "I'll bet Locke's an unholy mess."

"Don't be so sure," said Jefferson. "Locke is a ring-tailed roarer."

Wash opened the door and the two of them stood there with the moonlight flooding down on them. "My God," said Adams. "It looks like Sid Coates' slaughterhouse."

Wash wiped the blood from his mouth. "It was a draw," he said. "Get his horse, Monroe."

"Sure, Wash! Sure!" The kid ran to get the bay.

Rowan put on his undershirt, wincing as he pulled it past his face. He shrugged into shirt and coat. Jeff handed him his hat. Monroe led up the bay. Wash went into the barn and got his shirt. He bent and picked up something from the floor. For a moment he stared at it and then he looked quickly at Rowan. He put his hand into his jeans pocket and came out of the barn. Rowan thrust out his hand. "You're a good man, Wash. I still think it was your fight."

Wash grinned. "A man is a fool to fight," he said.

Rowan swung up on Jim. "Do I have the right to come and see Joan?" he asked.

Wash nodded. "Who's gonna stop you around here?"

"Thanks, Wash."

"Forget it. Good night, Rowan."

Rowan guided the bay to the lane and rode slowly to the road. He ached as though he had been used as a punching bag. He was on the Llano road when he suddenly thought of his marshal's badge. He thrust a hand into his inside coat pocket. The badge was not there, nor was it anywhere else about his person. Then he knew, with a cold feeling, what it was that Wash Donigan had picked up from the floor of the barn.

CHAPTER TWELVE

Two days after Rowan's brawl with Wash Donigan, Loco Dawson rode into Llano and found Rowan in Sim Short's general store. "Got to see you right away, Rowan," he said.

Sim peered over his spectacles at Loco. "Where the hell you been?" he asked. "I had a lot of hauling for you to do. You get thrown in the *calabozo* somewheres?"

"Yeh."

Short looked from one to the other of them. "What's going on around here?"

Rowan shrugged. "Too damned much for a cow town."

Short scratched his chin. "Slip Wellman vanishes. Sid Coates ain't been seen near his slaughterhouse. Loco was seen riding miles north of here with Sid Coates tied up like an Apache prisoner. Locke, sometimes I think you're something other than you make out to be."

"Such as?"

Short glanced at the door and then leaned across the counter. "Oscar Schwab told me who you are. Now, don't get riled at Os. I'm mayor here in Llano, and have been for two years, and just because nobody else wants the damned job I'll have it a long time, God help Llano. Now

I'm for law and order, you know that, Locke, and I want to help you. Fact is, I been waitin' for you to ask me. I'm a prideful man, and my feelings has been hurt because you didn't. *Now* I'm asking you."

Rowan glanced at Loco. The little ex-soldier nodded. "Sim ain't too bright," he said, "but he's honest."

"Last hauling job you'll get from me," said Sim.

Loco spat. "You don't pay enough, anyways."

"Shut up," said Rowan. "What was it you wanted to tell me, Loco?"

"Bad news. Sid Coates is dead."

"Hell!" snapped Rowan. "You didn't kill him, did you?"

"How you talk! We camped out in the brush the first night out. The next evening we wasn't too far from the Lazy LF. I decided to camp that night rather than try to ride all the way through in the dark. Made a fire and was getting ready to brew some coffee when somebody opens fire with a rifle. Sid gets skinned by the first shot. He jumps up and starts to run. Second slug hits him and breaks his damned neck."

"Maybe they were after you?"

"I was down at the waterhole and wasn't even in sight from where the shots came from, but I could see Sid. The bushwhacker was after him all right. I crawls through the brush and sees a man riding off through the scrub trees but it was too dark to make out who he was. I doused the fire, snared Sid's feet with my lasso and dragged him under cover. I hid in the brush all night and at dawn I buried Sid. Found these where the bush-whacker had been lying." Loco handed Rowan two empty hulls. They were .50/95's. They looked at each other. "Was it Pres?" asked Rowan.

"Like I said, I couldn't tell."

"Of all the damned luck. Well, we've still got Slip."

Loco waggled his head. "I went on to the Lazy LF. Your foreman told me Slip broke out of the Santa Rosa juzgado, stole a hoss and took off like a speckled frog with a striped snake after him. He won't be back. The big *ladino* was scared to death he was gonna get a hemp necktie."

Rowan smashed a big fist down on the counter. "And I needed those two long loopers for testimony!"

"I'm sorry, Rowan. I done the best I could."

"It wasn't your fault!"

Sim scratched his poll. "Now what?"

Rowan shoved back his hat. "Pres Ripsey is in on this. You keep your mouth shut about that, Sim."

"I'm an oyster. Why don't you snaffle onto him?"

Rowan shook his head. "I can't buck the Box R yet. Supposing I *did* take him in? Ripsey's gang would tear the town apart before they let me get him outa here."

"We could back you up, Rowan."

"No. You're all good men but we'd be outnumbered by far."

"What do we do then?"

"Sit tight for a time, waiting for the next move. There's another man in this mess. A man with brains enough to build up a first-class rustling ring. Smart enough to snatch cattle from John Ripsey and get away with it."

Sim looked speculatively at Rowan. "Who?"

Loco waved a hand. "I know. Dane Grenville."

"Good God," said Sim.

Loco took a letter from his pocket. "Hash gave me this. Mrs. Forbes left for Denver with the baby. Hash said he thought you ought to know about this."

Rowan opened the letter and studied the ragged writing.

Dear Rowan,

he read slowly,

Missus Forbes left heer with the baby after she tole me something witch might be of interest to you. You remember me talking with you about that hombre what came through heer before Larry went to Llano, the one what said something about Lazy LF hides being seen in Llano. Dane Grenville. Well, that ain't him, leastways that ain't his name. His real monicker is Lewis Theba. It pains me to tell you this but I taken pen in hand to do so. Missus Forbes, she gets worried about you getting kilt down there too. So she calls me to the house one night, she was crying like all get-out. Seems like she knew this Theba in Denver when she was just a kid and had some doings with him, not nice neither. Anyways, he leaves her and tells her he will be back, but he don't come, the dirty skunk, so she marries up with Larry, and comes heer with us. Theba shows up heer when Larry ain't around one time, we was all out branding, and wants she should run away with him but she says no she won't go and says she is happy. So this skunk looks around and likes the Lazy LF. So he sneaks back onct and tells Larry about them Lazy LF hides in Llano. He figgered Larry right, for Larry goes down there and don't come back. Missus Forbes keeps her mouth shut when you are heer, but gets worried like I said and tells me to write to you when she is gone back to her folks in Denver with the baby which all us boys miss. So there is what I have to say. I hope it will help. Give that skunk Theba what for. Hope you are in good health. The ranch is fine and the cows fat.

Your friend,
Hash Bryce

Rowan crushed the letter in his hand and looked across the street at the Union. He started to walk to the door of the store, but Loco gripped him by an arm. Rowan threw him off. Sim ran down behind the counter and jumped in front of Rowan. Rowan shoved him aside, but Loco gripped Rowan by the gunbelt.

Rowan reached out with a hand as though feeling in the dark and gripped Sim's shoulder so tightly that Sim yelled out in pain. The sound seemed to snap something in Rowan. He shook his head and looked strangely at the two frightened men. "It's all right," he said in a low voice. "Thanks. Thanks for stopping me."

Sim walked behind the counter. "Give me some spit-or-drown chewin' " said Loco. The storekeeper placed the tobacco caddy in front of Loco, but his eyes never left Rowan. "Loco," he said, "you see that look? The bars of hell was down."

Rowan rolled a smoke and lit it. Grenville, or Theba, knew a lot about what was going on in the Llano area. He had Pres Ripsey where the hair was short, stealing cattle from his own father to pay off a gambling debt which must have been run up in a fixed game. He had eliminated Larry Forbes, or at least had had the job done. Yes, Dane Grenville knew a lot in his devious mind, but there were three things he didn't know. The first was that Rowan Locke was a U.S. Marshal; the second was that Rowan was Larry Forbes' cousin; *the third, that Rowan was going to kill him.*

Loco cut off a chew and stuffed it into his mouth. "Never did ask you how you got your face looking like that, Rowan."

"Fell up a tree."

"Yeh. Yeh."

Dane Grenville rode up the center of the street on a fine dun. He dismounted in front of the Union and went in. "Loco," said Rowan, "take a look at that saddle gun on the dun. Don't make it too damned obvious."

Loco left the store and wandered across the street. He leaned against a post and began to whittle a stick. He looked into the Union and then stepped off beside the dun, keeping it between him and the saloon door. Quickly he pulled the gun partway out of the sheath and slid it back in again. Then he wandered off down the street, to reappear at the back door of the general store.

"Model '76 Winchester. Pistol grip. Tang sight. Fancy

bit of hardware. Breech walls all fancy-like, with pictures of birds and stuff, a .50/95."

"Pres Ripsey's rifle."

Sim Short looked through the dusty front window. "Funny thing," he said over his shoulder, "I never seen Grenville carry a saddle gun before."

"Me neither," said Loco. "Say, Rowan! You think he was the *hombre* what drygulched Sid Coates?"

"I'll stake a heap on it."

"You figure on running him in, Rowan?" asked Sim.

Rowan shook his head. "I've got the rustling pinned on him and Pres, but I haven't found out who killed Larry Forbes."

"You can pin that on the Black Donigans."

Rowan shook his head. "I doubt that."

"It was shotgun work. Near the Donigan land. Wash Donigan sold Lazy LF beef to Os Schwab. What else do you want?"

"It's all circumstantial."

"Men have been hung for less than that."

Rowan waved a hand impatiently. "It's all too pat, as though someone was trying to make it look like the Donigans were behind it."

"Yeh," said Loco. "Now that you mention it, I can see what you mean."

"Loco, you go out to Coates' slaughterhouse. See if those steers are still there."

"And if they are?"

"Drive them into town; come around east of town and put them in those pens down by the river."

"I might get picked up for rustling."

"Let me worry about that."

"Yeh," said Loco, "I'll let *you* worry about it if I end up with a hemp necktie or a slug through my belly. I'll go, but I'll damned well do my *own* worrying!" He vanished through the back door.

"Fussy little man, isn't he?" said Sim. He peered through the window. "Say! There's Pres Ripsey!"

Rowan walked to the window and watched the man dismount. Pres walked over to Grenville's dun, looked up and down the street and then took the fancy Winchester from the sheath and slid it into his own empty sheath. He looked up and down the street again and then went into the Union.

Rowan left the store by the back door, skirted behind the livery stable, cut across the street and rounded behind the Union. He peered in through a dirty window. Pres and Grenville were seated at a table playing cards. Rowan went around to the back of the saloon. A pile of empty boxes blocked sight of him from the street. An open window was just behind the table occupied by Pres and Grenville. Rowan flattened himself against the wall and listened.

"It was easy," said Grenville. "Sid was killed with the second shot. Little over a hundred yards."

"Hell, that rifle can hit dead center at three hundred."

"I wanted to make sure."

"I could have done it."

"You're sure proud of your rifle shooting."

"You want to match me sometime?" demanded Pres.

"Don't act like a kid."

"What happened to Slip Wellman?"

"I don't know. He's vanished."

"I don't like it, Dane."

"You think *I* do, you idiot? We'll just play it quiet for awhile. Did the boys get those steers over to the Rio Grande?"

"As far as I know."

"Then let them know we won't have any more for them for awhile."

"Look, Dane! Why don't we forget about the whole thing? You've made plenty off of Box R cattle. We'll make a slip and there'll be hell to pay."

Grenville's voice was cold. "Look, Pres. You still owe me plenty."

"You've made double what I owe you."

"Yes, damn you, but *I've* had to do the work! Supposing I tell your father how much you owe me?"

"You wouldn't dare!"

Grenville laughed. "Supposing I tell him about meeting Laura in different towns?"

"He'd kill you!"

"Not the way I'd work it."

Pres laughed without mirth. "Yes, I agree to that. You can work out *any* kind of a dirty deal."

Rowan heard the cards being shuffled swiftly. "Some day," said Dane Grenville softly, "I might take it in my mind to kill you, Pres."

In the silence that followed Rowan heard the riffle of the cards. Glasses clinked. "Anyway," said Pres, "we got rid of one of the Donigans."

"A helluva messy way. Why do you have to be so damned dramatic? Firing your own father's barn to make it look good. Couldn't you have gotten rid of him some other way?"

"I figured I could pin the burning on Madison."

"I knew he was sweet on Laura," said Dane. "I told you that long ago. You could have dropped him anywhere by just sending him a message, supposedly from her, and then waiting for him with that rifle of yours. The Donigans will make you Ripseys pay, one way or another."

"I think they've had their bellyful of fighting."

"You're wrong. They'll wait their chance with you. Locke is another one who'll wish he'd never been born when they're through with him."

"I can't figure him out. You think he's a lawman?"

"*Quién sabe?* He's too smart to be working for the salary they pay lawmen. There's something up his sleeve besides a good punching arm."

"I'll kill that cold-eyed Locke some day."

Grenville laughed. "It'll take a heap of killing. Let's play cards. I'm sick of this damned intriguing."

Rowan padded silently around the back of the Union. He still didn't know who had killed Larry Forbes, but Pres Ripsey would be brought to account for the murder of Madison Donigan. Rowan went to his room and dropped on his bed. The Donigans knew he was a lawman if the two in the Union didn't. It was another facet to the many-sided problem that faced him. Rowan rolled a smoke and lit it, placing his hands beneath his head. He watched the tobacco smoke drift through the open window. Joan Donigan. She would be a prize to bring home to the Lazy LF, providing Rowan lived through the Rio Mescalero mess.

CHAPTER THIRTEEN

Dane Grenville left Llano the same evening Rowan had overheard his conversation with Pres Ripsey. Rowan found Loco in the livery stable, pounding his ear on a pile of straw. Rowan shook him awake.

"Grenville pulled out of town five minutes ago, heading north. Trail him. I have an idea he's going to contact his men in the hills," he said.

Loco cursed. "You want I should get killed?"

"I've seen you work before, Loco. As an old Apache hunter you should be able to stay out of his way."

Rowan saddled Loco's horse as the little man got his rifle. He waved goodbye as Loco headed north out of the dark town. Rowan lit a cigar and crossed the street to the Union. Dandy scowled as he saw him. He jerked his head toward the rear of the big saloon. "Pres Ripsey is likkered up," he said. "Don't rile him."

Rowan eyed the drunken rancher in the mirror behind the bar. Pres was sprawled in a chair, staring moodily at the bottle in front of him. "I won't start anything," said Rowan.

"I'd appreciate it if you'd leave. He don't cotton to you, Rowan."

Rowan downed his drink. "The feeling is mutual," he said dryly. He paid for his drink and left the bar. The streets were busy, and he realized with a start that it was Saturday night, the time when the ranchers came in to let their womenfolk shop while they idled in the bars and streets talking cows. A buckboard came to a stop in front of Short's General Store. Rowan saw Joan and Jeff Donigan step down. He crossed the street and took off his hat. Joan eyed his battered face. "You've been fighting again," she accused.

Jeff grinned. "Sure has," he said.

"What do you know about it, Jeff?"

"Joanie! It wasn't *me!*"

Rowan grinned. "No. Jeff and I understand each other now."

"Yeh," said Jeff, "but it took a heap of doing."

Joan glanced from one to the other of them. She touched her throat with a slim hand. "The morning after you left the farm," she said to Rowan, "Wash looked like he had had a battle, which is nothing unusual. Said he fell up a tree. I suppose *you* did, too?"

Rowan shrugged. "Danged trees are always in the way," he said.

She raised her hands in mock horror. "Men! Well, I've got to shop and get back to the farm before Dad misses me." She hurried into Sim's place.

Jeff leaned against the buckboard. "You left something out at the place," he said.

"Yeh. Blood and a tooth or two."

Jeff shook his head. He reached in his pocket and took out Rowan's marshal's badge. He handed it to Rowan. "Wash says you've got enough guts to be a Black Donigan," he said.

Rowan took the badge. "Does this make a difference?"

Jeff spat. "Look, Rowan," he said, "us Donigans have done our share of lawbreaking, but we aren't worried about you. Another thing: Larry Forbes wasn't killed by one of us. That shotgun deal was a plant to get us in trouble. We didn't even see the man until his body was found on the road in front of our place."

Rowan nodded. "I think I know who dry-gulched Forbes."

"Who?"

"It can wait."

The batwings of the Union crashed open. Men turned to see Pres Ripsey swaying in the yellow lamplight. He looked across the street at Jeff and Rowan, said something to himself and swayed over to his horse, where he stood for a time holding onto the saddle horn. "Drunk as a coot," said Jeff.

"We'd better move."

"Move, hell! He don't bother me."

"Have you got a gun?"

"Shotgun under the seat."

"Leave it there. Go somewhere else."

Jeff laughed. "I'm staying right here."

Pres stood up and glared at the two men. He made as if to mount and then pulled his rifle from its sheath. The lamplight glinted from the silver-chased breech. Rowan gripped Jeff by the arm. "Get out of sight. He's drunk enough to do anything."

"He worries me."

Pres suddenly flipped the rifle up, gripping the lever, charging the chamber. He swayed a little. Then he raised the rifle. "Hey, Donigan!" he called. "Try this for size!"

Rowan whirled, shoving Jeff to one side as the fine weapon roared. Jeff grunted and went down. His straw hat flew off and blood ran down his face. Rowan dropped in front of the fallen man and reached for his Colt. Pres darted into the alleyway south of the Union. The big rifle spat flame. The slug whipped into the side of the buckboard. The mules whinnied and reared. Men scattered into the shadows, diving through open windows or dropping flat on the ground.

Rowan cocked his Colt. Pres fired again. Boots thudded on the hard earth. Rowan looked down at Jeff. He had been hit alongside the head. Rowan thought he was dead. He got to his feet and crossed the empty street. A rifle roared on the far side of Denton's Feed Store and the slug slapped into the side of the Union. Rowan hit the dirt, thrusting his gun arm forward. Pres sped across the street, laughing like a fool. Rowan snapped a shot out as Pres crashed through the batwings of the Stockmen's Bar. His rifle crashed again. Smoke drifted out into the street. Men cursed. Two of them came through the door and ran across the street.

Rowan ran down the alleyway, passed behind Denton's and sidled up to the street, flattening himself against the wall. He could see into the smoky saloon across the street. Pres was in there alone, knocking glasses off the bar with the smoking Winchester. The rancher's son threw a bottle at the big harp lamp and shattered it, plunging the saloon into darkness.

Down the street, Sim Short dragged Jeff Donigan into his store. Rowan watched the dark saloon. Glass tinkled to the street as Pres thrust his rifle muzzle through it. The .50/95 flamed, knocking an ornamental wooden ball from the top of Denton's. It flamed twice more, knocking the second ball from the roof and then smashing the china doorknob of the feed store. Rowan inched back.

Drunk or sober, Pres was a heller with the long gun.

The street was as empty as a ghost town. Rowan darted across the alleyway to jump behind a shed. The Winchester kicked up dirt inches behind him. Rowan passed behind the shed, crawled in through an open window and stopped in the shadows of the interior where he could see the Stockmen's Bar. A shadowy figure jumped out through the batwings, fired twice and then darted back under cover again. Glass fell into the street where a slug had whipped through a side window of the Union.

Rowan mentally checked the number of shots Pres had fired. *Ten.* He had at least two shots left, figuring the size of the big cartridges. Rowan wiped the sweat from his face. Pres rested the gun barrel on the window ledge and fired twice up the street, shattering a window in Luna's Chili House and breaking a wooden support which held up the Union saloon sign.

The big Winchester must be empty, but Pres carried two nickel-plated Colts on his *buscadero* gunbelt. Rowan eased through the back window and padded down the alleyway, cutting across the street to stop in front of the adobe livery stable where Chisos Ahrens had met his death. Rowan inched along the front of the building and then sprinted down the alleyway between the livery stable and the Stockmen's bar. He stopped in the shadows and crouched beside an open window. Odors of burned powder, coal oil and whiskey drifted to him. Pres was at the front of the saloon talking to himself.

Rowan peered into the saloon. Pres was crouched on the floor, slowly filling the magazine tube of the rifle. Rowan eased himself through the window and stopped behind a pilaster, with just enough room to conceal himself. Pres finished loading the weapon and fired three times up the street. He laughed and then pumped three shots through the shed where Rowan had been just a few minutes before. Pres stood up and walked to the bar, rolled over it and gripped a whiskey bottle. He shattered the neck on the edge of the bar and drank deeply, the whiskey flowing down his chin and soaking his shirt and coat. He wiped his mouth and picked up his rifle. Four times the heavy weapon roared in the dark saloon, smashing into ceiling and walls. Ten shots. Two left. Pres drank again and leaned against the bar holding the rifle. He walked to the door and peered

up the street, then he walked unsteadily toward the
back of the saloon. "Yellow-bellied townfolk," he said.
"Afraid of a real rifleman!" He fired into the piano
which stood against the back wall and then turned to
snap a shot from the hip toward the front of the
saloon.

Pres hiccupped and levered the empty out to reload.
He pulled trigger and the hammer fell on emptiness.
Rowan darted out, gripped the hot barrel of the rifle and
whirled Pres about. Pres cursed. Rowan swung his Colt to
buffalo Pres, but Pres swayed out of the way. Rowan
jerked the hot weapon from Pres's grip and hurled it
across the room. Pres dropped both hands for a double
draw but Rowan stepped in close, drove in a battering
left and followed through with a cut at Pres's head with
the Colt barrel. Pres went down on one knee and freed a
Colt. Rowan jumped back and booted the drunk alongside the head. The spur raked Pres from temple to chin.
He groaned and tried to get up but Rowan booted him
again viciously. The high heel thudded against Pres's jaw,
snapping his head back. He crashed down into a litter of
broken glass.

Rowan shoved back his hat and wiped the sweat from
his face. He jerked the fancy twin Colts from their
sheaths and threw them behind the bar. Then he gripped
Pres by the collar and dragged him to the door, heaving
him out into the dusty street. Men came from their
hiding places and looked down at the bloody face of the
drunken man. "He went loco," said a cowpoke. "Plumb
staring loco."

"A high lonesome if I ever seen one," said a store
clerk.

Sim Short came down the street. "You all right,
Rowan?"

Rowan wiped his mouth with the back of a hand.
"Yeh. What do we do with him?"

"Let him go," advised the cowpoke. "You jug John

Ripsey's son and you'll have the whole Box R *corrida* in Llano to spring him out."

"He killed Jeff Donigan," said Rowan quietly.

Short shook his head. "Just a crease. Lucky you shoved Jeff to one side or he'd be as dead as Mad Donigan."

"Let him go then," said the clerk. "Long's he didn't kill Jeff."

Sim Short raised his head. There seemed to be a change in him. "No!" he said flatly. "We'll jug him! By Godfrey! No man is gonna tree Llano and get away with. To hell with John Ripsey and the whole Box R!"

The cowpoke swallowed. "Well, I'm due back at the ranch," he said, and trotted off to his horse.

The clerk ran a finger around beneath his collar. "Just remembered I ain't seen my brother George in quite some time. Guess I'll take off tonight for Carrizozo." He walked swiftly away.

Rowan gripped Pres by the collar and dragged him along the street. Coon Ellis came out of the *calabozo* and helped Rowan drag the bleeding man into a cell. They dumped him on the cell floor and Coon clanged the door shut and locked it.

"This will cause a war, Rowan." Rowan wiped his hands and rolled a smoke. "Maybe it's about time somebody broke the Ripsey hold on this country," he said. He left the jail and walked down to Sim's store. "Where's Jeff?" he asked.

"Joan has him in a room at the hotel, Rowan." Sim was loading an ancient shotgun. He looked at Rowan. "Might as well get ready."

Rowan went to the hotel and up the stairs to the room occupied by Jeff. The doctor had just finished bandaging Jeff's head. He smiled at Joan. "He'll be all right in a day or so. He'll have a headache to beat all headaches, but at least he'll be alive to enjoy it." He left the room.

Joan came to Rowan. He kissed her warmly. She placed her head against his chest. "You saved his life," she said.

"Have to protect my in-laws," he said.

She looked up. "Can't we leave as soon as Jeff is able to get about?"

He held her close. "I've got a nice place up north," he said. "Fine grass, plenty water, well sheltered. The Lazy LF. You'll like it."

"Let's leave tonight!"

He shook his head. "I've still got a job to do. You know I'm a marshal."

"You can quit! There's been enough bloodshed."

"No!"

She kissed him. "I should have known better."

"Stay here with Jeff."

Rowan left the room and walked down the hallway. There would be hell to pay now. As soon as John Ripsey heard the news, he would come into town primed for war, for John Ripsey still believed he was kingpin in the Rio Mescalero country.

CHAPTER FOURTEEN

Rowan slept well and awoke late. As he dressed, he glanced out into the street. It was empty of life, and Rowan suddenly realized it was Sunday morning. He checked his Colt carefully and cleaned it, reloading it and slipping it into its sheath. He took a stingy gun from his war bag, a .44/40 Colt with a sawed-off two-inch barrel. The front sight had been filed off and the front of the trigger guard cut away for easy access to the trigger. All corners that might catch on his clothing were rounded off with a file. He loaded it and slipped it beneath his waistband. He polished his boots for want of anything better to do and when he had finished he heard light footsteps on the stairs. Someone rapped on his door and he opened it.

Laura Ripsey stood there, dressed in a gray riding habit, a pert bonnet on her light hair. She pushed into the room and shut the door behind her. "You've got to let Pres go," she said breathlessly. "Dad heard the news this morning. He has sent out men to get all the Box R men. He's coming in to get Pres."

"Pres will stay in the cooler," said Rowan.

"You don't know what this means!"

"I think I do."

She bit her lip and paced back and forth. "Please," she said, "let him go."

Rowan shook his head. "There comes a time when a man goes too far, even if he is Pres Ripsey, son of the cattle king."

"What's in it for you? Get him out of jail. Dad will pay you."

"I get my pay."

"What do you mean?"

Rowan turned his coat front to show her his badge. "Pres is in deep. Not only because of attempted murder, but because Mad Donigan is dead, and I know Pres killed him."

"You lie!"

"You know he did. Because Madison was seeing you."

She flushed. "He forced himself on me."

Rowan laughed. "Does any man have to force himself on you, Laura? Mad Donigan? Dane Grenville? Me?"

Her hand lashed out, striking Rowan across the mouth. He gripped her wrists. She struggled wildly and then quieted down. She rested her head against his chest. "Let him go," she said softly. "I'll go away with you. You can have anything you want. Money. A ranch. *Me!*"

Rowan shook his head. "Get back to the ranch and tell your father to stay there. Tell him I'll arrest him and his boys if they try to free Pres."

She tore her hands loose and gripped him tightly. "Oh, Rowan! You're not like the others. I know we'd be fine for each other."

Someone tapped on the door. It swung open. It was Joan Donigan. "Rowan," she said, "I . . ." Her voice trailed off as she saw Laura pressed close against Rowan. For a moment her eyes seemed to glisten and then they flashed with the frosty Donigan light and she turned, slamming the door behind her.

Laura stepped back, adjusting her smooth helmet of

hair. "The little farm girl," she said with a laugh. "Don't tell me you worked your charm on *her,* too?"

Rowan slapped her hard across the mouth. Bitter rage filled him.

She slowly raised a gloved hand, touching her bruised lips. "You'll die for that," she said coldly. "Before God, Rowan Locke, I'll see you in hell before tonight!" She turned and left the room.

Rowan looked down at his hand. He shook his head. He looked out of the window. Laura plunged down the front stairs of the hotel and swung expertly up on the sorrel mare that waited for her. She circled the horse and set steel to it, riding like fury for the bridge.

Rowan left the room and walked down the hall, tapping on Joan's door. "Joan!" he called

There was no answer.

"Joan! Open this door!"

Rowan waited a moment and then walked down the hall, down the stairs and out into the morning sunshine. Dust was still settling on the road beyond the bridge. He walked down the street to Sim Short's store. Sim was seated on a bench, polishing his double-gun. He looked up. "That was Laura Ripsey," he said.

"Yes."

"The Box R bunch coming in?"

Rowan sat down and rolled a smoke. "Yes. But not for some time, I imagine. They have to round the boys up. John will want a large *corrida* when he comes in here."

Sim nodded. "Looks like I'm all alone, Rowan."

Rowan lit his smoke. "Oh, I don't know," he said easily.

The street was quiet. A mongrel scavenged through a box beside Schwab's Butcher Shop. The sun glinted from the shallow Rio Mescalero. A mule brayed from a corral. "Quiet, ain't it?" said Sim.

"Too damned quiet."

"No church this morning. Preacher says the weather is too hot."

"It will be."

Sim scratched his head. "You know Loco never did find them steers out at Coates' slaughterhouse."

"I didn't expect him to. Somebody choused them out of there. More evidence gone."

Sim spat. "You figure you'll get some evidence today?"

Rowan nodded. "All I'll need."

"Yeh. If you live."

Rowan stood up. He walked south toward the bridge, his spurs muffled by the dust. He stood there for a long time watching the puffs of clouds send racing shadows along the dun slopes to the west. The Rio Mescalero purled over the smooth stones of its bed, with sunlight glinting from the clear water. The hills to the west were hazy and unreal. Rowan saw no trace of dust on the road to the Box R. He walked slowly back up the street. When John Ripsey came it would be like a planned campaign, with all the odds on his side. He had the odds, too—his own imperious courage; the backing of Box R *vaqueros;* the fear which he had developed in the people of the Rio Mescalero country for sixteen years.

The sun was at its highest when a lone horseman raised the dust south of town. Rowan stepped into the shade of the Union awning and watched the lone man before he realized it was Loco Dawson. Loco rode into town and slid wearily from his sweat-lathered mount. "Trailed Grenville into the foothills and lost him. I went to the place where we saw those rustled cattle but there wasn't anyone there. I cut through toward Encinosa but saw nothing. I'm sorry, Rowan."

"Forget it, Loco."

Loco looked up and down the street. "Where the hell is everybody?"

Rowan told him the story. Loco shoved back his sweat-stained hat and whistled. "No wonder I seen a half dozen of the Box R waddies jumping up a lot of dust heading for the ranch."

Rowan handed the makings to Loco. "They'll be along as soon as John gets enough of them together."

"What do we do?"

"You can leave."

"I'll stay. They won't *carajo* me outa Llano."

"Suit yourself."

Sim Short came across the street trailing his shotgun. "Coon Ellis took off," he said. "Skited outa here like a Nueces steer on the prod."

"Where's Deputy Busch?" asked Rowan.

Sim spat. "Gone like the snows of yesteryear."

A horseman clattered across the bridge. "Levi Burrows," said Loco. *"Cocinero* at the Box R."

The cook drew rein in front of the three men. "Hell," he said, "ain't you *hombres* gone yet? John is feeding his boys redeye. They aim to leave pretty soon. I high-tailed it. I want no part of this thing."

"How's Old John?" asked Loco.

"Got a hogshead of blood in both eyes. *Adios!"* The cook spurred his jughead and hammered north out of town.

Sim wiped the sweat from his face. "Maybe we'd better let Pres go?" he suggested weakly.

"No," said Rowan.

Sim's hands shook a little. "I ain't got the nerve to try and stop Old John."

"You'll have to put up or shut up," said Rowan.

"You can talk!" jeered Short. "You can leave any time. I gotta stay. Look!" He turned the lapel of his coat. The sun glinted from the marshal's badge he had pinned to it. "I'm the mayor, the dogcatcher, the jailer and the marshal. All alone. I'm *Llano!"*

Rowan stood up. "Give me the badge," he said quietly. He took it from the older man's shaking hand. "Get under cover. Loco, you go to the hotel. Stay with Joan Donigan and her brother. I'll be at the *calabozo*."

Rowan walked down the street to the squat jail. It was well built of adobe. He walked into the office. Pres Ripsey looked through the bars of his cell. His battered face was sickly in color. "Let me out," he said.

Rowan dropped into a swivel chair and swung it around to face the cell, propping his feet up on the desk. "You'll sit there until you go to trial, Pres."

"My old man will get me out."

"He might try."

"You won't stop him!"

"I'll sink my navel into the sand trying to."

"You talk big."

Rowan helped himself to a cigar from a box on the desk. "You damned near killed Jeff Donigan," he said as he lit up.

"I wish I had."

"Just like you killed Madison, eh?"

"You can't pin that on me!"

"I will."

"Who the hell do you think you are?"

Rowan placed his hands behind his head and leaned back. "I've got two titles right now. City marshal of Llano."

"Some job!" interrupted Pres. "None of 'em last more than a week. You won't last today."

Rowan blew a smoke ring and idly watched it drift toward a window. "I'm also Deputy United States Marshal for this district of New Mexico, sonny. Play that on your mouth harp."

Pres swallowed. "You're a liar!"

Rowan took his badge from his pocket and held it in a beam of sunlight. Pres shifted on his bunk. "What are you going to do?"

"Find out who killed Larry Forbes."

"I don't know anything about that."

"You know a helluva lot about rustled cattle, though."

Pres laughed. "Me? Why should I rustle cattle? My father has the second largest herd in this territory."

Rowan inspected his cigar. "Does he know about the money you owe Dane Grenville?"

Pres flushed.

"Does he know about Sid Coates and Slip Wellman brand-blotting Box R cattle and selling them right here in town? Does he know about the cows you've driven over the Capitans and Jicarillas, through the Sierra Oscura and across the Jornado to the Rio Grande? Maybe he'd be interested in knowing about the Seven Rivers sticky loopers who have been working with you?"

Pres touched his mouth with a shaky hand.

Rowan yawned. "Sid Coates was knocked off with that fancy rifle of yours, handled by Dane Grenville. Slip Wellman talked like a parrot when we sweated him out up at Santa Rosa. Pres, you are in one helluva spot right now."

Pres wiped the sweat from his face. "My father will get me outa here."

"I still have evidence."

"Yeh. If you live through the Box R gunfire."

Rowan idly polished his city marshal's badge. "Oh, it doesn't really matter, Pres. I have sworn statements, testimony from reliable witnesses, everything I need to spin a rope for that neck of yours. Hidden away. In case I die, you'll be well taken care of. We can have a hand or two of draw down in hell when you join me."

Rowan got up and began to check the rifles and shotguns in the rack near the front door, whistling "The Devil's Dream" as he did so. There were four old Henry rifles, a long-barreled Greener double-gun, and two sawed-off shotguns. Rowan found cartridges for the Henry rifles and loaded them with flat-nosed .44s. The sawed-off guns were twelves but the Greener was a ten gauge. He loaded them and placed the Greener just inside the door.

Pres rattled the door of his cell. "Say, Locke," he called, "I'll make a deal with you. Supposing I make a statement about what I know?"

"Might be interesting."

"I'll write it up and sign it. You let me go free. Then you got the case cleared up. You take off and I'll be gone, too."

"Supposing I don't?"

"You know my old man will be in town before long."

Rowan rubbed his jaw. "Well, it's a deal." He got paper and pen and slid them through the bars. Pres sat down and began to write. Rowan checked the back door to see that it was locked and distributed his arsenal near the various windows. He set a pot of coffee going on the little oil stove. Pres finally looked up. "It's all here," he said. "How we worked the whole deal."

"You sign it?"

"No."

"Do it."

"You let me out first."

Rowan shook his head. "Sorry."

"All right, damn you, I'll sign." Pres signed the paper, waved it to dry it and then held it toward the bars.

Rowan took the paper and read it. He nodded. "Very nice."

"Let me out now."

Rowan's eyes turned frosty-gray. "You double-crossing skunk," he said. "My word is as good as yours, which is worth nothing. Sit in there until hell freezes."

Pres cursed and thrust a hand between the bars, snatching at the paper. Rowan reached a big hand between the bars and gripped Pres by the shirt front. He jerked him toward the bars, smashing the battered face against the steel. Pres moaned and staggered back, holding his bleeding nose. "I'll kill you! I'll kill you!" he shrieked.

Rowan folded the paper and thrust it behind a picture hanging on the wall. He whistled as he turned up the flame beneath the coffeepot.

Someone ran along the street. The door banged open. It was Sim Short. "The Box R *corrida!*" he said. "Old John and ten riders, armed for bear! Rowan, we still got time to pull freight for the tules!"

Rowan shook his head. "Find a place to fort up in," he said quietly. "I'm staying pat."

Sim Short shook his head and scuttled for cover. Rowan tightened his gunbelt, glanced at the moaning prisoner, and then stepped out on the low porch in front of the jail.

CHAPTER FIFTEEN

Eleven mounted men paced slowly north on Front Street. One man waited for them in the shade of the ramada in front of the squat adobe jail. John Ripsey rode easily, his hands resting on his saddle horn, holding the loose bridle reins. Hoofs rattled on the hard street like pebbles in a gourd. Saddle leather squeaked as the grim man leading them held up a gloved hand. The ten Box R *vaqueros* drew rein and hunched in their saddles, watching Rowan Locke with slitted eyes. John Ripsey rode forward and reined in his horse twenty feet from Rowan.

"Is my boy in there, Locke?" he asked quietly.

"He is."

"I want him."

"You'll have to get a writ."

"I want him, *writ be damned!*"

Rowan folded his arms and leaned against a post. "He stays."

John Ripsey kneed his horse forward, glancing up the street lit by harsh sunlight. Not a soul stirred along the three blocks of ugly buildings. "You're not forted up, are you, Locke?"

Rowan smiled. "You figure it out, Ripsey."

"In other words, you're alone."

"I may be."

"You know, I think you would have made a good gambler, Locke."

"I've made money over the green cloth."

Ripsey reached slowly inside his coat and drew out a silver cigar case. He extracted a cigar and bit off the end, lighting it and eyeing Rowan over the flare of the match. He puffed at the cigar and hunched his shoulders. "The boy was drunk," he said.

"Loco, I'd call it."

"You've been drunk yourself, I daresay."

"I have, and so have you."

"Let the boy go."

"Maybe you don't understand. Pres shot up the town, creased Jeff Donigan, endangered many people. God alone knows why no one was killed."

"No one *was* killed."

"Madison Donigan was."

In the silence that followed, one of the Box R men drew out his saddle gun and placed it across his lap.

Ripsey puffed at his cigar. "What has the death of Mad Donigan got to do with my son?"

"He killed him."

"You're a liar!"

Rowan shrugged. "I'll prove it. I'll also prove that Pres Ripsey and Dane Grenville have been rustling you blind."

John Ripsey placed his hand on the ivory butt of his Colt. "Come on, boys. He's loco." He touched his horse with his spurs and rode forward. His men crowded up behind.

Rowan stepped back and reached in for the Greener. He leveled it and swept back both hammers with his left hand. "Now, John," he said pleasantly, "there's eighteen buckshot in here with split wads. Come on."

"You won't get all of us."

"I'll take a few of you to hell with me."

Ripsey eyed the twin muzzles and then looked into the frosty eyes above the gun. "You know, Locke, I think you would." Ripsey rode south on the street, halted and dismounted two hundred yards from the jail. His *corrida* dismounted. Ripsey spoke swiftly. The men scattered behind the buildings. Ripsey looked up the street at Rowan for a moment and then stepped behind a building. The horses were bunched together. Not a man was in sight.

Rowan stepped back into the *calabozo* with cold sweat streaming down his sides, pasting his shirt to his body. He closed the door behind him and placed the bar across it. Pres was standing by his cell door, holding onto the bars. His eyes never left Rowan.

"You're scared gutless right now," he said with a sneer.

Rowan filled his coffee cup and placed it on the desk. He picked up a Henry rifle and loaded the chamber. He sipped at his coffee, waiting for the first shot. He didn't have long to wait. A rifle cracked in the street running north of the jail and the slug whined between the bars of a window, smashing into the wall behind Rowan, scattering plaster all over the desk and into Rowan's cup. He emptied it and refilled it. Another slug thudded into the thick, bolt-studded door of the jail. Four or five others smashed into the outer walls. Rowan finished his coffee and walked leisurely to the rear of the jail. He looked through a rear window from the side. A *vaquero* was eyeing the jail from behind a post. Rowan raised his rifle and fired. A splinter from the post lanced into the cowpoke's cheek. He yelled and ducked down an alley.

Powder smoke swirled in the jail. Rowan walked from window to window, occasionally snapping out a shot. A slug whined from a cell bar and flattened itself against the ceiling. Pres promptly dived to the floor and rolled under his bunk.

The firing died away. Rowan looked across at the

hotel. There was a furtive movement at an upper window and he saw the worried face of Loco Dawson. A slug slashed through a window and skinned Rowan's face, drawing a trickle of blood. He saw a broad-shouldered waddie peer from around the corner of the hotel. Rowan peeled a foot of pine splinter from the hotel wall. The Box R man jumped back.

For an hour the Box R men kept up a steady fire at the jail. The floor was powdered with plaster. Broken glass crunched under Rowan's boots. The stovepipe was holed in three places.

Rowan heard a scuffling noise at the rear door. He paced toward it. Then he heard a faint fizzing noise. He dropped flat just as a deafening explosion blew the door in, driving a thick cloud of smoke in on him. A piece of adobe smashed against his jaw. He cursed, peering through the swirling smoke. A gun blossomed orange flame in the center of the smoke. Rowan rolled to one side, ripped his Colt loose and pumped two shots into the belly of the man who had hurdled the fallen door and thrust a six-gun toward him. The man hit hard, smashed against Rowan and lay still. Rowan jumped behind a post and fired twice. A man grunted in the alleyway, dropped his rifle and gripped his left shoulder. Blood dripped through his taut fingers. He staggered out of sight.

Rowan reloaded his Colt with shaking hands. There was no movement in the alleyway. The dead man lay across the fallen door, his fingers dug into the litter of plaster, the dripping blood soaking into the powdery floor covering.

Rowan walked to the front and ducked involuntarily as a slug whipped the air inches above his head. He peered through a front window and nearly choked. Joan Donigan was coming down the front stairs of the hotel as casually as though going for an outing. She walked up the empty street to the livery stable. She went in. A few minutes later she came out, riding a blocky claybank, her skirts high on her shapely legs. She turned the claybank to the south and rode easily out of town. No one made a move to stop her.

There was a bumping noise at the front door of the jail. "Damn you, Kelly!" a man said. "Light it!"

Rowan thrust an arm through a window and fired downward. Two men sprinted for the corner. A six-gun spat flame from an upper story of the hotel and one of the men pitched forward and lay still. The other made good his retreat. Rowan jumped to the far side of the door and pressed himself flat against the wall. The explosion blew the door open, leaving it hanging awkwardly on one hinge. A cloud of smoke swirled through the jail. Plaster rained from the ceiling in a dry patter. The draft through both shattered doors carried the smoke through the battered building.

Rowan picked up a rifle and thrust it through a window, churning it dry at a shed across the street. The big slugs whipped through the thin walls. A man dived out of a side window, gripping a shattered arm.

Rowan coughed. The air was thick with an acrid odor. He drank deeply at the water can and wiped his mouth. The odds were high and the going rough. Suddenly he knew he couldn't hold them off. It was just a matter of time now.

Rowan placed the Greener on the desk and picked up a Henry rifle. Through the open door he could see two Box R men near Schwab's Butcher Shop. One of them raised a rifle. There was a spurt of flame and smoke from the shop. The rifleman gripped his chest, turned slowly and went down, lying still in the middle of the sunny street. Big Oscar Schwab stepped out in front of his shop, firing a stubby Spencer. Rifles and pistols cracked steadily and Schwab jumped back into his shop. A slug brought his big front window down in jagged shards. Rowan grinned.

A shotgun bellowed from Short's store. It roared

again and a Box R man sprinted for cover, dropping his rifle. Sim Short had joined the battle. Loco Dawson peered out of a second-story window of the hotel and ripped out three shots from his Colt.

Rowan peered through a side window. The Box R men were drifting back toward the Union. He hurried them up with a few shots. Rowan walked toward the back of the jail carrying a Henry rifle. A whining ricochet made him jump and drop the repeater. He darted back, drawing his Colt, snapping two shots at a running Box R man.

Rowan walked to the front of the jail. Dust rose on the road. Three horsemen thundered over the bridge holding shotguns across their laps. They dismounted and scattered for cover as the Box R men opened fire. They were Washington, Adams, and Monroe Donigan. Joan Donigan halted her horse on the far side of the river and stood up in her stirrups to watch her three brothers join the fight.

A Box R man pitched out of the loft of the livery stable. Suddenly Rowan realized that Ripsey's forces had been badly cut up. There must be five or six of them dead and several wounded. He snatched up the Greener and jumped out into the street. The three Donigans yelled as they saw him. Rowan jumped into a doorway. Loco scuttled down the steps of the hotel and ran across the street with slugs skipping across the hard earth at his boots. Oscar Schwab panted up the street. "We got them holed," he said. "We close in. *Ja!*"

Sim Short ran across the street with his shotgun at the trail. "Now what, Rowan?"

Rowan cocked the Greener. "Close in on the Union," he said. They moved slowly in, taking advantage of every bit of cover. Now and then a gun flatted off. Schwab fired from the shoulder and dropped a cowpoke who jumped out of a doorway and sprinted for the saloon.

The three Donigans crossed the street in a quick

rush. Adams grunted as a slug skinned his shoulder. Rowan crossed to the side of the Union, reached a window, and thrust the Greener through the glass. He fired as it tinkled about his feet. A man screamed inside the echoing saloon. Rowan threw the Greener down, drew his Colt and smashed the rest of the glass. He crawled in. Two Box R men lay groaning on the floor. Two others raced for the front door. John Ripsey was braced against the back wall with ready Colt, a bloody hand at his left side. The Donigans came through the front door, threw down their shotguns and closed with the two panicked punchers. Wash drove a big fist hard against a waddie's nose, dropping him like a pole-axed steer. Monroe hit the second *vaquero* with a hard one-two and followed through with a crisp uppercut that snapped the man's head back and sent him down for the long count.

John Ripsey raised his Colt. He coughed hard and lowered it. He looked at Rowan. "Calf rope," he said quietly. "I'm licked, Locke." He dropped the Colt and pitched to the floor.

Rowan walked to the old man. Ripsey opened his eyes. "Damn you," he said. "If you'da worked with me, we could have made a cattle kingdom as big as the whole territory." He closed his eyes.

Rowan dropped down beside the old man. The hard eyes were glazing. Rowan stood up. "He's gone," he said, and somehow he felt as though he had ended something, unscrupulous as it was, that somehow had the essence of greatness about it.

Somewhere down the street a rifle shattered the quiet half a dozen times. Schwab walked toward the jail. He went in and a moment later he came out, running heavily. "Pres iss gone!" he yelled. "Blew off the door lock yet!"

Rowan remembered the Henry rifle he had dropped near the cell door. He drew his Colt and cut through the back room of the saloon to jump out into the alley. There was no sign of life. He walked cautiously toward the battered jail and looked in through the back doorway. The jail was empty. He climbed over the shattered door. The cell door gaped open with a shattered lock. Empty brass hulls littered the cell floor.

Rowan scouted through the back ways of the town, but Pres had vanished like the morning mist along the Rio Mescalero. He went back to the Union. Schwab met him at the door. "Is bloody victory, Rowan. We get five of them killed and four wounded. Two of them unconscious."

Rowan sheathed his Colt. "Get the doctor for the wounded. It looks like none of our boys was hurt seriously."

"There will be no more trouble in Llano. I am glad. Yet it iss not good to see a man like John Ripsey die at his age in saloon with bullet hole. Ach!" Schwab shook his head.

Rowan clapped the Donigans on the back and left the saloon. Joan was waiting for him on the far side of the street. She held up her face for a kiss. He grinned. "I'm a mess."

"Kiss me!" she demanded.

He held her close. "I've got to get on the move," he said.

"Why?"

"Pres Ripsey got away. Dane Grenville is still loose. They caused the deaths of many good men, even the men of the Box R. John Ripsey had a great hold on them. Too bad they had to die for a skunk like Pres."

"You can't turn away a man like John Ripsey, Rowan."

"No. I must admit I admired him."

Rowan turned as Loco limped up. He pinned the marshal's badge on Dawson. "Take over," he said. "I'm leaving."

"You ain't going alone!"

Rowan nodded. "The job isn't done." He walked into

the livery stable and got Jim. As he led him out into the street he saw the townspeople coming out from hiding, looking curiously at the wreckage of the jail and the human wreckage in the bloody street. He swung up on Jim and kneed him toward the bridge. He looked back as Jim moved along. Joan was watching him from in front of the hotel. He waved and turned the bay onto the road leading to the Box R.

CHAPTER SIXTEEN

Rowan left Jim in a motte of cottonwoods half a mile from the ranch buildings of the Box R. Shadows were already creeping down the slopes. Rowan took his rifle and field glasses and worked his way toward the buildings. He stopped in a ditch and focused his glasses on the house. The huge cottonwoods shrouded the house in shadow. Rowan examined the house and grounds inch by inch. There was no sign of life. No smoke rose from the chimneys. Not a horse or other animal was in sight. Rowan crawled along the ditch until he was even with the grove of trees. He studied the house again. The place seemed deserted.

He was just about to go to the house when he saw a thread of dust at the base of the purple hills. He crawled beneath a clump of brush and waited with spidery patience. Years of experience in hunting the most elusive of all Indians, the Apaches, had taught him to take his time in the most dangerous game—hunting men.

The sun was almost gone when a lone horseman topped a low swale west of the ranch buildings and drew rein, leaning forward in his saddle to study the scene before him. Rowan shaded his glasses with his hat and saw the lean, saturnine face of Dane Grenville swim into view. Then Grenville kneed his horse to the south and rode down toward the river. He was evidently planning to approach the brooding house under cover of the river bank.

Rowan left the ditch and followed a low rise in the ground until he reached the adobe wall which closed off the north side of the house. He stood there for a few minutes looking at the house. Then he eased himself over the wall and padded softly to an embrasure beside a partially opened window. He waited again, testing with all his senses for signs of man. Hoofs rattled on the hard earth behind the house. Rowan slipped through the window into a large dark room. He crossed the carpeted floor and stopped at the door. The door was open a few inches. He eased it back and looked into the dark hall-way. Light showed in the living room. A door creaked a little down the hall. Rowan drew back, leaned his rifle against the wall and drew his Colt.

Feet scraped the floor of the hallway and a tall figure passed cautiously. Grenville. Rowan watched him stop at the entrance to the living room, his tall figure outlined by the light. Something crashed on the floor.

"Damn you, Grenville!" said Pres Ripsey. "You gave me a start, standing there like a damned ghost."

"What happened in town? I heard John took some of the boys in to break jail for you."

"There was a hell of a fight."

"John must have won. You're here."

There was a moment's silence. "I don't know. I broke out of jail and came back here."

Grenville walked into the living room. Rowan padded down the hall and stepped into the deep doorway of a room. He could see Pres Ripsey standing by the fireplace. Sweat beaded his battered face. His hands were bleeding. Grenville was lighting a cigar. "What are you looking for, Pres?" he asked.

"Money! Damn it! I'm breaking for Mexico."

"Why?"

"Locke is a United States Marshal."

"What has he got on you?"

Pres laughed harshly. *"Everything!* He knows I killed Madison Donigan. He tricked me into writing out a confession about everything."

"What do you mean by everything?"

Pres wiped his mouth with the back of his right hand. "The rustling. The deal we had driving cattle to the Rio Grande. *Everything!"*

Grenville's hands shook a little. "You chicken-gutted fool!"

"You can talk! Where were *you?"*

"If you had stayed away from the liquor, you wouldn't have gone loco and shot up the town. You haven't got the brains of a jackass."

Pres spat. "It's too late now. There's money hidden somewhere around this fireplace." Pres looked at his bleeding hands. "I've been prying at these damned stones for over an hour and haven't found it yet."

"Who else is around?"

"Laura is in her room."

Rowan felt a cold finger trace the length of his spine. Laura's room was the next one to his left.

Pres worked at the stones. Suddenly he stiffened. There was a grating noise. He lifted out a stone and thrust eager hands into the hole, bringing them out holding a tin box. He looked over his shoulder at Grenville. "See?" he said triumphantly. "I knew the old man had *something* hidden in that damned fireplace!"

Grenville relit his cigar. He leaned against the fireplace and watched Pres pry off the lock. The lid snapped open. Pres threw out some papers and gripped a canvas bag. He slit the draw cord with his case knife and dumped the contents out on the table. Yellow gold shone in the lamplight. Pres yelled for joy. "By God, I can live like a king down there!"

Grenville rubbed his lean jaw. "You sure messed up a fine rustling deal, Pres. We had it made."

"*You* did, you mean," said Pres over his shoulder as he poured the coins back into the bag. "I'm glad it's over."

"It isn't over," said Grenville softly. "You still owe me plenty. I'll settle for that gold."

Pres whirled, his knife in his hand. "Damn your greedy soul! You bled me white! You queered me with my father! He changed his will! I know he did! He left the ranch to Laura! This is mine!"

Grenville smiled thinly. He raised his slim hands level with his shoulders. "Put up the knife."

Pres threw the knife to one side and jerked open a desk drawer. His right hand came up, steadying a double-barreled derringer. "Get out of here," he said. "I've taken my last order from you."

Grenville shrugged. He raised his hands higher. Pres laughed. "I'm the boss now," he said.

Grenville's movement was so quick Rowan hardly saw it. His right hand slid up the cuff of his left sleeve. When it snaked out again there was a stingy gun in it. It spat flame. The soft-nosed slug rapped into Pres, raising a puff of dust from his coat. He dropped the derringer, swayed and then gripped the bag of gold coins. For a moment he stood there facing Grenville and then he hit the floor, spilling the coins at the feet of the man who stood there with a smoking gun in his hand.

A door creaked open next to Rowan. Grenville stooped and gathered up the coins. He moved swiftly, stepping out of an open window. Boots grated on the hard earth outside. Rowan stepped out of cover, heard a movement behind him and whirled to see Laura Ripsey, wearing a wrapper, not ten feet away from him. She came forward. "You! Where is Pres?"

Rowan stepped aside. She walked to the doorway of the living room and turned her head quickly away. "Why did you kill him?" she asked.

Rowan came up beside her. "Dane Grenville was here. He did it."

"You hated Pres! You hated my father! You hate me!"

"I swear to God I didn't do it!"

She leaned against the wall and placed her hands behind her. "I suppose you will kill me, too? My father will hunt you down!"

Rowan shook his head. "Your father will never hunt anyone down, Laura. He was shot to death in town this afternoon."

Her face grew tense. "Ever since you came to Llano there has been blood."

Rowan came toward her. "Look! Dane Grenville is getting away while we stand here. He killed Pres. I'm going to get him."

She came close to him and placed her arms about his neck. "We can still have everything, Rowan. I'm rich now! The ranch is mine! Don't you want me? I'm yours if you do."

"You were Madison Donigan's, too, and Dane Grenville's."

She turned away. Suddenly she stopped and snatched up the derringer Pres had dropped. Rowan's fist caught her as she turned. She dropped without a word. Rowan turned and ran through the dark hallway to a back door. He eased it open. The area was shrouded in shadows. The dry wind soughed through the trees and scrabbled at the thick walls of the house. Rowan cocked his Colt. There were no sounds of hoofbeats. He stepped out into the open and froze as something hard rammed against his back. "Marshal Locke," said the calm voice of Dane Grenville, "move along, please. Drop that Colt."

Rowan dropped the Colt and raised his arms over his head. He walked toward the great blackened area where the barn had stood.

Grenville laughed. "I stopped outside for a last look at Laura. I didn't expect to see *you*, Marshal."

Rowan reached the edge of the burned area and stopped. Grenville poked him with his gun. "Thanks to Pres Ripsey I have enough money to get by very well in Mexico for a time."

"You'll be hounded down."

"I'll make it. Keep walking."

Rowan reached the gate and passed through, walking up a slope toward a motte of thick willows.

"One thing I never could understand, Locke. You seem more than just a lawman. You seem to have a very personal interest in this whole mess."

Rowan stopped in a shadowy clearing.

"How do you want it, Locke? Back or belly?"

Rowan whirled, smashing his right forearm against Grenville's gun arm. He clipped the tall man with a left chop as the Colt roared, shattering the quiet and awakening the echoes. Grenville cursed. Rowan dived through the trees and hit the dirt just as the Colt spoke again, sending a searching slug over his head. He rolled back and felt his feet drop over an embankment. He looked to right and left. He was at the edge of the cutaway bank of the Rio Mescalero. There was no retreat.

Grenville moved in the trees. "You won't get away," he said.

Rowan eased his hand inside his coat and gripped the butt of his belly gun. He slipped it out. Grenville was down the slope a little. "You might as well come out," he said. "The grass is as dry as tinder. One match and you'll cook like a barbecued beef in there."

Rowan eased through the dry brush beneath the trees.

"This will be my last killing," said Grenville. "I've cleaned up enough to get by for some time." There was the snap of a match. In a few minutes Rowan saw a bright glow and heard the crackle of the dry grass and brush. In no time at all he would be forced out of cover, and he still couldn't see Grenville in the shadows waiting for him to come out.

Rowan worked his belly gun down behind his coat collar at the back of his neck. He called out. "Calf rope," he said. "I'd rather die by a bullet."

"Your choice."

Rowan stood up and raised his hands. He walked past the crackling flames. He could dimly see the gambler in among the trees. Grenville shifted a little. "I still don't know why you're so interested in this case, Locke."

"Larry Forbes was my cousin."

Grenville was silent.

Rowan lowered his hands a little. He still couldn't get a clear view of Grenville. Sweat dripped down his sides.

"Wash Donigan killed Forbes," said Grenville.

"You're a liar."

Grenville laughed. "All right. I did it. Used a shotgun to get rid of him."

"Because of Marion Forbes."

Grenville shifted again. It was easier to see him now. "You know a great deal," he said. "I changed my mind about her. I was shooting for the Box R, even if I had to take Laura with it."

"Nice fella," said Rowan dryly.

Grenville coughed. "Getting smoky. Time to go," he said.

"Theba, you're a no-good, lying—!"

The name triggered Grenville into action. Rowan dropped to bring the gambler up against the skyline even as the Colt roared. The slug smashed into Rowan's right bicep. He was sickened with pain. Grenville jumped to one side and fired again. The slug spurted dirt where Rowan had been lying. He rolled into a hollow, sick with pain and green slavering fear. He reached up with his left hand and ripped the Colt free, cocking it clumsily. He lay still. Grenville came forward. Rowan raised the belly gun and squeezed it off. The big slug caught the gambler

squarely in the gut, doubling him forward. He fired his
Colt with reflex action. He lay still.

Blood ran down Rowan's arm. Thirst seemed to grip
at his throat with husking hands. The ground tilted up,
leveled and lowered swiftly as waves of sickness poured
over him. His head sank and he passed out.

Then stench of burning cloth and flesh aroused
Rowan. For one awful moment he thought the fire had
him. He opened his eyes. The motte was ablaze with
light, streamers of fire climbing the dry trees. He looked
about him. He was cut off. He gripped a tree and pulled
himself to his feet. He staggered toward a wall of flame
and then recoiled as it seared his face. Clumsily he ran
toward the river bank. Grenville lay in the midst of the
roaring flames, his fine clothing ablaze. Rowan took
another step and plunged off into space, landing with a
crash at the bottom of the steep cutback bank. Gravel
cut his face and hands cruelly. He got to his feet. Shots
cracked out, one after another, panicking him until he
realized it was the heat exploding the remaining
cartridges in his belly gun.

Rowan ran awkwardly east along the river bank.
Flames licked down the bank ahead of him, and he
turned and waded into the shallow waters of the river,
plunging across as a wave of heated air reached him. He
dropped flat on the far bank.

Rowan worked out of his coat and ripped off his shirt
sleeve, binding the wound with his bandanna. He got to
his feet. The wind was from the west, driving great sheets
of flame toward the ranch buildings of the Box R. The
bunkhouse and a shed were already ablaze and great
sparks were soaring toward the ranch house. He ran
down the south bank of the river, but there was no
chance of getting to the house. Even as he watched, fire
licked up on the broad flat roof. He stood there helplessly as the house began to blaze. She was still in there.

Rowan crossed the river a quarter of a mile east of the

burning ranch and stood there a long time watching the holocaust. He shook his head and felt the bile rise in his throat. He limped to his horse and mounted, sitting hunched in the saddle watching the end of John Ripsey's feudal kingdom. Then he kneed the bay toward the road and rode slowly east toward the Llano road.

There was no feeling of the avenger in Rowan as he rode away from the burning Box R. Rather a soul sickness. He eased his wounded arm as he reached the Llano road and looked back again at the pall of smoke, lit by the flickering flames, far behind him. The people of Llano were in the streets looking westward at the conflagration. A slim young woman ran from the crowd toward Rowan. It was Joan Donigan. Her face was pale and drawn. He slid from his saddle and held her close, leaning heavily against her. "It's all over," he said.

"Thank God you're still alive."

He kissed her with his dry, scorched lips. The whole quest had been hell, set off by the flaming guns and burning buildings. Suddenly a wave of longing for the Lazy LF came over him. He limped up the street with his woman. It was a hard country but it was *his. His and Joan's to make something out of.*

THE LONELY GUN

To my nephew, Ronnie

*No man travels
far in the desert
who cannot rest
in the shade of
his arrows...*

Paiute Saying

CHAPTER ONE

The desert comes alive at night with the ceaseless battles of hunter and hunted. The bobcat hunts the dainty kit fox while the kit fox in turn pursues the pocket mouse. The horned owl hunts the spotted skunk while overhead the leather-winged bats look for moths.

All night long the desert is the arena of swift and deadly battles for existence, and when the ice-chip stars wink out one by one the animals vanish into their day hideouts. No sooner has the last of them disappeared when the cycle of day begins with the appearance of the false dawn and the arising of the birds to begin their search for food.

It was just such a dawn at the watering place in the desert. The faint moon still hung low in the western sky and a cool wind swept across the land swaying the long-stemmed ocotillos, the mesquites and the creosote bushes. Only the gaunt saguaros were motionless, holding their arms up against the graying sky like warning sentinels.

The brown-hued water in the shallow rock pans was dappled by the wind which swept through one of the openings in the rim of yellow rock surrounding the water hole. The yeso-covered dome of the long-abandoned mission shone faintly in the pale, watery light.

There was one place the night hunters had shied away from during the darkness. Some of them had seen what lay there, while others, with their keen sense of smell had identified it as an odor they hated and feared ... that of man.

Case Hardesty raised his head and looked up the barren slope ahead of him toward the jagged ring of rocks. There would be water there; there had to be water there. The two hundred yards between him and the rocks would be the last two hundred yards he would ever travel if the tinajas were dry.

He rested his head on the cool sand and then thrust out his arms to claw at the ground, slowly and painfully inching his way toward the water hole. There didn't seem to be a drop of water left in his gaunt body. He was suffering from the deep thirst, the third and final thirst: the intolerable thirsting of the bones.

The desert was deathly quiet now. In a short time, the sun would be up, and Case knew that if he did not find water there the sun would finish him off.

He inched on, dragging his body, hardly feeling the sharp stones dig into him. He dug in his worn boot toes and pushed himself along as he pulled with his bleeding fingers.

The sun had tipped the eastern range of mountains and had begun to flood the desert with its light. There was a softness to the light, for it was yet too early for the harsh metallic brightness that kills as easily as any weapon. It was the time of year when the heat, which is the very blazing core of the desert summer, is at its worst.

He reached the outlying rocks and stopped to rest. He slowly turned his head to look back to the north. There was no sign of dust on the desert, for which he was more than grateful. The border was miles to the south, across the deadly Spanish Desert, difficult enough for a mounted man to reach and almost impossible for a man on foot. Case Hardesty knew well enough he would never make it in his present condition.

He lay there, now and then lifting his heavy head, trying to see the water, or at least smell of it; but the desert was playing with him in its last cruel jest, holding off on him until the last possible instant to let him know whether he would live or die that day.

He wormed his way across the flinty rocks and then saw the water in the rock pan. He closed his eyes and doggedly worked his way forward until his raw questing fingers touched the blessed coolness of the water. It was not a mirage. He dropped his head and his hands swept back the floating algae so that he could thrust his face beneath the brownish fluid and sip a little of the gamy water. Then he rolled away from the pan and fainted dead away.

The late morning sun beat down into the bowl of rock. Case opened his eyes and felt as though he were stretched on a griddle, sapping what little life was left in him. He crawled toward the shade of an overhanging rock. A gila monster, occupying the shade, hissed at him from its purple mouth. Case threw a stone at it. "Move, you bastard," he croaked. "I'm taking over. Git!"

The gila monster studied him with unwinking eyes and then moved sluggishly away to vanish into a cleft. Case reached the shade and pulled himself up into a sitting position. The sun glinted from the shallow water and seemed to lance into his reddened eyes.

He felt in his shirt pocket for the makings and rolled a smoke. He drew a match across the rock and lighted the cigarette. The tobacco smoke seemed to score his throat, but he needed the harshness to awaken feeling.

He studied his place of refuge with slitted gray eyes. The old building which occupied one side of the large oval-shaped area was in sad disrepair. Yards of plaster had fallen from the walls revealing the field-rock construction. The facade was pocked with what looked like bullet holes. The crudely carved pillars on the front of the structure were scored and worn by the sand-laden winds. Mesquite shrouded the base, and the sun shone on the whitened dome. He smiled a little as he eyed it. It was the guide he had used to find the watering place.

The hardy Jesuits who had raised the building long ago had built it well, but now it was an abandoned shell, open to the winds. A wooden cross, silvered by the sun, hung precariously from the dome. Case had heard of the lonely water hole and of the building there. Apache raids had swirled about it in the old days. Papagos had fought beside Spanish soldiers to defend it. The Papagos had built the place in the faith that it would serve them well and nurture the vine of Christianity, and it had—for a time. But even the hardy Papagos had left that barren country long ago.

He got to his feet, wincing as the hot rock seemed to burn through his worn boot soles. He walked unsteadily to the tinaja and knelt beside it. The water was brown from droppings and pinkish-hued bladders floated in a tiny cove at one side. He looked at the bloated body of a snake floating in the scum. He fished it out with a stick and cast it behind the rocks.

He couldn't be particular. He drank deeply and then walked to the old mission building. Case wondered why in God's name it had been built there. It was much bigger than he had imagined.

He peered inside and saw that there was little left of the interior furnishings and decorations. The niches which had been the stations of the cross were empty. Holes had been smashed into the walls and dug into the hard-packed earth of the floor. At the far end he could just make out the sanctuary with traces of the decorations still showing faintly.

He walked inside and turned into a small, thick-walled

room. There was a door and a narrow staircase leading up to the old bell tower. He walked up the stairs and into the place where the bells had hung long ago. There was only one of them left, about two feet in height, and it must have weighed well over a hundred pounds. He hit it with his hand, and the soft tone was sweet and lingering.

He stood back in the shade and looked to the north. There was no sign of dust or smoke. A wind devil moved aimlessly across the yellow sands and vanished even as he watched. The distant mountains rose from the level ground like dislocated bones, and already there was a purplish haze about them. It was the same in each of the cardinal points of the compass. Vast wastes of sand stippled with thorny vegetation, distant hazy mountains, intolerable heat and not a sign of life.

He followed his trail with his eyes. Somewhere along the way his horse lay dead. There was food in the saddle bags, his Winchester, and a salt sack stuffed with money ... twenty thousand dollars in bills of high denomination. Five thousand of it was supposed to have been his for his share in the holdup of the bank in Cottonwood Station. Five thousand was Chip Gilbert's, five thousand was Leonardo Janos' split, and the remaining five thousand should have been Floyd Hanks' share.

Floyd Hanks was dead with one of Case's forty-fours in his head. Chip Gilbert and Leonardo Janos were somewhere in the Spanish Desert looking for him, if they had not died of thirst or been picked up by Sheriff Dade Maslin and his posse. Case had been feigning sleep when he had heard Floyd say he would take care of Case. He had come unwound from his blankets with his Colt in his hand, firing an instant before Floyd. He had made it to his horse and off into the darkness with the loot, followed by the other two. At dawn the next day his two pursuers had split up to outride the posse. None of them had wanted to try the Spanish Desert, and that was why

Case had gambled on it. He had damned near lost the gamble.

There was only one way for him to go. The die was cast. Somehow he must make it on foot to Sonora but even then the odds were well nigh impossible. It was the Devil's Highway, named so in grim jest by contemporaries of Father Kino. A land forgotten by time, brooding and baking under the hot sun, swept by sandstorms which could erase a trail in a matter of minutes. There were water holes to be sure, but this was the time of the year when most of them were dry. Beyond the imaginary border line there was the Gran Desierto, more dangerous than the Spanish Desert.

To the west were mountains between him and the Colorado. To the east was desert and more desert. To the north were his enemies and one of two fates; a bullet or a stretch in Yuma Pen.

He leaned against the side of the opening and rolled another quirly. The hot wind moaned through the bell tower. Some sacrilegious bastard had left a sign of his passing long ago; a pile of fecal matter. Case kicked it from the tower. Someone had cut a message in Spanish into the thick plaster. "There is nothing but death here," he read. He grinned crookedly. "Bull crap," he said. Spaniards and Mexicans always seemed preoccupied with death. *Muerte, muerte . . . muerte.*

He went down the stairs and out into the blazing sunlight. There was no time for him to sit and brood, placidly waiting to die. He was a fighting man, a Missourian by birth, and for the last ten of his thirty years he had become accustomed to violence and death. He was as isolated as a castaway on an island in the Pacific, but a castaway couldn't walk on water like Jesus, while Case could walk on the desert. It would take some figuring on how to do it, and one little mistake would make the difference between life and death; and he aimed to live.

Twenty thousand dollars would be a fortune in Mexico. A man could have his pick of fine ranches, food, and women if he liked. He would invest the money, then pay back the bank. After all, it was only a loan, with no interest to be paid unless they caught him and sent him to Yuma, and he'd go down fighting before they did that. He'd never live through imprisonment.

He drank again and then squatted in the shade to think. Cactus wrens fluttered in the mesquites. A white-rumped shrike pursued a whip-tailed lizard across the bowl and struck it hard to kill it. It scuttled off with the lizard hanging from its mouth. Case was hungry. There was a movement yonder by a flat rock and he saw a plump chuckwalla nibbling at a pear cactus.

Case moved slowly until he was within five feet of the big lizard and then he kicked it with his foot. It squirmed as he crushed its head.

There was a flash and another shrike darted toward the lizard. Case struck at it and the vicious bird sank its beak in his hand. He tore it loose and cast it away and it flew out reviling him noisily. He wiped the blood from his hand.

He made a fire of dry branches and twigs and skinned the lizard. He had served with the Fifth Cavalry for a time and had been friendly with the Apache scouts, who had taught him how to live in a country they knew well. They could be dropped on the desert miles from anywhere and could live easily. More than once that knowledge had served him well.

He roasted the chuckwalla and ate half of it, saving the remainder, hungry as he was. He found a cracked olla behind the mission and filled it with water, forming a sling from his bandanna. He pulled off his boots and washed his filthy socks. They were dry in a matter of minutes. He studied his sunburned hawk's face in his steel pocket mirror. His reddish beard was thickening. It would change his appearance a little. He needed clothing and a horse. He hated the thought of venturing out into the blazing desert, but there wasn't enough time for him to waste sitting there waiting for the sun to go down. He soaked his hat in the water and put it on, grateful for its temporary coolness.

He backtrailed, eyeing the furrows he had cut into the sand with his body during his painful journey to the water. He estimated that his horse was about five miles from the water hole. At least he would be able to travel back after sundown. Case struck off steadily, a gaunt lath of a man without an ounce of surplus flesh on his six-foot body.

———

THE CLAYBANK WAS ALREADY BLOATING when Case found him. He stripped the carcass, cutting off the best parts of the meat, and drawing out the big intestine. He coiled the greasy tube and wrapped it in one of his old shirts. It was another Apache trick. They would ride a horse to death, cut off the edible portions and use the intestine for a canteen.

The sun was low over the western mountains when he finished hiding the carcass with brush and sand. The sweat poured from his body as he carried his gear back to the south. There was still no sign of life on the desert except for a great ragged vulture who wheeled high overhead watching him, waiting for him to fall.

He found his Colt lying in the sand two miles from the wells. It had fallen from his holster the night before.

The dying sun tinted the white dome of the mission with a soft pinkish hue. The dome could be seen for miles and he knew well enough his pursuers would use it for a guide as he had done.

He reached the water hole and stripped off his stinking clothing. He bathed and dressed himself in his worn army trousers and gray flannel shirt. The remains of the lizard was his meal for the night and he cleaned his guns in the dusk light.

Now and then he looked at the old mission. There was an eeriness about the place in the darkening light. The wind moaned through the openings. The place seemed haunted by those who had passed that way, some of them to die and others to bless it for its water and then to forget it shortly thereafter.

He thought of Mexico as he found a hollow high on the rock wall for his bivouac. He smoked as he squatted there looking to the south. It had been five years since he had been in Sonora. Hermosillo was a pleasant memory. He wondered if Dulce was still there, Dulce of the flashing eyes and blue-black hair, whose firm little body and tapping heels had called him back many a lonely night in the desert. Maybe she was married and covered with fat, with a brood of snotty-nosed kids following her about.

He had buried his partner Lew Gillis just south of Pitiquito along the Rio Magdalena with a Rurale bullet in his chest. That was one time Case had been running again, this time to the north, with the Guardia Rurale combing the hills for him. It had been Lew who had killed the Mexican in a fight over a cantina bitch at Pozos del Datil. The Rurales never forgot a man once they wanted him, There was no use in trying to tell them Lew had killed the Mex. They had a saying when they executed a man down there if they weren't quite sure he was guilty: God will sort the souls.

It was another hazard he had to face, the Guardia Rurale. But once he got beyond Sonora he would be all right. He could buy protection down there, change his name and maybe become a Mexican citizen. It was a cinch he'd never buy off the Rurales. Most of them were ex-criminals or revolucionarios who had bought their freedom by agreeing to serve in the Rurales, and they served well.

"Damn you, Hardesty," he said. "Your ex-partners are thirsting for your blood. Sheriff Maslin is hunting you. The Rurales will be waiting for you. Anything else you can get into?" He laughed.

He raised his head quickly as he heard the faint tone of the bell. Case grabbed his Winchester and levered a round into it as he slid down the rocks and faced the mission. It was a dim, ghostly bulk. Cold sweat worked down his sides as he heard the bell again. He walked to where he could see up into the tower. There was no one there. "The wind," he said. But even as he said it he wondered whether the shade of a padre had come back to ring for evening prayers.

There was little religion left in Case Hardesty. He had seen too much of the seamy side of life. But he looked up at the cross atop the dome, lowered his rifle and took off his hat. He needed help, and not from man, but from a higher power. If he could, he would have gone back to Cottonwood Station and returned the money, but he knew that was impossible.

There was a strange, uneasy feeling in him when he went back to his hollow and dropped to the ground. Now and then he looked at the bell tower, but the bell did not ring again even though the wind was stronger, sweeping across the desert and whispering through the openings of the mission.

CHAPTER TWO

C hip Gilbert raised his big cloth-covered canteen
and shook it. There was about a pint of water
left in it. He uncorked it and filled his mouth
with water, swilling it about, then squirting it back into
the canteen. He did not look at Leonardo Janos as he did
so, for the Mexican was down to his last swallow of
water.

Janos looked at the big man he rode beside. There
was little love in him for Chip Gilbert and now he hated
the man. Chip was big of bone and heavy of body and he
took a sadistic pleasure in making others suffer. There
had been no sorrow in him when he had left the body of
Floyd Hanks to chase Case Hardesty. He had soft-talked
Floyd into trying to kill Case. Floyd had died so quickly
from the gun of Case Hardesty it had sent a chill
throughout Leonardo.

Case had been the brains of the quartet. It was he
who had thought up the idea of robbing the bank at
Cottonwood Station. It was he who had stopped Chip
from killing the cashier after he had rung the alarm.
Twenty thousand was a lot of money. A man could do
well with a quarter of that sum in Mexico. Now Leonardo
knew his share would be ten thousand if they ever caught

up with Hardesty. But facing that man was not to Leonardo's liking. If they did find him and kill him Leonardo was not sure what would happen to him when he was alone with Chip. The man would wait his chance and kill him as he would a fly.

"How far?" asked Chip.

"*Quién sabe?*"

"How far, damn you!"

The Mexican's face darkened with an angry rush of blood. "*Más allá*. Farther on."

"You been saying that all day."

Leonardo looked to the southeast. The old mission was somewhere there in the darkness. They had not seen it that day, which worried him, but he had not admitted it to Chip. It was a big country. They had ridden hard to the west and then along the base of the mountains to throw off the posse. But the detour had cost them time and water and their horses were worn out.

"You sure you know the way?" asked Chip.

"Yes."

"You ain't lying?"

"My life is at stake too, amigo."

"We can't go back now."

"No. There is only one way to go."

Chip digested this. It was hardly worthwhile to kill Leonardo for the little water he had. Besides, the Mex knew that country, or at least claimed he did. That was why Hardesty had brought him in on the deal. Hardesty had planned well. He had thought of loading a burro with water kegs for the journey over the Spanish Desert, but the damned burro had bolted because of the gunplay between Hanks and Hardesty.

They had seen too many dried bones that day to suit Chip Gilbert. Bones of horses, oxen, mules and men. It was a trail of death, the Devil's Highway.

"Supposing the water holes are dry," said Chip.

Leonardo crossed himself. "God forbid," he said quickly.

The big man laughed. "You think God is worried about *us*?"

"Do not say such things!"

"Bull crap! Chip Gilbert believes in himself."

Leonardo looked at his companion. The man was as hard as the basaltic rock of the mountains behind them.

"*Vamonos!*" said Chip. He kicked at his coyote dun and jerked his head at Leonardo. All day they had ridden with Leonardo just ahead of Chip. The big man took no chances. Leonardo had the uneasy feeling that either Chip or Case would kill him before too long if he did not get away. But there was no other way to go. All trails led to the scattered water holes, forcing travel to them, and in this case there was only one water hole within their reach, and if that water hole was dry....

———

LEONARDO'S SORREL shied and snorted. He reined it in and looked about. The moon was rising in the east, casting silvery rays across the desert.

"What is it?" demanded Chip.

The Mexican did not answer. He slid from his saddle and drew his rifle from its ornate leather scabbard. He levered a round into the chamber and walked toward a pile of brush. He kicked the brush aside and looked down at the hacked carcass of a horse. Whoever had left it hidden had taken care to hack off the brand.

Chip dismounted and walked to Leonardo. "Fresh," he said.

Leonardo nodded.

"Hardesty's?"

"Yes."

"You sure?"

"I know horses," said the Mexican.

Chip walked about. He could see no tracks. He looked to the south. There was a faint patch of lighter color miles away. "What is that?" he asked over his shoulder.

Leonardo shrugged. "Caliche, perhaps. White rocks."

The wind stirred the brush. Gas escaped from the body of the horse. "Jesus," said Chip.

Leonardo drew out his slim-bladed cuchillo and squatted beside the carcass. He began to cut strips of flesh from it.

"You loco?" asked Chip.

"We will need food."

"From that stinking thing?"

The dark eyes studied Chip. "There are no butcher shops out here, amigo. Meat is meat. See, Hardesty has taken some of the meat. He is wise that one."

"Let it alone!"

"A thousand Jesuses! Do you think *I* like this?"

"Damn fool Mex will eat anything."

Leonardo hefted his knife. He could cast it overhand or underhand and hit an apple at twenty feet with it. It would be so easy to kill Chip with it, take the water and strike out for himself, but he needed Chip with him if he was to get his share of the dinero.

Chip spat dryly. "Hurry up."

"Why? It is senseless to go on tonight. The horses are tired."

Chip walked over to Leonardo. "Hardesty can't be far away. That horse ain't been dead too long. How far would Hardesty get carrying his gear? Maybe a few miles, no more."

"As you say," said the Mexican. He carried the meat to his horse and led it to the south. The whitish area was plainer now. Then he remembered what it was and his heart seemed to skip a beat. It was the dome of the old mission at the haunted wells. Strange things were told about that place. Bells would ring softly with no one pulling on their ropes. Ghostly voices would sound in the secret words of the mass from the preface to the pater. "*Dios en cielo!*" he said.

"Don't talk spic!"

Leonardo turned a taut face toward the big man. "There is our water," he said.

"The white place?"

"Si. It is the dome of the old mission."

"Good."

Leonardo swallowed. "It is not a good place. It is haunted."

"Bull crap."

"I swear by the saints, Chip. One does not go there at night."

"If Hardesty is there I'm taking off right now. Pronto!"

"You are mad! Men have vanished there. Others have gone out of their minds."

Chip gripped the Mexican by the front of his shirt and drew him close. "I'm going there," he grated, "and you're going with me!" He shoved the smaller man back and stood there like a great bull with lowered horns, stupid and dangerous.

Leonardo crossed himself. "Por amor de Dies, Chip, do not make me go there tonight."

The piggish eyes of the big man were almost closed. There was no superstition in Chip Gilbert, but the abject fear etched on the Mexican's face started him to thinking. "How far would you say it was?" he asked.

Leonardo shrugged. "Four, maybe five miles."

Chip scratched his bristly chin. "He ain't got a horse. He had to walk that five miles in the heat. Maybe he walked a helluva lot farther than that too, because he's the kind of a soft-hearted bastard who'd try to save his horse."

"That is wrong?"

Chip spat. "A horse is transportation, not any love

affair with me." He looked toward the whitish patch of
the mission dome. "He didn't have no more than a small
canteen on his saddle when he got away. He'd likely share
it with his horse. That means he'd be plenty dinked if he
made the wells. He'd still be there, resting, figuring out
what to do."

"If there is water there."

Chip laughed. "If there ain't water there he's dead and
we can take the loot off of his carcass."

"*Si, amigo ... si ...* but if there is no water there then we
too are the same as dead."

Chip swallowed a little. The hot wind moaned
through the brush. He wasn't afraid of facing Case Hardesty, with or without the help of Leonardo, for there was
no fear in him for gunplay or rough-and-tumble work,
but the thought of dying of thirst was something else.

"It is not a good place, Chip."

"You got any other place to go?"

"No."

"Then shut up. We'll get a little rest and go on just
before dawn."

Leonardo nodded. He squatted by his horse and
looked toward the mission. There would be no rest for
Leonardo Janos that night.

CHAPTER THREE

C ase Hardesty opened his eyes and placed his right hand on his Winchester. The wind was cooler now and the moon silvered the naked desert, etching clearly the shadows of brush and rock. He sat up and looked about. The facade and dome of the mission shone in the moonlight. If anyone was within five or six miles of the mission they would see that dome.

Disquieting as the lonely place was at times, he was loath to leave it. There was a peacefulness there he had not experienced in many years, and he was tired. Tired of body but even more tired of mind. He was thirty years old and had never been able to save a dime and he knew now that if he had taken his five-thousand-dollar share of the loot he would have gone through it in record time.

He rolled a smoke and crouched down behind the rocks to light it. A lighted match could be seen for miles in that country. He cupped his hand about the cigarette as he smoked it, looking to the south and wondering what the odds were.

Something seemed to warn him to leave that place and yet something made him want to stay. He tried to drive the first thought from his mind but he could not do so.

He ground out his cigarette and stood up to look to the north. A feeling came over him that there was danger out there. He gathered his gear and walked down to the pool, a silver mirror in the moonlight. He filled the horse intestine and tied the end. He filled the water olla too and covered the wide mouth of it.

Maybe he was carrying too much weight for the journey through hell. He hefted the salt sack. Each extra pound would heighten the odds against his making it through to safety. He took a thousand dollars and re-placed the rest of the money in the bag. A thousand dollars would pay his way for a long time in Mexico, and eventually he could come back to the water hole to get the rest of it. He cached the salt sack and his surplus gear and when at last he was ready to leave he carried his weapons, water, food and money.

Case climbed up to the bell tower and looked to the north. The desert seemed as deserted as the moon. He turned to look to the south and it seemed to him as though he saw a spark of fire out there, but it happened so quickly he wasn't sure. He tapped the big bell for good luck and went down the stairs.

He did not look back as he passed through the far opening in the rock ramparts which surrounded the watering place. The Spanish Desert spread out before him and it was a place of beauty that night.

He walked with a long, smooth swinging stride, and the cool wind dried the sweat on him. He felt good, but always in the back of his mind, like a cholla needle stuck into the flesh, was the thought of the next day when the desert would turn into a yellow hell. Now and then the urge came over him to run for a time, to try and beat the daylight, but it was senseless. It was no place for a man to lose control of himself. The desert was as patient as a spider and would bide its time until he fell. It had won these silent battles before and it would win many others after it had defeated him.

CHAPTER FOUR

Sheriff Dade Maslin stood on the sand knoll holding the reins of his sorrel. The road was behind him and his posse of nine men. The road ran as straight as a string from east to west, and there wasn't one branch road trending south for forty miles that he knew of. Sure, there were trails in the Spanish Desert, plenty of them, but they had a damned disconcerting way of dying out into barren llanos.

They had found the body of one of the men who had held up the Cottonwood Station bank, neatly drilled with a bullet. They had found a sturdy burro laden with tightly calked oval water kegs. They had found the tracks of two men who had ridden to the west and of one man who had ridden to the south.

Dade could feel the sweat work down his sides. He was itchy and he was dirty, and he had no stomach for the Spanish Desert at any time of the year and least of all at the very core of summer. But there was a deep pride in Dade Maslin; the pride of a law man who stayed on the trail until he caught his quarry or killed him. It had to be one way or the other.

It was said of Dade Maslin that he had saved the county a lot of money by bringing back proof that he had killed the criminals he had been chasing. Sometimes it was his quarry's horse and sometimes his guns, but he always brought back proof and it was also a fact that the man he had been chasing was never seen again, leastways in Dade Maslin's bailiwick.

Dade felt for his cigar case and lighted a long nine. He could hear the men of his posse talking in low voices at the foot of the knoll, eyeing each other and then looking up at him, tracing meaningless signs in the sand with their boot toes. None of them wanted to chance the Spanish Desert and he was damned if he could blame them, but he knew they'd follow him if he led the way.

They were situated right in the middle and northern terminus of a vast trough of sandy wastes. The mountains far to the right and to the left rose almost directly from the flats and they looked forbidding enough at night without seeing them through a veil of haze during the torrid days.

Dade thought of the three men out there. Chip Gilbert, Leonardo Janos and Case Hardesty. They were all rawhide tough and hard. If Maslin had been asked what three men he would avoid trailing if he had the choice, he would have named the three of them, and of those three it was the man Hardesty who was the most dangerous because he had more than average intelligence.

"Antonio!" called out the sheriff.

A short man stood up from where he had been squatting apart from the others and came silently up the slope. The man could walk on broken glass and not make a sound. He was a mixture of several breeds. White and Indian was Antonio and his specialty was in tracking down men. Some said he was part Apache while others swore he was part Yaqui. Dade thought he was of the Arenenos or Sand Papagos, the wild cousins of their people, but even he wasn't sure.

The tracker stopped beside Dade. The moonlight glistened on the silver cross he wore suspended by a leather thong about his corded neck. Even his eyes seemed to glitter in the light. "*Patrón?*" he asked in his soft voice.

Maslin swung out a thick arm as though to encompass the brooding desert spread out before them. "Water?" he asked.

The breed seemed to digest the thought for a time. There was no use in trying to hurry him. At last he spoke, almost as though to himself. "Charcos dry. Pozitos dry. Tinajas, some with water, but maybe not."

Maslin shoved back his hat. Charcos were water holes scooped in clay basins; pozitos were dug in the sand washes; tinajas had been eroded in the granite mountains and held water most of the year. But the way Maslin wanted to go was straight down the middle of the vast valley ahead of him, and it wasn't the terrain for tinajas.

"No water then?" asked the sheriff.

Antonio touched the cross at his neck. "There is a place which might have water. Many miles south. It is said the Men With Black Robes built a mission there."

"You've been there?"

"Long ago."

"If there is a mission there then there must be water."

Antonio shrugged. "The mission was abandoned even by the Papagos long after the Black Robes left."

Maslin nodded. He knew the Papagos and the Pimas. They could live where no one else could, and if they had finally left the place it must be hopeless indeed. Still, it was something.

Maslin looked at the tracker. "You can find this place?"

"Yes."

There was no use in taking the others along. They would be frightened, not so much of the men they were hunting as of the implacable and deadly desert. If there was anyone who could find those outlaws it was Antonio.

"You'll lead me there, Antonio?" asked Maslin.

The dark eyes studied the big sheriff and then dropped.

"Yes, patrón. But the others."

Maslin nodded. "Heaney!" he called out.

A lean man detached himself from the group at the foot of the knoll and trudged up to Dade Maslin. Linus Heaney was the best deputy Maslin had ever sworn in. "Yes, Dade?" he said.

Maslin relighted his cigar, eyeing Heaney over the flare of the match. "I'm going on with Antonio. You take the rest of them back to Ocotillo Springs. Make that a base camp. Send pairs of men east and west to see if any of them try to backtrail. If I need you I'll send for you."

"But, Dade"

Maslin cut off the deputy with a wave of his big hand. "Antonio knows where the water is."

Heaney eyed the breed with distrust. "So he says."

Antonio did not move.

Maslin looked to the south. "There's some water hole out there with a mission near it."

Heaney laughed without mirth. "Jesus, Dade, you goin' to buy that pig in a poke? There ain't no such place."

"You've been out there?"

"Sure I have!"

"All over out there?" persisted the sheriff.

Heaney flushed. "Why, hell's fire, a man can't cover every inch of that hell hole."

"Antonio can."

"Dade," pleaded Heaney, "that mission story is a cock-and-bull tale just like the Dutchman's Lost Mine and the Lost Adams Diggings. I've heard about the place but I ain't never talked to any man who saw it."

"Then talk to Antonio... he has."

Heaney held out his hands in despair. Dade Maslin had been like an older brother to him. "Then I'll go along," he said quietly.

"You'll do as you're told."

The moon was at its zenith. The wind whispered through the brush and the whispering sounded secretive and evil.

Heaney walked down the slope.

"Give me three or four of your canteens," said Dade. "You can make it easily to Ocotillo Springs on what you have left."

Heaney brought up the canteens and stood there looking at Dade. Then he thrust out his hand and gripped the sheriff's. He did not speak as he turned away, nor did he look at the breed who squatted like a horned toad on the warm sand.

The men watched the two of them move into the desert. "Maslin has guts," said Charley Logan.

Red Hastings spat. "Guts and no brains," he said.

Heaney hit Red just once, on the point of the jaw, and when Red hit the ground and clawed for his Colt he suddenly stopped as he saw the look in the deputy's blue eyes.

The posse rode toward the east along the old rutted road. Red Hastings nursed his swelling jaw. Linus Heaney rode silently with an unlit cigarette pasted to the corner of his mouth. He wasn't sorry for hitting Red after what he had said. The hell of it was that maybe Red was right after all. Dade Maslin was zealous, sure enough, the bulldog breed, but no one would ever say he was brilliant.

Antonio padded through the brush with a long, swinging stride, followed by Maslin on his big rawboned sorrel, with the saddle hung with full canteens. He chewed at the stub of his cigar as he rode and his eyes probed ahead.

The moonlight lay on the desert like a silvery blanket of finest weave and there was not a trace of cloud in the sky. For the first time in his career as a law officer Dade Maslin wondered if he was doing the right thing. It had always been so easy before. Find the trail and stick onto it like a leech, brushing all obstacles aside until the final showdown when the irons were slipped on the hunted's wrists or he went down in rifted gunsmoke.

"*Ándale Va!*" said the tracker over his shoulder.

Maslin came out of his reverie with a start and saw that he had lagged behind. The tracker moved swiftly and effortlessly with hardly a sound beyond the husking sound of the Apache *n-deh b'keh* he wore on his tireless lower legs. He could go on like that for hours. To *what?*

CHAPTER FIVE

C ase Hardesty glanced over his right shoulder. The moon was a pale silvery gray now, working down from the zenith, lighting the far slopes of the western range.

The terrain had changed now, with rolling waves of sand undulating ever onward to the south, stippled with thorny brush which seemed to reach out clawing hands to slow him down and at last stop him.

He looked back and wasn't sure if the whitish patch he saw dimmed by the wash of the moonlight was the mission or not.

How far? How far? The thought pounded incessantly through his brain.

The moon was seemingly resting on the top of the mountains to the west, and it would be flooding the valley of the Lower Colorado and the Gulf of California.

He saw the distant flicker of light to the southeast, an instant's illumination and then it was gone as quickly as it had come like some mysterious and eerie message from the unknown.

He stopped in his tracks. He knew there were small placitas near the border but from his calculations they would be much farther to the east. Quitobaquito,

Sonoyta, Agua Dulce and Agua Salada, but these would be shielded by the mountains. The Camino del Diablo, the notorious Devil's Highway, was far to the south too, meandering on both sides of the border. Too far for him to see the campfire of travelers on that hell's highway.

Case shifted his small pack and eased the greasy gut canteen away from his raw neck. He had always played the lone wolf. His venture with his three late companions had been planned that way because he had needed them, and now, when he needed help, he could not bring himself to approach other humans out on the Spanish Desert.

He padded on, feeling the sweat work itchily down his sides and trickle down his long legs. Fear had come to stride along just behind him. The night was fairly friendly, but the daylight would reveal his enemy to the fullest ... the deadly, sun-scorched desert.

Scraps of a poem filtered through his mind. Mr. Saylor, his platoon commander in B Company of the Fifth, had been struck in the breastbone with a sagittate flint arrow driven by an Apache bow in the Swisshelms. The man had been dying as Case had carried him out of danger. For two days Case had fought to save the man but there had been nothing he could do and, near the end, when the officer had been delirious, he had said that poem which Case had really never forgotten; but the sequence of words came hard to him now in his tired condition.

He tried to fit the words together. It had been something by Coleridge.

Mr. Saylor had been given to reading poetry. Case minded the time he had been supposed to be teaching a class on map reading on a scorching day and instead he had taken his class out beneath the paloverdes and had read Milton to them.

It had been something which had stirred in the young

officer's mind as he had been dying, with the clarity of vision such a man has at the time.

Case did not look back. Lonely as the desert was, there was still something there; something alien and horrible, and then the words of the poem fitted themselves neatly into place and they did not help his peace of mind.

> *Like one that on a lonesome road*
> *Doth walk in fear and dread....*
> *Because he knows a frightful fiend*
> *Doth close behind him tread.*

The moon was gone, leaving but a faint wash of pale light against the sky.

Case slogged on, wanting a drink but knowing full well he'd need every drop for the hell of the coming day.

The wind shifted and brought with it a faint, mingled odor he knew well. Bitter wood smoke and the smell of horses or mules.

The camp was close.

Case sank down to the ground to get off the skyline. It was an automatic reaction with him.

He lay there against the cooling sands, easing off his pack and gut canteen. Then he raised himself up and worked his way to a knoll thatched with mesquite. He crawled up it and looked to the southeast. There was nothing to see but more desert, dominated, if the word can be used, by a low formation of black volcanic rock. Then he saw a dull winking eye of red light and knew it for an ember in a bed of ashes.

The urge was in him to get his gear and move out at the double, making tracks between himself and the unknowns, because he felt by now that no man was his friend.

There were bandidos in that country, and hard-bitten revolutionaries, and it was known and haunted by the fierce Yaquis, blood brothers to the Apaches, who had never been tamed. Even the Sand Papagos wouldn't hesitate to club him to death for his weapons, for they were worth more than money in the Spanish Desert country.

He slid down the slope and got his gear, then padded to the southwest.

The woman's scream stopped him in his tracks as though he had been pole-axed.

There was a moment's pregnant silence and then the woman screamed again from the very bottom of her chest. It echoed for a fraction of a second and then died away.

Case dropped pack and gut canteen and ran silently toward the rock formation, but he did not charge in as another white man would have done. Apaches had taught him that trick. They said a white man would run directly toward a shot or some noise, while an Apache would circle around until he knew what was happening and whether they were friends or enemies.

He cut to the south, past the littered base of the rock formation, running like a deer.

He cut in again from the south and dropped to the harsh ground to look down into the hollow behind the rocks.

There was a sagging buckboard standing there and beyond it two mules. A man and a woman stood near the ashes of the fire, struggling for something. The man backhanded the woman and she went down hard, striking the fire bed and rolling free with a grunt of pain.

Case arose and ran down the slope. The man turned as he heard the slapping of boot soles. He dropped something and clawed for his revolver, but Case swung up his reversed Winchester and drove the steel-shod butt hard against the man's jaw, felling him like an ox.

Case turned as someone moved toward him and his reaction was so swift and sure he had struck down a woman before he realized who it was.

He stepped back and looked down at the two unconscious people.

"Who are you?" the first woman asked as she got up.
The first thing she did was to pick up the big canteen the
man had dropped to try for his six-gun.

"Never mind. What's been going on here?"

She looked down at the man. "He wanted the water. I
awoke and saw him with it."

"You scream very well," said Case dryly.

She shook her head. "It wasn't me. It was her."

"You get burned?"

"A little."

"What is this place?"

She laughed shortly. "Do these places have names?"

"Some of them do."

Case eyed her. She was tall and well built and he had
seen a pair of beautiful long legs as she had rolled free
from the fire. Her hair had been bound back behind her
head and he could see that it was beautiful too.

Case looked about the meager camp. "What are you
doing here?"

"Are you an officer of the law?"

His head seemed to snap back to look at her because
of the cool manner in which she had asked him. "No," he
said.

"What are you doing out here, Mr. No-Name."

"Heading south."

"On foot?"

"No law against it, Miss No-Name."

She laughed. "We're following the Camino to Yuma."

He eyed the sagging vehicle and then the two worn
mules. "You're a long way from the Camino."

"That's not true!"

He nodded. "You're a good twenty miles or more
from there."

She had not lost her composure when she had been
struck down nor when a strange, wild-looking man had

plunged into the camp, but now a change came over her. She did not even look down when the man groaned at her feet. "But we need water," she said quietly.

"You won't find it around here."

"There's Tule Tank and other watering places."

He shook his head.

"Where are they then?"

He thrust out his rifle toward the southwest. "Mas alia ... farther on, between the Tules and the Cabeza Prietas."

"But this is the way!"

"No."

In the silence which followed the man sat up and felt his jaw. "Water," he said.

The woman did not offer him the canteen. Instead she knelt by the other woman and examined her. She spoke over her shoulder. "She'll be all right. You strike well, mister."

"I've had experience," he said dryly. He suddenly reached down and jerked the pistol from the man's holster. He stepped back as the man stood up. He was as tall as Case and of heavier build, but even in the dimness Case could see there was a softness about him.

"Who are you?" demanded the man.

"Call me Case."

"Well then, Case, who are you?"

"Traveler," said Case. "Who're you?"

"Phillip Davis."

The woman looked up at him and then at Case. "Help me with her," she said.

Case hesitated. Davis had a bitter look on his face.

The woman stood up. "He won't bother you," she said.

Case leaned his rifle against the ancient buckboard and lifted the woman. She was smaller than the first woman and lighter of build, but she was damned pretty too, with her dark hair and skin, as compared to the more Nordic beauty of the other woman. Case carried her to where a blanket was spread on the sand. He lowered her gently, and as he did so she opened her dark eyes.

Case stepped back and let the blonde woman take care of her companion. "*Mi Corazón*," she said quickly.

"Her heart," said Case quickly.

The blonde woman stood up straight. "No," she said. She walked toward the fire as Phillip Davis walked to the other woman and knelt beside her.

Case approached the tall woman. "I see," he said. "Her husband?"

"No."

"Sweetheart, then?"

"Yes."

There was something strange about her as she stood there while Davis held the woman close. "What's wrong?" asked Case.

"Nothing."

"You're sure?"

"Damn you!" she said quickly. "I'm Madeline Davis! He is my husband!"

CHAPTER SIX

They sat together in the pre-dawn darkness, and although Madeline Davis must have been concerned about the two dim figures seated on the blanket thirty feet from her and Case, she did not show it as her thoughts wandered from her conversation with Case. Their subject was vital to all four of them, but it was Case and Madeline who talked about it, and as they did so, fear seemed to settle down out of the darkness and made a fifth addition to the party.

"You had better turn back the way you've come," said Case quietly. "Where was the last water hole you stopped at?"

"I don't know the name."

"That doesn't matter."

"There was just enough water there for the mules and one filling of the canteen," she said.

Case touched his dry lips with his tongue. They were too far from Tule Tank to make it on foot and he knew those two mules would never make it without water. His own water lay out there in the darkness, and he had not mentioned it. There was enough there for him to make it to the south, and he'd be damned if he'd turn back to the north and the mission water hole. Chip and Leonardo might be there, and perhaps Dade Maslin as well.

The man and woman murmured in the darkness. Case glanced at Madeline. The dark woman was called Dulce, the same name as Case's old amor at Hermosillo. But there was a difference. Case's Dulce had been well named . . . sweet, pleasant, agreeable. This Dulce had the fires of lust and passion in her dark eyes.

"And the next water hole beyond the last one?" asked Case.

"*Quién sabe?*" she said.

"Dammit! Don't you know?"

"It was night. Phillip lost the way for a time. We found the last water by luck. The camino led on from there, or at least we thought it did. It ran out somewhere in the black rocks. Dulce. ..." Here she hesitated as though the very name was anathema to her. "Dulce claimed she had been over the Camino del Diablo before. She was afraid to go back and so was Phillip. I was afraid to go on but I couldn't let them wander out here."

"Why?"

She shrugged. "They are weak. I'm strong."

"But him...?"

She eyed him. "I know what you are thinking. There isn't any love left in me for him, that is sure, but they need me."

"This is loco!" he said fiercely. Damn all women! He wished to God he had not let the screaming arrest his flight to the border. He had thought at first it had been Madeline who had done the screaming but now that he knew her he was sure she was the type who would fight as fiercely and silently as a man would ... as he himself fought. It had been Dulce who had screamed.

"You know this country," she said.

"No man knows this country."

"It is always the same. Don't lie to me, Case."

"You're wrong. I'm not lying. The mountains and the desert seem the same, but the winds sweep across the trails in the winter covering them and uncovering old trails, emptying some water holes and filling others."

"So you took the long chance of running south right through this country you fear."

"What do you mean ... running?"

They eyed each other.

"Why else would you be out here?" she asked at last.

He nodded. "And you?"

She looked away. "We can't go back," she said quietly.

Phillip and his Dulce were not speaking now and Case wondered if they were doing what he suspected. The man was like an animal and the girl was little better.

"Was it murder, Case?" she asked.

"No. Do you believe me?"

"I think so."

He stood up and looked down at her. "And why are you running? Because of murder?"

She stood up and looked up into his hard face. "Perhaps."

"What does that mean?"

She looked to the east. "Perhaps not because of a murder committed, but of one which may be committed."

"I don't understand."

"Perhaps you will."

Phillip Davis came through the darkness. "How much water do we have?" he asked his wife.

"Two quarts, perhaps."

Davis looked at Case. "And you?"

"Don't worry. I don't need any of it."

"You have water then?"

"Yes."

"How much?"

Case shifted his rifle. "Enough."

The man ran a hand across his cracked lips. "You'll have to share it with us."

"So?"

"I can't force you to, Case, but you must do it in the name of humanity."

"Jesus God!" The ejaculation burst from Case before he realized it.

The man reached out a hand toward Case. "We haven't enough to reach Tule Tank."

Case moved back. "There isn't enough water in my possession for one of us to reach Tule Tank."

"We can travel at night when it is cooler."

Case looked past the man. The breeze had died away. There was the faintest suggestion of light in the eastern sky. "Look," he said.

"Es el dia!" called out Dulce. She came toward them, drawing her shawl over her head. "The mules must be hitched."

Case leaned on his rifle and watched the strange trio of beings he had met in this God-forsaken hole. It wouldn't take much for him to walk away from Davis and the Mexican girl, but Madeline Davis bothered him.

No one moved.

"Es el dia!" repeated Dulce.

"Yeh," said Case dryly.

The wind returned, this time from another direction and it moved over and about them with inquisitive invisible fingers, loosening a lock of hair here and a flap of clothing there. Playing with them before the hell of the day broke over the eastern mountains with its greenish-gold light to forecast what was really in store for them all.

Madeline Davis walked to the mules and led them to the sagging buckboard. "Leave them be," said Case.

"What the hell do you mean by that?" demanded Phil Davis.

"Ride them. They'll never haul that contraption through the sand. They won't last long anyway, but it will be longer if you ride them with spells of walking ... lots of walking."

Davis looked uncertainly about. "But our luggage," he said.

Madeline walked to the back of the buckboard and dumped the luggage on the ground. 'Take what you really need," she said.

Dulce hurried to one of the valises. "My dresses," she said.

"Wear what you have on," said Case. "Take cloth to bind over those flimsy shoes."

Case turned to speak with Madeline and something hard struck him just below the left ribs. He turned to look into the taut face of Phil Davis and then down at a double-barreled derringer nuzzling his ribs.

"Take me to the water," said Davis. "Leave that rifle."

Case dropped his Winchester. Dulce ran to it and picked it up. For a moment she eyed Madeline and then she looked back at the two men.

"Vamonos!" snapped Davis.

Case walked ahead of Davis until he found his gear. He picked it up and walked back to the camp. Davis looked at the horse-gut canteen. "That thing full?" he asked.

"Yes."

"Give it to me!"

Case handed it to him. Davis jerked his head at Dulce and Case heard her work the rifle lever to load the chamber. Davis stepped back and thrust his derringer into his pocket. He fumbled with the end of the Apache canteen. "How do you open this crazy contraption?"

Case untied the end and Davis raised it to his mouth. He sucked at it and the gamy, greasy water ran down his chin. He gagged a little as he took it from his mouth. "What kind of thing is this?" he demanded as he raised it to his mouth again.

Case shifted his feet. "Made out of fresh horse guts," he said quietly.

The man spat a mouthful of the water all over Case. He dropped the horse gut and the water gurgled from it. Case jumped forward. "Damn you!" he said. He felt the Winchester ram hard against his back.

"Stay where you are, hombre," said Dulce.

Madeline darted forward but Dulce swung the barrel of the rifle and struck the taller woman, driving her to one side as the last of the water ran from the deflated intestine.

Phillip Davis spat again and again and then he slashed at Case's face with both hands. "You dirty sonofabitch!" he grated. Then he hit Case with all his strength. Case fell back against the buckboard. He slowly wiped the blood from his face. "I'll kill you for that, Davis," he said softly.

"You said it was water!"

"It was, you damned fool!"

"Water? You're loco."

Case straightened up. "That might have been the difference between living and dying," he said.

The man was badly frightened now. "I didn't know, Case. Before God, I didn't know! I thought you were trying to poison me."

Case shook his head. "No," he said quietly. "Besides, it's too late for that."

"Too late for what?"

"Poisoning you." Case walked away and spoke back over his shoulder. "You were poisoned when you got here."

"What shall we do?" screamed Dulce. "He will be coming soon."

Davis glanced at Case. "Shut up," he said.

Case turned slowly. "Who will be coming soon?"

Phil Davis drew out his derringer and cocked it. "Never mind," he said.

The blood was salty in Case's mouth as he stood there. There was something furtive about the two of them. Madeline Davis stood quietly by the dusty mules.

"What are you going to do with that toy?" asked Case.

Davis waved the stingy gun. "You know the wells, Case. You're going to show us where they are."

It was light enough now for Case to see their features clearly. He walked to his pack and picked it up. Then without a word he started walking south.

"Stop!" yelled Davis. "Stop, or I'll shoot! Give me that rifle, Dulce!"

Case kept on until he was within twenty feet of the water olla he had shoved under a mesquite bush with his foot when he had gotten his gear at gunpoint.

"Stop, damn you!"

Case thought he could make it across the border with the water he had cached.

"You hear me, Case!" screamed Davis.

The eastern sky was awash with pale light.

Case turned slowly and looked at the three of them but the only one he really saw was Madeline. "Get your things together," he said.

———

CASE LED the way on foot, followed by the two women riding the weary mules while Davis brought up the rear carrying Case's heavy Winchester. The water olla bobbed steadily at Case's left hip. Madeline had the big canteen.

An hour after they left the camping place the sun was already making itself well known to them. There was no misty haze about the mountains as yet.

Madeline rode up beside Case. "He might have killed you," she said.

He glanced up at her. "I would have gotten both of them before they killed me," he said. "I had my six-gun."

"I believe you, but they might have wounded you; crippled you."

"That was why I came back." She nodded. She knew. It was not because of his fear of being wounded that he had come back. He had come back because of her, for without his help she would have died alone in the desert.

CHAPTER SEVEN

They could plainly see the round dome of the mission protruding above the rock formation but there was no sign of life that they could see. Chip Gilbert drew his rifle from its scabbard and loaded the chamber. Leonardo Janos wet his lips. He had a feeling that Case Hardesty was holed up in those rocks, or perhaps in the old bell tower, watching them over the sights of his rifle. It would be easy shooting. One man could hold off many from the water if he so desired.

"I don't like this," said Leonardo at last.

Chip jerked his rifle toward the east. "Who does? But I ain't going to sit out here while that sun comes up and bastes me in my own sweat. You move around to the far side and see what you can see."

"No."

The rifle muzzle covered the Mexican. "Git!" said Chip.

Janos led his horse slowly toward the south, all the time seeming to feel Case Hardesty's hard gray eyes following his progress. There would be a single ringing report and the impact of a soft-nosed forty-four and then nothing but a dead man lying on the sands with powder smoke drifting from the tower.

A spotted night snake moved sluggishly away from Leonardo's path. A crissal thrasher broke into rich song and then stopped abruptly as Leonardo's horse kicked a rock. Cold sweat greased Leonardo's rifle stock and barrel where his hands gripped the weapon. He looked at the tilted cross atop the dome and spoke softly as he walked. "With the favor of God I will live."

Chip Gilbert walked forward with his horse between him and that silent bell tower, peering under the horse's neck, waiting for a telltale movement. If luck was with them they'd find Case Hardesty dead or unconscious with the loot still on him. There would be enough water to make the Sonoran border. Leonardo knew the way. Once into Mexico Chip would invest a bullet in Leonardo and profit handsomely.

Leonardo was out of sight now and the thought came to Chip that the Mexican might invest a bullet in Chip, but Leonardo wasn't too good a man with the long gun and if he missed....

The Mexican was to the south of the rock formation now. There was no sign of life on the lightening desert. He took his courage into his hands and walked swiftly toward the rocks, leaving his horse behind him. One of his boots kicked a stone ahead of him and it clicked sharply against a rock. He worked his way up the slope and saw the side wall of the mission. A moment later he dropped flat behind some brush which crowned the rock wall surrounding the pool.

The place seemed deserted. A cactus wren fluttered aimlessly about the large tinaja which was almost in the center of the wide oval area below the Mexican. There were no signs of tracks, a fire or anything else which showed recent occupation by man.

Leonardo's dark eyes surveyed the mission. The bell-tower opening which faced him was still dark within, but there was no movement up there. His eyes studied the desolate graveyard sited some yards behind the mission.

The nameless dead rested there. Perhaps he too would rest there without benefit of a mass. Try as he would he could not defeat the brooding thoughts which had infested his mind since he had seen Floyd Hanks die so quickly, and the thoughts had made less of a man of Leonardo Janos.

"May God favor me," he said as he stood up and worked his way down the steep slope.

He eyed the water as he stopped at the bottom of the slope. His throat seemed as though it had been scoured by sand and he wanted a long drink, but it was a bad position to be caught in.

Something scraped against rock and he whirled, raising his rifle only to see Chip Gilbert standing in the rock passage to the west. The big man laughed. "Ain't no one here. You scared?"

Leonardo scowled. He turned away and knelt beside the water, drinking sparingly, but all the time he did so he kept thinking of that mission at the far side of the oval. Even in the early morning light it was not a pleasant place.

Chip Gilbert dropped beside Leonardo and sipped a little of the gamy water. "Jesus," he said. He fished a dead beetle from the bottom of the pool.

They sat there looking at the mission. "You suppose he's in there watching us?" asked Leonardo.

"Hell no! If he had wanted to stop us he would never have let us get this far. Go on in there and see."

"No."

"You heard me."

"No!"

Chip stood up. "Yellowbelly," he said.

The big man walked toward the front door of the building. He glanced back with a grin when he reached the door but Leonardo noted that he had his Winchester ready when he suddenly leaped inside.

The Mexican could hear the faint crushing of boot

soles as Chip prowled about the interior and then they faded away. It became too quiet to suit the Mexican. Minutes ticked past and still there was no sign of life, and all the eerie stories Leonardo had heard about such places came home to roost.

Chip Gilbert reached the top of the stairway in the bell tower. He moved softly as he walked about, until he could look down and see the Mexican beside the pool. It would be easy to kill him, but the loot was still missing and Chip figured he might still need Leonardo's help.

Chip looked to the south. The sun was up now and the desert was being revealed clearly. The wind was rising a little and there was a faint streak of dust against the southern sky, but whether it was a wind devil or sign of travelers he wasn't sure. Besides, it was to the southwest of his position, and if it had been Hardesty he would have probably struck off straight for the south. Still, there were tinajas in those mountains to the southwest.

He walked around the big bell and looked to the north. Nothing but sand and brush. *Bueno!*

"*Hola!*" called Leonardo.

Chip grinned as he stepped back. The Mex was scared.

"*Hola, amigo!*"

The words echoed back faintly from the rocks. "*Hola, amigo! Hola ami. . . Hola ... Ho . . .*"

Chip saw Leonardo standing fifty feet from the front of the building. Chip picked up a chunk of plaster and flipped it out over Leonardo's head. It struck in the pool and Leonardo jumped nervously as though he had backed into a jumping cholla. Then he sprinted for the rock passageway with his boots drumming dully on the rock surfaces.

Chip held his sides. He saw Leonardo vanish into the desert. The big man hurried downstairs and out of the building. He took up a post to one side of the passageway and waited until he at last heard a movement at the outer end of the passage, the stealthy approach of the Mexican.

Leonardo was almost even with Chip when the big man stepped out. "Where you been?" he asked coldly.

Sweat trickled down the Mexican's face. "I went for the horses, *amigo*."

"Yeh? Where are they?"

Leonardo turned away to get the horses. Some day I will kill this big man he thought, after we get the dinero.

Chip was squatting beside the pool idly smoking when Leonardo returned. "What do you think?" he asked.

"*Quién sabe?* It is evident that he is not here. Perhaps he went south."

Chip thought of the dust he had seen. "Yeh. Well, he ain't riding, that's sure. We'll stay here until the horses get rested, then push on in the late afternoon."

Leonardo watered the two mounts. Now and then his eyes strayed toward the mission.

Chip placed a blanket in the shade of a boulder and lay down to rest, but he wouldn't sleep.

The Mexican began to gather mesquite twigs and branches. He placed them against a rock.

"Don't make no fire out here," warned Chip.

"We must eat."

"No smoke, dammit!"

"Where can I make it, then?"

"In the mission."

There was no use in arguing with Chip Gilbert. Leonardo gathered the wood and took the meat. He walked toward the mission and inside of it, scared to death, but too proud to let Chip know about it.

The interior had been gutted. The gilded reredos was long gone. The carving had been smashed about the niches. The five altars had been demolished. Holes were everywhere.

It was cool in the long nave as he walked toward the

sanctuary. High above him he could see the outlines of the plaster palm fronds under the faded dome of the sanctuary. His feet grated on the battered floor as he walked into the sacristy. The place had been subjected to an orgy of filthiness. The walls were stained with the smoke of fires which had been kindled in there by travelers. Ashes, rags and dung, both animal and human, had dried on the flagstone floor. The sun shot a shaft of light through the door which opened to the east. There was a feeling of unutterable loneliness and tragedy about the place.

He crossed himself before he set about making the fire. He had been an altar boy many years before in his native Durango. One did not forget those things easily.

CHAPTER EIGHT

The sun was up high as Dade Maslin called a halt. The tracker squatted in the shade of the horse. He had refused water, and instead he had bound tighter the buckskin band about his forehead and dark hair, for it had become loosened by his sweat.

Maslin sipped a little water and eyed the tracker. The man had gone on for hours. He had folded his thigh-length Apache desert moccasins about his knotted calves. The man could outrun a horse on the side of a mountain. Dade had heard such runners had been trained to run a mile and back again at top speed with a mouthful of water and be able to spit out the water when they had finished.

Dade lighted a cigar and looked out across the desert. There was a misty haze in the distance where the land seemed to slant upward, but there was no sign of a mission such as Antonio had mentioned.

The sweat soaked through Dade's shirt and dripped from his florid face. The horse stood there with his head low. Dade took off his hat and gave the horse some water.

"How much further?" he asked the tracker.

"*Más allá.*"

That was all ... *más allá* ... farther on. Always *más allá*.

There was no use in stalling. It wouldn't get any cooler nor would they have any more water until they reached the water hole. "Let's go, Antonio," said Dade.

Antonio walked to a clump of catclaw and cut a switch. Methodically he beat his dusty calves until the blood flowed, then he cast aside the switch, drew his belt tighter and started off at the same tireless trot as though he had not been running for hours.

The sun was at its zenith when the tracker stopped and shaded his eyes with his hands. "There," he said.

The light seemed to probe into Dade's reddened eyes as he peered in the direction Antonio looked. At first he could see nothing and then he made out something shining in the sun. Something domed and white. He closed his eyes. When he opened them again the distance seemed to swim in a reddish haze and a shaft of pain seemed to lance into his throbbing head. He swayed a little, gripping his saddle horn. The heat seemed to press down on him as he stood there doggedly trying to clear his brain and then suddenly he fell full length on the ground.

He opened his eyes to see the dusty legs of the tracker close beside him and then he passed out completely.

———

"PATRÓN ... PATRÓN ... PATRÓN..." Antonio said.

Dade Maslin opened his eyes. Thank God it was dark, but the heat had not abated. The sand burned through his clothing and even the water with which Antonio bathed his face was hot. Dade looked upward, trying to distinguish the features of the tracker. He gripped the man by the arm. "How long have I been lying here?"

The man did not answer.

"How long?"

"Not more than an hour, *patrón*."

Then Dade Maslin knew the truth. He had gone blind.

"What shall I do, *patrón?*"

A weaker man might have accepted his disability but Dade Maslin was not a weak man. He was muy hombre; very much of a man. To such a man a thing like this was a crushing blow. He tried to think but nothing was clear and the heat was hellish as though the gates of hell had been opened.

"Perhaps there is someone at the water hole?"

Dade sat up. He knew who would be at the water hole if anyone was there and he'd get short shrift from any one of the three of them. But there was nothing else to do. Antonio could go on to the water hole and ask for help but they would kill him like a fly. Perhaps if the tracker got him there they would let the two of them alone. They'd laugh of course and maybe beat them, but they might go on toward the border knowing their pursuer was absolutely helpless. On the other hand, the dead cannot speak.

"Help me up," said Dade.

He stood there holding onto the saddle horn. "*Ándale!*" he said hoarsely as he mounted his horse.

Antonio took the reins and led the sorrel toward the distant mission. Now and then he looked back at the taut face of his patron. Antonio had always depended on Dade Maslin for the simple necessities he required. Now his *patrón* depended on him.

CHAPTER NINE

There comes a time when a man thinks the chips are down for him, and it is then he thinks of what he might have done and might have been had things gone differently. It is as though his entire past life is revealed in its nakedness and he knows terror because of what unseen powers can do with him, either to save him or destroy him, and there doesn't seem much rhyme or reason in what they do.

The thought was Case Hardesty's as he plodded northward, leading Madeline Davis' mule. She rode with bowed head. They had not spoken for a long time, but something had happened between them in the few short hours they had been thrown together. Some subtle understanding for each other which neither of them had mentioned but which each of them now knew for a certainty.

Case had not yet solved the riddle of the three people whose lives were now bound inexorably with his. Madeline seemed simple and forthright. Phillip Davis was a weakling who cared nothing for the laws of human decency although he would be the first to plead for mercy because of those unwritten laws. Dulce was of the earth, thinking only of herself and her pleasure, taking a cruel delight in the fact that she could flaunt her conquest of the big, handsome Yanqui in front of his patient wife.

There was a wall of black rock a mile from them, rising almost sheer from the sandy earth, and it seemed as though the top of that rock wall was the edge of the earth and beyond that was space, for they could not see over it nor around it and there was nothing but the blazing blue sky to mark the crest of the wall like a straight knife slash.

Case was worried. He had not remembered that wall of lava rock. He had not descended it the night before. The way had been free of such an obstacle.

As they neared it Phillip Davis came forward wiping the sweat from his reddened face. "You sure you know the way?" he demanded.

Case did not answer.

"Well, do you?"

Case eyed the man. "You lead the way if you think you can."

Davis did not answer Case's challenge. He had been used to bullying people and getting away with it but his reputation as a hardcase vanished quickly enough when he met men like Case Hardesty or a woman like his wife.

"We'll have to climb it," said Case quietly.

"Why, in God's name?"

Case waved a hand. "Look, Davis, there isn't a break in that wall as far as we can see. We don't know what is on the far side of it, but the water hole is to the north. That I know for sure."

Davis looked to the southeast. He was always looking that way and so was Dulce. "Let's get on with it, then."

Case led the way and when he reached the foot of the black wall, he had his misgivings. A horse could never get up that slope and it would take a damned nimble mule to do it. Their mules were about on their last legs.

Madeline dismounted and stood beside Case. "Can they make it?"

He shrugged, gripped the reins and started up the slope while she raised her skirts and followed him, never looking back at the other two. They were halfway up when the mule slipped and fell, tearing the reins from Case's hand. The exhausted animal made no effort to get back onto its feet. It rolled over and over and struck with a dull thud against a sharp ledge of rock. Dust floated up from the ground. Case knew the mule was dead.

"Bring up that other mule!" he called out.

Davis stared up at them. Dulce stood beside him and she was talking rapidly in her native tongue. The man at last started up the slope, picking his way with care and punctuating each step with a muttered curse.

He reached the two of them and they helped him with the sweat-drenched, struggling beast until at last they reached the top. They stood there dripping with sweat and their intense thirst seemed to grip them tighter by the throat.

Dulce stood a quarter of the way up the slope and she looked up at them. "Help me!"

Phil Davis dropped in the shade of the mule.

Case turned around and looked north. He looked at a curious phenomenon. They were on level ground, stretching as far as the eye could see. Sand stippled with mesquite and ocotillo, while behind them was the steep wall dropping down to the rocky surface of the desert. The wind must have drifted the sand up against this natural barrier. He looked to the east and his heart sank. There was no sign of the mission.

"Help me, Pheel!" the Mexican girl screamed.

He did not answer. "Water?" he asked Case.

"Later. Go get your *preciosa*."

"Let her make it herself."

Dulce had dropped to the surface of the slope and she beat her little fists against the black rock.

Madeline looked away. She too was looking for the mission. Dulce was screaming. *"Diós en cielo! Santa Madre de Diós!"*

Case wiped the sweat from his face. He stripped off his pack and started down the slope. The girl was silent when he reached her. He picked her up and slogged up the rough slope and he could feel the strength drain from him as he did so. At last he dumped her beside Phil. Madeline handed him the canteen. "You need it," she said.

"What about me?" demanded her husband.

She did not answer.

Case pushed the canteen back. "Let's go," he said. "Northeast."

Davis looked northeast. "Where's this damned mission?"

"There may be a fold of land between us and it."

"Yeh ... maybe..."

They plodded on with Case leading the staggering mule. For a short time they were etched pitilessly against the skyline like figures cut from black paper, and then they were gone.

Far to the southeast a lone rider suddenly drew rein. He could see the long black rampart of rock. He had been seeing it for hours, but now he saw tiny figures moving along the top of it until they vanished. He nodded in satisfaction.

He was slender and young, not more than twenty or twenty-one years of age, and his face was tanned by the sun. It was his eyes which would draw notice. They were icy blue in startling contrast to his brown skin.

A Winchester was sheathed in a saddle scabbard and he carried an ivory-butted Colt tied down to his right thigh. Three large canteens hung from the saddle.

He had found last night's camp of the three people he had been following and knew positively it was their camp, not only because of the abandoned buckboard but because of the bag of clothing which lay beside it. Dulce's clothing. There was no doubt about that, for he had bought these clothes for her himself.

Somewhere along their flight they had picked up another man but that fact did not bother the kid. One man or a dozen wouldn't stop him from finding Dulce and Phillip Davis and when he found them he'd kill both of them. The country was strange to him but he had a crude map drawn by a man at Agua Salada who knew the country. The man had known El Jabonero, the Soapmaker, who had found and lost a fortune in gold in the Cabeza Prietas, or claimed he had. It had cost the kid twenty dollars in gold to get the map. It didn't matter how much it cost him to find those two fugitives.

The thing which puzzled him was that Madeline was still with them. She had helped them escape, but why she had done it was beyond reasoning, for the kid, in any case.

The black rock rampart stretched for miles to the west. The kid had seen his quarry traveling easterly. He eyed his map, then turned his rangy bay to travel due north. There was a water hole there, or so the map showed. The old man had been vague as to whether there would be water there. It didn't make any difference to the kid. He'd taken chances before and he would take them again, and to him revenge was almost sweeter than life itself.

———

THE SUN WAS low in the west and there wasn't a breath of wind. The whole world seemed waiting for that brass orb to travel west and bring the relief of darkness.

Case Hardesty was confused. They should have seen the mission dome by now. Dulce rode the worn-out mule with her head shrouded in her black shawl and her bare legs gripping its sweating barrel. Madeline trudged behind Case. Far behind them was Phillip Davis.

"You're lost," said Madeline quietly.

Case shook his head. "Stay here and rest. Let me go on ahead for a spell."

She eyed him. "You're worn thin," she said.

"Not thin enough to sit here and die like a sheep."

"No... you wouldn't."

"Let them have a mouthful of water. Help yourself too."

"And you?"

He grinned crookedly. "I'm part lizard and part Apache."

He slogged off up a rise of ground, followed by her eyes.

The ground seared through his thin boot soles. He thought of buying a fine pair of figured boots from old Bartolomeo, the leatherworker of Hermosillo. That and a new Stetson. A man wasn't a man without good boots and a fifty-dollar hat.

He glanced back as he reached the top of the rise. The women were crouched in the shade of the mule. Davis lay flat on his face. "Bastard," said Case. It made him feel better.

There was nothing beyond the rise but another identical rise. He squatted on the far side of the crest from the three-waiting people. He could feel the weight of his packed wallet against his chest. The whole thousand dollars couldn't buy him a bottle of Mex beer or a cup of gamy water.

He scanned the sterile ground between him and the next rise. There wasn't a trace of a trail, but there were plenty of scattered rocks. He eyed a curious rock formation and then stood up quickly, running down the slope to the formation.

Rocks had been carefully formed into a curious symbol. The top part of it was a cross based on what looked like a blunted arrowhead. He wiped the sweat from his face and looked in the direction in which the rock cross was pointed. Southwest. The arrowhead pointed in turn to the northeast.

"A grave?" he questioned himself.

Tule Tank was miles to the southwest, or so he reasoned.

He walked to the northeast and reached the top of the rise. The sun shone on the white dome of the mission four or five miles across a llano. "*Gracias a Diós!*" he said quietly.

He turned on a heel and walked back to his companions. Madeline approached him out of earshot of the other two. "Phil says he can't go on."

"Leave him then. I've found the water hole."

She swayed a little and he caught her by the arm. "I'm sorry," she said.

They walked back to the others. Case rolled the man over. "Get up," he said.

Phil shook his head.

"Get up!"

"No."

Case turned. "Go on ahead," he said to Madeline. "Cross the first rise. You'll see a rock formation on the sand. Beyond that is another rise. You'll see the mission dome from there."

Dulce climbed up on the mule. Madeline took the reins and led the mule toward the first rise.

"Get up, you bastard," said Case.

"Go to hell!"

Case pulled the tall man to his feet. "Listen," he said harshly. "There is water within five miles. Now move!"

Davis wiped the sand from his sweaty face. His eyes seemed suddenly to focus. "I've seen you looking at her," he said. Case stared at the man. "You loco? Dulce or Madeline?"

"Dulce."

Case threw back his head and laughed. "Dulce? That *puta?*"

Davis swung so suddenly he knocked Case to the ground. He raised a boot and drove it against Case's jaw. Case shook his head as the sky reeled. He was booted three more times before he gripped a leg and up-ended the tall man. Davis hit the ground with a grunting cry.

Case threw down his pack and rifle "Get up," he said thinly.

"No."

"Get up!"

He dragged Davis to his feet, set him, measured him and then hit home with a jolting, savage one-two, belly and jaw. Davis staggered back and raised his hands, but the lean man was on him with a hurricane of smashing, ripping blows which smashed him flat on the ground.

Davis clawed for his Colt but a boot instep ground down on his gun wrist and he released the six-gun. He got to his knees and butted Case in the belly. The wind went out of Case with a rush and he fell back. Davis rushed in driving wild erratic blows. Case covered up and retreated. Davis revealed his teeth in a wolfish grin as he hammered blow after blow.

Case felt a tooth crack. His mouth filled with blood. It spurted from his nose. Davis was like a man possessed, drawing on a hidden reserve of strength. Case was hurled to the ground. He tried to rise and was kicked alongside the jaw. He lay still.

Davis stepped back. "I'll finish you, you bastard."

But Phil Davis had never met a man of the Hardesty breed. The lean man was up on his feet with blood dripping from nose and mouth. Hard fists battered down Davis' weak guard and smashed at his face until blood blinded him. The knockout punch was so fast and hard he never knew what hit him.

Case wiped the blood from his face. He looked down at Davis. Leave him here to die and rot, he thought.

He looked toward the rise. The women were out of sight. A wraith of dust marked their slow passage.

Case rubbed his skinned knuckles against his filthy shirt. His breath was harsh and dry in his scored throat. Leave him.

Then he remembered the rock cross beyond the rise. It had saved them. Saved him, at least, when he really didn't deserve it.

He shrugged. He slung his rifle over his shoulder and lifted Phil Davis, resting him across his shoulders. The drama wasn't over yet. The third and final act had yet to be played.

Case Hardesty turned and walked slowly across the scorching ground bearing his heavy burden.

The women were waiting for him at the foot of the second rise. Dulce did not turn. She was looking at the distant dome of the mission, crossing herself and praying. Madeline looked at Case's battered face and then at her unconscious husband as Case dumped him to the ground. She knew.

Case had overdone himself and there was a great weakness in him. He should have let Phil Davis lie there to die, but he knew the woman would have gone back for him. Not Dulce, of course, but Madeline. She was beyond his reasoning.

Case lifted the man with the help of Madeline and placed him across the mule. He took the reins and led the mule to the northeast. Dulce stumbled along behind them, dropping farther and farther back, but she would make it. There was a toughness in the small woman which her lover certainly lacked.

Madeline walked beside Case. "He would have left you there," she said.

"I'm getting to be as big a fool as you are."

"Thanks," she said dryly.

"What are you running from?"

"I'm not running from anything."

"But they are."

"Yes."

"Tell me about it."

"No."

He gripped her by the arm. "Look, woman, I've got enough on my mind as it is without wondering what drove you three out here."

She jerked her head. "Dulce's sweetheart is following us."

"I thought you had furnished her with a sweetheart."

Her eyes cut him like a lash. "Damn you!"

"I'm sorry."

"You should be." She touched her burning face. "Dulce was my maid back in Nogales. Phil is a gambler and not too successful at that, but he thought he was. I was in love with him once. Oh, he can be nice ... when things are going well.

"We had a fine *casa* back there. Phil made enough money to keep us comfortable. Then one day he brought Dulce to the house. I didn't need her and certainly didn't want her, but she gave us a pitiful tale of running away from home in Nacozari or some place. I took her in and treated her like a sister. I suppose I was blind. She was all sweetness and light to my face, but behind my back she was making love to Phil. I don't know whether he loved her or not, but Phil is like a child, craving affection because he is weak, I suppose.

"But *she* isn't weak. She can assume the part, but there is a hard core in that woman."

The sun was almost gone but its light still glistened from the mission dome. Case eyed it. There was no smoke; no dust. There was a chance left to get water and strike out again to the south. It would have to be afoot again, and he wondered what he would do about Madeline.

Madeline stumbled and his hand was quick to help

her. She smiled tiredly. "You seem always there to help, Case. The Good Samaritan."

"I'm not always this way."

"Why are you helping us?"

He looked away. The touch of her had excited and pleased him. "You didn't finish your story."

"There's not much left. A young man appeared. A tough, willful young man, with good looks and money. That's all Dulce needs, good looks and money to turn her weathervane head, and I'm sure she can make do with an ugly man who is well-heeled."

"Figures."

"You sound bitter."

"I've been around ... too much, perhaps."

"Yes. Dulce played around with this young man. Phil didn't know it for a time. I was ready to leave him but I stayed because I didn't want trouble between the two men.

"The young man showered her with gifts and clothing. He fell in love with her. He asked her to marry him. I tried to tell him about her, but it was no use. She was torn between the two of them, but the choice was easy enough. The young man didn't have a wife to block his way. I think she was actually going to marry him when he went away to make more money.

"When he came back he found the two of them together. I stopped a murder right there. I had him arrested to cool him off. But his return had frightened them. Now it was all Phil with Dulce because she knew the young man would never forgive her, and Phil at least could get her out of town.

"The night they planned to leave the young man broke jail. I was afraid he would kill them so I helped them. We made it to Magdalena one jump ahead of him. I wanted Dulce to return to Nacozari but Phil would have none of it. He went on to Caborca, hoping to strike south to Hermosillo but we heard he had gone ahead thinking we would go that way.

"We turned back and reached the border. Dulce sweet-talked Phil into trying the Camino del Diablo. I knew nothing of it and Phil knew little more. We had to leave when we heard the young man had been seen within a few miles of where we were.

"You know the rest, Case."

In the silence that followed he glanced at her. "You think this man is still following you?"

"He won't give up. He means to kill them."

"And you?"

"He won't bother me."

"Why didn't you let him have them instead of risking your life to save them?"

"It isn't them, Case. It's him. I don't want him to commit a double murder. He has killed before, but killing a woman is different than killing a man, in the West at least."

"Who is this young man?"

"Some people call him simply the Kid. Some call him the Conchos Kid."

"Jesus," said Case without thinking. "I'm sorry."

"You know him then?"

"Enough to keep away from him. I saw him in Globe about a year ago. Even the hard-case miners left him alone. I can see now why you believe he will kill them."

She glanced back at the two of them. "As I said, it isn't them so much I'm worried about as it is him."

"Why? Let him hang."

"No," she said quietly. "You see, I left out one fact, Case."

"So?"

"The Conchos Kid happens to be my brother."

Case faltered in his stride. He stared at the calm woman at his side.

There was the faintest ghost of a smile on her sunburned face. "You see?" she asked.

He nodded. She had the character of a person who could use inherited strength and power to do good or evil and do a first-class job of it either way. She had gone the right way while her brother, and Case, had done just the reverse. Yet she was trying to save her brother from committing two more crimes.

The mule stumbled and then fell heavily. Phillip Davis grunted in pain as the heavy animal landed on his belly. He opened his eyes, beat futilely at the weight atop him and then mercifully fainted dead away.

Case got down on his knees and threw a shoulder against the sweat-slick hide of the beast. He strained and felt his power wane within him. Madeline got down beside him and they tried together. Dulce ran to the unconscious man and cradled his head in her arms.

"God dammit!" rasped Case. "Get down here and help! *Carajo!*"

The three of them finally managed to roll the dead mule off the body of Phil Davis. Case checked him. "Nothing broken," he said at last, but he knew the man had been injured internally. He looked at Madeline. "I'll have to carry him again."

"No, Case! You're worn out!"

"I can't leave him here."

Their eyes met like touching blades and then softened. "Yes," she said.

They helped him raise the man. It might not have helped him to lift him so, but there wasn't any other alternative. Case shifted his burden and nodded. "Let's go," he said.

They walked toward the mission in the gathering dusk. Somewhere off in the distance a coyote howled. The mountains seemed to move in on them.

Phillip Davis coughed and a moment later Case felt something warm run down his sweating back. He said nothing to the two weary women. He did not look up. He did not want to see how far the mission was from them, for the sight might make him lose what little strength he still had left. It would take a long time for him to get the unconscious man to the water hole, and that didn't mean anything. It would save the lives of Madeline, Dulce and Case, for a time at least, but Phillip Davis might join the unknown dead in their desolate graveyard behind the mission.

CHAPTER TEN

Antonio wriggled through the baking rocks with as little feeling as a desert spiny swift. He peered down into the place where the water hole should be and nodded in satisfaction. There was plenty of water for him and his *patrón*. His dark eyes surveyed the area. It was almost dusk. He had left his *patrón* a mile from the watering place, for Antonio was always suspicious in the desert. There was no telling who might be waiting at the water hole.

There were a few faint tracks in the sand at the far side of the open area beyond the *tinaja*. The mission building seemed to stare at him with blank eyes of narrow windows. He had scouted patiently all about the area but he would not go into the mission, nor near it. It had been said that there were *chisos* and *espectros* haunting the place. Nothing other than the desperate plight of his *patrón* would have forced Antonio near the place after daylight.

He lay flat on his lean belly. The place seemed deserted, but in the back of his mind there was a subtle warning. He was a child of the desert and knew its changing moods, its benefits and its perils. He had been born a heathen and converted to Christianity, but the old teachings and the old ways were still strong within him. It was not the way of his people to camp near water in dangerous country. That was the way of the White-Eyes.

He studied the mission and his skin crawled. The far mountains had at first glowed golden in the dying rays of the sun, then changed to rose-red while he had lain there. They were now a deep violet and in a little while, before the rising of the moon, there would be mysterious darkness peopled by the spirits of those who had died without benefit of the last rites.

He did not want to be alone there in the darkness. His *patrón* was blind, but he was strong, and he would stand between Antonio and the unknown.

The tracker worked his way down the slope. His throat was dry with their thirst but it had not occurred to him to drink ahead of his *patrón*.

He vanished into the darkness as silently as he had come.

Chip Gilbert got up from his meaty belly and let down the hammer of his rifle to half-cock. He had had the breed in his sights for ten minutes, an easy shot. He knew the man. It was Sheriff Dade Maslin's human bloodhound.

Chip looked to the north in the direction Antonio had gone. How many possemen were out there?

The big man walked downstairs into the dark, echoing nave. He whistled softly.

Leonardo came out of the sacristy where he had stayed with the horses, quieting them, holding their windpipes to prevent them from nickering as the tracker had prowled silently through the darkness. "He is gone?"

"Yeh."

"What shall we do?"

Chip spat. "Sit tight."

"*Porque?*"

"For why? I'll tell you why. If Maslin and his men are

out there they'll be along here in a short time. They need water and we got the water. *Comprende?*"

Leonardo digested this. "But he has many men. They will root us out of here."

"Bull crap. By the time they get here the moon should be up. We can hold them off as long as we like. I can sit in that bell tower and hold off a company of cavalry."

"Then what happens?"

"Easy." Chip grinned. "We run Maslin off. By the time we pull out of here and head for Sonora, they won't be in any shape to chase us. *Comprende?*"

Leonardo's dark face broke into a hesitant smile. "*Yo comprendo!*"

"The canteens are full?"

"*Sí.*"

Chip rolled a smoke and handed it to the Mexican. He fashioned one himself and then scratched a lucifer against a niche which had been one of the stations of the Cross, sending a chill over Leonardo. He lit Leonardo's cigarette and then held the match to the tip of his smoke. The flickering light depicted his broad face in an unholy glow. "Here's the play: We sit tight. I'll get up into the tower. You stay with the horses. When I make my pitch, you leave the horses and circle around to get behind them. You come up the passageway and we'll have them between two fires."

The Mexican nodded. It was clear enough. Chip would be safe in the tower with easy access to the horses while he himself would be in the open afoot with perhaps half a dozen Yanqui gunslingers to handle if the going got too rough.

Chip sucked at his cigarette. "We don't want Hardesty to get too good a lead on us, but I'll be damned if I want Maslin and his boys breathing down our necks."

"*Sí.* It is a good plan."

Chip nodded. "And you and Floyd thought Hardesty was the brains of us four. Now look at us. Floyd dead; me and you in a good position to find Hardesty and get dinero and then jump up the dust for Mexico."

"Yes . . . Mexico."

"You sound like you don't think this is a good play."

"I wonder if I'll ever see Mexico again."

"You can leave now if you feel that way, *amigo*."

The Mexican shook his head. He did not like this business of using the old church as a post of ambush and as a stable. No good would come of it.

"Get moving, then."

Leonardo vanished into the darkness, but Chip could see the glow of his cigarette as he turned in the sanctuary for a moment as though to look at Chip and then he was gone. Chip took a canteen and walked up into the bell tower, carefully shielding his cigarette glow in his big hand.

———

"IT IS ME, *PATRÓN*."

The soft voice came through the darkness which held Dade Maslin in helpless bondage. "*Gracias a Diós*." said Dade.

"There is no one there."

"Water?"

"Enough."

"*Bueno.*"

Antonio led the big sorrel to the south. He would have to tell his *patrón* that he would see that he was safe there and then he must backtrack to find Linus Heaney. There was nothing else he could do.

Antonio raised his head as he saw the moon touch the east side of the dome with a magic brash of silver. It looked unreal as though the whole thing was a dream brought on by eating peyote. He stopped and looked at the rock formation.

"*Ándale!*" said Dade.

Antonio never carried a gun, only his knife. He was not a man who depended on a gun and he had never been able to master the art of marksmanship. Besides, the guns were too noisy, scaring the game whether it be man or animal. He was a past master in the use of the knife and bow and could use the sling well. It was all he needed.

"*Ándale!*"

Antonio turned and looked up into the face of his *patrón*. "A gun, *patrón*."

"Why? You said no one was there."

"They may have come there since I left."

Dade hesitated. The tracker was more dangerous to himself and his friends with a gun than he would be to his enemies. Finally he drew his Winchester from its sheath and held it out. Antonio took it and without another word he led the sorrel on.

He stopped at the west end of the rock passage to smell the air. There was a faint aura of something there. Not the gamy water and the heated rock; not the pungent odor of mesquite, but something vague and indefinable which bothered him.

The tracker shrugged and then led the sorrel through the dark passageway until they stood there before the pool in the faint light of the rising moon. Antonio helped the sheriff to the ground. He led him to the water and carefully pushed aside the floating algae. "Kneel *patrón*," he said quietly.

There was a movement in the bell tower and the tracker's head went up like a startled rabbit. He heard the unmistakable sound of the lever of a repeater being worked.

"Stand where you are!" the harsh voice called down. Antonio darted to one side and raised the rifle. He pulled the trigger and was rewarded with a dull click. At the same time something hard rammed up between his shoulder blades. He dropped the rifle and raised his hands. He had forgotten to load the accursed rifle.

Dade Maslin slowly raised his hands.

Chip stood up holding his rifle and grinning like a baboon. "Yeh, Maslin!" he called. "Walk right into it like a blind man, eh?"

Maslin felt the cold sweat work down his heated sides. The voice was unmistakable. It was Chip Gilbert, a man he had sworn to catch and bring back to justice, and the big outlaw held the winning hand. All Dade had was the black ace.

Leonardo stood behind the tracker. Suddenly he raised his rifle and smashed it down on the head of the tracker, felling him.

Maslin stood there with his eyes wide open, seeing nothing but Stygian darkness.

"Cover him, *amigo!*" called down Chip.

Maslin felt the rifle muzzle nuzzle his kidneys.

In a little while he heard the grating of boots on the hard ground and then he could smell the sour, sweaty odor of the big man. Tobacco smoke crept into Dade's nostrils. Chip was close. Maslin turned, gripping the rifle muzzle in one big hand and forcing it upward while his right fist caught the Mexican flush on the jaw, hurtling him back against the rocks. Maslin swung the rifle toward where he thought Chip Gilbert stood. "Don't move," he said quietly.

There was no sound from the big outlaw.

Maslin moved his head from side to side, hoping he was looking right at the man.

It was as quiet as the tomb.

Then Chip spoke. "I can kill you before you pull the trigger."

"You always did talk up a storm and flood a spit," said Maslin.

There was a movement behind Dade. He moved to one side. "Don't move, Mex," he said.

Chip stared at the sheriff.

The noise came again.

Maslin swung the rifle barrel. "Get over with your amigo," he said.

Chip Gilbert's head tilted forward and he moved closer to the sheriff. Suddenly he darted in, gripped the rifle and tore it from the sheriff's grip. Gilbert laughed. "You law bastard," he said. "You can't see a damned thing."

Maslin dropped his hands. "How did you know?"

Gilbert laughed again. "It was your breed boy who moved," he said.

Antonio raised his head and felt for his knife, but Chip Gilbert moved swiftly for one of his bulk. His right boot heel struck the tracker behind the ear, dropping him cold.

Gilbert leaned his rifle against a rock. He reached for Maslin's six-shooter and quickly drew it out. He threw it on the sand and then dragged Leonardo to the tinaja, slopping water on the unconscious Mexican. Leonardo groaned. He opened his eyes. "Have mercy," he said huskily.

"Get up, you bastard," said Chip. "Cover the tracker and don't let him flatten you like the sheriff done."

Leonardo took the rifle. He stared at Maslin. Chip nodded. "Blind as a bat." Chip unbuckled his gun belt and dropped it to the ground. He spat on his palms and balled big murderous fists. "Jesus God," he breathed. "What a setup."

Chip hoisted his filthy trousers and padded forward on the balls of his feet. "Put 'em up, Maslin," he said.

"I'm sun-blind, Gilbert," said the sheriff quietly.

"No? Hawww ..."

Chip hit Maslin in the guts with a left and caught the down-coming chin with a crushing right uppercut which snapped Maslin's head back up again. He staggered back with outflung arms and was hit three times with blows that would have grounded an ordinary man. He hit the rocks and grunted as he felt a point drive against his kidneys. He stood up and raised his fists with blood dripping in a dark spate from nose and mouth.

Chip danced about in the moonlight, shadow boxing, throwing vicious punches, rights and lefts, inches from the battered face of the law man. "Enough," said Leonardo.

Chip spat. "Shut up," he said. "You know where I learned to spar, *amigo?*"

"No."

"In the prison at Yuma five years ago. A man sent me there to rot. You know who he was?"

"No."

"Him!" Chip punctured the word with a right hook which carried all the weight of his heavy body behind it. Maslin went back and hit the ground. There was no outcry from him. He knew the big man would beat him to death, but he'd never get a plea for mercy from Dade Maslin.

Maslin got the boot a half a dozen times. He passed out and was thrown into the shallow water of the tinaja, dragged out and slapped about for a good three minutes with blood and water dripping from him and spattering the rocks and the sadistic outlaw.

Leonardo looked away. There was a cruel, bloodthirsty streak in him too, but nothing like this. The big man was *muy loco*.

Maslin went down and Chip stood over him, snarling, "Get up, you tin-starred bastard, and fight like a man."

"Enough ... enough. ..." said Leonardo. *"Diós en cielo, amigo!"*

In the silence that followed, the wind shifted to the south and a wailing cry came to them faintly on the breeze.

Leonardo shivered. Chip Gilbert buckled on his gun belt and gripped his rifle. He darted up into the bell tower. A moment later he hurried down. "Christ," he said. "Talk about luck! They's four people heading this way from the south. Two wimmen and two men and one of the men is carrying the other."

"So?"

Chip grinned. "The man doing the carrying is none other than our old companero, Case Hardesty. Drag that breed into the mission!" Chip lifted the unconscious, bloody sheriff up onto the sorrel and led the horse into the mission. He let Leonardo lead the sorrel into the sacristy and then he hurried outside to erase all traces of humans being there.

There was a lopsided grin on his broad face as he looked about and then ran back into the mission. This was more than he had ever hoped for. Dade Maslin, Case Hardesty, twenty thousand dollars and two women. Most of all he wanted Case Hardesty. What the sheriff got would be nothing compared to what he would do to Hardesty, and he'd let the lean outlaw meet him man to man. He wet his thick lips and seemed to shiver all over in anticipation.

CHAPTER ELEVEN

It was Dulce who was bemoaning her fate. There were times when she prayed loudly, then she would lapse into silence only to break out into a stream of invective. It was annoying to Case Hardesty, but there was nothing he could do to shut her up. She seemed to have forgotten everything but her own discomfort, but she did not go ahead of Case and Madeline to reach the water. As much as she hated them, she needed their presence to bolster her weakening courage.

"Can you make it?" asked Madeline of Case.

He grunted. His throat and mouth were so dry he could not make an articulate sound. Phillip Davis moved a little now and then, and when he coughed Case could feel the blood seep through the back of his shirt. The injured man would never leave the water hole alive without medical care.

Dulce passed them, staggering a little in her haste. She did not look at them but only at the dome of the mission where the cross stood out against the sky. She vanished around a point of rocks.

"Faithful to the end," said Case at last

"She's weak, Case."

"In a way."

There was no further sound but the husking noise of their feet on the hard earth and the steady breathing of Case as he labored on. He knew Madeline was getting in a bad way because of thirst but she walked along beside him, helping him over the bad spots and leading him through the tangled growths, giving him a strong moral support which kept him going on.

He glanced up to see the eroded wall of the building just ahead of him. His sweat almost blinded him and he thought of nothing but getting Davis to the water. Still, there seemed to be a subtle warning emanating from the place; something alien and dangerous, but he shrugged off the thought. They had to have water. There was one place to get it. Whatever happened after that would be taken care of in turn.

Dulce lay on her belly sucking noisily at the gamy water, oblivious of anything else. She rolled over to look at the others, wiping her open mouth with the end of her shawl, and then suddenly she vomited violently, spewing forth the water she had just taken in.

Case lowered the man to the ground with the help of Madeline. "Take only a little," he said.

"And him?"

Case wiped his face. "Wait a bit. Bathe his face and wring out a little water from a cloth into his mouth."

"How bad is he?"

Case turned and touched the back of his shirt. "Look," he said quietly.

"Good heavens."

Case sipped a little water and then turned to look at Davis. The man opened his eyes. "Water," he said.

Case nodded to Madeline. She took a handkerchief and wet it, wringing it out, then wetting it again to bathe the dirty face of her husband. He opened his mouth and she squeezed the cloth to let a few drops trickle into it. "More," he husked.

"No."

"Damn you!"

She sat down beside him and bathed his face. Dulce felt in her bodice and drew out a pack of sweet Mexican cigarettes, lighting one, watching Davis impassively.

Madeline looked about "How far to the next water hole, Case?"

"Which way?"

"North."

He shrugged. "Thirty or forty miles."

"And west?"

"Tule Tank, I think."

"How far?"

"About the same, or maybe a little closer. Beyond that is Tinajas Alias. There's always water there but it's too far for us."

"What do we do?"

He drank a little more water. "We might just sit here for a time. Someone will come."

She looked about at the surrounding rocks and the old mission. "Friends or enemies?"

He grinned crookedly. "No friends of mine."

"Can you go for help?"

He inspected the thin soles of his worn boots. "Yes...."

She eyed him. "But you won't."

"I didn't say that."

"Who are you running from, Case?"

He stood up and peeled off his shirt and undershirt. He threw them to one side.

"Case?"

He looked down at her. "It doesn't matter."

"But you don't want to go back?"

"No."

"You can make it to the border."

"I know."

"Then you'd better leave us here."

He did not answer. Conflicting thoughts clashed in

his tired brain. The man would die alone there if he took the woman with him. Dulce would be saved by Maslin if the big sheriff got there. If Chip Gilbert and Leonardo got there first, the story would be different. They would use her and then kill her. The dead do not talk.

It was Madeline who bothered him. He was tough. Pity had been burned out of him long ago. Better to leave her there and trust that Maslin would find her. But if his two past partners got there first....

"I can't leave him here," she said at last.

She could almost read his innermost thoughts.

Case exercised his arms and shoulders, trying to loosen them up. "The Kid will be along, I imagine," he said.

Dulce stood up and walked to the shelter of a big rock. She huddled there with her shawl over her dark hair. She was crazy scared.

Madeline stood up. "I won't let him kill Phil, Case."

"From what I've heard of him, I think otherwise."

Case suddenly looked at the mission. His alertness was returning. He walked toward his rifle.

"Stay where you are, Hardesty," the voice said from the shadows inside the mission door.

Case turned slowly as Chip Gilbert came from the mission with his rifle in his big hands. There was a movement atop the rocks to the south of the water hole. Leonardo Janos stood there with his rifle held at his shoulder as he squinted down the sights.

Gilbert paused twenty feet from Case. Chip held the aces but he wouldn't take chances with Case. He knew him too well. "All trails lead to water in the desert," said Chip.

Leonardo scrambled down the rocks. He eyed Dulce in appreciation. He came up behind Case.

Chip grounded his rifle. "Where's the *dinero?*"

"*Quién sabe?* said Case. His Colt was at his side, but

Leonardo would have a .44 in his back before he could draw and fire.

Chip's small eyes wandered from Davis to Dulce and then to Madeline. He whistled softly. "Nice," he said.

The moon was up high and Case could see every line of the big outlaw's broad face. There was no pity there. He would take what he wanted from them and, knowing his tastes, Case could foresee violence, lust and death.

"Where's the *dinero*, Hardesty?" asked Chip in a low voice.

"Lost."

"You lie!"

Case shrugged. He cursed himself for a fool. He should have known Chip Gilbert would have followed him there. There was no other place the man could have gone. Leonardo knew that country. He would have led Chip to the water hole.

Chip rubbed his bristly jaw. "Where'd you pick up the wimmen?"

"South."

"Making for the border, eh?"

"You figured it, Chip."

"We would'a caught you anyways."

"Maybe."

Chip jerked his head. "Get away from the water."

Case walked toward Chip. Leonardo was close behind Case. Suddenly Chip swung a big arm and hit Case on the jaw, knocking him flat. Case lay on the ground and felt the blood flow inside his mouth.

Chip spat. "Now, where is the *dinero?*"

"Lost."

The boot heel struck Case on the chest, driving him flat again. Chip grinned. "I got the aces," he said. "There are ways of making you talk. No water. A helluva beating. A little knife work by Leonardo. You see?"

Madeline looked toward Case's rifle but she knew she would never get her hands on it.

Chip squatted beside Case. "You sure are a bullhead." He jerked his head at Leonardo. "Look through his shirt."

Leonardo took out the wallet, packed with the thousand dollars. He counted it eagerly and his dark face grew darker. "Just a thousand, amigo."

Chip nodded. He eyed Madeline and Duke. "Mebbe they got it."

"No," said Case.

Chip rubbed his jaw again. "We kin strip 'em," he said with a loose grin. "Save time both ways."

Case wanted to attack the big man but he knew he'd never get away with it. "I cached the *dinero* out in the desert, Chip."

"Yeh? How far?"

"Ten miles, maybe."

"Yeh ... maybe..."

Chip stood up. "I know you, you hard-headed bastard," he said. "I could beat you half to death and you wouldn't talk." His eyes wandered to Madeline. "Now I figure you came back here to help them. Right?" He eyed the woman's full figure. "You always had a soft spot for horses, dogs, and wimmen."

Leonardo wet his lips. This would be something to see. Chip walked to Madeline and gripped her by the arm. Her hand caught him full across the mouth but before she knew what had happened he had forced her to her knees and ripped her dress from her shoulders. The moon shone on her smooth white flesh. "Jees," said Chip.

There was no fear on her face. He pulled her to her feet and dragged down the dress exposing her full breasts. "Some *chichonas*," he said with a leer.

Case got to his feet "All right," he said quietly, "you win."

Chip walked away from the woman. She pulled up her ragged dress to cover herself.

Case wiped the blood from his mouth. "Maslin will be along soon, Chip," he said.

"Yeh."

"You know he never gives up."

"Yep."

There was something about the big man which made Case suspicious.

Chip waved a hand to Leonardo. "Escort the two ladies into the mission, *amigo*," he said. "It ain't polite not to let our guests meet each other."

Chip withdrew Case's Colt from its holster and shoved Case toward the mission.

They walked through the echoing nave. The odor of horses came to Case. They passed through the sanctuary into the sacristy. Chip leaned against the wall. "Hardesty, meet Maslin and his breed tracker."

Case looked at Dade Maslin. The sheriffs face was a nasty battered mess. His hands had been tied behind him. Antonio lay to one side and he had been lashed to a timber balk which was against the wall. Maslin opened his eyes.

Chip kicked the sheriff. "Blind as a bat," he said cheerfully.

Leonardo lit the fire. The flickering light filled the room and made grotesque shadows on the peeling walls.

Chip beckoned to the two women. There were two rickety chairs near the steps which led up to the pulpit. They sat down. Chip squatted in a corner with his six-shooter in his hand and Case's Colt thrust through his wide belt. "Now we're all here," he said. He rapped against the wall with the muzzle of his Colt. "Meeting will come to order. I got the floor."

Case studied his old riding partner. There had always been a streak of cruel madness in Chip Gilbert.

Chip grinned. "Now we got six prisoners, Brother Leonardo. We got enough horse flesh to get us to Sonora and Brother Case here will give us the dinero. We got two fine fillies there on them chairs. Too bad we ain't got some likker.

"Maslin was looking for us; we was looking for old Case here; Case was looking for a hole to hide in. Now, we're safe from Maslin and we got Case."

A branch snapped in the fire. Maslin wet his bruised lips. "You won't get far," he said.

"No? Hawww!"

Chip leaned forward and the firelight showed all the cruel viciousness of the man. "We take the dinero and the wimmen. We take care of you, Maslin, and the breed. From the looks of that hombre out there he won't live long."

He had not mentioned Case.

Chip eyed Case. "That leaves you, Hardesty. I always had a hankering to kill a man with my bare hands. Anyways, a bastard like you who double-crosses his old amigos."

"What about you putting Floyd Hanks up to trying to kill me?"

Chip waved the gun. "I wanted to get rid of both of you. I figured one of you would get it back there. Didn't make no difference to me."

Leonardo's dark eyes flicked toward Chip. He would be next. Leonardo didn't give a damn for the others. With all that money he could buy and sell all the women he wanted in Mexico.

Chip nodded in satisfaction. "Yep, Old Chip has the aces." He looked up quickly. "Where's the dinero, Hardesty?"

"I'll show you on one condition."

"Yeh? What?"

"Leave the women alone."

"Sure, Case, sure. I was only joshing."

Like hell, thought Case.

Chip stood up. "Come on," he said.

Case led the way outside. He pointed toward the low, mounded graves, "In there," he said.

"Which one?"

Case looked puzzled. "Damned if I know."

The big man's face underwent a change. "You better remember."

Case walked to the nearest grave. "Maybe this one."

Case picked up a piece of board and began to dig at the mound. He was waiting for a chance to get at Chip, but Chip wouldn't have much patience and Case knew the moment Chip saw the money he'd put a slug into Case's back. The big outlaw stood well back from Case and his six-gun was raised and ready. Case was down about a foot into the hole when he saw Leonardo come out of the sacristy and stand there against the wall of the building watching them.

"Get inside and take care of them wimmen!" said Chip.

"I tied them. I stay here."

"You don't trust me?"

"Maybe ... maybe not."

"Wrong grave," said Case.

The two outlaws eyed each other. Case leaned on the piece of board. If he could get close enough to Chip he'd break the board over his thick skull.

Chip turned. His eyes seemed to glitter in the moonlight. "Which grave?" he asked.

Case wiped the sweat from his face. "I'm not sure."

The hammer of the Colt snicked back. "So?"

"Do not kill him, amigo!" called out Leonardo. "Wait!"

"Come here," said Chip to Leonardo.

The Mexican trotted over to them.

"Get out your knife."

Leonardo shifted his rifle to his left hand and drew out his *cuchillo*.

Chip grinned, revealing his stained yellow teeth.

"Now, amigo," he said to Case, "I'll give you ten seconds to find the right grave or Leonardo here will carve you. You'll live, of course, because he's an expert with the blade."

Case looked up at them from the hole. They weren't bluffing. They meant it. He'd live too, as long as they wanted him to.

"One," said Chip. "Two. Three. Four. Five."

Case could see the white face of Madeline looking at him from the window of the sacristy.

"Six. Seven. Eight."

It was no use. He had to do it.

"Nine."

"Ten!" said a cool voice from the eastern entrance into the circle of rocks.

They looked up. A smiling young man stood there with his arms folded across his chest. The moonlight glistened on the silver conchos he wore on his hatband and on his wide leather gun belt. It shone too on the ivory-plated butt of the six-gun hanging low and tied down on his right thigh.

Chip Gilbert's jaw dropped. Leonardo cursed beneath his breath.

"Don't move," said the young man.

Case glanced at the sacristy window from the corner of his eye. Madeline was gone. As far as Case knew, Phil Davis still lay helpless beside the water hole. The newcomer was the Conchos Kid, all right.

CHAPTER TWELVE

The Kid whistled shrilly and a big bay walked up beside him, nuzzling his shoulder. The two of them came forward, and the young man's head turned constantly from side to side as he watched the three silent men beside the grave and the moonlit mission with its dark empty windows and doors.

He stopped at last fifteen feet from the three men and glanced down at the grave. "Burial?" he asked quietly.

"No," said Case.

"Grave robbers, then?" There was the faintest ghost of a smile on the man's face.

Chip Gilbert spat. "Who are you? What do you want?" he demanded truculently.

"I'm looking for two women and a man," said the Kid. *"Who are you?"*

"The name is Steve Wallace. Most people call me the Kid."

Chip raised his head. "The Conchos Kid."

"Yes."

Leonardo wet his lips. The stranger was as well known in Sonora as he was in Arizona. It was said that he had ridden with Lopez when he was only eighteen years old. If that was true, then he was indeed *muy hombre*, for Lopez and his men, both gringos and Mexicans, were the toughest *corrida* west of the Rio Conchos in Chihuahua.

Wallace eyed the mission. "Where are they?" he asked.

Leonardo wanted no part of this soft-spoken smiling gringo. "Inside," he said.

"Go get them."

"Wait a minute!" said Chip. "I'm running this show."

"Maybe. You go about your business. I have mine to take care of."

"Such as?"

The Kid slid a hand down alongside his holstered six-gun. "Phil Davis is going to face me."

Case got out of the hole. "The man is badly injured, Kid."

"So?"

"He might die."

The smooth face darkened a little. "He will, but not naturally."

There was a movement just within the rear door of the mission and the Kid turned a little, crouched, and his Colt seemed to leap into his hand. "Come out!" he said.

Madeline Davis appeared in the doorway. "Phil is badly hurt, Steve."

"And Dulce?"

"She's inside." Madeline rubbed her wrists. "I got loose and untied her too."

The cold eyes swiveled to look at the three men. "Who tied you, Sis?"

Leonardo swallowed. His eyes stared at the leveled six-gun. "Wait," he said quickly. "I tied them. It was Chip who told me to... I swear it."

"Chip?"

"Me," said Gilbert. "No offense, Kid."

Steve Wallace looked at Case. "I've seen you before."

"Yes, in Globe, about a year ago. I'm Case Hardesty."

"I've heard of you." Wallace sheathed his gun. "Who else is in that building?"

"Sheriff Dade Maslin and his breed tracker," said Case.

The Kid's head jerked. He reached for his sheathed Winchester.

Chip grinned. "He won't bother you, Kid. I got him and his boy tied up tighter than calf for the castrating."

"What's the game here?"

Chip waved a big hand. "Me and some of the boys did a job at Cottonwood Station. Case here double-crossed us, killed one of my men and run out here."

"How much loot?"

Leonardo glanced at Chip. The big man was trying to run the show and the Kid had thrown a crowbar into the machinery. Now Chip Gilbert's slow-working brain would have to figure a way out of this mess. Leonardo knew Chip would have killed the Kid if he had had the chance, but not in a showdown draw between them. Even Hardesty would have his troubles trying to outdraw and outshoot the Kid.

"How much loot?" asked the Kid again.

"Twenty thousand."

The young outlaw felt for the makings and rolled a smoke. "Where is it?"

Chip jerked a thumb at Case. "He cached it. We was looking for it when you come up on us. Help us find it, Kid, and me and the Mex will ring you in on the deal."

"How much?"

"Three ways all right?"

"Hell yes!"

Wallace lighted his cigarette. He walked toward Madeline. There was no show of affection between them. She had strained their relationship too far. "Well?" he asked.

She looked up into his set face. "You can't kill Phil,

Steve. Dulce is nothing but a little fool who plays the field. It isn't worth it to kill her."

"She played in the wrong field this time."

"But she isn't worth it, Steve! Take me away from here."

"Who brought you here?"

"Case Hardesty."

The Kid turned to look at the three watching men. "He sure stuck his neck out. Once they get their hands on that money they'll kill him."

"He didn't have to come back. He would have been safe from them if he had kept on alone."

"Why did he do it?"

She looked back over her shoulder. "It wasn't because of them, Steve. It was because of me."

He seemed to soften a little. "Why didn't you let Phil and Dulce run away together? I would have found them."

"For more killing?"

"No man was ever killed by me unless it was a fair fight."

She shook her head. "How many men have a fair chance with you, Steve?"

"A man's got no business packing a gun if he doesn't know how to use it, and expect to use it"

"Some day your turn will come."

He smiled thinly. "Maybe."

"Men talk of you in the same class with Hardin, Billy the Kid and others. Someone always wants to try you top guns and there will be a day when they get you, Steve."

He laughed and then turned to look at the others. "Find that dinero, Hardesty. Pronto!"

Case shrugged. He turned back to the grave and kicked the loose dirt aside. He took the sack from the hole and tossed it at Chip's feet. "Pick it up and hand it to me like a little gentleman," jeered the big man.

Case picked it up and handed it to Chip. Chip swung a big fist and knocked Case down. He raised a foot to boot Case but the action was cut short by the Kid. "Enough!" he snapped coldly.

Chip turned. "We got it," he said.

"Bring it here."

"Just a minute!"

"Bring it here, hombre."

"Yep," said Case dryly as he felt his bruised jaw.

Chip muttered under his breath as he walked toward the young outlaw. "I'm running this show, Kid," he said sourly.

"So? Then why are you bringing the dinero to me?"

"I made a deal."

"Yeh. . . ."

Case watched the two of them. The Kid had dealt himself into the game, which would save Madeline sure enough, but it left Case in the same situation he had been in before the arrival of her brother. Chip Gilbert meant to kill Case, there wasn't any doubt about that happening, and he'd kill the Conchos Kid too if he could get away with it. Not in a stand-up gun fight but in the dirtiest way he could. The thing that made Case wonder was what the Kid was thinking.

The Kid hefted the bag. "Nice," he said. "What's the catch?"

Chip held out his big hands, palms upward. "There ain't any."

"There's a posse out somewhere, isn't there?"

Chip shrugged. "Maslin came on alone. *Muy hombre*, or at least he thinks he is. Take a look at what I done to him."

"I'll do just that. You first."

Chip walked inside and threw more wood on the fire.

Leonardo waved his rifle at Case, and Case walked to the mission to follow Madeline inside. Dulce had vanished.

The Kid looked at the smashed face of the sheriff.

"Jesus," he said quietly. He looked at Chip. "You did that to him and didn't get anything back?"

Case leaned against the wall. "Chip forgot to tell you that Maslin was sun-blind when Chip worked him over."

The young man turned slowly and taut lines formed themselves at the corners of his mouth. "You dirty. ..." he said softly.

Leonardo had his rifle at waist level and the muzzle swung gently back and forth covering both Case and the Kid. Chip's hard eyes studied the young gunslinger. Case watched for any telltale warning of what Steve Wallace would do and he was prepared to take advantage of it. But the Kid idly swung the sack back and forth. He was smart enough not to make any breaks, and he was smart enough to know too that Chip and his amigo weren't quite ready to get rid of him.

"Well," said Chip.

"It's your business."

"No," said Maslin clearly. "It's mine."

Chip laughed. "Listen to him," he jeered.

Case studied the sheriff. The man was bullheaded. There was no need to rile Chip any further.

Antonio, the tracker, lay quietly, but his eyes were steel hard as he looked at Chip. He would never forget what the big man had done, and God help Chip Gilbert if Antonio got him in his power. There were ways he could draw out the outlaw's last hours. The ways of the desert people. Staked out naked on an ant heap with honey smeared in a path to his mouth and eyes. Wrapped in a green hide and left to lie under the blazing sun. There were many ways....

"Where's Davis?" asked the Kid.

"Outside," said Chip.

"Let him alone, Steve," said Madeline.

The Kid did not answer. He walked into the sanctuary and stalked through it to the nave and thence to the great front door. "Gone," he said. His voice echoed and died away in the vast empty building.

It was instinctive for him to move quickly to one side and draw out his Colt He thumbed back the hammer and stood there studying the moonlit area with slitted eyes, waiting for a sound or a movement which would trigger swift and deadly action.

Chip walked into the sanctuary, glanced quickly back at Madeline and Case, and then stepped behind a wall pillar. The Kid still had the money sack in his left hand and he was a dim figure near the front door. Chip hoped to God Davis would kill or wound him.

The Kid came back a ways and then darted to the south side of the nave, close to the baptistry door. Then he was gone.

"Where is he?" called out Leonardo to Chip.

"Shut up! Davis ain't out there."

There was a movement in one of the deep niches along the south side of the nave. Chip drew his Colt and fired. The hard echo slammed back and forth between the walls. A woman screamed.

"Jesus!" said Chip. "It was the Mex filly!"

Dulce stepped out into the nave. "Before God, *señor*!" she cried out.

"You hit?" he said in a tense voice.

"No."

"Then git back here, dammit! Don't never do something stupid like that again!"

She scurried toward the sanctuary. "I was afraid of him."

"So is Chip," said Case dryly.

Chip whirled and thumbed back his Colt hammer. "You open that big mouth once more and I'll stop it up with a slug."

The stinking powder smoke drifted through the nave and flowed toward the front door.

Chip's breathing was harsh in the deadly quiet.

"Go get him," said Case.

"You think I'm afraid?"

"You? *Not* Chip Gilbert."

Still the deathly quiet. Chip moved a foot and it grated on fallen plaster.

There was the muffled crack of a six-gun somewhere up in the area of the bell tower. Chip hit the floor and thrust his Colt forward. He fired blindly and then rolled behind a pile of fallen masonry.

The smoke drifted aimlessly about and then moved slowly toward the front door.

There was a soft movement behind Case and he turned to see the Kid standing there. The Kid looked down at Chip. "Looking for something?" he asked quietly.

Chip stood up. There was a vacuous grin on his broad face. "Jesus, Kid," he said, "I thought he got you."

"Yeh?"

Chip holstered his Colt.

The Kid leaned against the wall and began to roll a smoke. His hard gray eyes studied Chip over the flare of the lucifer. "He's holed up in the tower," he said quietly.

"He won't go far," said Chip.

"No. Who were you shooting at?"

"The Mex girl."

The Kid took the cigarette from his lips and turned slowly. He saw her crouching beside the breed tracker. Her body shook in a spasm.

The Kid turned to look at Chip again. "And the second shot?"

"I got excited when I heard your shot."

Madeline came close to her brother. "Steve! You didn't...?"

He shook his head. "It was him, shooting at me."

Chip wet his lips and looked toward the tower. "I'll help you root him out of there."

"No."

"Why not? We're partners now, ain't we?"

"I wouldn't trust you in the dark, hombre. Besides, he won't go anywhere unless he jumps. There's a gateway in the staircase. I wedged it shut He'll be there when I go for him."

"What do we do now?" asked Chip.

The Kid sucked at his cigarette and the soft glow lit up the sharp planes of his face. "I'm taking my sister out of here when I take care of Davis."

"We'll split the *dinero* now, then."

The Kid shook his head.

"What the hell do you mean?"

"Just this: You'll always be waiting to get me, hombre, that is, as long as I have the dinero on me."

"That ain't so!"

"You're a liar."

Chip raised his huge hands and then dropped them helplessly.

Case eyed the soft-spoken gunslinger. The Kid had Chip buffaloed, and Case wondered just how much of it was sheer bluff.

"Where's the dinero?" asked Chip quietly.

The Kid glanced at Case. "I took a leaf out of his book. I cached the loot. Now, as long as you don't know where it is, hombre, you're going to stop waiting for a chance to put a slug into my back."

The wind whispered through the nave. It seemed to speak with the voices of the long dead who had once built, lived and worshiped in the place. Voices of warning.

CHAPTER THIRTEEN

ase Hardesty lay on the filthy floor of the
sacristy and worked steadily on the bonds
which lashed his wrists together. It had been
Chip's idea to tie him, and the Kid hadn't argued with
the big outlaw. Chip was sprawled asleep in the sanctuary
while Leonardo sat in a chair with a rifle across his thighs
watching Case, Maslin and Antonio. Dulce had crawled
into a hole somewhere, away from the cold eyes of the
Kid. Madeline was asleep, or at least she was pretending
to be asleep while the Kid sat in a chair tilted back
against the wall, smoking steadily, looking into the dying
embers of the fire.

Suddenly the Kid got up and walked outside. His
boots grated on the hard ground and then the noise died
away. Leonardo shifted a little in his chair.

"The Kid sure outfoxed your new boss," said Case in
Spanish.

"Shut up!" snapped the Mexican. "He is not my boss!"

"No? You know what will happen to you when he gets
his hands on that *dinero*."

The dark eyes flicked toward the sanctuary. "I am a
man," said Leonardo.

"Yeh. But you should have known better than to come here and desecrate this place."

"We have done nothing!"

"No," said Case dryly, "nothing but bring horses in here. Defiling the sanctuary. Beating up helpless men. Thinking evilly of women. Don't you think those things are desecrations?"

"This is no longer a holy place. It is nothing but an empty building. There are many such in my country. They are nothing ... nothing."

Case squirmed up so that he could rest his back against the wall. "You really think so?"

"Yes."

Case shook his head. "That's not what I know."

Leonardo rolled a smoke and lighted it. "What do you mean, *hombre?*"

"Forget it."

'Tell me!"

"Make me a quirly first."

The Mexican rolled a cigarette and placed it between Case's lips. He lighted it. "Go on."

Case eased his back and sucked in on the cigarette. "I heard the bell," he said.

"When?"

"When I was here alone."

"The wind ... no more."

"There wasn't any wind, amigo."

The night wind moaned softly through the nave. Leonardo shifted a little. He wet his lips.

Case nodded. "I was up in that tower. One of your countrymen had written something there."

"So?"

"There is nothing but death here, it said."

"Bazofía!"

"It is *not* garbage. You saw the many graves. The last resting places of the old padres, the converts, the travelers who reached here only to die."

Case knew that Leonardo had more than his share of superstitions. He also knew the outlaw had once been an altar boy and that he was alternately torn between his lust for gold and his yearning to return to the religion of his youth. The Mexican was tough. He had killed his share of men. He had guts in a fight, but the unseen had always frightened him. Work on your enemies' weaknesses, thought Case.

"It was quiet," said Case. "So quiet I could hear the rustling of the little mice in the brush. The mission was a dim bulk in the darkness. There was no wind, of that I assure you, amigo. Then the bell rang, just once, faintly and sweetly. The echo died away softly, softly, softly...."

"You lie!"

"There was no one in the tower, amigo. Not one who could be seen, that is."

"*Diós en cielo*! Be quiet!"

Case felt one of his bonds loosen a little. He spoke no further, letting the seeds he had planted in the Mexican's mind sprout and nourish.

Chip Gilbert was snoring. There was little he had to worry about, with the exception of having been outwitted by the Kid. Chip had captured Maslin and Case easily enough. Leonardo was still his ally. The Kid couldn't stay alert all the time; and then Chip would get him and work on him to a fare-thee-well.

Case eased a hand through his bonds. He spat out his cigarette. Leonardo prowled into the nave and then back again. The dim, echoing place was too much for him. He passed silently through the sacristy and out into the graveyard behind the building. The Kid worried him. Case Hardesty's story of the mysterious bell ringer worried him. Chip Gilbert worried him. Leonardo padded toward the rocks and vanished among them.

The Conchos Kid squatted in a hollow where he could see the bell tower. There was no sign of life up there. Phil Davis had a gun and a canteen of water but maybe his life was ebbing away. The Kid had wanted to see the bastard die with a slug in his belly, but maybe this way was better.

Leonardo paused to look for the Kid. There was a movement near him. He whirled quickly and raised his rifle.

"It is me ... Dulce," said the woman.

"What do you do here?"

"I am afraid, Leonardo."

He grounded his rifle and eyed her figure in appreciation.

"Sit here beside me, Leonardo."

He sat down. "What is it you want?"

"Look," she said quickly. "We are both Mexicans. These gringos hate us. There is money hidden down there. You are much of the man. Go down there. Kill the big gringo friend of yours. Kill that Case man. Capture the Kid and force him to tell you where the money is hidden."

He spat. "And what will you do, little rabbit?"

She dropped her shawl and moved closer to him. Her cheap perfume came to him mingled with her sweat. He could see the dim outline of a smooth brown shoulder. "We will take the money and the horses and ride south to Sonora. Think of it, Leonardo! All of that money and the two of us."

He passed a hard hand over the smooth, inviting flesh. "Yes," he said softly, "the money and the two of us."

She wriggled a little closer to him and he felt the soft and yet firm pressure of her breasts against his arm. "You will do this thing?"

"You are clever, Dulce, but not clever enough. Do you not think I will probably fail? They are all strong men and good with the guns and fists. If anything happens to me, you will run to the man who wins and give him your body while I will lie here and rot in my grave, forgotten by everyone."

She sat up straight. "You garbage!"

"Wait," he said quickly. "I will see what can be done."

He stood up and drew her to her feet. He ripped down the bodice of her dress and pawed at her, then crushed her lips against his. He shoved her down again and leaned over her. "But if you betray me, little rabbit," he said fiercely, "I will fix you with the knife so men will not spit on you in passing."

He took his rifle and disappeared amongst the jumbled rocks.

She drew up her bodice. "My pretty dress," she said brokenly. She touched her bruised lips. "Garbage!"

Leonardo paused. The bell tower was plainly in sight and a cold shiver crept over him.

"Looking for someone?" the quiet voice asked.

Leonardo did not move. He felt his Colt being taken from his holster and heard it clatter into a rock crevice. His rifle was taken from his hands. He turned to look into the smiling face of the Kid.

The Kid stepped back. "Get out of here," he said.

"I was not looking for you."

"You lie. Beat it!"

Leonardo scuttled down the slope. The woman arose from the rocks. "Did you do it? I heard no shot. Did you use the knife?"

He did not answer.

She looked up the slope and saw the Kid standing there. She opened her mouth to scream and then shut it. Her heart thudded against her ribs. Then she turned and scuttled away. Dulce knew what the Kid would do to her. She had failed again.

Leonardo walked toward the mission. Then suddenly he dropped to his knees, looked up at the cross on the dome and began to pray for the first time in many years.

———

CASE RUBBED HIS WRISTS. Chip was still snoring. Madeline moved. "You freed yourself?"

"Yes."

"I was waiting for a chance to do so."

"Thanks."

"What will you do now?"

"Get a gun."

"Free Maslin and his tracker."

"No."

"Why not? They can help us."

He shook his head. "Maslin would get me, one way or another."

"He's blind, Case!"

"You don't know the man. I could give him back the money, but it wouldn't make any difference. He came after me and the others. The only thing that will stop him from getting us is for him to die."

"You're cruel."

He shrugged. "This is a cruel world, Madeline, and this is the center of cruelty. Some of us will die before long. A bullet, a knife, or thirst."

Chip rolled over. Case stepped into a niche. "Be quiet," he said softly to the woman. His hip struck something and he felt it with his right hand, touching the barrel of a rifle. He eased it up and passed his hand along the stock. He felt a deep dent near the buttplate. It was his own Winchester .44-40.

"He's still asleep," she said.

He nodded as he stepped out of the niche. He picked up his cartridge belt from the floor and swung it about his hips. His holster was empty and so were the belt loops. Leonardo had appropriated the cartridges. But the magazine still held twelve rounds, because it had been fully loaded when it had been taken from him, and no rounds had been expended. He felt like a man again.

"Where did the Kid go?" he asked.

"I don't know.

There was a deep-set doorway cut into the south wall of the sacristy. Case padded toward it and eased open the door. A draft of cool air fanned his face. He walked through the doorway. Faint light came from a small window high on the wall. There was another doorway to his right. Then he realized there was a whole series of rooms along the south side of the big building.

He walked back to the sacristy door. "Come on," he said.

"Where?"

He leaned on the rifle. "You going to stay here with that skunk sleeping there?" He jerked his head toward the sanctuary.

"But what about my brother?"

Case grinned wryly. "He can take care of himself. Coming?" He did not wait for an answer. Time was precious. He tried the door in the west wall. It grated a little as it opened.

Madeline hesitated for a moment. Then she knelt beside Antonio. She cut his bonds. "Go," she said quickly. "Get help."

He looked up at her.

"Do you understand?"

"Yes."

"Go, then. Quickly!"

"But my *patrón*."

"He can't go. He is blind. I'll try to help him. But you must go quickly." She handed him the knife.

He stood up and bowed his head a little to her. "*Gracias!*"

"*Ándale!*"

He walked toward the sanctuary with the knife in his hand.

"No!" she said.

He turned and bowed again, then walked to the rear door of the sacristy. In a moment he was gone as silently as a hunting cat.

She walked into the room beyond the sacristy and closed the door behind her. Case came from the west door. "Follow me," he said. "Don't be afraid."

He closed the second door behind her. The room was very dark, with a faint patch of light high on the south wall from a tiny window. "Where are we?" she asked.

"*Quién sabe?* The old padres built well. I didn't realize how big this place was."

He led the way through two more rooms, with his boots kicking aside the accumulated trash of years, left there by those who had used the place and then had vanished, never to return again.

CHAPTER FOURTEEN

Phillip Davis lay flat on the floor of the bell tower. The moon was almost gone, but he did not dare look out of the tower. He had cursed himself for being foolish enough to have climbed up where he was, but there had been no other place to go. They had left him to die beside the water hole, but he knew he had not been hurt that badly. His side ached, and now and then he could taste blood in his mouth, but he would survive.

He had heard someone softly climbing the stairs and had fired blindly, and the flash of the pistol had revealed the taut face of Steve Wallace, but the bullet had missed.

Davis eased his way along the floor to the stairwell. He walked cautiously down the stairs in the darkness and full into an unyielding gateway of hard wood. He tested the gateway. It had been locked or wedged shut. He stood there in the darkness with cold sweat trickling down his sides. There was one canteen of water between him and death, nothing more, and the time would come when the heat of the next day would force him to drink and drink until he had used all of the water. There was no chance that the Kid would leave the place and let him alone. His one hope was that Madeline would intercede for him, and it was not much of a hope at that. He had seen

Madeline looking at the strange man, Case, who had come so mysteriously out of the desert and had saved the lives of the three of them, for a time at least. It was a cinch he had not done it for Phil or Dulce.

Dulce! She had shown herself for what she was. She would work any man if she had the chance. The one thing Phil was sure of was that the Kid would never take her back. There was too much of Madeline in him.

He shook the gate gently and knew it was hopeless. Even if he managed to open it he knew the Kid would be waiting for him, and then it would be six-shooters for two and breakfast for one, and the odds were mountain-high against Phil gunning down that smiling killer.

He walked back up into the tower and flattened himself against the side wall, trying to look down toward the water hole. There was a flash of orange-red flame from the rocks beyond the water hole and a slug thudded into the plaster just above Phil's head. He cursed as he dropped flat. The bastard had eyes like a cat.

The echo of the shot died away and smoke drifted from the rocks.

CHIP GILBERT HEAVED himself to his feet as he heard the shot. "Leonardo!" he yelled. He drew his Colt and ran toward the sacristy.

The sacristy was empty except for Dade Maslin who had raised himself to a sitting position and now looked at Chip with unseeing eyes.

"Where are the others?" demanded Chip.

"I don't know. I've been asleep."

The big outlaw thrust his gun muzzle against Maslin's head. "Damn you! Where are they?"

Maslin looked calmly up at Chip. "How would I know?" he asked quietly.

Chip smashed the gun barrel down on the sheriffs

head and then he ran to the outside door of the sacristy. It was dark out there now but there was no movement that he could see. "Leonardo! Leonardo!" he yelled hoarsely.

Leonardo could hear Chip plainly enough. His voice was enough to awaken the dead. But Leonardo knew what was in store for him if Chip found out that he had left Case Hardesty and that the Kid had taken Leonardo's guns. The Mexican slid down a slope and found a wide cleft to crawl into. Things were going from bad to worse with no prospect of getting any better.

Antonio had heard the shot too. He stood there in the darkness beyond the outer rim of rocks and looked toward the bell tower and dome which rose above the rock ramparts. Maybe his patron was in trouble again. He could not leave him alone there with those people.

The tracker walked silently toward the rocks and vanished among them like a lizard.

Case and Madeline had heard the muffled noise of the gun. She gripped his arm. "Where did it come from?"

"West, I think."

The room was dark and smelled of dust and filth.

Case struck a match. There was something white in a corner. Madeline gripped his arm tighter and looked away. It was a skull grinning at them from a pile of rags. Boots protruded from the other ends of the rags, but there was nothing but bones inside of them.

"He won't bother us," said Case.

He walked past the gruesome relics and tried a door. It was shut tight. He estimated that they must be somewhere just behind the room which was at the bottom of the bell tower.

He threw a shoulder against the door but it would not budge. Sweat broke out on him as he tried again and again. It was no use.

"What shall we do now?"

He turned. "I hoped to get out of here and get horses and strike off to the south, perhaps to Tule Tank."

"Everyone will be alert now."

"Yes."

"We can't stay here, Case."

"No, but by this time Chip and Leonardo know We've gotten away, for a time at least. But now, if we go back, I might get met with a bullet when I try to get through that door into the sacristy."

They stood there in the darkness, and the hopelessness of their situation weighed down on the woman. "Perhaps Steve will help us?" she suggested.

Case did not answer. She was a loyal fool to believe in her brother. It was Case's thought that he'd killed Phil Davis and Dulce and then jumped up dust getting out of there with the bank money. If Case didn't have Madeline to worry about he'd take a chance on working with the Kid, at least long enough to find out where the loot was hidden. Case was damned if he was going down to Sonora as broke as he was now, with twenty thousand dollars, which had once been in his hands, going to line the pockets of the Conchos Kid.

"Why don't you forget about me, Case? Go on. Get out of here. I'll be all right."

It was a good thing she could not see his face. He had gone through hell's suburbs to reach the water hole with the money, and then had made the return journey because of her.

Then he felt her arms about his neck and she drew him close. "I'm sorry," she said softly. She knew.

Steve Wallace had moved his position after he had fired up at the bell tower. He lay amongst the warm rocks, watching and listening. He had not seen Phil Davis in the tower, but there had been some movement up there. Maybe the bastard wasn't as hurt as he had made out to be. He had fired quickly enough when Steve had started up the tower stairway. The bullet had fanned past Steve's right ear.

The smart thing for him to do was to get the money and get Madeline away from there, but that wouldn't be so easy. He should have killed Leonardo when he had found him snooping about. Yet it wasn't his way. The Mex hadn't done anything against him; not yet, in any case. The Kid had no sympathy for the blind sheriff and his breed tracker; the sheriff would have shown no pity for the Kid. It was the man known only as Case who bothered the Kid. He was rawhide tough and dangerous; a man to be reckoned with. Yet Madeline seemed interested in him. She had a weakness for such men, probably because she had married such a weakling.

The Kid wanted a smoke, but he knew better than to roll a quirly and light it. He'd probably get a bullet along with the solace of the nicotine. It was dark now but the dawn would be along soon enough and then it would be the time for a showdown.

The warm wind whispered past him as he lay there. "Dulce. Dulce. Dulce ..." it seemed to say.

Dade Maslin opened his eyes but could see nothing. He felt that he had been left alone. Blood trickled down his face from his cut scalp. "Antonio?" he asked softly. There was no answer and somehow he had expected none. The tracker was faithful enough in his way, but even he might have seen the handwriting on the wall and escaped while he had the chance. Dade cursed the darkness which made him helpless. He got to his feet and worked at his bonds. His back was against a door and it swung open behind him. He fell heavily and then got up to kick the door shut again.

His sweat greased the rawhide thongs which bound him and he managed to slide one wrist through them. Dade quickly untied the remainder of the lashings and rubbed his half-numb wrists.

He had no idea where he was. His boots kicked aside

trash and fallen plaster, and the musty odor of dust hung in the still air. He was weaponless and blind and the one ally he had had was gone, God alone knew where. Maybe Antonio had gone for help, but there wasn't much consolation in that fact. Even if Antonio reached the posse and brought them back the whole issue would be settled long before they reached the water hole. About all they could do would be to bury Dade and try to catch the others.

Dade felt along the wall until he found another door. He eased it open and felt his way into the next room. Then he stopped with a feeling that he was not alone. He waited a while hoping to hear some noise but the place was as quiet as a tomb. The thought made him shudder a little. He was not an imaginative man, but he was sure he would never leave that place alive.

There was a movement near Dade and he felt his heart thud against his ribs. Then something hard was pressed against his back. "Don't move," said Case Hardesty. "It's Maslin," he said.

"Let him stay with us, Case," said Madeline. "The man is helpless."

"You know what he'd do if he found me helpless."

"You're not the sort of man who'd let those others kill him."

"I told you what he'd do to me."

Maslin wet his dry lips. "Help me, Hardesty," he said quietly.

"Why? You tracked us across the desert with that human bloodhound of yours. You've got guts, Maslin, but you're not too bright."

"Thanks."

"Do they know you came in here?"

"I was alone when I found my way in here. My tracker is gone."

"So?"

"I freed him," said Madeline.

"Won't do much good," said Case. "By the time he

gets back here with help, which isn't likely, this whole bloody mess should be settled."

"You can't let this man die, Case."

Case lowered the rifle. He lit a match and looked at Maslin. "Good God," he said. "Your face is covered with blood."

"Chip Gilbert buffaloed me. He's outside looking for Janos."

Case flipped the match into a corner. "Time for me to get busy," he said quietly.

"What will you do?" asked the woman.

"Quién sabe? The Kid is watching Phil, I expect. It looks like it's between me and those other two."

"They'll kill you!"

"Maybe. I can do a little killing myself if I have to."

Maslin wiped the blood from his face. "Look, Hardesty: I haven't got a chance to get away. I'll make a deal with you."

"Go on."

"Take Gilbert and Janos. Find me that money."

"What's in it for me?"

"Go back to Cottonwood Station with me as my prisoner. I'll do the best I can for you."

"Yeh ... ten years in Yuma pen."

"I might get you off easy."

"You've got a great sense of humor. Supposing I did what you ask and was lucky enough to get both of them, do you think the Kid will let me take that money? It's hidden. He isn't that much of a fool to hand me twenty thousand dollars and let me ride away from here."

"I can talk to him," said Madeline.

"I wonder."

"We can't stand here and wait for them to come after us," said the sheriff.

"You can. You can't do a damned thing, Maslin. It's all up to me."

"Where are we?"

"In a row of rooms on the south side of the mission. No water. There's only one way out as far as I can see and that's the way we came in. I can hold them off if they want to get in here."

"Maybe they'll let us alone?" said Madeline.

Case leaned back against the wall. "Chip Gilbert? Don't fool yourself. He'd wait his chance to get me, and you too for that matter, Madeline. The man is loco. He double-crossed me willingly enough, but now he thinks it was me who double-crossed him. The man isn't right in the head. Maslin knows that. Look what Chip did to him."

Maslin nodded. Madeline helped him to a bench which ran along one wall. "Thanks, ma'am," he said.

Case rested his rifle against the wall. He walked into the next room. There was a pile of trash in one corner. He stepped up on it to see if he could peer through the little window high on the wall. The trash collapsed and his heels struck wood. He shoved the trash aside and felt a trap door. There was a huge iron ring set into the tough wood. Case gripped it with his hands and tried to raise it, but it was impossible. "Maslin," he said, "give me a hand here."

Madeline guided the sheriff to Case. Case placed the big man's hands on the ring. They squatted and heaved on the ring together. The door moved a little.

"Once more," said Case.

Madeline hurried to the east door. "I thought I heard voices."

"Heave," said Case.

The door grated a little and then was flung back against the wall. A draft of cool musty air flowed about them. Case got his rifle and walked to the east door. He listened. He heard footsteps in the next room and he slid his rifle barrel through the door ring and against the wall an instant before someone tried to open the door.

The three of them stood there in the darkness hardly

daring to breathe, and then they heard the grating of footsteps and the faint noise of the other door being closed.

"Now what?" asked Maslin.

Case walked to the trap door and looked about until he found materials with which to make a torch. He felt his way down masonry steps in the darkness until he could light the torch without fear of the light being seen from the window.

He was in a low tunnel made of heavy masonry. The dust rose about him as he looked about. It might have been built as a refuge from Apache and Yaqui raids. Many of them may have swirled about the old mission in other days. He put out the torch and returned to the room.

"Where does it go?" asked Madeline.

"Quién sabe? I'll explore it."

He got his rifle and barred the door with a thick bar he found under the bench. "Stay here," he said.

Case walked down the stairs and relighted the torch. He coughed because of the smoke and dust.

The tunnel ran both ways from the foot of the steps. He walked to the east until he entered a low vaulted room. Two empty coffins stood on trestles, and he figured he was somewhere under the nave or the sanctuary where the old padres buried their dead. Four thick candles stood on a low table near the dusty coffins. He lit one of them and extinguished the torch. There was an eerie feeling in him as he stood there in the flickering light. His boots rang on the flagstones as he walked along the tunnel to the west.

Relics of the past lay underfoot. Ollas and pots, rags, tools and broken relics of the church. A robe hung on. a peg, just as though the owner had left it there to come back for it. He wondered how long it had been hanging there in the Stygian darkness.

He figured out that he must be somewhere near the front of the mission when he reached another room, only partly walled with masonry neatly piled to one side. An unfinished arched doorway was at the far end of the room.

He passed through the doorway and into an earth tunnel. A small animal scuttled down the passageway ahead of him. Water trickled down the damp walls, and puddles of it dotted the slimy floor. His boots rang as he crossed a place where the passageway had been cut roughly through rock. Then he waded through several inches of water, thrusting the thick candle ahead of him to drive back the oppressive darkness.

The tunnel slanted upward and he felt a draft on his face. He put out the candle and felt his way along, seeming to feel the weight of the earth over his head. Then he could see a lighter patch in the gloom ahead of him.

He stopped to listen, hearing the faint splashing of water behind him in the tunnel.

The air was warmer now and a breeze felt its way into the tunnel. He walked softly, placing each foot with care and holding his rifle ready.

Now he could make out objects with greater clarity. He could see boulders beyond the end of the tunnel. A door hung askew at one side and the outer face of it had been cleverly painted a dun color to fit into the color scheme of the surrounding rocks.

He paused at the mouth of the tunnel to listen again, but all he heard was the rustling of the brush in the wind.

Case stood there a long time until at last he walked outside with a feeling of intense relief. It took him a few minutes to orient himself. He had come out in a deep gully to the south of the mission, although he could not see the building itself.

The breeze felt good on his face. Somewhere not too far from him would be Chip Gilbert, Leonardo Janos and the Kid, and he knew he had to kill the first two at least to get free from the mission. The Kid was the unknown factor, but he knew Case had probably saved Madeline's life and that might make a difference; but twenty thousand dollars might swing the balance the other way too.

Something moved in the brush. Case reversed his rifle, ready for a butt stroke. It was a man, standing there looking to the east, and he did not wear a hat. It was Antonio, Maslin's breed tracker.

Case debated with himself on what to do. The tracker was fiercely loyal to Dade Maslin. Case had heard of that loyalty long before he had ever seen the breed. Case wasn't worried about Maslin—the man was helpless—but the breed was something else again, and he could use a knife as fast as some men used a gun.

Suddenly the tracker turned and looked full at Case. "Don't move," said Case softly.

Antonio had no gun, but he had the knife Madeline had given him. He knew too that this hard-eyed man facing him could shoot fast and well before the knife reached him.

"Put up your hands. Come here. *Comprende?*" said Case.

Antonio slowly raised his hands and came forward.

Case walked behind the man and placed the muzzle of his rifle against the tracker's kidneys. "Walk," he said.

"In there, *señor?* No ... no ... no. ..."

"Go on!"

Antonio shivered a little as he walked into the dark tunnel.

"Now listen, *hombre*," said Case. "Your *patrón* is safe, for a time at least. He has nothing to fear from me as long as he doesn't try anything with me. You understand?"

"Yes."

"I'll take you to him, but if you try anything you will both die. *Comprende?*

"*Yo comprendo.*"

"Bueno." Case looked back over his shoulder. "Did you see any of them?"

"The man Janos is hiding in the rocks. The woman is there too, but they are not together."

"You did not see the big man Gilbert?"

"No, but the other man, the young one, is among the rocks watching the tower."

"And the *caballos?*"

"They are near the graveyard."

"Walk on, then."

Case found the candle and lighted it. The dark eyes of the tracker studied Case and then looked furtively along the damp tunnel.

"You will help your *patrón*, but in order to save his life you must trust me as I'll trust you."

"Sí! Sí!"

"Walk beside me, then, Antonio."

They walked on until they reached the big room under the sanctuary. The tracker's eyes widened as he saw the coffins. He hesitated but Case shoved him on. "There is nothing to fear," he said. "Nothing but those men outside who would kill all of us if they have the chance."

They returned to the room where Maslin and the woman waited for them. The tracker placed his hand on Maslin's shoulder. "I have come back, patrón" he said simply.

Maslin felt the tracker's face with his big hands. "Gracias, Antonio," he said.

Case put out the candle. "There is a way of escape," he said, "but we'll never make it until we take care of Chip Gilbert and Leonardo Janos, and that won't be easy."

"What do you want Antonio to do?" asked Maslin.

"Help me capture or kill them."

The tracker nodded. This was the way of his people. Those two men must die for what they had done.

"And my brother?" asked Madeline.

Case rubbed his jaw. "I don't know what he'll do. I only know this: I don't want him behind me out there."

Maslin looked toward Case. "I don't want him," he said, "unless he insists on keeping that money."

"You're not in a position to want anybody, Maslin. Keep your mouth shut and do as you're told and we'll get out of this mess. One more thing: Get any ideas out of your head that you're going to take me in." Case gripped Maslin by the shirt front. "Is that clear?"

"Yes."

"Bueno."

The wind whispered through the little window, but there wasn't another sound; almost as though the four of them were alone at the mission.

CHAPTER FIFTEEN

Leonardo Janos raised his head and looked toward the gully where he had seen two men. One of them was the tracker Antonio, but he had not made sure who the other one was. It had been either Maslin or Case Hardesty. They had vanished as though they had dropped into the earth.

The Mexican slid down into the gully and walked toward the end of it until he saw the tunnel entrance. There was no sign of life there, but he was sure he could smell candle grease and it reminded him of his days when he had been an altar boy. A wave of superstitious fear crept over him, but he fought it off. They had been men of flesh and blood, not supernatural beings.

He stepped into the end of the tunnel. It must lead under the old mission, but he wasn't going to find out. He had heard Chip yelling for him and the big man was somewhere to the west. Leonardo wasn't about to let Chip know he had lost his weapons to the Kid. Chip had a beast of a temper and was quick to lash out when he had been crossed.

The Mexican hesitated again. Perhaps he could trail those two into the tunnel and get a weapon, or at least find out what they were doing in there, but he had no idea what he would find in there. He wiped the cold sweat from his face. Then he remembered that the dying man in the bell tower had a gun. Perhaps he was unconscious or had died. It was worth the risk of a bullet going up there for the gun; a lesser risk than facing Chip Gilbert and knowing what the big man would do to him.

Leonardo left the tunnel entrance and worked his way back through the gully, placing each foot with care and sweating icily every time he heard a noise. The moon was gone but it was light enough to see a little.

The wind whispered dryly through the gullies and it seemed to Leonardo that they warned him of danger. He skirted the outer rim of rocks and walked softly down the northern side of the strange rock formation. He could see the dark, warning finger of the tower and the faint shape of the big dome behind it.

He again worked his way through the rocks and to the back of the big mission. There was no one in the sacristy. He had no idea where the three men prisoners and the American woman had vanished. Perhaps spirited away by the ghosts of the padres. There was nothing for him to do but walk into the gloomy sanctuary and thence into the echoing nave.

He padded softly, having removed his spurs, and carefully avoided striking ahead with his feet, lifting each foot carefully and thrusting it gently forward until he reached the door of the baptistry.

He eased into the dark baptistry and something moved. Fear spurred him on. His hand struck a body and he slid his hands up to the small, soft throat. Then the mingled odors of perfume and sweat came to him and he knew he held the woman Dulce helpless in his dirty hands. "Quiet," he hissed.

Leonardo drew her into a corner. "What do you do here?"

"I was trying to get to my man."

"Which one?"

"The one in the tower."

"Why?"

"Because the other one will kill me."

He digested this. She was like a little rabbit, soft and trembling, but he knew she could be as hard as steel, and he had no other ally.

"You know where the money is, Leonardo?"

"No. But it is not of the money I am thinking. I have no weapon but my knife. I must have a gun or Chip will beat me and perhaps kill me for failing him."

"Be a man!"

"I *am* a man!"

"Then prove it! Phillip Davis has a gun. He is badly hurt. Let us go up into the tower and get that gun. The horses are picketed behind the mission. We can lead them quietly into the desert and ride south."

"But the money!"

"You think any of them will hesitate to kill you if you look for it? These gringos will kill anybody for that amount of money."

"That is true."

"Is not life more sweet to you than money?"

"Listen," he said softly. "The Kid is out there watching the tower and also watching for the rest of us to try him. If we make one mistake he will come. We must be quiet. If necessary we must kill the man in the tower."

"Yes," she said quickly.

He looked down at her dim face. "But you once loved him, Dulce."

"Don't be a fool!"

That was enough of an answer for Leonardo Janos. "Come," he said.

He led the way to the foot of the stairs and looked up into the darkness. The Kid had said he had wedged shut the door or gateway which was part way up the stairs. Leonardo drew out his knife and tested its edge. Then he padded up the narrow staircase with the woman close behind him.

He thrust out a hand and felt the hard wood of the gateway. There was no sound in the tower except the soft breathing of the woman and the faint moaning of the wind.

Leonardo removed the wedge and eased on the gateway. It opened softly. He swallowed hard and started up the stairs. There was no sound from the man above them. Perhaps he was dead.

He could distinguish the faint light from the openings in the bell tower. There was a movement above them.

Leonardo stood with his head and shoulders level with the floor, knowing damned well he wouldn't have a chance if Davis fired down on them.

The soft noise came again.

Leonardo suddenly pressed himself against the side of the stairwell as he heard the unmistakable clicking of a gun hammer. Then the bell tower was blasted with flame and smoke and the slug seemed to hiss past Leonardo. The woman grunted and then fell. Leonardo threw himself into the tower.

The man stood there with the smoking gun in his hand, but the Mexican was too fast for him. The knife flicked out and drew blood. The pistol was dropped and snatched up by Leonardo. He slammed a shoulder against the swaying gringo and drove him to the floor.

A rifle cracked flatly from the rocks and the slug rang sharply against the bell. Leonardo jumped to one side, lost his footing and plunged from an opening with a sob of fear. He struck the roof of the mission and hung there at the edge, still half-blinded from the explosion of the pistol.

The rifle cracked again. Leonardo scrambled across the littered roof and around the side of the dome with cold sweat greasing his hands and face. He dropped flat and lay there with his shoulders heaving and trembling, unable to go any further.

It was quiet again. Leonardo checked the hot weapon. There were four rounds left. He reloaded the two empty cylinder holes from his gun-belt loops.

The woman was dead or wounded. No matter. Leonardo was safe for the time being. It didn't matter to him if both of them were dead. He wanted to get out of that place of death as fast as he could.

———

CHIP GILBERT HAD SEEN the gun flash from the tower and the two following flashes from the rocks, but both of the last two flashes had come from different places. The Kid was too smart to fire always from the same place. But what puzzled Chip was that he had seen a man leap or fall from the tower and land at the edge of the roof, only to vanish like a great ungainly bird. It had looked like Leonardo. Perhaps the money was cached in the tower.

Chip let his rifle hammer down to half-cock and walked quietly to the rear of the mission. Hardesty, Madeline and Maslin, along with the breed tracker, had vanished into thin air, but the horses were still there, shying and blowing, pulling nervously at their taut picket ropes.

Chip stepped behind a wide outer pilaster and waited. He needed Leonardo. There had been a time when he had held the reins in the situation, before that grinning, cold-eyed bastard of a Kid had showed up. The Kid had taken over easily. He had the money cached. But maybe he was so damned determined to get at Davis he might get careless, and that was when Chip and Leonardo would take over again. This time there would be no slip-up.

There was a grating noise above Chip. Pebbles and plaster rattled down about him. He looked up to see a man hanging from the roof eaves. The man dropped and as he hit the ground spraddle-legged he stiffened as the muzzle of Chip's rifle was jabbed against his kidneys. *"Diós en cielo!"* he gasped. Would this hell never end?

"Yeh," said Chip dryly. *"Diós en cielo?* Where you been, you bastard?"

Leonardo turned. "The Kid got my guns. I had to get another."

"In the tower?"

"Si!"

"You're more loco than I ever figured you was."

Chip jerked his head and led the way into the jumbled rocks behind the mission. "Where's the Mex woman?"

"Dead, I think."

"And Davis?"

"Quién sabe?" Leonardo shrugged. "Maybe dead; maybe alive."

"He don't matter. The others do. Where are they?"

"You know where the Kid is. The others are still in the mission."

"Yeh? Where? How do you know?"

Leonardo wiped the sweat from his face. He told Chip of what he had seen at the tunnel.

Chip scratched in his beard. "I got enough of this damned monkey business. We got to get the Kid."

Leonardo paled.

Chip looked toward the mission. "But I ain't so sure the Kid might not get help from Hardesty and that damned breed. So, we got to get them first."

"This will not be easy."

"Dammit! I know. But the breed don't carry a gun. I don't think he even knows how to use one."

"Hardesty does."

Chip did not answer. He had no stomach for going into that tunnel with Hardesty and the breed waiting for him and perhaps the Kid walking quietly in behind him. He cudgeled his slow brain into action. They had to get

Hardesty and Antonio first, then force the Kid into revealing the money cache.

"I figure Hardesty and his friends are hiding in some of them damned rooms on the south side of the mission," said Chip. "I also figures that tunnel opens into them rooms. We'll split up. One of us goes into the mission to block that way; the other goes into the tunnel."

Leonardo swallowed.

Chip nodded in satisfaction. "That's it! I go into the mission. You go into the tunnel."

"Before God, Chip!"

"You afraid?"

"I am a man!"

"Then you go into the tunnel. You're always blowing about being a man. This time you can prove it."

Leonardo wet his lips. He didn't know if he was more afraid of the tunnel than he was of Chip Gilbert.

"Here," said the big man. He thrust a candle into Leonardo's wet hands. "You got matches?"

"Si."

"Scared?"

"No."

"*Bueno.*"

"It is getting darker, Chip."

Chip nodded. "We'll sit tight until the false dawn. Here we can watch the horses. Ain't no one going to get at them!"

Leonardo nodded. He looked toward the dim mission. One of the little group which had met there through the mysterious hand of God was probably dead. The woman Dulce. Perhaps the gringo in the tower was dead. It was said such things happened in threes. Who would be next?

CHAPTER SIXTEEN

C ase Hardesty eased his way into the sacristy. The room was empty of life and there was no sound from the nave. He had heard the shooting from somewhere near the front of the mission and hoped to God Chip Gilbert or Leonardo had earned a slug in the belly or head, but he wasn't anxious to go and find out.

His undershirt and shirt lay soggily in a corner of the room. He pulled them on and flattened himself against the wall to peer outside. He could see the horses dimly against the rock walls east of the graveyard. Case knew better than to try for those mounts.

If he could only find the Kid and talk to him, he might enlist him on his side, but the Kid was determined to get Davis. Maybe he had already. Maybe Davis had got the Kid, but it wasn't likely.

The quiet mission got a little on his nerves. He picked up a canteen and some of the little store of food which lay on a bench in the sacristy. Case walked back into the south-side rooms and tapped three times on the second door and then three times again.

Madeline opened the door for him. He closed it and barred it.

"What's up?" asked Maslin. The tracker sat at his feet like a faithful dog.

Case handed the canteen to Madeline. "Drink," he said. "Here is food too."

"No," she said. "We must save water."

"There's water in the tunnel. At least we're ahead on that score."

"If you can get back into the tunnel without being murdered."

"I'll have to go down there again with Antonio anyway."

Maslin shook his head. "One man with a rifle and my tracker with a knife. By God, Hardesty, if I could see and I had a gun! We'd root them out."

"Maybe. I don't trust you with a gun behind me anyway, Maslin."

"*Gracias!*"

"You're more than welcome."

"What was that shooting about?"

"I don't know. The horses are still there. I didn't see anyone else."

"What do we do now?"

"It's getting pitch dark out there. Can't see much and it will get worse."

"Antonio can find his way about in the dark like a cat."

"I know, Maslin, but *I* have to see to shoot. We've got three triggermen out there, and they'll shoot fast if anything bothers them."

Maslin nodded. "Then you'll wait until dawn?"

"Just before. I hope I can get one of them or both of them."

"Yeh."

Madeline gave the sheriff and the tracker some of the food. She shared hers with Case. They sat silently in the darkness until they had finished eating.

Maslin suddenly laughed.

"What's the joke?" asked Case.

"I was just thinking that all of you hardcases might kill each other off and take my tracker to hell with you."

"So?"

"Here I am, Dade Maslin, the man-hunter, sitting here with a woman, blind as a bat, waiting for other men to do my fighting. If you don't come back, what then?"

"Yeh ... *what then?*"

Madeline spoke up. "I'd take care of you, sheriff."

He looked toward the sound of her voice. "I've never seen you, ma'am, but from the sound of your voice I believe you would. Gracias . . . gracias."

Case rolled three smokes. He placed one in Antonio's mouth after he lighted a match, and placed the second cigarette in Maslin's mouth. He lighted all three cigarettes and then sat down on the floor. He passed his big hands over the cool metal of his rifle.

They were a strange quartet. The silent, loyal tracker; a woman who had hoped to save her faithless husband from being murdered by her brother; a top man-hunter who never quit a trail in his law career until he had killed or captured his quarry; Case Hardesty, a hardcase outlaw who had suddenly realized he might be in love with a woman he had known only for a few hours, and who had suddenly found his conscience again. *The gods must be laughing up their sleeves.*

————

THE CONCHOS KID was still watching the dark bell tower. He had no way of knowing what had happened up there unless he went up there himself, and like all men of his caste, he did not like the idea of walking into a trap. Somewhere in the darkness, too, were men who might be stalking him even now. The big brutal outlaw and his Mex side-kick, and perhaps Case Hardesty. It would be dangerous to expose himself, but the dawn would be along quickly enough and then it would be showdown time.

The tower seemed to draw him like a magnet. He had not trailed Davis and the two women clear down into Sonora and back up into the Spanish Desert for nothing. He had come for the bittersweet taste of vengeance and he meant to have it. The cached money meant nothing to him. He had hidden it to make sure Gilbert and Janos let him alone to do what he had to do. After that, well, things would settle themselves.

He worked his way through the warm rocks and around to the north side of the mission, then dropped to his belly to work his way toward the building, inching along and stopping often to look and listen. The place was quiet; it was too damned quiet to suit him.

The Kid made it to the dark doorway of the mission and inside, pausing at the deep doorway of the baptistry to listen. There was no sound, so he padded into the room and to the foot of the stairway. His right boot toe struck something soft. He stepped back and lowered his rifle, and then the unmistakable odor of Dulce's perfume came to him.

He knelt and felt her warm body, and as he touched her face he felt the stickiness and he knew it was blood. He thrust his left hand inside her bodice and felt her soft breast. There was no heartbeat.

He stood up and gripped his rifle. He had been a fool to fall in love with her and he had been warned about her by Madeline, but still the little Mexican girl had been gay and vivacious, full of passion and intrigue. He had meant to kill her in his first hunger for vengeance but he knew now he could never have done it.

He looked up the stairwell and then stepped over the body of the woman. He worked his way up the stairs with his finger on the trigger and the rifle at waist height. The acrid odor of burnt gunpowder hung heavily about him.

The Kid reached the top of the stairs and paused.

The wind whispered through the bell-tower openings. "Davis," said the Kid quietly. He moved quickly to one side to avoid the bullet he expected, but nothing happened. His shoulder bumped against the bell as he moved about trying to find the man he hated and had solemnly sworn to kill; but the man was gone.

The Kid went down the stairs and stepped over the body of Dulce. He did not stop until he was outside of the mission in the warm, windy darkness.

———

CHIP GILBERT RAISED his head as he heard the soft tone of the bell. "Someone's up there, *amigo*," he said.

Leonardo winced. The words of Case Hardesty came back to him. *You should have known better than to come here and desecrate this place.*

"The wind, I guess," said Chip.

I heard the bell, Hardesty had said, *when I was here alone.*

"Still," said Chip quickly, "there ain't enough wind to move a heavy thing like that, is there?"

Leonardo did not answer. The words were written up in the bell tower. *There is nothing but death here.*

"Maybe Davis is still alive," said Chip.

It *was* quiet, Hardesty had said softly, *so quiet I could hear the rustling of the little mice in the brush. The mission was a dim bulk in the darkness. There was no wind, of that I assure you, amigo. Then the bell rang, just once, faintly and softly. The echo died away softly, softly, softly. . . There was no one in the tower, amigo. No one who could be seen, that is....*

Por amor de la Virgen Santísima. Hardesty had not been lying then.

"Maybe he's dead, then," said Chip. "Hawww!"

"A thousand Jesuses, Chip! Be quiet!"

The big man stared closely at his companion. "Don't tell me you believe this place is haunted?"

"No!"

"Bull crap! You *did* say it was haunted. You said men had vanished here and others had gone out of their minds."

Leonardo passed a shaking hand across his face.

Chip was beginning to enjoy himself. "You yellow belly! You little goat with horns! You ain't got the guts to be a real man. You won't go into that tunnel."

"I am a man! I will go!"

"You'll swear on that?"

Leonardo hesitated.

"Well?"

"I swear, then."

"On what?"

"Damn you! On the corpse of Christ. In the name of Christ."

"You sure you're not afraid?"

Leonardo snapped his fingers bravely. *"Nada. Nada."*

A grin passed over Chip's broad features in the darkness. He hadn't been sure of this partner of his, but he knew the man well enough to know he would go into that tunnel when the time came. Chip lay flat and slanted his hat over his eyes. "I'll sleep awhile, partner. Keep a good watch." He was quiet for a time and then he rolled over on one elbow. "By the way, before I forget...."

"Sí?"

"If that Gawd-damned bell rings again you go up and see who's doing it."

"Curse you!"

Chip laughed softly as he lay down to sleep. Things were getting better. They'd smoke out Hardesty and Maslin and get the Kid too. After that, well, Chip could make it to Sonora alone with the dinero. He fell asleep thinking of what times he'd have with all that loot.

————

PHIL DAVIS BELLIED into the brush near the water hole. His clothing was soaked with sweat and drying blood. The Mexican had ripped him a little with his knife across the right forearm, with the tip of the blade raking his belly. Then the Mex had fallen from the tower with Phil's Colt in his hand. There was nothing for Phil to do but try to make it out of the mission and hope to God the Kid wouldn't find him. It had been close enough.

He shuddered a little as he thought of how he had fallen over the body of Dulce. Instead of the Kid killing her, it had been Phil's bullet which had let the life out of her scheming little body.

Fear seemed to crawl out of the darkness behind him and settle on his back, comfortably and surely as though it knew where it had a victim. There was no place to go and no way to defend himself, but there was a core within him which made him want to keep his miserable life in the worst way.

Madeline didn't give a damn for him, nor any of the others. They were thinking of their own miserable little lives. If he could get a horse he'd make it out into the darkness of the desert and take his chances on finding water. But he had no skill in such matters. In the Southwest border country a man had to be good in everything he did or he could not survive. If he carried a gun he had to know how to use it. He had to ride well. If he gambled he had to be good at it. Phil Davis had drifted into gambling because he liked it, not because he was really good at it, and he had had a run of fair luck for a time. That was when he had taken up with Dulce and she had cost him everything, he thought bitterly. He was damned sorry for himself but not for anyone else. It just wasn't his way.

The desert country frightened him. He was a town man and the desert with its threat of death as the price for carelessness had always unnerved him.

He looked back at the mission. He'd have to hold out

somehow until he could get a horse and some water. It would take a long time to get those two tickets to further his life and he didn't think it was possible for him to do both before daylight.

He wormed his way further into the brush and into a gully shrouded by brush. He could go no further.

There was a brooding, menacing quality about the quiet desert night. The real desert dwellers, the bobcat and the kit fox, the mice and the birds, had left the area of the water hole or stayed in their holes and burrows. There was bigger game afoot and they wanted no part of it. Man the destroyer had taken over, as he had done in the past, but in time man would die or leave and then the desert cycle of life would resume as it had for hundreds of years.

CHAPTER SEVENTEEN

Leonardo Janos opened his eyes as the hard hand covered his mouth. He looked up into the dim face of Chip Gilbert. "Time to get going," said Chip.

Leonardo shivered in the cool pre-dawn wind which seemed to search through his sweat-damp clothing. "So soon?" he asked.

"We've wasted enough time already. Dammit! You should have a rifle, but we ain't got time to forage for one."

Leonardo sat up. The horses were restless. They had been too long without water and it bothered him. He had always been more concerned about animals than about his fellow humans, although he doubted if Chip Gilbert was really human. *"Diablo,"* he muttered as he tightened his belt buckle.

"What's that?"

"Nothing."

"You mentioned the devil."

"Sí. Even the devil would shun this evil place."

"Yeh. Hawww!"

Leonardo shivered again, and not from the damp.

Chip placed his mouth close to Leonardo's ear, and

his foul breath sickened the Mexican. "You Indian along the north side of the rocks, then cut in toward that tunnel you was talking about. Go in and try to flush them out."

"And you?"

"I got to stay in the open until I see what happens."

"*Sí...* of course you do."

Chip nodded. "Now, if you see the Kid, try to take him."

"Just like that, eh, *amigo?*"

"Yeh ... just like that. But don't kill him. *Comprende?*

"*Sí*. We must find the money."

Chip clapped Leonardo on the back. "*Vámonos!*"

The Mexican worked his way through the brush and rocks until he was on the open desert to the north, then he padded west until he reached the boundary of the great rock oval. He paused there and then went on to the south side of the rocks. There was no sign of life.

He slid quietly down into the gully and eased both knife and Colt in their sheaths. The tunnel entrance was a dark, irregular outline at the end of the gully, shrouded by waving brush which seemed to claw and pull at him as though to hold him back from some nameless and unseen horror.

In his own way Leonardo was a brave man and he knew it; but this was something else. Everyone has courage in some ways and cowardice in others and no one can say why. He stepped softly into the tunnel and stood there with the cool draft flowing about him.

A mouse scuttled for cover right at his feet and his heart jumped and skipped a beat or two. "*Valiente,*" said Leonardo softly as though talking to someone else to encourage him. It was his other self to whom he spoke, the self which knew better than to trust itself in that silent, looming tunnel.

He walked in, feeling his way carefully. Chip had said they needed light to shoot and Leonardo suddenly realized that it could be brassy daylight on the desert and there would be no light to shoot by in the permanent darkness of the tunnel. But it was too late to go back now. He had to prove to Chip and to himself that he was *muy hombre*. There was some pride left in Leonardo Janos.

The tunnel floor slanted downward and suddenly his feet splashed in water. He stopped to listen, peopling the darkness with phantoms who seemed to whisper ghoulish thoughts. He would light many candles in the cathedral at Durango if he ever got away from this haunted place.

He waded through the water until his questing hands struck masonry. He knew now he must be somewhere under the mission. There was nothing else to do but strike a light and hope he didn't have his life snuffed out faster than he could snuff out the candle. He struck a lucifer on his belt buckle and tried to light the candle, looking nervously beyond the pale, flickering glow of the match so that he failed to ignite the wick.

It took two more matches to light the candle, but the feeble glow did little more than to show that he stood just beyond an unfinished arched doorway. He stumbled over a cut masonry block before he reached the far side of the low vaulted room in which he stood.

There was no sound other than the steady dripping of the water from the ceiling of the tunnel and the faint moaning of the draft through the passageway.

The Mexican hesitated. It would take time for Chip to get the daylight he wanted before he went into action; therefore, it was best for Leonardo to wait a little while. Perhaps he should retrace his steps to the mouth of the tunnel; but he had come that far. He was a man! He would wait in the room for a little while. Meanwhile there would be no harm in having a cigarette to steady himself. He needed just a little steadying, you understand.

He rolled a smoke with shaking hands and lighted it from the candle. He snuffed out the candle and stood there in the darkness to one side of the yawning mouth of the walled tunnel, puffing at the cigarette, lighting up his taut dark features.

_____

CASE HARDESTY AWOKE with a feeling of danger in his mind. It had happened to him before, an acquired sense from his years in the service and as an outlaw. The room was still dark but he sensed the coming of the dawn.

Someone moved close to him in the darkness. It was the tracker. "The time is now?" asked Antonio.

"Soon."

"What do you want me to do?"

"Can you go down into the tunnel and scout toward the way out?"

"Yes."

The man had guts, thought Case. His mixed breeding might have built a strong strain of superstition in him, but he did not show it

"I wish I had a gun for you, amigo," said Case.

"I do not handle them well. The knife is better."

"Yes. Go down then. You know the way?"

"I never forget," said the tracker with quiet pride.

"Go with God then, *amigo*."

"May God favor you too, *señor*."

The tracker walked into the room of the trap door. Case heard him lift the door. He hurried to the breed and placed a hand on his shoulder. "Wait," he said. He cut his candle in half and gave it to Antonio along with some lucifers.

"I do not need the light, senor."

"Perhaps, but you might need it."

The tracker walked down the steps into the pitch darkness. He shook a little with the cool dampness.

He felt his way along until he reached the room of the coffins and he paused to light a match to orient himself. He was impassive as he looked at the coffins on the trestles. He walked as quietly as a hunting bobcat until his outstretched hand struck cloth material. He felt it. It was a robe of some sort, of heavy material, and he was cold. He walked back to the room with it and shook it. The dust rose about <u>him</u> in the darkness. He pulled it over his head. There was a cowl to it, and he raised it to rest it about his head. The robe was a little musty, but it kept the chill from his half-naked body. He would return it when he did not need it.

Antonio walked back into the tunnel, pausing often to listen. He heard nothing, but then his nostrils picked up the faint odor of burning tobacco wafted down the tunnel.

Antonio drew out his knife and held it blade down as in meeting a man. It was like an extension of his own hand, his best weapon, and with it ready he feared no man nor animal. He walked silently along the passageway waiting for a movement or sound to warn him and trigger him into swift action.

———

LEONARDO HAD GROUND out his cigarette. He wanted another one but there was not time. The job had to be done. He felt for the candle and scratched a match on the stone to light it, changing it to his left hand while he drew his Colt and cocked it with his right hand. Now was the time. He was a man. He would show Chip Gilbert that he was frightened of nothing, not even the *chisos* and *espectros* of the darkness.

He stepped into the tunnel and raised the candle to view his way. Then he saw the dark-robed figure within ten feet of him, moving quickly forward. His heart seemed to fail within him and he opened his mouth to cry out in horror, but no sound came from him. There was no face to be seen within the shadow of the cowl and he knew it would be a horrible grinning skull.

The glittering blade moved out and struck hard into Leonardo's upper belly. Leonardo raised his Colt as the steel jerked back and forth carving a big figure 7 in the Mexican's lean belly. His last act was to smash the heavy barrel of the Colt down on the cowled head. The candle dropped into the water and was extinguished. Two bodies fell heavily.

———

"HE SHOULD HAVE COME BACK by now," said Case.

Maslin nodded. "Perhaps, but he always takes his time. You can't hurry him, Hardesty."

There was a faint suggestion of light in the little window.

"I'll take a look-see outside," said Case.

"You'll walk into an ambush."

"Can't stay here, Maslin."

"Yes."

Case grinned. "Maybe it would be better if the three of us killed each other off. Then you could go back to Cottonwood Station and write us off the books. Another successful man-hunt accomplished by Sheriff Dade Maslin."

"Go to hell!"

"Maybe I won't have any choice."

"You would have made a good law man, Hardesty."

"I'm not sure if that's a compliment or not."

"It is."

"Gracias."

Maslin waved a hand.

Madeline came to Case. "Let me go with you, Case."

"No."

"I can shoot."

"We only have one gun."

"Perhaps I can get my brother to help you."

"Him? He's got the blood hunger eating at him. He'd let all of us die, even you, to kill Davis."

"That's not true!"

He shrugged. "There's one way to find out. Try for the showdown."

He walked through the room to the door which led into the room which in turn was next to the sacristy. She followed him. "Case," she said softly.

He turned to meet her arms rising to encircle his neck. She kissed him. "Come back," she said, then she was gone.

Case touched his lips with his left hand. He had wanted to free himself from the water hole and the mission, get his money and ride to Sonora, but now he knew there was more than that involved. He wanted Madeline Davis more than the money; more than anything else he had ever wanted. She wanted him and made no bones about it.

The nave was empty. Faint gray light showed in the eastern sky. There wasn't much time. He stayed well back from the window and looked out at the horses. They were nervous. They needed water, and the dawn wind brought the odor to them. The rocks beyond them seemed as devoid of life as ever, but someone might be waiting there with ready rifle to put a slug into him if he was foolish enough to step out into the open.

He padded through the dark nave and stopped just short of the great doorway. There was a darkness in the open area where the water hole was, but the area too seemed empty of life. A bird called softly from the brush and then fluttered off.

Case needed Antonio to scout for him, but it would take time to go down into the tunnel and get him, He walked into the baptistry, wondering if Phil Davis was alive or dead in the bell tower. His eyes fell on something dark at the foot of the stairway. He walked forward and knelt beside the body of Dulce, then he looked up the dark stairwell. A man could see most of the area from that tower and from the roof behind it.

Case went up the stairs with his Winchester thrust forward and his finger holding back the slack of the trigger. He didn't trust Davis any more than he did Chip Gilbert.

The place was empty except for the big bell. It wasn't light enough yet to see anything. A man could see a lot up there, but he was also a clay pigeon for a good marksman.

He flattened himself against one of the thick supporting pillars and studied the rocks to the north and east but saw nothing. He moved to another pillar and looked to the south, but there was nothing there but rocks and brush with the dark desert beyond. He sensed, rather than saw, a movement west of the mission above the natural rock passageway which led out to the desert.

A man crawled out of the brush and bellied along until he found a canteen. It couldn't be Chip, as the outlaw was half again as big as he was, and it was not Leonardo Janos. The man crawled toward the water hole and began to fill the canteen. Now and then he looked back over his shoulder as though watching for someone. At last he had the canteen full. He got to his knees to stopper it. Then Case knew it was Phillip Davis.

Davis began to crawl toward the rocks. A man stood up in the brush. The wind carried his voice to Case. "Davis," he said clearly. It was the Kid.

Phil Davis stood up. "I'm unarmed, Kid," he said.

"You didn't think I'd kill you like that, did you?"

Davis dropped the canteen. "For the love of God, Kid, Dulce is dead! It's all over!"

The Kid moved closer with his rifle at hip level. "No," he said. "You and I have a reckoning."

"I'll go back to Madeline. I'll make a good husband to her. You'll see. Give me a break, Kid."

"I will."

They stood there facing each other.

Case padded about the tower. Maybe Chip and Leonardo would see the two men facing each other for the showdown. If they came out and showed themselves there wouldn't be any hesitation in Case. He'd kill them both.

The Kid raised his head. "I never yet killed a man who didn't have a fair shake of the dice against me."

"You have two guns. I'm unarmed."

The Kid let down the hammer of his rifle and walked forward. He placed it on the ground ten feet from Davis. Then he deliberately turned his back and walked ten paces. He turned again. "Rifle against six-gun. I won't draw until you have that Winchester in your hands."

"How do I know it's loaded?"

"It is. It's a chance you'll have to take. One of us won't leave here, Davis."

The wind waved the brush. It was getting lighter so that Case could see the conchos on the Kid's belt and hat.

Davis walked forward and stopped. "Jesus," he said. "What chance have I got?"

"Better than getting shot down in cold blood."

"Let me get the rifle in my hands."

"O.K."

Still the gambler stood there. The Kid folded his arms across his chest. Case shook his head. There was romance in the Kid. Too much, perhaps. He'd die under the gun of some harder man who'd brag about his kill until hell froze solid.

"Make your play when you're ready, Davis," said the Kid.

"Maybe Madeline can settle this thing."

"You married my sister, you bastard, and played around with that little bitch even after you knew I wanted her."

"You didn't love her."

"You know a lot, don't you?"

Davis felt the cold sweat run down his sides. He was weak from loss of blood. But there was no way to go. The odds were stacked, but still a man with a rifle had a fair chance with a man firing a six-gun.

"Make your play, Davis!"

Case was fascinated, but not fascinated enough to forget to look for Gilbert and Janos.

Davis bent to pick up the rifle, watching the Kid all the time. He breathed harshly as he stood erect with the heavy rifle in his hands. He thumbed back the hammer.

"Now!" called out the Kid. He went into a crouch and swept his hand down for the draw, whipping out his Colt and cocking it.

Davis threw himself flat and fired at the same time the Kid's Colt roared. The Kid grunted in savage pain as the soft-nosed .44 hit him in the gun wrist. The Winchester flashed again as the Kid did the border shift and jumped sideways. The second slug whipped through his hat. His Colt cracked. Davis jerked and rolled over.

The echoes slammed back and forth between the rocks. The horses whinnied in fear. Smoke shrouded over the water hole.

Phil Davis stood up. He shook his head. He picked up the canteen and walked unsteadily toward the rock passageway to the desert. The Kid stood there watching him with the smoking Colt in his left hand and his right hand covered with blood which dripped onto the rocks.

"Stay where you are," said the Kid.

Davis shook his head. He staggered a little as he walked. Then he stopped at the entrance to the passageway. He turned to look at the Kid. "Damned near got you, tinhorn," he said and then fell flat on his face.

The Kid walked to him and hooked a boot toe under him. The gambler rolled over with outflung arms and lay still. The Kid spat and then awkwardly reached across his body to sheathe his six-gun. He felt his smashed wrist and the sickness came over him. He retched violently and then walked toward the pool.

A rifle cracked from the rocks and the slug slammed into the pillar inches from Case's head. He fired twice at the flash and then jumped back.

The Kid sprinted for the brush and rocks and disappeared from sight.

There was nothing in the graying light but drifting powder smoke and the body of Phil Davis.

Whoever had fired at Case was in the chaotic mass of rocks south of the mission and in such a position that he could cover both ends of the mission with the exception of a small blind area at each end; but he could move fast enough to cover those blind areas, too, if he must.

Case wet his lips. He had expended two rounds when one would have done as well, and he knew the odds of hitting the hidden rifleman under such conditions were a thousand to one or higher.

It must be Chip Gilbert who had fired. Janos wasn't that good with the long gun. In a little while the top of the bell tower would be flooded with light and no man could fire from there without being a perfect target.

Damn Antonio! Case needed his help now. The Kid was out of action and Maslin was helpless. If the tracker was out among the rocks he might get close enough to the rifleman to put a knife into him; but there was no way of Case knowing where the breed was, or even if he was alive.

He stood at the top of the stairs. He had to get down out of that tower, but there was no way of knowing whether someone might be waiting down below for him.

Case walked slowly down the dark stairwell until he reached the bottom. He stepped over the cold body of Dulce. The baptistry was still dark. He walked past the heavy carved-stone baptismal font and peered from the deep-set window. There was nothing to see but the dull leaden-hued waters of the tinaja and the stiffening body of Phil Davis.

Case hesitated. He was safe enough in the thick-walled room. There were two ways to get at him: the window and the door, unless one of his stalkers could get up into the tower, and he discounted that fact.

There was only one thing to do and that was to get out into the open and use all his tracking skill to get at his two enemies, and he had to do it quickly before it got much lighter.

Case walked into the nave and stopped to listen. There were no windows cut into the east wall of the great room, so it was still very dark in there.

Case picked up a piece of plaster and hurled it with all his strength out into the open area in front of the mission. It struck and shattered. Two shots ripped out and the slugs keened from the rocks. *Bueno!* The rifleman was still holed up south of the mission.

There was a blind spot at the northwest corner of the mission. He'd have to take a chance to get into the rocks. He took in a deep breath and sprinted as silently as he could for cover, momentarily expecting a slug between the shoulder blades.

He reached the rocks and dived for cover, flattening himself as he turned and raised his rifle. Nothing happened. Where in hell's name was the other one?

CHAPTER EIGHTEEN

Chip Gilbert replenished his magazine as he watched the front of the mission. He was waiting for Leonardo to make his play. The Mexican should be into the mission now. Chip grinned. If Leonardo got Hardesty it would be easy enough for Chip to get Leonardo. The Kid was out of action. Chip could work over him to find the location of the money.

The big man moved quietly through the rocks, first to the west to see the front of the mission, then to the east to see the back of it. No sign of Hardesty.

Chip crawled to where he could see the horses. They were still there, restless because of lack of water, but the picket pins still held them.

The sun was just below the eastern mountains. Chip squatted under a ledge and scanned the rocks to the northeast. Nothing moved. Maybe Leonardo was stalking Hardesty. Maybe he was still in the tunnel. Chip wasn't too worried. He'd never face Hardesty for a six-gun showdown, but he knew he was as good as Hardesty with a rifle, maybe a shade better.

Chip thought of the tall, long-legged woman in the mission. She was a looker, and smart too. She had no use for Chip Gilbert now, but if they were left alone, with him having twenty thousand dollars in his war bag, she might change her tune. If she didn't, well, Chip could have a high lonesome with her before he left for Sonora, and then take care of her too.

The Kid was in agony. The soft-nosed .44 had struck the wrist bones and had coursed upward to smash between both bones of his forearm. The slug was still under the swollen skin of his inner forearm. Cold sweat dripped from his face as he awkwardly bound his bandanna about the wound and drew it tight with his teeth. Nausea poured over him. Somewhere in the jungle of rocks and thorny brush the others were stalking each other.

He knew well enough what would happen to him, and Madeline, if those two, Gilbert and Janos, found him like this. He had played high and mighty with them in order to get Phil Davis, and he knew he'd never leave there alive if the two hardcase bastards found him like this.

He crawled for deeper cover and looked back to see if he was being followed. His left hand gripped a crumbling ledge of rock. The rocks shifted and he pitched forward, clawing at thin air until he struck hard at the bottom of the gully, landing on his shattered wrist. There was a fleeting moment of excruciating agony and then he seemed to fall still further into a pit of Stygian darkness.

———

DADE MASLIN PACED A FEW STEPS. "GOD," he said. "I should be out there helping Hardesty."

"There's nothing you can do," said Madeline quietly.

"What is he to you?"

She looked up into his unseeing eyes. "A man," she said.

"An outlaw with a price on his head. A killer."

"He's trying to save our lives."

"He means a lot to you then?"

"Yes."

"And your husband?"

She made a gesture of futility. "I loved him once, or at least thought I did."

"How did you happen to come here?"

She told him the story.

Maslin shook his head. "You're a fool, woman. Why didn't you let the Kid get at them?"

"He's my brother."

"Is there a price on his head too?"

"No."

"He has killed, though?"

"He doesn't notch his gun," she said. "I've heard stories about him. He was always wild and unruly. Somehow I think he could have made his mark in the world. He has everything to do so."

"It's a little late for that, isn't it?"

"He's only twenty-one years old."

"With a record."

She walked to the doorway. "I'm going to look outside."

He moved swiftly, felt for her in the darkness which shrouded him, and gripped her by the upper arms. "No," he snapped.

"He may need help, sheriff."

"There's nothing you can do but pray."

He released her and she leaned against the wall. She had faith in Case Hardesty, but she had had faith in Phil Davis too, a faith which had been deliberately destroyed.

———

CASE RAISED HIS HEAD. The horses were just below him, but he was downwind of them. They were nervous enough as it was.

A rifle cracked from just south of him and the slug ricocheted from the rocks near him. Flecks of lead lanced into his face, drawing tears from his eyes. He dropped flat and rolled over and over until he found a place where he could thrust his rifle between two rocks.

There was a movement in the brush across the open space. He fired twice and was rewarded with a hoarse grunt.

The smoke drifted downwind. One of the horses jerked free from his picket line and galloped toward the front of the mission.

Case knew now it was Chip Gilbert firing at him. Janos could never shoot that well under such conditions. But where was the Mex?

Case crawled behind a ledge of rock and peered beneath a creosote bush. There was nothing to see. Another horse broke loose and moved to the front of the mission.

Case had eight rounds left and no record to show for the four expended rounds but a grunt which might mean anything. Maybe he had killed or wounded the big bastard.

The rifle rapped again and the bullet sang thinly just over Case's head. Chip was all right, damn him to everlasting hell!

Maybe he could circle around and outflank Chip, surprise him or meet him face to face and shoot it out.

Case bellied along, cursing the spiked vegetation and the keen-edged rocks which made a bloody shambles of his knees and elbows.

He moved to the west at a slow rate until he was at the front of the mission. The two horses were placidly lapping water.

Case kept on until he was just over the natural rock passageway which opened on the western desert. He slid down into it and scrambled hurriedly up the far side to drop into the brush and wait for a movement or a sound to alert him.

He wasn't too far from the tunnel but he wasn't of a

mind to chance going into it and meeting Leonardo Janos in the darkness.

The sun had tipped the eastern mountains now and was pouring a flood of light across the awakening Spanish Desert.

Case slid down into a gully and followed it until he saw the sands stretching to the south. He stopped there and looked to the east. Nothing.

He kept close to the rock wall until he found another eroded gully. He moved up it until he found a place to scale the steep wall. Something moved behind him and he whirled. There was a man lying there, feebly moving his head. Case raised his rifle and sighted.

A shot crashed out above him and to his right and the slug smashed against the breech of his rifle, numbing his hands. He jumped back and saw the grinning face of Chip Gilbert wreathed in the powder smoke.

He jumped back again as the rifle spat flame and smoke. He dropped his own rifle and fell heavily. There was nothing else to do but scuttle for cover without his only weapon.

"Got you now, you bastard!" crowed Chip.

Two more shots missed Case by inches as he plowed through brush and loose rock and darted into the gully he had left before Chip had surprised him. He ran up it, scrambled over the far side, rolled down a rocky slope and into a rock cleft barely big enough to conceal him.

Chip held the aces now and he'd make the best of it. Case crawled until he was near the western end of the passageway. The Kid's rifle lay near the body of Phil Davis, but there was no chance to get it without drawing half a dozen slugs and Chip wouldn't miss.

"Come on out, Hardesty!" roared Chip.

The damned arrogant fool had given away his position. He was still right where he had surprised Case.

Case wiped the sweat and blood from his face. He picked out some of the shards of lead. He could run from

Chip for a time and maybe elude him, but Chip had
everything under control.

He looked at his bleeding knees. His trousers had
been fixed with antelope skin between the thighs and at
the knees, and the good leather was in sad shape. He
eyed the leather. Something came back to him; a trick he
had learned from the Apache scouts he had served with
while in the cavalry. They could be dropped down into a
hostile desert, foodless, waterless and weaponless and
still survive by using their native skills.

It was a long shot, the plan which formed in his mind,
but his back was against the wall and there was no other
way for him.

Case worked his way through the brush and rocks
until he found a place where he could look out on the
open area before the mission. He saw the rifle lying
there. So near and yet so far.

He took out his clasp knife and rapidly cut the
leather away from his right trouser leg, heedless of
slashing his flesh.

His hands greased the leather with sweat as he
worked. He quickly cut out a diamond-shaped piece of
leather and pierced four holes through the median line of
its width. He carefully cut two leather thongs and rolled
them on a flat rock, looping an end of one of them. Then
he attached the thongs to the diamond-shaped piece of
leather, one on each side. He put his knife away and
placed the loop about the middle finger of his right hand
and the free string between the thumb and first finger.
Case nodded in satisfaction. He carefully selected three
smooth stones about two and a half inches long and an
inch thick.

It was a real Apache sling. He had competed with the
Apache scouts and even old Jack Rabbit, who was said to
have no peer in the slinging art, had admitted that Case
was as good as any young buck with the ancient weapon.
Case had watched the younger scouts play a rough game

with the slings, facing each other in two teams across a wide, cleared area and hurling the stones at each other, The scouts had learned this game as boys while undergoing warrior training before they were taught the art of bow-and-arrow shooting.

The stones would whirl through the air at you. It was dodge and duck, cast your missile, snatch up another and try to avoid a stone coming at you, wait your chance and cast with skill and strength. There was no protection other than the ability to dodge. More than one buck had been dropped in the deadly game. Broken bones were not uncommon.

He crawled behind a ledge and peered toward where he had last heard Chip. It was one thing to face a sling in the hands of an eager warrior, knowing his weapon was no better than yours. It was quite another matter to use the crude weapon against a skilled marksman with a rifle in his hands.

The sun was higher now and the desert was awash with golden light. Already its heat was beginning to be felt.

Case moved slowly toward the mission. Inside its walls he would be safe for a time if he wasn't caught in a cross fire between Chip and Leonardo. The absence of the Mexican plagued him. What chance had Antonio against such a man armed with rifle, pistol and knife?

He slid down a slope facing the north side of the mission. There were fifty yards of sunlit ground between him and those thick walls.

He stood up, held his right hand partly raised at his side with the stone held ready in the sling. There was no sign of life. He started quickly across the open space with his heart thudding like an Apache tom-tom.

He was twenty feet from the rear of the mission when he heard the shrill whinnying of one of the horses at the water hole. He turned to see Chip Gilbert standing near the front of the mission with his rifle at hip level pointing at Case. "Calf rope," said Chip with a broad grin.

Case slowly raised his hands hoping to God the dumb bastard wouldn't notice the sling and stone in his right hand. The icy sweat trickled down his sides and he tried to ease his harsh breathing.

Chip came forward. "Damn you," he said. "I'll make you pay, Hardesty."

Case said nothing. He didn't want to anger Chip into firing.

Case slowly turned his hands so that the backs of them were toward Chip. If he missed with the sling he still had a reserve stone in his left hand and a third stone ready in his left shirt pocket.

Case tried his bluff. "Hardcase, Chip," he said dryly. "You with a rifle and me bare-handed."

Suspicion clouded the broad face of the outlaw. "Yeh, Hardesty. You was always so smart. The brains of the bunch. Well, where are you now? Trapped, that's what you are. I got the edge on you, Hardesty, and I'll get the dinero too." The big man paused to take a breath and he moved a little closer to Case.

Case had him started now. It wasn't like Chip Gilbert to miss such an opportunity to crow over Case.

Chip spat. "You was so smart! Well, hombre, you run your luck out. I always thought it was luck instead of brains what got you by."

The sun was warm on Case's back and shining into the eyes of Chip. Chip was twenty feet away from Case by now and winding up for another spiel of bombast.

Case turned a little to the right, set himself and eased back his right arm.

"Hawww!" jeered the big man. "'Look at you! You're even falling out of them fancy pants you wear."

Chip moved a little closer. "How do you want it? Belly or head? Or maybe I oughta let you sweat while I think where I'll put the slug."

Case suddenly drew back his right arm and threw it forward, loosing the unlooped string. The stone whispered through the air and caught Chip with a dull thud, squarely in the middle of his low broad forehead. His hands loosened on his rifle. He staggered back and opened his big mouth.

Case placed his second stone in the sling, gripped the unlooped string and hurled the heavy stone. It thudded against Chip's jaw. He dropped the rifle and fell heavily against the mission wall.

Case dropped the sling and sprinted forward. He kicked the rifle out of the way and gripped Chip by the front of his filthy shirt. He looked into the glazing eyes of the big man and then released his grip. Chip sagged sideways and fell flat on his back. His mouth and hands worked but there was no sound from him as he died with a fractured skull.

Case wiped the sweat from his face. He took Chip's Colt and the rifle. He stepped back and looked for Leonardo. The place seemed as deserted as when he had first come there.

He walked to the rear of the mission. The last two horses stood there with sagging heads. Time enough to water them when he took care of Leonardo.

The sacristy was still cool when he entered it. He walked into the room next to it and then through to the second room. He tapped three times with the butt of the rifle and then three times again.

"Case?" asked Madeline through the door.

"Yes."

She opened the door and gripped him by the arm.

Maslin looked at Case. "How did you make out?"

"Chip Gilbert is dead," he said quietly.

"And Leonardo?"

"That I don't know." Case grounded his rifle. "Where's Antonio?"

"He hasn't showed up."

"I'll look for him."

"Be careful. Janos is a dangerous man."

Case grinned sarcastically. "As if *I* didn't know that."

"Have you seen my brother and Phil?" asked Madeline.

"Yes."

She looked quickly up into his face. "Tell me," she demanded.

"Phil is dead, killed by your brother."

Her face worked a little and then she looked away. "I knew it."

"Your brother is badly wounded. He'll live, though."

"Leave me that Colt," said Maslin.

Case gave it to him. "Lots of use that will be."

"I can shoot," said Madeline.

Case walked to the trap door and stood there listening. There was no sound from the dark hole below him. He didn't care much about going down there, but it was better than walking outside to find the exit of the tunnel. Leonardo might be waiting to dry-gulch him near there.

He eased his way down the stone steps into the room below and felt his way to the room where the two coffins rested on their trestles. He stopped again to listen, but there was no sound except the soft sighing of the strong draft through the tunnel.

There was nothing else to do but light a candle. The pale light guttered in the draft, throwing patches of light on the walls and shrouding other parts of the room in shadows.

He checked the rifle and held it in his right hand at waist level while he walked on holding the candle up high. The water splashed about his boots and the damp air chilled his heated body.

Then he saw the two bodies on the tunnel floor and noted with a start that one of them wore a padre's cowled gown but the feet which protruded from beneath the robe were encased in moccasins, and he knew he had solved the mystery of Antonio's disappearance.

He leaned the rifle against the wall and knelt beside the two men. The tracker had a livid welt across his forehead but he was breathing. Then Case turned to Leonardo. The man was dead, with a look of fear still etched on his dark face and in his staring eyes. Case looked at the man's belly, and his guts churned within him at what he saw and a taste of bile came up into his throat.

He carried the tracker to the room of the coffins and placed him on a bench. He went back for his rifle and then wet his bandanna in the water. He went back to the tracker and dripped water on his face. He wiped the man's face and was rewarded with Antonio opening his eyes.

"You did well, amigo," said Case.

"*Gracias!*"

"There is nothing to fear now. The big man is also dead."

"*Bueno.*"

Case helped Antonio to his feet, but the man was weak and so Case hoisted him across his shoulders and carried him up into the mission. "Here's your tracker, Maslin," said Case. "He killed Janos and got a buffaloing in the process. He's all right."

"Thanks, Hardesty. Thanks, Antonio," said Maslin.

"It was nothing, *patrón*," murmured Antonio.

Madeline looked at Case. "My brother," she said.

"Yes."

"There are medicaments and bandages in one of my saddlebags," said Maslin. "Get them and help him."

"Can I go too?" asked Madeline.

"Why not?" asked Case. "There's no danger now."

They walked outside into the bright light of the sun. Case led the two horses to the water. Madeline looked at the body of Phil Davis, and Case cursed himself for not hiding the body.

"Kid!" called out Case.

"What do you want?" The voice was faint and weak.

"Come to help you, Kid."

"Let me alone, Hardesty."

"Steve!" called Madeline. "You need help. There's nothing to fear."

There was a moment's hesitation and then the Kid called out. "All right, Sis."

"Come on," said Case. "The quicker the better."

They walked up the slope and found him in the gully. He fainted dead away as Case picked him up to carry him to the sacristy.

CHAPTER NINETEEN

The morning sun was beating against the thick eastern wall of the mission, adding to the heat of the fire in the sacristy. Case had honed several knives to a razor's edge and had sterilized them in boiling water. With the help of Madeline he had cut out the bullet lodged in the Kid's arm. Luckily the Kid had fainted again as he felt the tearing of his flesh.

Case had managed to set the bones, and it would do until a doctor examined the wound. He bound the two holes with bandages and then sat back to roll a cigarette.

Madeline sat beside her brother, bathing his face and chest. "Will he be all right?" she asked.

Case shrugged as he lighted the quirly. "*Quién sabe?* I know one thing, unless he can train himself to draw and shoot as well with his left hand as he could with his right, he'll never be feared as the Conchos Kid again."

"Perhaps it's just as well," she said quietly.

Case stood up. Antonio was taking care of the horses. Maslin was sitting in the nave. "I have another job to do," he said.

"You're worn thin, Case," she said.

He grinned. "Hard to wear me out, Madeline."

"Yes."

He had found a battered spade in one of the rooms
while the water had been heating. He picked it up and
walked outside. With the help of the tracker he carried
the bodies of Davis, Dulce, Chip and Leonardo, to the
graveyard and covered them with blankets. Then he set
to work in the loose soil of the graveyard to prepare a
common grave.

The sun was up high when he and the tracker finished
the grave. Case wiped the sweat from his naked upper
body. "All ready, *amigo,*" he said.

"Yes."

"Help me with them."

They carried the bodies to the grave and lowered
them in. Case placed Dulce beside Phillip and the two
outlaws together a little space away from Davis. They
covered them with the blankets. Case picked up the
spade.

"Wait," said the tracker. The sun flashed from the
cross which hung at his throat.

"Why, *amigo?*"

"Something should be said above them."

Case looked at the serious face of the tracker. "Yes,"
he said. "Get the others."

Antonio went into the mission and came back with
Madeline and the sheriff.

"Who'll say the words?" asked Case.

"I'm not very good at these things," said Maslin.

Madeline shook her head.

Case looked at the shrouded bodies. What was there
to say? There was no remorse in his mind for any of
them. They had reached trail's end because of what they
had been.

The tracker came forward. He bowed his head. Softly
he said the Lord's Prayer and then stepped back. "Requi-
escat in pace" he said. He picked up some earth and
threw it into the grave. Each of the others did likewise.

Case picked up the spade and swiftly filled in the

grave. He threw the spade to one side and walked into the mission.

"Now what happens?" asked Madeline. She took the sheriff by the arm and led him to the door of the sacristy. Case was feeling the Kid's pulse. "He'll live," he said cheerfully.

"Yes," said Maslin. "Step back from there, Hardesty."

Case turned quickly. Maslin held a cocked Colt in his big hand. "Don't make a move," he warned.

Case eyed the law man closely. "You can see!"

"Yes. The time I spent in that dark room must have helped. I could see a little this morning."

Case nodded. "I should have known when you asked me for that Colt. I was wondering a little later on how you knew I had one. Too tired to understand, I guess. Well, Maslin, what happens now?"

"I came here after four men and twenty thousand dollars. Three of those four men are dead."

"Leaving me to take in, eh?"

"Yes."

"You haven't got the twenty thousand, Maslin."

Madeline raised her head. "Steve told me where it is. He hid it in the baptismal font in the baptistry."

"Get it, Antonio," said Maslin.

The tracker silently left the room and was back in a few minutes with the sack of money. He placed it at Maslin's feet.

The Kid opened his eyes and took in the scene. He looked at the money sack. "Game's over," he said weakly.

Maslin nodded. "I don't want you, Kid. Your affair with Davis has nothing to do with me."

"Thanks."

"You can leave when you feel better and take your sister with you."

"It isn't fair," said Madeline. "Case risked his life to save us, sheriff."

"I know."

They watched the law man. Case knew him of old. He never quit a trail until his quarry was captured or dead.

Maslin rubbed his bristly jaw. "They offered five hundred dollars apiece for you, Case, Gilbert, Janos and Hanks. Two thousand dollars reward."

"I'm shocked," said Case dryly. "I figured I was worth more than that."

"You always did have a high opinion of yourself."

Case shrugged. "Can't help it, Maslin."

A branch snapped in the fire. Antonio watched them. The ways of such men were beyond him.

Maslin tapped the gun barrel against his left wrist. "However, there are extenuating circumstances, as they say."

"Go on," said Case.

"I figure this way: As I said, three of the four men who held up the bank in Cottonwood Station are dead. I can write them off when I get back. That leaves you, Hardesty. You killed Hanks and Gilbert, so I take no credit for that. Antonio here killed Janos. But I can't very well go back there and say you're not dead."

"You aiming to kill me too?" asked Case.

"No. But there are three men buried out there. Hanks is buried where you killed him. Now we five know that Gilbert and Janos are in that grave with another man. That man, with apologies to Miss Madeline here, could very well be you, Hardesty, in case anyone is damned fool enough to want to come out here and check my story, which ain't likely."

Madeline's breath seemed to catch in her throat.

Maslin sheathed the Colt. "I'm leaving here tonight on my horse. Antonio always goes afoot. I'm taking eighteen thousand of that money and if they ask me where the rest is I'll say I lost it and to take it out of the reward money I have coming."

"You interest me strangely," said Case.

Maslin looked at the three of them. "I'll give you a week's start out of here. Go anywhere you like, but don't stay in Arizona Territory. Understand?"

Case grinned. "Keno!"

The Kid nodded. "I bought a small spread in Colorado some time ago. It isn't much but it has possibilities. My gunslinging days are over. I'll take you there too, Sis, if you like."

She nodded. "You'll need help to get there, Steve, and a foreman too, and that shouldn't be hard to figure out."

"How about it, Hardesty?" asked the Kid.

"Suits me," said Case. He smiled at Madeline.

Maslin nodded. He picked up the sack and counted out two thousand dollars. He handed the money to Madeline. "A wedding present, I hope," he said with a broad smile.

"All's well that ends well," said Case.

———

THE MOON WAS UP HIGH. The wind whispered about the mission. The Kid was resting quietly.

Case and Madeline stood at the rear of the mission. They had just said farewell to Maslin and Antonio and the hoofbeats had died away to the north. The moonlight shone on the four peeled crosses Antonio had placed on the grave.

They walked to the front of the mission and looked at the moonlight sparkling on the water. Case drew Madeline close and kissed her. As they looked at each other the bell rang softly, just once, and the sweet echo died away on the dry night wind.

TAKE A LOOK AT LAST TRAIN FROM GUN HILL AND THE BORDER GUIDON:

Two Full Length Western Novels

Owen Wister and Spur Award winner Gordon D. Shirreffs spins tales of the old west that are exhilarating and bigger than life. You'll find two such full-length tales in this double volume that are sure to please even the most discerning consumer of Western fiction.

In *Last Train From Gun Hill*, no one dares cross the powerful Craig Belden— that is until his son rapes and murders Matt Morgan's beloved wife in cold blood. Now Matt, armed with a six-shooter, deadly precision aim, and white-hot rage, won't stop shooting until justice is done. The bullets fly, and God help whoever gets caught in the crossfire...

In *The Border Guidon*, the last Union soldier left alive in the treacherous Arizona wastelands knows he has one final mission to complete before he can rest. It's up to him to ferret out a valuable cache of ammunition stolen by the Confederates. He'll complete his mission come hell or high water—even if he has to blow up the whole territory to do it.

"The joy of reading Shirreffs' work is in his mastery of pacing and his tough, gritty prose." – James Reasoner, author of Outlaw Ranger.

AVAILABLE AUGUST 2022

ABOUT THE AUTHOR

Gordon D. Shirreffs published more than 80 western novels, 20 of them juvenile books, and John Wayne bought his book title, Rio Bravo, during the 1950s for a motion picture, which Shirreffs said constituted *"the most money I ever earned for two words."* Four of his novels were adapted to motion pictures, and he wrote a Playhouse 90 and the Boots and Saddles TV series pilot in 1957.

A former pulp magazine writer, he survived the transition to western novels without undue trauma, earning the admiration of his peers along the way. The novelist saw life a bit cynically from the edge of his funny bone and described himself as looking like a slightly parboiled owl. Despite his multifarious quips, he was dead serious about the writing profession.

Gordon D. Shirreffs was the 1995 recipient of the Owen Wister Award, given by the Western Writers of America for "a living individual who has made an outstanding contribution to the American West."

He passed in 1996.